MARIA DEAN

BEAUTIFULLY BEASTLY

Love isn't always beautiful. Sometimes, it's beastly.

BEAUTIFULLY BEASTLY

MARIA DEAN

HOT TREE PUBLISHING

Beautifully Beastly is a work of fiction. All names, characters, events and places found therein are either from the author's imagination or used fictitiously. Any similarity to persons alive or dead, actual events, locations, or organizations is entirely coincidental and not intended by the author.

For information, contact the publisher, Hot Tree Publishing.

WWW.HOTTREEPUBLISHING.COM

EDITING: Hot Tree Editing

COVER DESIGNER: BookSmith Design

E-BOOK ISBN: 978-1-923252-56-1

PAPERBACK ISBN: 978-1-923252-57-8

It only felt right to dedicate this book
to a true Stephen King fan,
so Kristin Scearce, this one's for you.

ONE

FENRIR

I'M A TRAINED KILLER. I CAN KILL PEOPLE WITH A SIMPLE bullet to the forehead, a quick cut to the femoral artery, or a powerful fist to the temple. But if looks could kill, there'd be a dead man at the bar right now. He's wiry as fuck, with slicked-back hair and a tan that looks like it came out of a bottle. He has no business being in this bar—let alone on this earth—and I want nothing more than to bury him, but I have my orders, and dealing with him isn't one of them... yet.

The starched white collar cuts into my neck, the fabric stretched tight across my pecs. It makes me look smart and in control, but I'm as uncomfortable as a madman in a strait-jacket—and the asshole at the bar is doing nothing to calm my agitation. This isn't attire I'm used to, not the terrain I've been trained for. The beat of the music in the club is so loud, I feel the bass reverberate off my ribs, like the bass player is strumming the strings across my chest. The lighting is dim, smoke swirling across the dance floor as if it's guiding the clubbers on how to move. I can barely make out my hand in front of my face, but despite the poor visibility, I can see *her*.

An avalanche of dark hair.

Beautifully luminous eyes.

Lips that so very rarely smile.

It's a blessing that I have a licence to stare, to watch her intimately. It is, after all, my job. The only reason I'm here.

To keep her safe.

To keep her alive.

Taking a step forwards, a man knocks into me, his hands gyrating in the air to the infernal pound of the music. He turns, hackles raised, about to berate me for not watching where I'm going, even though he's the one who is blind.

"Hey, man—" His words die on his tongue as he registers my gigantic stature, my immovable breadth, and if this isn't enough, his eyes finally reach my face. His pupils expand when he clocks the scarring that runs up the left side of my neck and claws its way over my cheek.

His jaw drops as he holds his hands up in defence. "Sorry, man. My fault."

I pay him no heed; his reaction is nothing new. My sights are on Hayami, who is perched on a stool, the slimy scumbag sitting opposite her, his greasy hand having found its way onto her upper thigh where the split of her dress exposes her like a gash. I see red, a thick bloodred as I march over to them.

"Fenrir." Willa's warning erupts through my earpiece, echoing against the sound of her voice not three feet to my left. "Don't overreact."

"Define overreacting," I reply as I slam my fist into the scumbag's face, sending him flying off the stool.

"What the…?" Hayami cries as Willa pulls her away from my fury. This isn't the first time Willa has had to intervene when I've lost my head, and I'm sure it won't be the last.

"You don't touch her. No one fucking touches her." Grabbing the dickhead by his shirt, I haul him to his feet. A tiny bead of blood pools at the corner of his lips.

"What the fuck?" the slimeball says, wiping his mouth with the back of his hand.

"What the hell are you doing?" Hayami fights her way out of Willa's hold.

"My job," I spit, still eyeing the fucker as I cling onto the shoulders of his shirt.

"Your job?" Hayami shouts above the music. "Did it look like I was in danger, Beast?" Her hands are on her hips, the split of her dress having ridden further up her leg.

Reluctantly, I let go of the creep.

Seemingly recovered, he touches his mouth, surveys the blood on his hand, and laughs. I want to punch him so badly that my hand aches.

"I think we all just need to calm down," Willa says, inserting herself between me and the cretin. "Everything is fine, Fenrir." She glares at me with a look I've seen countless times before. "Hayami is fine, aren't you?" she asks, glancing at Hayami for confirmation.

"Yes, I'm fine. Just trying to have a good time like a normal twenty-year-old until this fucking beast steamed in." Hayami rolls her eyes.

"It's okay," Willa reassures her. "You can go back to having a good time. We'll be here." Willa places her hand on my chest, exerting a gentle push that, in normal people, would cause them to step back, but I don't move, not even an inch, until she stares at me with pleading eyes that are asking me just to be a good dog and do as I'm told.

Although there's no official hierarchy where Hayami's bodyguards are concerned, Willa has been doing this far longer than I have, which means she has a degree of authority over me that I try to respect.

I swallow my fury as the fuckwit I just punched straightens his shirt and smirks before climbing back onto the stool like a little lord clambering back onto his pedestal. Even through my blaze of anger, I can't help but be impressed by the guy's resilience. Most men don't stay within a mile of my presence when they see me, let alone laugh at me, but this guy is either very brave or extremely stupid.

I put money on the latter.

"What is with you?" Willa hisses through gritted teeth. "You know you can't pull this shit."

"He was touching her." I back off, fists still clenched, eyes like lasers on the jerk.

I want to add that she is Hayami Devall—daughter of gang lord Barrett Devall, one of the richest, most influential, and most powerful men in Rothkor. No one rivals him, except perhaps the Castro family, who've been vying for control of this city ever since Devall took the reins more than thirty years ago.

Bottom line? No one fucks with a Devall.

But I'll be damned if I use the Devall name to define Hayami. That's not the reason I punched that slimy fucker.

"She's a consenting adult who's allowed to have a man touch her. Our job is to keep her alive. We only act when there's a threat to her, or have you forgotten that?" Willa's eyes narrow. She's one of the few people who isn't scared by my looks, and she can give as good as she gets. Her bark is worse than her bite, sure, but she's not someone to be messed with. Then again, neither am I.

Hayami is back on her stool, looking far more regal than the fucker with the fat lip who's leering at her as if he's just won her at a fairground stall. He pulls his stool closer, and I have to fight the monster inside me not to explode and bring the walls of this place down around us all.

"Besides," Willa says as she brushes her hand down her starched shirt and tugs on the lapels of her black jacket, reminding me that I'm not the only one trussed up in a smart suit, "this isn't the kind of venue where you can let your fists do the talking. Have you forgotten where we are?"

As if this suit could let me forget.

The club is new, recently opened by one of Barrett Devall's business cronies, probably furnished with dirty money and decorated in blood. From the outside, it's a high-class, swanky club for the super-rich. On the inside, it's just another laundrette.

Of course, Hayami has a pass to the premier suite—one she refused. She chose instead to stay on the dance floor with the regular crowd, and I can't blame her. The premier suite will be full of wealthy assholes whose sole purpose is to flaunt their riches.

"No, I haven't forgotten."

"Good." Willa pats me on the chest like the good mutt I am.

Blending into the darkness, I retreat into the shadows. The beat of the music drops, and I try to slow my heartbeat to match the rhythm as I watch Hayami. Willa nods, like she's congratulating me for doing as I'm told.

She knows what I'm like. Knew it the first day we met, six months ago, when I was introduced as Hayami's new bodyguard. She sniffed at me and muttered something about not being able to take the hound out of the dog.

This bodyguard business isn't how I began working for Barrett Devall.

A year ago, after leaving the army—where I'd served for just over ten years—I walked into the large warehouse known as the Kennel with blood-encrusted fingernails, a black eye, and sore knuckles.

The Kennel is the headquarters of the Hellhounds, the

name given to Devall's foot soldiers—the muscle behind all his business dealings. A motley crew of people who wear their battle scars like armour. We're the messengers, the heavies who handle the dirty work. We are your worst nightmare.

After being dragged into the warehouse by a couple of Hellhounds patrolling the site, I was dumped before Callan Croft, the head of the Hellhounds, a hulk of a guy with tattoos on his face and dark hair like a wire brush. He asked me what I was doing on his turf. I told him I was looking for work.

He took one sweeping look at my bloodied knuckles, snarling teeth, and knotted scars before he slapped me on the back, called me one ugly motherfucker, then introduced me to the rest of the pack, who were as unsightly as I am. Background checks happened, but Callan had already known I'd fit in. I was welcomed with open arms and wagging tails.

It felt like fate—working for the Devall family, the biggest rivals of the Castros, Rothkor's second-largest gang. I never questioned it.

Not until six months ago.

That's when it all changed.

When I swapped my dog collar for a shirt collar.

TWO

FENRIR

SIX MONTHS AGO

I'M PRETTY SURE A HELLHOUND HAS NEVER SET FOOT INSIDE Devall Mansion, yet here I am, standing in the foyer, palms sweatier than they were in the desert during an eight-mile ruck with a twenty-five-kilo pack, plus water, rifle, and helmet.

The mansion lives up to its name: pale marble flooring, a glistening chandelier, and a split staircase that looks like a musical set—minus the sequinned dancers flanking the steps. I feel as out of place as a homeless man in the Ritz.

I'm greeted—if you can call it that—by an airbrushed woman in a dress suit. She stares at me, clearly certain it isn't the thirty-first of October, until I tell her I've been summoned by Mr Devall. Only then does she cautiously usher me to follow her, turning as soon as she can to avoid looking at my face.

She knows the same thing I do: I don't belong here.

Callan, head of the Hellhounds, had been as shocked as I was when the message came through that Devall wanted to see me in his home. I didn't waste any time thinking it over; he's not a man you keep waiting.

Sharp suit, dark hair speckled with silver, Devall's still handsome even in his late sixties. Combined with a fierce expression that could make a man lose control of his bowels, he's a man who can make any sceptic believe in the devil.

The woman leads me out of the foyer and down a long corridor, her ponytail swinging as she walks. No conversation. No small talk. She's probably wondering—like I am— what the hell I'm doing here. She'll know about the Hellhounds—everyone in Rothkor does. But I'd bet good money she's never come face to face with one, especially not a face as brutal as mine.

We take a right, and I'm met with the scent of chlorine and humidity that swathes my face in a sickly heat. There's a glass wall to my right, and on the other side, the rippling of dark blue water. The pool room. Because every mansion has an indoor pool, right?

At the end of the corridor, Barrett Devall stands with a group of four men. Three of them look pale and nervous, like they'd rather be anywhere else. The fourth is Markus Flint, who's been with the Devall family for years. He started as a bodyguard before working his way up the ranks to head of security. His greying hair and worry lines speak to his loyalty as much as his age.

Markus eyes me cautiously as the woman announces my arrival.

"Ah, Fenrir Therion," Devall says, seemingly unaffected by my appearance—unlike the three other men, whose eyes trace the scarring down the side of my face and neck, probably wondering how far down my body my scars travel.

I see it written all over their faces: the inner dilemma, the silent tug-of-war. They know they shouldn't stare, should avert their gaze, but they can't.

I'm the car crash at the side of the road.

"I see you got my message." He cocks his head, but there's no handshake, no pat on the back, which I can live with.

"Yes, sir." I nod, placing my hands behind my back, feeling scruffy in my dark combats and black T-shirt, especially next to his immaculate suit, which probably cost more money than I'll ever make.

Devall turns back to Markus. "We're done here," he says, ever the gentleman, patting Markus on the back, who nods. "Take the new recruits to the systems room. Get them acquainted with the tech and then report back to me in—" He flashes a gaudy watch. "—an hour."

"Of course, sir," Markus replies before Devall stops him with the palm of his hand on his chest, then signals with a nod for him to step aside. The pair form a huddle as Devall speaks quietly into Markus's ear, divulging something that clearly isn't for the likes of us, leaving me with the newbies.

I'm starting to feel the weight of the shifting glances from the recruits—presumably the newest additions to Devall's ever-expanding security team. This man has always had enemies. He always will. You don't run a city with such a ruthless regime like his without stepping on a few toes.

The Castro family remains Devall's biggest thorn. Headed up by brothers Vincent and Robert, they've been trying to move into Devall territory, aiming to dominate the nightclub scene. Tensions have been rising since Tyrone Miller, one of Castro's men, was found dead last week in a multi-storey car park with a bullet between his eyes.

Suspicions wouldn't have been raised if the guy hadn't been brokering a new alliance with a foreign businessman— one with money and resources far beyond the realms of Devall's illegally gotten gains. Naturally, all fingers pointed to a Hellhound hit.

But every action has a repercussion. A gang war is brewing.

So, yeah, it makes sense that Devall's hiring more security.

To unburden myself from the weighty glares, I glance through the glass wall of the pool room.

Sunlight blares through the external window, casting diamonds across the surface of the water. The pool glistens with an almost surreal tranquillity—until I register the mass of black hair, arms, and legs sprawled out from the faceless body floating at its centre.

There's a beat.

A fleeting moment where I'm caught in the serenity—the fluidity of the water—almost like the stopping of time.

Until I come to my senses.

Like the trained soldier I am, I move—fast and efficient.

I crash through the door to the pool room and dive in, instinct over memory. It's nothing like the cold lakes from army survival training. Back then, we were drilled to *never* jump in unless absolutely necessary. Always assess. Always use a tool. Rescue from a safe distance.

But there's nothing here to help me, and no time to waste.

I don't even notice there's an entourage behind me, Markus abandoning the recruits in the corridor to follow me, until I've hauled the body from the water and dragged her onto the side of the pool.

"What the hell?" Devall's voice thunders over my shoulder.

From the coughing and spluttering, it's clear I don't have a dead body on my hands, so there's no need for CPR. Still, I hold her upright, resting her body against my knees, allowing her to catch her breath.

An anchor drops in my stomach as I realise who I've just

pulled out of the pool: Hayami Devall, Barrett's only child and heir to his empire.

Hayami is a Japanese name, presumably chosen by her mother, Junko, Devall's third wife. It means "rare beauty." But how could they have possibly known? How does anyone see the beauty of a woman in a babe in arms? But I see it now. Even in her bedraggled state, her beauty seeps from her pores. Her skin is drenched, but it doesn't dull the pale glow, the luminosity that seems to radiate from her.

And yet there's something else.

An eerie darkness clings to her, but doesn't quite touch. It hovers over the surface of her skin like a shadow waiting for permission. Waiting to take hold.

I should be shocked by this, but I'm not. It's something I've been able to see for the past fourteen years. I've never told anyone. How could I? Where would I even begin? Because this isn't the first time I've seen this shadow. I've seen it more times than I can count—on strangers in the street, fellow soldiers in my squad, even on myself.

I knew what it was the first time I glimpsed it in the mirror. It was months after the incident, when I finally dared to look—really look—at the reflection of my new face. The shadow shimmered around my periphery, as if it wanted to introduce itself. As if it knew the time wasn't quite right... but almost.

There's no doubt what that dark mark is: the shadow of death. The whisper of its breath.

It only haunts people like me, who have been on the brink of dying and somehow survived. We're now coated in this darkness, stalked by its obscurity, reminded of where we would be had fate not intervened.

This is why I'm under no illusion as to what Hayami was trying to do, where she was about to be taken.

Because I've been there myself and lived to tell the tale.

And now, so will she.

Clad in a tiny swimsuit, she feels impossibly delicate in my roughened hands—like porcelain. I almost drop her, overcome by the fear that I shouldn't be touching something so beautiful, so exquisite.

"Willa, we need you in the pool room, now," Markus speaks into his cuff, then adjusts the earpiece that I imagine is permanently attached.

Hayami coughs up some more water. Instinctively, I rub her back, then stop when I remember who she is, where I am, and who's watching. It's when the coughing ceases and she clears the water from her eyes that she finally looks at me.

Beautiful. Fucking beautiful, but I don't have time to appreciate them as her eyes widen, her pupils dilate, and her mouth drops open. Her reaction tells me exactly what she's thinking.

Horror. Revulsion. Fear.

Same old, same old.

She claws her way from my grasp, and I don't blame her.

"What the fuck?" she splutters.

"Princess." Barrett nears, Markus joining him but keeping a respectable distance. "What happened?"

"I don't know." She shakes her head as Markus grabs a towel from the lounger and tosses it to her. "I was just floating in the water, and then this goddamn monster pulled me out and nearly drowned me."

Six pairs of eyes regard me as Hayami wraps the towel around her shoulders.

"She was facedown in the water. I thought...." I don't finish because there's no point. They all know what I thought, what anyone would think if they saw a person like that.

"You were floating on your front?" the gang lord asks Hayami.

"Yes," she replies. "I always float this way. It's relaxing—until some fucking ogre drags me from the water. Who the hell even is this beast?"

"It's not important, my princess." He dismisses her question.

I am not important.

"Yeah, well, he needs firing, right now."

"Leave things to me, Princess." He looks up, his eyes narrowing as a Black woman arrives in full security uniform —white shirt, black trousers, a Taser strapped to her belt.

"What's happened?" She kneels beside Hayami, concern etched across her brow.

"Why weren't you watching my daughter?" The humidity in the room rises as Devall glares at the woman, who I presume is Willa.

"We don't watch her when she's in the house, sir," Willa answers confidently, then looks to Markus.

"There's no need to whilst she's in the safety of the house, although we do monitor the security cameras. Normally, this includes the pool room, but Hayami asked for it to be switched off this morning, as she wanted privacy whilst swimming," Markus explains.

Devall scratches his chin and eyes Markus, and I swear the sides of his eyes blink like those of a viper.

"My daughter doesn't pay you. I do. You take orders from me. I want a female security guard to monitor the cameras in the pool room when my daughter swims, is that clear?"

"Daddy, there's no need—" Hayami begins, but she stops the minute her father's eyes land on her.

Surprisingly, she holds his gaze, but only for a few seconds before her head dips.

"Markus, dismiss the new recruits." He gesticulates in the direction of the three men abandoned in the corridor, who just stare beyond the glass wall. Markus looks as if he's ready to argue, then thinks better of it before Devall turns his attention to me.

"You. My office. Now," he barks. "Markus, once you've escorted these men out, come and join us."

I've often wondered how inmates feel on death row, and now I know, because Devall might as well have signed my death warrant.

The walk to his office is cumbersome, the term *dead man walking* ringing in my ears.

If I wasn't worried before, I am now. Everything has changed. I've manhandled his daughter and dragged her out of the pool for what seemed, to her, to be no apparent reason, although I'd argue otherwise. But what if I was wrong and she was simply floating on her front like she said? She hadn't been struggling. She hadn't been calling for help.

Yet there was the shadow that shimmered around her, marking her with her brush with death.

What will he do to me for touching his daughter?

I know how he deals with people who anger him. I'm a Hellhound. I'm the messenger who metes out the wrath of Barrett Devall, who delivers his disappointment in whatever way is necessary. He's not a man to be trifled with. He doesn't fight fair, rarely fights his own battles, and invariably uses violence to do the talking.

Enter the Hellhounds, the irony of which doesn't escape me. What will my fate be for pulling his daughter from the pool? And who will be brought in to dish it out?

Flexing my fingers, I wonder which he'll cut off first; I've laid them upon his daughter for no good reason, so therefore they will be removed from my body—a permanent reminder to never touch what does not belong to me.

And then there's Hayami's reaction. She was angry—clearly—but it was more than that. There was revulsion.

Distaste. I saw it when she called for my dismissal, as if my scars had offended her. As if I don't belong in her world.

And in the fleeting moment between her father calling her "princess" and her demanding I be fired, I understood exactly who Hayami Devall is.

A spoiled heiress who always gets what she wants.

The gang lord pushes open a large oak door and leads me —and Markus, who's caught up with us—into his office. The plush burgundy carpet blends with the dark mahogany furniture that wouldn't look out of place in a museum.

"How long have you been with us, Fenrir?" Devall asks.

I stand with my hands behind my back, chest out, and head high. This isn't the opener I was expecting. Maybe he's just drawing it out, toying with me. I wouldn't put it past him. "Six months, sir."

He eyes me as if assessing the truthfulness of my answer whilst also trying to read my scars.

"Your face?" Devall flings this question at me.

"A fire, sir."

"Whilst you were in the army?" He arches his eyebrow.

"Yes, sir," I lie.

"Ah." The noise comes from his mouth as if it's an expulsion of air.

"Why did you jump into the pool?" He changes tact.

I wonder if he's stalling—not to draw out my fear, but for another reason entirely. Maybe he's already sent out a signal to the Hellhounds and is just waiting for them to charge into the room and tear me apart, limb from limb. Bloodthirsty bites. Fearsome claws.

Will it be the Cyclops—one of the Hellhounds who had his eye gouged out in a fight? Or Freddy, with a blade for a finger on his right hand, after one of Castro's men bit the original clean off?

Whoever it is, I just hope they show me some mercy for being one of their own.

"I saw her body, sir. Thought she had drowned. I just reacted."

He glares at me and then looks at Markus.

"I called Fenrir here today because I had an assignment for him. A delicate one that would have required his... how shall we put this? His face fit the job." He chuckles at his cleverness, but Markus shows some restraint, his face remaining impassive. "But after this little fiasco, I've decided that I want Fenrir Therion on my daughter's security team."

Silence devours the room, and I don't know who is more shocked, me or Markus.

"I…. Sir, Fenrir is a—" Markus begins but doesn't finish. He doesn't need to.

He was going to say that I'm a Hellhound—one of the most fearsome, grotesque people to walk this earth. We're the ones hired to inflict pain, teach lessons, and carry out Devall's dirty work. We're nothing more than dogs, tethered beasts who do the monster's bidding.

"I don't give a fuck who he is or where he currently works," Devall snaps. "This man thought my daughter had drowned. He was the only one who not only noticed her but did something about it." He levels his gaze on Markus, voice like steel. "Now, if this isn't the kind of person I need protecting my only heir, then who the fuck else is going to do it?"

Markus looks on the brink of despair but seems to remember his place and nods. "Of course, sir. I'll add him to the team right away, sir."

And with that, I'm ushered out of the room with both hands still attached.

Hayami's security team. What the actual hell?

I'm supposed to protect the woman I've just dragged back

from the brink of death—a death, I presume, she chose for herself, no matter how much she protested afterwards.

She may be beautiful, but Princess Hayami strikes me as the kind of woman who's had everything served to her on a silver platter... and still finds it lacking. She comes across as a spoiled brat. She *wanted* to die.

And I stopped her.

And just like her father, I suspect Hayami doesn't like it when she doesn't get what she wants.

But none of that matters now, because I've just been handed a pardon, and I'm not sure how I feel about it. Maybe I've been exonerated in Devall's eyes, but there's little doubt in mine: Hayami isn't going to like the newest addition to her team.

Not one little bit.

THREE

FENRIR

THE MUSIC IN THE CLUB SOUNDS LOUDER AND FASTER, THE rhythm pumping into my veins as I watch the scrawny fucker leering at Hayami, who is oblivious to his slimy tongue and clawlike hands.

She only sees the beast in me.

It's been twenty minutes since I punched him. My hand still throbs, and I hope his lip does. But it doesn't seem to have served its purpose, as he's still pawing at her. Right now, I'd love nothing more than to look away, turn a blind eye, but that's not why I'm here. Not what I'm paid to do.

Hayami leans in and whispers something in his ear, which seems to expand his sneer and widen his eyes. He nods at her, then slides off the stool and heads to the bathrooms before throwing me a sickening, taunting grin that needs wiping off his fucking face.

I want to follow him. Teach him a lesson. Break every finger that's touched her skin. But he's not my priority.

She is.

After a few minutes, Hayami slips from her stool and heads to the bathroom.

I glance at Willa, who's already following Hayami, signalling with her eyes that she's got this, though I doubt she does—not by my standards, anyway.

"Make sure you go in with her," I say into my cuff mic.

"I'm not going into the cubicle with her. She doesn't need me to wipe her ass," Willa replies.

"But he's in there waiting for her." This isn't the first time she's pulled this stunt—asked some guy to go into the bathroom to wait for her in a cubicle.

As we arrive outside the women's bathroom, anger rumbles through me like the tremors of an impending earthquake at the thought of what that scumbag could be doing to her right now.

"You've gotta cut her some slack," Willa says, placing her hand on the door before turning to me.

"Like fuck I do. Do you not remember the time she asked a guy to meet her in the cubicle, and he tried to slip her those pills? If anyone is going to kill her, that would be the easiest way."

She rolls her eyes. She knows I'm right.

"Okay, I'll check on her."

She pushes open the bathroom door just as a horde of women flood out, lips thick with freshly applied gloss, hair tousled and smoothed, ready to flock back into the thick of the club. They clock Willa, pay her no attention, then lock eyes with me. Their reaction is like it always is in dark places. They see my size, take in the muscles, notice the dark hair, the perfect side of my face that showcases my good looks, and they giggle, elbowing one another, getting ready to say something flirtatious—until I turn my head and they gasp, lean into one another, and scurry off.

I hold the door open and watch Willa disappear through

another internal door, which swings shut behind her, leaving me blind to the situation.

Fuck.

"What's going on? I have no visual," I ask.

"It's fine. She's fine."

"Is he in there with her?" My skin starts to prickle as my mind begins to create images, and they're always of the worst-possible scenario. Hayami being strangled. Hayami being beaten. Hayami being molested.

There's no answer. It means that fucker is in there with her.

Fuck.

Willa is too soft. She doesn't see the danger. She tries to give Hayami her space, tries to let her live as normal a life as possible, where women get touched up by strange men in clubs, but I can't picture anything other than his fucking hands on her. All I want to do is charge into the bathroom and rip his fucking head off, but that'd be extremely unprofessional.

Adrenaline floods my veins.

What is he doing to her? Why is she letting a slimeball like him touch her? When will she realise that she's worth more than him? She's worth more than all of us.

My feet are over the threshold, and I imagine Willa already berating me for overstepping the mark, which stops me. I've no just cause to barge in there and kill that guy with my bare hands. I have to let Hayami live her life.

Sweat coats my back. Rage boils beneath my skin. Then, just when I think all is lost, my earpiece crackles as Markus's voice travels through the airwaves. I hear two words that normally strike the fear of God in me, but right now, they're music to my ears.

"Code red. I repeat, we have a code red."

FOUR

HAYAMI

THE SHOPPING CENTRE IS BUSTLING WITH LATE-NIGHT shoppers all getting their retail thrill at the end of a boring day at work. I've been at university, Bastian babysitting me for that little stint, and now it's the Hellhound's turn to watch over me.

He's been on my security team for a few weeks now—despite my insistence that my father get rid of him. I'm still reeling from him pulling me from the clutches of the water I believed was the answer to everything. But the Beast decided otherwise.

No one's told me he used to be a Hellhound, but it doesn't take a fucking genius to work it out. He's not your average businessman—not with a face like that. But fuck me, I never would have thought my father would let a Hellhound onto our estate, let alone in our house.

The day I took that swim now feels surreal. The conversation with my father the night before had been the start of it, the beginning of the nightmare that doesn't feel like it'll ever end.

After that catastrophic meeting, I'd lain awake all night, fear drenching my cold yet clammy skin, revulsion and anger fermenting into a furnace I couldn't control. I replayed his every word, even though I never wanted to hear them again.

I'd stood in his office like a petulant child, rage building beneath my skin as my father unveiled his master plan, the project he'd been working on for the last few years.

He smiled, like he'd done me a favour, bought me a pony, given me a castle when all he'd done was curse me.

How dare he?

How dare he barter with my future?

How dare he treat me like one of his fucking business deals?

The scream welled in the back of my throat, but I swallowed it like I've done so many times before. Screaming isn't the way to deal with my father. He'd have summoned Willa and Bastian, who would've manhandled me back to my room and probably sedated me. Although, sedation felt like a nice option then, because the thought of what he'd proposed had made me want to vomit.

"I want only the best for you, Hayami, only the best. And this is the only way I can secure it." My father paused, and it took me a second to realise he was waiting for me to thank him, to bow my head and tell him how grateful I was for all he's done for me, for the fact that he controlled my future like a puppeteer.

But the words wouldn't come; they wouldn't betray me. So instead, I'd smiled as I plotted how I could sabotage his plan. There was no fucking way on this earth I was letting him run my life any longer.

I'd risen with the sun like a zombie, having stared at the ceiling for the entire night, and I knew what I was about to do despite trying to convince myself it'd be nothing more than a morning swim, even when I asked Markus to switch off the security cameras.

And I did swim. One last swim. One last quiet moment before I showed my father what he'd pushed me to. With each length, I could still hear my father's words, still see the look in his eyes.

I gripped the side of the pool to catch my breath. I'd stopped counting after fifty lengths. I'd stopped counting everything.

It was time.

I floated on my back, but the lights above the pool hurt my eyes. Even with them shut, I had felt their stare upon me as if they knew what I was about to do and were judging me, burning into my eyelids in a vain attempt to stop me.

So I'd flipped onto my front and was consumed by the water.

A loud droning filled my ears, the pressure surrounding me, making me feel like the water was holding me, cradling me in my hour of need.

It was the only way to be done with my father. So I let the water claim me.

The only problem with this plan was I wouldn't see the look on his face when he realised what I'd done. How much I'd cost him.

Pressure built in my chest as I'd held my breath and kept my mouth clamped shut.

The droning noise began to sound like humming, as if the water itself was shushing me, assuring me that it had me and would never let me go.

But before I could delight in this thought, the water exploded beside me, and I was pulled from its clutches and hauled onto the side of the pool.

My eyes were full of water, my mouth gasping, lungs

burning. It took several seconds before I could open them. But when I did, he came into focus—the man who'd pulled me from the depths, who'd put an end to my demise.

He knelt beneath me, my body draped over him like I was sprawled across a large chair, his dark trousers plastered to his skin. And as my eyes adjusted, I looked up at his face and was utterly convinced I'd succeeded—because this wasn't a man at all.

He was an angel. Beautiful.

A serene masterpiece, made of only the finest qualities, the likes of which I've never seen on this earth.

Yes, he was an angel, and he had come to take me.

But then he'd turned, slowly, slightly, the fraction of movement distorting the light and shattering the image of him. My angel disappeared. The smooth skin on the right side of his face gave way to something else.

Scars.

Ugly, snaking scars that roamed from his collar and clawed their way up his neck, touching the underside of his chin and nearly reaching his left eye—stopping just short of taking his sight.

The skin was mottled, warped. Nothing like an angel.

Every bit the devil.

I pushed away from him.

And I saw it in his face—the acceptance of my reaction. This was how it must always be for him. The response he was used to. Who wouldn't look at him and not think he looked like a beast, his perfect portrait slashed down one side?

I could imagine people were afraid of him. But it wasn't fear I felt. It wasn't the reason I pushed back from him, with what he must have taken for horror written across my face.

No. I saw something else.

A man who'd endured pain. A man who'd seen the worst.

A man who was as scarred as I am—except his scars were visible. A man who has been to hell and lived to tell the tale.

And he'd come to me, on the brink of death, as if fate had hand-delivered him.

Even now I wonder why he was sent to me. Why is he here? What job has he been tasked with doing?

I'm a logical thinker, someone who needs evidence and hard facts before forming opinions. I've never been one for fate and destiny and spirits, yet when he pulled me from that pool, I felt something, saw something I'm still having a hard time assessing.

My analytical brain is arguing that he was there by my father's design—that somehow, my father knew my intentions. That he'd tapped into my brain, seen what I was about to do, and that's why the Beast was there. And why he now stalks my every move.

Yet, it doesn't sit right. It isn't possible that my father knew what I intended to do. That's beyond the realm of science. Beyond the capabilities of man, even one such as my father.

A shopper brushes past me, and the Hellhound swings his arm out, bringing me out of my stupor. He's so close I can smell his spicy cologne, feel the energy radiating from him.

He makes me nervous—though not because of the brutal scars. I've grown used to those. I see them every night when I lie awake, remembering being held by him after he'd pulled me from the water. The beautifully beastly man who changed my life. Who intervened when I thought no one would. Who decided my time wasn't up—that I had more to give to this unfair world.

Strangely, I'm not repulsed by his scars. What I see now is how others respond to him—the faces of the shoppers as they pass. They catch a glimpse, grimace, move aside, or look down. They want to unsee him.

But I see him. Or at least, I *think* I do.

And every so often, there'll be that one person who doesn't look away from him, doesn't scowl at his face, the people like me who don't view him like he's just stepped out of a horror film. And I wonder what they see. Like me, do they want to know how he became the beast he is?

Selecting another dress from the rail, I fling it over my arm and then head to the dressing rooms. The Beast clears my path, his eyes sweeping the shop for danger. He's dressed in all black: combats and a tight tee that only accentuates his buff physique.

I reach the cubicles and note the heavy curtains, which hang across each section. I make my way to the furthest one at the end. Normally, it's Willa who shops with me, and she's quite happy to wait at the front of the row, but he follows me, checking the empty cubicles as we walk past them.

Reaching the last one, I step inside and then turn to face the Hellhound, contemplating just how much I can push him.

It's nothing personal—although I'm still harbouring some anger with him. I don't know whether he saved me or condemned me. I guess only time will tell. But whoever he is, I'm a bitch to everyone on my security detail; Willa and Bastian are just used to it. They know I don't mean half of the things I say. That it's purely the backlash of the lonely existence I endure. Willa laughs my sniping off, and Bastian ignores me. But the Beast? I haven't tested him yet. Now seems like the perfect opportunity.

"Are you joining me?" I ask, gesturing with my head for him to step inside. "You gonna watch whilst I undress, just to make sure no one attacks me in the dressing room or leaps out from under the curtain?"

I flick my tongue over my teeth, smirking as he stands, arms folded, his eyes as dark as thunder clouds. This could go one of two ways: He could ignore me, like Bastian, or he could laugh in my face and make it into a big joke. But he doesn't strike me as a comedian.

When he lowers his gaze, the air shifts.

"Do you want me to?" He doesn't smile, doesn't hint that this is a joke. He sounds deadly serious, and I can't ignore the heat that flares over my skin. From any other guy, this would sound leery, but there's nothing creepy about the way he's looking at me.

Just as I'm about to come up with a witty comeback, he says, "You think this is all one big joke, don't you?" There's no mistaking the deliberate tone of his words.

My mouth opens, but nothing comes out.

"You think I'm just here for show, the freak to scare off the real bad guys. But when I do a job, I do it properly, and right now, my job is to protect you. That means I'll do whatever it takes to keep you safe, no matter how spoiled or entitled you are. Now, I can wait out here, or I can come in there. It makes no fucking difference to me."

Spoiled and entitled? I should be reeling, but I'm too shocked that he bit back. Of all the bodyguards I've had, not one of them has ever stood up to me. They've always been too scared of my father. Not of me. No one is afraid of me.

With a hefty tug, I pull the curtain closed, banishing him from my sight.

He's annoyed me, but I'm also intrigued.

The heat doesn't leave my skin as I sit in the cubicle, not trying anything on. Just sitting on the small bench, imagining what would've happened if I'd let him come in with me.

FIVE
FENRIR

I SHOVE OPEN THE INTERNAL DOOR TO THE BATHROOM. Two women by the sink scream and grab their handbags as if they're shields.

Willa is by the end cubicle, appearing to be talking to the door, probably trying to explain to Hayami about the code red. She'll always try and use words first, but I don't have time for words.

"Move away from the door!" I shout, drawing my gun as I kick the flimsy lock, the door swinging open.

Fury explodes in my temples. Willa tries to hold me back as I see Hayami pressed up against the far wall, one strap of her dress lowered, as the fucking leech wipes his mouth with the back of his hand.

My anger is frenzied, unbridled, untethered, and I don't give a fuck about protocol.

I grab the guy by his hair, haul him off Hayami, and drag him out of the cubicle. His eyes are wide, the whites stark as he thrashes about like a flailing animal. I shove the barrel of my gun into his mouth.

"You want something to suck on, motherfucker? I'll give you something to suck on."

He makes a choking sound, which only makes me push the gun down further.

"Fenrir, calm down. There's no need. I'll deal with this," Willa urges, trying to contain me.

"What the fuck? What the actual fuck?" Hayami shouts, pulling the strap of her dress up.

Her voice is the only reason I remove the gun. But my anger still rages, and with one blow to the side of his head, the fucker is out cold on the tiled floor.

"You fucking animal!" Hayami spits, her face contorted with powerful fury.

"As I was trying to tell you, Markus has issued a code red, which means we have to get you out of here, now." Willa tries again with the words.

"A fucking code red!" Hayami shouts "When is there *not* a fucking code red? What is it this time?" She folds her arms.

"We aren't sure yet, but we need to get you back to the house." Willa gestures towards the exit.

Hayami's eyes flick towards the door before landing back on Willa. "No." She sounds in control, but I know this is only the calm before the storm as she stares at Willa and then at me. "I'm not going anywhere."

"Hayami." Willa draws out her name as if it will help to soothe her.

"I said no. I'm having a good time. Well, I *was* having a good time until this fucking beast charged in here, so no. No. No." She's spiralling, words shooting from her mouth, her eyes stern.

Nausea pulses in my gut, as I know there's only one way this is going to go.

"I'm not coming with you. I'm not leaving this club," Hayami continues to vent. "I'm going to live my life regardless of what you or him or Markus or my father says, because I'm sick of it. Sick of it. Fucking sick of it all!" She's shaking. Twenty years of being on a leash. Twenty years of doing as she's told. Twenty years of being shadowed by bodyguards.

"I hear you," Willa pleads, hands out in front of her, slipping closer to Hayami. "I do. I know what you must be going through."

"How do you? How do you know? I bet you didn't have two fucking bodyguards hovering over you every time a woman tried to touch your pussy."

"Hayami," Willa warns, but Hayami won't be silenced that easily.

"And you, Beast." She turns to me. "When was the last time someone touched your cock? I bet you didn't have two bodyguards watching from the sidelines... unless that's your thing."

I'd love to dwell on the fact that she's just mentioned my cock, but there's no time for daytime fantasies. I'm too focused on getting her out of this fucking club alive.

"Confirm location," Markus's voice booms in my ear like he's standing next to me.

"We're in the Latvia Club," Willa answers.

"Yeah, that's what the GPS says, and I gave you a code red almost five minutes ago, so why the fuck are you guys still there? Is there a problem?"

"Hayami was in the bathroom. She's just finishing up," Willa explains.

"I don't care if she has to piss in the fucking car. Get her back to the house now before Devall has all our balls in a vice, including yours, Willa."

"Yeah, well, I do have the bigger pair." She doesn't smile at her joke, just turns her attention back to Hayami. "We have to go, *now*," she says, this time with a little more force.

Hayami takes a step forwards. The look in her eyes, the way she holds herself like she's preparing for the opening of a dam lets me know we're all fucked.

"Make me."

Willa glances at me, a sadness in her eyes that it's come to this, because this isn't the first time Hayami has refused to do as we ask. Not even a close second.

I take a step forwards and brace myself as Hayami sharpens her gaze.

"Back off, Beast," she sneers, her top lip curling. Her eyes narrow, and I can't help wondering who looks more of a beast now, me or her.

I take one more step towards her.

"Here we go," Willa says as Hayami launches herself at me.

Her nails are sharper than the last time she tried to claw my eyes out, and whatever she's been doing in the home gym must be working, as her kicks are strong. The only thing that remains the same is the volume of her screams.

"I hate you! You're a fucking monster!" Her cries bounce off the tiled walls as I pick her up, her fists punching my back, her legs whipping blindly.

I back up from the cubicle to give Willa some room, because we can't take Hayami out through the club like this. There's only one way we're going to get her out, and it kills me to do it.

Willa reaches into the small bag she keeps around her waist and pulls out the sealed packet.

"You got her?" she asks, her face stern, though weariness fills her eyes.

I turn so Hayami's thigh is facing Willa. "Yeah."

I hate this, just as much as Willa does. Hate the feeling of

Hayami struggling against me. Hate her scream when the needle goes in, the way her thrashing slows, her body going limp, how she hangs over my shoulder as all the fight leaves her. I hold her tightly, wishing I could rub her back, tell her that it's okay.

"Do you think there'll ever be a day when she comes quietly and we don't have to resort to this?" Willa asks, pocketing the needle and heading to open the door for me.

I pull Hayami off my shoulder and cradle her to my chest. She looks like she's passed out from too much drink, which is exactly what the clubbers will think.

"What about him?" Willa cocks her head at the comatose scumbag on the floor.

"Fuck him," I say as I carry Hayami out of the club and into the waiting car, relieved we've managed to get her out before she did anything she would regret. But my relief is short-lived as I remember the code red.

What the fuck has happened now?

SIX

FENRIR

I'M ON EDGE, AND IT'S NO WONDER, TRUSSED UP IN THIS fucking penguin suit. I'm used to action wear: combat trousers and heavy boots. Clothes that make you disappear into the night. This shirt and jacket feel claustrophobic.

Markus insisted that if I'm to protect Hayami at this evening's ball, then I have to abide by the dress code, whether I like it or not. I'm pulling at the cheap cufflinks he lent me when Hayami arrives at the top of the staircase.

She looked beautiful drenched in water after I pulled her out of the pool, and in the shopping centre when she was wearing sweats and a hoodie. But tonight, with her dark hair coiled into a pleat, claret lips, dazzling eyes, and a red figure-hugging dress with a split that stops mid-thigh, she is fucking devastating.

The only things marring this exquisite sight are the scowl on her face and the darkness that still surrounds her that only I can see. I'm thrown by her expression. I thought a woman like Hayami would love nothing more than to attend one of these functions. That she'd flaunt her name and her status amongst the other wealthy patrons.

But she looks as happy about this as I do.

In the two months I've been her bodyguard, I've yet to see Hayami smiling, laughing, relaxed, or laid-back, even when shopping. I'd been preparing to work with a spoiled princess, a diva of the worst kind, but slowly, I'm beginning to realise that she's nothing of the sort.

Okay, I'll admit, she has her moments—the snarky comments, the goading, the way she tries to bait me at every opportunity. But as the weeks have passed, I understand where this comes from and why she behaves the way she does. She's just as caged as the rest of us.

I thought she would be a social butterfly, but she doesn't go anywhere other than university and shopping. I'm sure this is because she isn't allowed to go anywhere without Markus knowing in advance and the location being vetted by him before it's approved. She's on a very tight leash.

She also doesn't appear to have any friends. I'm not sure if that's due to the restrictions or whether people don't want to be associated with a Devall. So, I kind of under-stand where the grumpiness comes from—and I'm receiving no special treatment when it comes to her temper. I'm sure she's still harbouring some resentment over the fact that I stopped her from killing herself. She certainly isn't treating me like her knight in shining armour.

Willa and Bastian are also fair game. She thinks nothing of barking at them. Willa, I think, quite enjoys the sparring, as if Hayami is her annoying younger sister.

And I won't lie: I don't mind the fierce Hayami—the snap of her tongue when she bites back. It's the only time I see a spark of life from her. An energy that reminds me there's a person in that shell.

But tonight, there's no spark. Tonight, she looks downright terrified.

Her father approaches, and I swear she bristles as he touches the crook of her elbow and leans in. "You look stunning, princess. Good job." He smirks.

Good job? I don't understand his choice of words, but Hayami appears to, as her brow furrows.

"Let's get a move on. We don't want to be late." Devall ushers us from the foyer.

I wait for Hayami to move, but she hesitates, stalling the inevitable. She clearly doesn't want to attend this ball as much as I don't, but we're all at the mercy of her father.

Her shoulders drop as she heads towards the exit. As she passes me, I wait for a snide comment—something about a beast being dressed up in a monkey suit—but she says nothing. And somehow, that breaks me more than it should. I lose my professional self and ask her if she's okay.

She stops and glares at me as if no one has ever asked her this question before. Just when I think she's going to spit in my face or throw one of her witty comebacks at me, she tilts her head and says, "Do me a favour, Beast—don't let anyone touch me tonight." Then she walks out the front door.

I follow her to the waiting car and open the door for her to climb into the back. Her cryptic request dances in my brain as I clock Devall getting into a car ahead. Markus nods at me as he holds open the door. He'd insisted the pair travel separately tonight, since tensions are rising between Devall and the Castros.

Returning Markus's nod, I climb into the front seat—the look on Hayami's face and her request sitting heavy in my gut.

By the time we arrive, the tension hasn't eased.

The venue is everything I hate about the rich. Gaudy chandeliers, designer outfits, a ballroom full of wealthy predators who prey on whatever takes their fancy. Hayami stays close, which is unusual, but I see the looks the men give her. See the hunger in their eyes. See the lust on their faces, the flick of their tongues as they imagine what she tastes like.

And I want to kill them all.

I hold myself together, keep my anger in check, but there's something about this function that sets me on edge. I've never been to a fancy ball, but I can imagine it's supposed to be a social event. People catching up on the latest business deals, boasting about their most recent luxury holiday or grand purchase. An event for the wealthy to showcase their worth.

But this doesn't feel like that kind of show.

The men are prowling, like hunters with guns. They aren't here for the orchestra, or to dance the foxtrot, or sip the champagne. They appear to be here to ogle Hayami and the nine other young women in attendance.

A couple of the women are basking in the attention, but the rest mirror Hayami: startled, afraid, and deeply unnerved.

We stay on the periphery, me glaring at anyone who dares to even look at Hayami. But then one fucking jerk-off in a suit approaches, and my scowl—and scars—aren't enough to deter him.

"May I have this dance?" he asks.

Hayami answers before I do.

"Absolutely not," she spits, but then her father arrives from nowhere.

"Come now, Hayami, that's not the way to speak to Mr Javier." His voice is slick like oil, and he turns to Javier. "I apologise. Hayami is a little nervous this evening. I'm sure a dance will loosen her up." He nods at Hayami, his slippery tongue retreating as he throws her the sharpest look that screams *obey or pay*.

Hayami gulps, lowers her head, and takes a step towards Javier, who is positively licking his lips. He takes Hayami's hand and leads her to the dance floor, and all I can do is watch.

The dance is never-ending. With each spin, Hayami's eyes land on me as I track her every movement. Javier tries to talk to her, but she doesn't appear to respond, only gazes at me as if waiting for me to throw her a lifeline.

Eventually, Devall disappears with some of his cronies, and I take my chance just as Javier's hand lowers to cup the curve of her ass.

I cut through the crowd like a scythe, pushing the dancers apart, already making up some bullshit excuse as to why I have to intervene.

But she's way ahead of me.

As I reach them, hand on my gun, she dips her head towards Javier's ear and says, "I'd move your hand if I were you, before he moves it for you." And then she looks at me, Javier following her gaze to where I loom behind him, like the Grim Reaper ready to collect what's mine.

"You heard her," I growl.

He smiles at me, but I see the fear as he registers my scars, wonders what battle I fought and what testament it is that I'm still standing.

Needless to say, he doesn't ask her to dance again, and neither does anyone else.

SEVEN
FENRIR

PRESENT

DEVALL'S OFFICE IS SICKLY HOT, AND IT HAS NOTHING TO DO with the six bodies occupying the space.

We stand in a row, facing the gang lord, who sits behind his desk like a man about to press the launch button on the atomic bomb. Markus is all official, hands clasped behind his ramrod-straight back. Bastian Ford is tanned, with watery eyes that are preoccupied—like he's counting down the days until his retirement. Willa appears exhausted, which is understandable—she has a tough job and a pregnant wife at home.

I'm not sure what I look like—other than my usual hostile self.

The only other person who's sitting—*no*, hunched is probably a more accurate description—is Junko Devall, Barrett's third wife. He brought her to Rothkor and married her after a business trip to Japan over twenty years ago. I imagine that once, she stood tall—her hair glossy black, eyes sharp and focused, skin as fresh as Hayami's.

But here, now, she looks haunted. Her skin is a pallid grey. Her hands wring something invisible. Her eyes are cloudy, as if misted over to unsee the things she must have witnessed over the two decades of being married to a man like Barrett Devall.

And if that isn't enough to add to her sorry state, there's a hint of a dark shadow cocooning her—a shadow I know only too well. It looks like the Grim Reaper has nibbled at her.

Like mother, like daughter, they both carry the death mark.

Coincidence? No.

They both share the Devall surname, and some curses come with more than just a reputation.

"Markus, update me." Devall steeples his fingers as the head of security steps forwards.

"Robert Castro is dead," Markus replies, letting it land in the room before Devall picks it up.

"You sure?"

"Positive. He was shot yesterday, sniper style, from long range whilst entering the Kaleidoscope, one of his clubs down on Gorring Avenue. He was taken to a private hospital, where he died later on in the evening."

Devall shifts his gaze for a second before firing it back at Markus. "And the sniper?"

Markus shakes his head. "No one has any idea. It appears to be a lone gunman, someone working on his own. But my sources are dry, and Callan has heard nothing through the grapevine. No one knows a thing, or if they do, they aren't saying anything."

Devall tuts. "Who the fuck would have the balls to take out Robert Castro?"

"That's the million-dollar question, sir, and unfortunately, the Castros think they have the answer." Markus waits a beat before continuing, the room hanging on his every word. "An email came through to one of your business accounts—the Amalfi bar you own on the southern side of town. Our IT guys are trying to trace the email, but there's so much encryption it's going to be nearly impossible to track."

"I don't give a fuck about the technicalities." Devall slams his hand on his desk. "Robert Castro is dead, and you called in a code red, so what the fuck is going on?"

"The email was a direct threat, sir," Markus says, then pauses.

I'm not sure if it's for dramatic effect, but Devall is about to open his mouth, so Markus quickly pulls his phone from his pocket and scrolls until he finds what he's looking for.

"It says, 'Devall will fall. It starts now. This blood is on your hands. And the next to be spilled will be the blood of your heir.'"

Fuck.

"The Castros think we shot Robert," Devall says.

"It certainly looks that way."

"But we didn't," he confirms. "I never made such a call."

"No, but I'm not sure how we're going to convince the Castros that this wasn't us. Not after Tyrone Miller's death six months ago. And we can't forget Morris Hamlin several months prior."

Devall raises his eyebrows. "Hamlin was in a brawl outside a nightclub," he says. "There was no evidence to suggest it was gang related."

"No, but no one was ever found responsible for his death, despite how hard the Castros looked. Add his death to Tyrone Miller's, and we have three members of the Castro gang all dead within a year of each other. You have to admit, it looks suspicious."

Markus waits as Devall appears to be thinking. When it's clear he isn't going to say anything, Markus takes up the thread.

"There's more, sir."

Devall's eyebrow arches.

"We lost surveillance on the cameras in the Premier Suite at the Amalfi around seven o'clock this evening. The security team down there headed to the suite to see what had happened and found every single person with their throats cut. They're all dead, including the staff. This was just before the email came through."

Silence clings to the heat in the room, making it feel sickly and claustrophobic.

For the first time, the gang lord looks uncomfortable behind his desk. Finally, he speaks. "Are you suggesting we're all in danger?" he asks Markus.

"I would say yes—it certainly appears that way, sir. The Castros have launched a very open and violent attack on us, which is understandable considering Robert Castro is dead."

Devall nods. "Vincent will want heads on fucking platters."

"He's made that clear, sir, with a direct threat to Hayami," Markus replies.

"Then we leave for one of the safe houses tonight." Devall slaps his hand on the desk, making Junko jump.

"If I may, sir, from a security angle, I wouldn't recommend the family moving together. It'll only make you more of a target and more vulnerable," Markus points out.

Devall surveys the room, and I wonder if he's weighing up the odds, working out just how much the safety of his family means to him. "Then what do you suggest?"

"I suggest you all leave for one of the secure houses, but separately. Vincent will send his best recruit from outside if he has to, so we need to make it as difficult as possible for his men to find you. I suggest some of the more remote locations you have."

Pursing his lips, the gang lord responds, "Fine, Junko can

leave tonight and go to Hanover House. Her team leaves with her. I'll stay here. I'm not going to be threatened out of my own home by Castro's men."

"And Hayami, sir?" Markus enquires.

Devall looks to Willa and then to me before replying. "You two will take her to Belial House."

The air crackles as Junko sits up as if she's just been electrocuted with a cattle prod. She hasn't reacted to anything she's heard in this room. Not the threat on her family, not the throat-slashing of some of their employees, nothing. Only now does she sit up and take notice.

"Belial, sir?" Markus asks, his face changing from very sure of himself to suddenly being thrown into the ring.

"Yes, you heard me. Belial. She's the target, after all—the email explicitly said 'the blood of your heir.' If it were me, I'd go for Vincent's children first and make him suffer their deaths before having to face his own. She needs to be somewhere that no one will find her. There's nowhere safer and more remote than Belial House."

"No." The word is so quiet, so small, we barely hear it, but Junko stands. Devall shoots her a look that would put anyone back in their place. "You can't send her to Belial House." Junko shakes her head and puts her hands out towards her husband, pleading with him. "Anywhere but Belial."

"Enough," Devall snaps, then nods at Markus, who moves towards Junko and rests a nonthreatening but very commanding hand on her shoulder. "There's nothing to discuss. She'll be safe at Belial House."

Junko looks like she's about to cry, but Markus's hand remains on her shoulder as Devall rises from his seat.

"You two will go with her." He motions to me and Willa. "No one else. The fewer people who travel, the less we'll draw attention to the fact that she's being moved. You leave within the hour. Get my daughter ready."

"There might be a problem with that, sir," Willa pipes up. Devall glares at her, and I'm sure we can all feel the sharpness of his stare. She quickly explains, "When the code red came through, Hayami was reluctant to leave the club. We had to sedate her to bring her back here."

Devall considers this before saying, "All the better to move within the hour, before she has time to come round."

Willa stares blankly at him. It comes as no surprise to him that we've had to sedate his daughter. After all, he was the one who suggested that we resort to sedation when we reported to Markus that she was becoming volatile and difficult to handle.

"Do you understand what I've just said?" the gang lord barks.

"Yes, sir," Willa replies quickly.

"Good."

The room feels uneasy, as if the walls are waiting to pounce.

"Then what the fuck are you waiting for?" He whips his head around to me. "You have fifty-eight minutes before you need to be on a fucking plane, so get a fucking move on."

"Yes, sir," we chorus.

Willa is the first to move. I follow as she marches down the hallway. Jogging to keep up, I grab her by the arm. She turns, eyes wet, face ashen.

"Are you okay?"

"No. God, this is the worst." She sniffs. "Marta is eight months pregnant. I can't be flying to some godforsaken shithole because the family has had some shitty death threat. What if Marta needs me? What if she goes into labour?"

"It'll be okay," I tell her, even though I know it isn't.

"And of all the fucking places, we're being sent to Belial House."

Willa swipes at her face with the back of her sleeve. I've

never seen her like this. She's always the pillar of calm and control. She must register the confusion on my face. "Has no one ever told you about Belial House?"

I shake my head. "No."

"It's a monstrous house stuck in the mountains, where all it does is rain and snow. It used to be where the family would go to get away from everything—to take a break, be cut off from the world and everyone in it. That was until…." Her lips quiver.

"Until what?"

She hesitates. "Forget it. I shouldn't have said anything."

I'm about to push her on this, but then I remember the ticking clock.

"And where exactly is Belial House?" I ask.

Willa stares at me, her usual warm smile nowhere to be seen.

"Hellion Ridge, above the town of Hellion Vale." She laughs—but it's not a funny laugh, more hysteria than humour. "No surprise that the names start with 'hell,' because that's where we might as well be going."

EIGHT

HAYAMI

THREE MONTHS AGO

Selecting a book from the shelf, I feel the Beast hovering behind me, probably scoping the bookshop for nonexistent stalkers, red dots on my forehead, or booby-traps planted amongst the thriller section.

"Do you read?" I ask him, placing the book carefully back on the shelf.

"No." His eyes remain alert, glancing at me quickly.

"Have you ever read a book?" I trail my fingers over the spines and select another one.

"Not since school." This time, he doesn't look at me, just stares at the doors to the main entrance as if a gunman is due any moment.

"I find that very sad."

He looks at me. "Why is that sad?"

"I can't imagine a life without books," I tell him, brushing my hand over the cover of a beautiful hardback that looks too nice to be read.

He glances down at the book in my hand. "What makes them so special?"

I inhale, contemplating my answer, before deciding that honesty is the best policy. I can't lie when surrounded by books.

"They're my friends." I glance at him. At his deepening scowl, I explain. "It may have escaped you, but I don't have a queue of people lining up at my door to hang out with me. Let's face it, who wants to be friends with Barrett Devall's daughter? I sure as hell wouldn't want to. So, the characters in these books become my friends."

He doesn't look convinced, so I try another angle.

"Do you ever want to escape?" When his eyes narrow, I ask, "Don't you ever just close your eyes and wish you were somewhere else?"

I don't think he's going to answer. Why would a Hellhound, trained only for one thing, have any understanding of what I'm talking about?

But then his shoulders drop, and he nods. "All the time," he says quietly, and my heart sinks. Of course he wants to escape; this poor, tortured creature isn't the nasty beast he pretends to be.

Holding the book flat in the palm of my hand, I lay my other hand on top of it. "These are my escape."

He glances at the book, uncertainty filtering across his face—unsure how something so small could wield such power.

"Here." I offer him the book.

He looks uncertain at first, hesitant to touch it. When he finally reaches out and takes it, his fingers brush mine as the book exchanges hands. And I can't help wondering what he wants to escape from. What life did he lead that brought him to my father's doorstep?

Exiting the plaza, I wonder if the Beast will read the

thriller I bought him or if it'll remain in the bag. I hope he gives it a chance. Right now, he looks pissed, which is normal, but it probably has more to do with the obscene amount of time I spent in the bookshop.

He hates shopping. But the urge to get out of the house has been too much—my father is in one of his more tempestuous moods, and my brain is refusing to let go of my impending doom.

After the foiled drowning, I set myself the task of finding another way to disrupt my father's plan for my future. I'll admit, with the arrival of the Beast on my security team, I've stopped focusing on coming up with a new plan.

But the ball last month has only heightened my campaign.

The revulsion I'd felt as soon as I walked through those doors had been enough to make me want to find the nearest lake and jump into it. Yet the Beast was by my side—something I was grateful for that night. It was the first time we had—how shall I put it—bonded?

He was exactly what I needed him to be, and I was so thankful that he was there; otherwise, I think I'd have thrown myself off the balcony.

Over the past few weeks, we've settled into a comfortable routine, but I'm restless today. My impending future keeps rattling in my brain, and the thought that I have no plan, no way of escaping, is starting to aggravate me. So a trip to the plaza felt like the only way I could get out of the house and feel even slightly normal.

Now in the car park, I try to keep a few steps ahead of the Hellhound. It winds him up when I don't stay by his side like a good girl, and my rebellious self is feeling undernourished.

I quicken my step, and I hear him huff behind me as he jogs to keep up.

"You're slowing me down, Beast," I tell him as I up my pace into a gentle run.

I'm almost to the car and enjoying this little game when a man dressed in black with his hood raised over a baseball cap steps out from behind a parked car and directly into my path.

We almost collide, but I jump back as he gets a good look at me.

"Hey there, you looking for a good time, little lady?" He tips the brow of his cap as his words roll in my stomach.

Little lady? The guy's a creep, but I don't have time to throw him an insult before the Hellhound is unleashed.

He dives on top of the guy, wrestles him to the ground, and punches him square on the jaw.

The guy is out.

The Beast turns to me. "You okay?" He hasn't even broken out in a sweat.

Clutching my shopping bag, I nod. "Yeah. I'm fine. Just some weirdo, that's all."

The Beast checks that the guy is still out, then takes a step towards me. He lowers his head, and I wonder if he's going to put his arm around me or stroke my back, but he does neither. Instead, in a low, heavy voice, he says, "Don't pull this shit with me, Hayami. This isn't a fucking game. You want to play games, I can play all day long, but not here, not now. Do I make myself clear?"

I should be furious. I should be punching him, telling him he has no right to talk to me this way—that I can do whatever the fuck I want. But those words have been doused by the arousal pooling in my stomach and the fact that all I want to do is ask, *What games?*

Trying to salvage the situation, I salute. "Understood," I say as he glares at me. We make our way back to the car, and it's in this moment—whilst I'm brushing myself down as if I'd been the one to dive onto the ground—that an idea begins to form.

A way that I can spoil my father's plans.

Like the Grinch, my grin must elongate my face. *Why the hell didn't I think of this earlier?* But it's going to be difficult. Impossible even. Not with the likes of the Beast on my back.

He's not going to like it. He definitely won't be happy. But fuck him. It isn't his future on the line. It's mine, and I'll be damned if I'm going to play ball.

NINE
FENRIR

PRESENT

"It's pretty basic, but it'll do the job. And I've packed you a few extras." Markus pats a large duffel bag. "There's a semiautomatic rifle in here along with a sniper rifle and an assault gun."

I raise an eyebrow, wondering what Markus knows that I don't. I already have my handgun, a Colt .45—a government model that's never let me down—and my personal gun, which only I know about. It's a Glock 19 9mm compact that I never go anywhere without.

"You think we'll need them?" I ask.

"I'd rather you didn't, but the mountain is home to all sorts of… animals. It might not just be the Castros you need to protect yourselves from." It's not the word *animals* that unnerves me but the pause beforehand, as if that wasn't quite the word he was looking for.

"Understood." When I stoop to pick up my bag, Markus puts his hand over mine, stopping me momentarily as he stares from under his baseball cap.

"Don't hesitate out there, Therion. Trust your instincts. You think something isn't right, you act on it. I'm not sure what the Wi-Fi will be like, but there are radios and our internal coms system. Someone will be on the other end, day or night. You keep in touch. Regular on-the-hour debriefs, do you understand?"

I'm used to Markus giving me the low-down, treating me like the newbie I still am. But this speech is different. His eyes hold me as if gripping my chin to make sure I'm listening to every word, words that sound like they mean something entirely different. Immediately, I'm reminded of Belial House, the way Junko reacted just an hour ago when Devall said its name. The way the blood rushed from her face, leaving it pale and lifeless, not dissimilar to the shade Markus is now.

Markus has been with the family for years. He started as a bodyguard, just like me, but worked his way up to head of the security team.

Has he been to Belial House? Does he know what awaits us?

"Yes." There's a brief second that I consider asking him why this place has such a bad rep, but the last thing I want is to feed my imagination. We're already bringing two shadows of death with us —my own dark mark along with Hayami's. There's no room for any more strangeness.

"I want to know everything that goes on out there, Therion. Everything. Because the last thing I need is the boss breathing down my neck when I'm in the dark as to what's going on with Hayami, do you understand?"

"Yes."

"Good." He takes his hand from mine and slaps me on the shoulder. "Don't let me down."

There's something final in his tone, like he's sending me off to war rather than up a mountain.

No more words are exchanged.

We load up in silence, the weight of whatever awaits us clinging to the air like static. The drive to the private airfield is uneventful, but my thoughts aren't. Markus's warning keeps circling in my head, echoing louder than the roar of the engines as the plane warms up on the tarmac.

By the time we're airborne, the mood has shifted.

Money means no questions asked. I've come to realise this in the six months I've worked for Barrett Devall. And this evening is no exception.

No one asked us why we were bundling a drugged woman onto a private plane. No one asked us where we were taking her or why. And when we landed, the guy who rented us the car never batted an eyelid at our comatose companion, who Willa is now supporting in the back seat as I drive us to the infamous Belial House.

Mountains surround the valley of Hellion Vale like two hands clasped together, holding us in their grasp. I'm not sure yet whether this feels safe—like a bird caught in human hands, unsure whether they're kind or deadly.

It's when we leave the flat terrain and start to climb the winding road up the side of Hellion Ridge that the atmosphere shifts. The rising altitude only intensifies the tension in the Jeep, the blacked-out windows sealing us in as the four-wheel drive pushes us higher up the mountain.

The sky is raven black, the trees swaying in the breeze as if they're tittering to one another.

Reminding myself that it has been a hell of a long night, I blink away the image of the gossiping trees as we head towards our destination.

It can't be much further.

The wheels grip the road like mountaineering boots, determined to get us to Belial House. Any higher and we'll need oxygen tanks.

As we round what feels like the twentieth corner, the road widens, and a clearing appears as the satnav announces that we've reached our destination.

I pull the car into the driveway and try to get a look at the house, but even with the headlamps, it's hidden amongst the darkness, which is so thick I can almost touch it.

I'm the first to get out of the car. There's no porch light to welcome us, no lamps in the windows, no cosy fire roaring from within. We're met instead by a towering structure: obsidian windows, a large, uninviting door, and a coldness I can already feel in my bones.

Any relief I felt at having finally arrived is quickly smothered by the sombre surroundings.

"Maybe we should be thankful it's night," Willa says as she climbs out of the car. "At least we can't see the house properly."

I pull Hayami from the back seat, where she's been unconscious for the entire journey. I clutch her to my chest, relieved she isn't awake to see this. The building is so still, which strikes me as odd—as if it's watching us, waiting for us to come inside before it reveals itself.

"What's the plan?" Willa asks, her eyes taking in the sheer bleakness of our surroundings—the tall trees, the dampness of the earth beneath our feet, the gibbous moon glowing above us—anything other than looking at the house we must enter.

"We'll take Hayami in, get some lights and heat on, and I'll bring the rest of the luggage in. You stay with her in case she wakes."

Willa looks at the sleeping Hayami in my arms. "She's going to freak when she wakes."

"She'll be groggy from the sedative," I say. She usually wakes up a bit cloudy and confused. "It'll be later, once she's fully come around, when it hits her."

"Something to look forward to." Willa exhales, and I note the new lines that have sprung up around her eyes. Worry's etched into her forehead, the gravity of her situation weighing heavily on her shoulders. "You ready?" She stares at the house as if she's gearing herself up to enter.

"We can't stand out here all night," I reply, wishing we could do just that.

We approach the house. Willa finds the keys in a key safe on the wall and pushes open the large wooden door.

The smell hits me first.

Damp. Cold. Forgotten.

"According to the plans, there's a large living area straight through those double doors," Willa says, wrinkling her nose. We spent some time on the plane studying the floor plan of the house and the map of the grounds Markus supplied us with, familiarising ourselves with the layout.

Outlines appear as my vision adjusts to the gloom. A large staircase snakes around the wall to the left of the grand entrance. Gilded frames catch on the sliver of moonlight that's dared to sneak through the windows, and a decorative table in the centre of the foyer is covered with a grey dust sheet. All the signs of a house once steeped in grandeur that, for some unknown reason, has been left to rot and ferment.

Willa trails behind as I push through a set of double doors and into a large room.

Like miniature mountains, the furniture is covered with more grey sheets. Willa proceeds to pull them off, setting off clouds of dust, revealing two large sofas, three easy chairs, and a coffee table.

"Lights?" I ask Willa as I lay Hayami down on one of the sofas, tucking her arms in and making sure she's comfortable.

"One second." She darts over to the far wall and fumbles with the switch.

The whole room lights up, casting a new scene before us. It would be tastefully decorated if we were living in the Victorian period. Dark wooden furniture, rich reds and purples embedded in the woven rugs, dark panelling lining the walls, and an open fireplace—I can almost imagine stockings hanging from it at Christmas. Three large sofas complete the room.

"It's not so bad with the lights on," she says with little conviction.

I want to argue. I preferred the gloom.

You can't fear what you can't see.

"Stay with her whilst I get the bags."

"Hurry, though," Willa says before I get to the door. "I've no idea how she's going to feel when she wakes up."

I quickly make my exit. Willa is right. What the fuck is Hayami going to think when she wakes up to find she's in Belial House with only me, Willa, and the darkness?

TEN
FENRIR

TWO MONTHS AGO

"WHAT THE FUCK ARE WE DOING HERE?" I HISS DOWN MY mouthpiece to Willa, who's watching Hayami as intently as I am.

Seemingly unaware of our unease, Hayami stands at the bar in five-inch stilettos and a figure-hugging black dress, looking like a peacock amongst a flock of pigeons.

"This is the bar she wanted to come to," Willa reminds me.

"Yeah, and I told you what kind of bar this is." I don't need to add that this isn't on the list of places that have been okayed by Markus for Hayami to visit—a list that consists of clubs and bars all owned by Devall. Willa already knows this and is turning a blind eye. She has a soft spot where Hayami's social life is concerned.

A man shimmies past me wearing a fishnet tank top, clearly showing his pierced nipples and tattooed chest.

"It's not our job to decide where she goes," Willa answers through my earpiece.

She's on the other side of the bar, watching Hayami from a different angle, ensuring that we cover all bases. She steps back to let a woman with a tray of drinks through the throng of people who are dressed—and I use the word *dressed* lightly—in short skirts, open shirts, tops that barely cover their breasts, and some that don't cover them at all.

"Unless it compromises her safety." I sweep the crowded room again but can't keep my thoughts at bay. What are we even doing here?

In the four months I've been assigned to Hayami's security team, she's never gone to a bar like this. Hell, she often doesn't leave the house unless it's to go shopping. She hates clubs and bars. Until now, it seems.

"How does this place compromise her safety?" Willa challenges me.

My eyes roll involuntarily. "People come here for more than a drink. Take a look around."

She doesn't follow my instruction, just keeps her eyes on Hayami. She must know what I'm referring to: the flesh on show, the gyrating hips, the wandering hands, and the adventurous tongues.

"I sense no danger here, and we don't have to worry about concealed weapons," Willa says. "Besides, she's an adult, and she's free to explore whatever things she wants to."

"You and I both know that's bullshit." I know what she's getting at, but this isn't Hayami.

Eight weeks ago, she asked me not to let anyone touch her at that stupid ball. Yet tonight, she walked into this bar despite me telling her what kind of place it is. I swear she hitched up her hem and flicked her hair over her shoulder like she was advertising herself, making sure everyone could see what was on offer.

But I'm still working on the rule that no one is to touch her.

Luckily, thanks to us being present, no one has approached her.

What is she playing at? Why are we here? If she doesn't want guys to look at her, then what the fuck is she doing in a place like this? I'm so confused, but I won't be deterred from my job. As far as I'm concerned, everyone is a threat.

"Hey, big guy." A person approaches me. I'm not sure what gender they are, as their hair is short with silver high-lights, their make-up bold and colourful, and their upper body is ripped under the tight Lycra top that's stretched across their chest. "How far down do those scars go?" They wink and trail their hand across my pecs.

I glare at them, and they drop their hand.

"It's always the mean-looking guys who turn out to be pussycats. Is that what you are, a pussy cat?" They laugh. "Is kitty not playing tonight?" They take a step back. "Such a shame. I would have loved to have played with you. Next time." They wink before gliding off into the crowd as I return my focus to Hayami, who is now on the move.

"I think she's heading to the bathrooms," Willa's voice advises down the earpiece.

"You better go scope them out. Fuck knows what's going on in there," I instruct Willa, who agrees and pushes on through the crowd.

I tail Hayami as she weaves aimlessly through the party-goers, appearing as if she's taking everyone and everything in. My stomach drops when she makes her way to the rear of the bar.

I've only ever been in this place once. I'd been sent to deliver a message to a guy who owed Devall money. I couldn't find him on the dance floor or near the bar but had been told that he was here. I'd pushed on through the back of the bar only to discover a bank of booths hidden in the dark-ness and shielded from prying eyes.

After bypassing the booth with a woman grinding on the lap of some guy whilst another guy next to him waited his turn, I found the scumbag I was looking for. He was huddled in the corner of a leather seat, having his cock sucked by a woman with a mop of blonde hair that could have been a wig. Needless to say, the message was an easy one to deliver with him having his crown jewels hanging out.

But Hayami is heading straight for the booths.

She reaches the first booth, and I want to grab her, pull her away, tell her that this isn't where she belongs. That this isn't what she's looking for. But there's something in her eyes. Curiosity. Intrigue. I can't bring myself to break the daze she appears to be in. She's frozen, like she's stepped into quicksand. Her eyes are trained on what's going on under the cover of the dim lighting and the rhythmic music.

It takes an effort to tear my eyes from her. When I do, I see what's caught her attention. A woman sits behind the rectangular table. Her eyes are closed, and her head sways. At a glance, anyone would think she's kicking back, enjoying the music and relaxing, until I clock the guy next to her. His hand snakes under the table and is clearly between her legs. Her nipples peak through her sheer top. She licks her lips, then opens her eyes and stares at Hayami.

Hayami's eyes widen, and I step forwards, ready to intervene, until the woman smiles at Hayami and softens her lips. I fight all my restraint to stampede over and drag Hayami away. Crooking her finger, the woman beckons Hayami to join them. She must sense Hayami's reluctance, as she then pulls the neckline of her top down, exposing her breast, and begins to play with her nipple in the hope that Hayami will be tempted.

And there's a second where I think she's going to go and join them, but then Hayami looks at me, her cheeks flushed, eyes searching. And I can't tell what she's thinking. Is she asking for my permission? Is she waiting for me to step in? What the fuck does she want me to do?

Just as I'm about to ask, Willa arrives and places her hand on Hayami's back.

"There you are," she says as Hayami is brought out of her trance. "I thought you were heading to the bathroom."

There's a beat where Hayami appears to be composing herself before she speaks. "Yeah, I was. I got lost."

Willa glances into the booth, the woman having covered herself up.

"Come on," she beckons. "I'll show you where they are."

Hayami doesn't look back at me as she follows Willa to the bathroom, and I'm left wondering what the fuck just happened.

ELEVEN

HAYAMI

PRESENT

THERE'S A BITTER TASTE IN MY MOUTH. MY TONGUE'S FURRY, like something's growing on it, and my head feels like my brain is loose and sloshing around in my skull. This isn't the first time I've woken up like this.

I try to recall what events led me here, but there's a new sensation, one I haven't felt before: a chill in my core, as if someone has frozen my insides, including my memory.

Flashes come back to me.

The club.

The beat of the music.

The guy's hand on my leg.

Following him to the toilet.

The widening of his eyes as he pulled down the strap of my dress.

The tingle of his tongue over my nipple.

And even though his touch felt like sandpaper and his lips like jelly, I wanted it. *It*—not *him*, just *it*. Because I want the touch of a man to be on my terms, not anyone else's.

Then the Beast arrived. The noise of the door being kicked in, the rage on his face as he'd ripped the guy from my body, and the quiver in my core as he'd shoved the barrel of his gun down the guy's throat.

I don't know what to make of the fact that the Hellhound shoving his gun down the guy's throat turned me on far more than the guy had when he flicked his tongue over my nipple. Despite the heat that'd burned between my legs, I cursed the Beast for interrupting us.

My throat swells as I try to swallow, and I recall screaming at him.

"I hate you! You're a fucking monster!"

There was no way I was leaving that club. No way I was having them dictate my life to me for one more second.

Then the Hellhound picked me up, threw me over his shoulder. The heat had brewed under my skin as I'd fought, kicked, punched—and then nothing.

And by my raging headache, blurry eyes, and fog surrounding my brain, I know they've bent to my father's will and drugged me, again.

There's anger somewhere amongst the haze. Raging, lethal anger. But right now, rather than burning brightly in my gut, it's smouldering under the aftermath of whatever shit they injected me with.

It's abuse. Plain and simple. But what police officer or doctor would listen to me, Hayami Devall? Which upstanding citizen would come to my rescue and arrest my father for illegally drugging me? Because, as much as I want to, I don't blame Willa or even the Beast. They're only following orders, and I know what would happen to them if they don't do as they're told.

It's my fault they end up drugging me. *My* defiance. *My* reluctance to do as I'm told. *My* resistance to fall in line with my father's demands. But it doesn't take the sting out of any of it.

Normally, after I've been sedated, I wake in my bed, but this doesn't feel like my soft mattress. Nor does it smell like the usual lavender I spray my pillow with. So, where the fuck am I?

I try to blink, but my eyes are sticky, like they know that when they open, they won't like what they see. But I force them to face whatever shit's awaiting me.

An orange glow greets me, along with a damp, musty smell accompanying the dark furnishings and rich colours.

Strange.

Blinking, I adjust to my surroundings. With the lull in my brain, I'm struggling to process that I'm somewhere I've never been before. If I have, I don't recall it.

"Where the fuck am I?" My voice sounds weird, a deepness to it that feels rough inside my ears.

"It's okay. It's okay." Willa's voice pierces the panic that's begun to balloon. Her hand's on my arm whilst her body blocks out the size of the room along with the enormity of my current predicament.

"Where the fuck?" I push up onto my elbows, taking in the large room, the dark cornices, the shadows that dance upon the darkened walls.

"It's okay," Willa repeats, using that voice she saves for when I've lost my shit and she's trying to calm me. "You're safe, and that's all that matters."

"Like fuck it does." There's a blanket over me, which I push away. My dress is gone, replaced with sweats and a hoodie. I glance at Willa, and then I feel him.

The Hellhound.

"What the fuck are you doing here?" I turn to face him, all of him.

The man who won't let me breathe.

The man who stalks my every movement.

The man who is ruining my life—albeit less than my father is.

"There was a code red," the Beast says.

"I remember." I lower my tone, signalling my annoyance at how they interrupted my night for a stupid code red. "We have a code red nearly every week."

"This one was different," Willa explains. "They made threats against you, specifically."

"And?" Again, this is nothing new. My life has been in danger since the day I took my first breath. Disgruntled gang members, people who have a grudge against my father (that list is endless), and anyone who opposes his reign on this city. I've been threatened by them all.

"Like I said, this was different." She swallows, which unnerves me. It takes me a second to realise why. I've never seen her like this. Hollow. Shaken. "They killed some people at one of your father's clubs."

"They?" I quirk my head to the side, but it isn't Willa who answers.

"Robert Castro has been assassinated," the Beast tells me, and my stomach plummets.

I try to keep out of the gang shit, but I know enough to understand the significance of this. Robert Castro is—*was*—the brother of Vincent Castro, the head of the Castro family, my father's biggest rivals.

"Of all the lame fucking ideas, that's got to be my father's worst," I say, looking back at the Beast.

"It wasn't his order. He's not to blame for Robert's death." The Beast eyes me cautiously.

The large grandfather clock in the corner of the room beats steadily as I gather my thoughts.

"Then why are we being targeted?"

"Because Devall is the obvious suspect."

"Why?"

He glances at the floor, and my hackles rise. "I'm not a fucking child. I deserve to know what's happening when my life is supposedly at stake because of this shit."

"Some of Castro's men have been killed. Tyrone Miller was shot six months ago, and before him, Morris Hamlin was beaten to death outside a club. The Castros have had us in their sights since then, and this has simply forced their hand. They have to blame someone, have to act; otherwise, they will appear to be weak," the Beast explains, flexing his biceps whilst Willa tenses her jaw.

She knows he shouldn't be telling me this stuff. But even though I loathe him, I do appreciate the fact that he seems to be the only one on my security team who doesn't shield me from the reality of my father's world. He keeps me up-to-date on the rumblings within the gang world. Maybe he's just unprofessional, or maybe he knows that knowledge can be powerful.

"They mean business, Hayami," Willa cuts in, but the Beast won't be pushed aside that easily.

"They killed a bunch of people in one of your father's clubs and then sent an email saying the Devalls will be next, specifically the heir." The Beast crosses his arms as Willa rolls her eyes.

"And that's why your father has sent us here," she adds, shaking her head at him.

"And where exactly *is* here?" I ask.

Willa sighs before she answers. "Belial House."

All I can do is laugh. It's manic, high-pitched, more of a shriek, but it's the only way I can respond to this shitstorm that's supposed to be my life.

"You've got to be kidding me." But by the look on Willa's face, I know this is no joke.

I glance once more at the room—its vaulted ceiling, the

enormous fireplace that houses crackling flames, and the oversized sofa I'm spread out on.

"So, this is the house of horrors?" I whistle through my teeth. "Well, fuck me. Things must be serious if my father has resorted to packing me off to this little hellhole. Or was this your idea?"

I look at the Beast, who glares from under his scowl, arms folded across his enormous chest like he's still standing guard over me—though there isn't a chance in hell anyone could get to me here.

He looks like the pillar of strength. Willa, on the other hand, fits the scene—her eyes wide, the whites ablaze like she's staring down the headlights of an oncoming vehicle.

But the Beast? He isn't afraid.

"Does he know about this place?" I tip my thumb at him.

"What's there to know other than rumours?" Willa bites her bottom lip. It doesn't suit her, this frightened rabbit look.

"She hasn't told you?" It's a question, even though Willa has just given me the answer.

My eyes lock with his, and I wonder what he'll make of it all. Willa is scared shitless. So why aren't I? I should be. Should be pulling the blanket up to my chin and asking the Hellhound to frighten the monsters away. Instead, I welcome something other than the shit show that is my life.

The Beast shakes his head.

"Well, why don't we pull up a seat, campers, and stoke the fire, 'cause this shit's about to get spooky." I rub my hands together, assessing my audience of two. But my skills are wasted on them. Willa is too fucking scared, and the Beast is… well, he's just the way he normally is—unaffected by everything and everyone, unless someone is trying to breathe near me.

"Believe it or not, this place used to be a holiday home," I begin. "We're talking years ago, at the time my father was married to his first wife, Eileen. I've been told they bought it because of how remote it is. A place for when they just wanted to get away from life for a bit. Sounds perfect if you ask me. But it wasn't. This place…." I glance around the room for dramatic effect. "My mum came here once with my father before I was born and swore she would never return, and they never have."

The Beast rolls his eyes.

"Am I boring you, big man?" I ask.

"No, but I'm guessing something happened? A shadow on the wall one night? A candle blown out during an important dinner?" There's a dry smugness to his voice, one he saves for talking about the super-rich.

"No, better than that." I widen my eyes and lower my voice to make it sound more sinister. "My mum didn't like the house from the minute she arrived, and she told me that she found out the previous owner had been a guy named Hollins who went mad here one winter when he got snowed in with his family. He started to see things that weren't there, rubbed his eyes with sandpaper until they bled, and scratched his skin off with a razor blade.

"His wife tried to get help, ran from the house with their two children in tow. But the snow was too thick, and they died of hypothermia on the mountain. Hollins remained in the house, unable to leave as the madness took hold. He was found weeks later, when the snow had thawed and one of the locals came up to see if the family were okay. Imagine their horror when they found his wife and two kids frozen to death on the roadside and then got here to find Hollins hanging from the chandelier."

Silence slithers over the room as Willa shivers.

"Shit." She exhales and hugs her body. "I'd heard rumours amongst the staff about this place and about how no one ever wanted to come here, but no one knew why. Did all that really happen?"

I hold it as long as I can before I let out a shriek of laughter. "No, but you should have seen your face!" I slap my leg, and Willa scowls. I'm laughing—really, I am—but the sound feels strange in this place, like it doesn't belong.

And maybe it doesn't, because beneath the laughter, something stirs—a memory. One I haven't thought about in years.

I remember the look on my mum's face when I was about eight years old and came across the photo of her at Belial House.

My mum was having a good day. I knew because her hair was tied back, and she kept smiling at me. I liked the days when she felt good. It made me feel good too. We were in my bedroom, looking at some photo albums. Most of the pictures were of me as a baby or a toddler, my dark hair in pigtails with chocolate smeared around my mouth. My mum wasn't in a lot of the photos, maybe because she was the one taking the pictures. But when I turned the last page, a photo slipped out and landed on my knee.

It was of my mum. She looked a little younger, her face not as lined, her cheeks rosier, and she was standing in the doorway of a grand house made from dark stone, with large ornate windows and a fancy roof. The building was surrounded by trees. It wasn't a place I'd seen before.

"Mummy, where is this?" I asked, holding the photo out. My stomach did that funny thing when I worried or when I had to eat something I didn't like.

Her happy face changed to one that didn't look like my mum's at all.

She snatched the photo from my hand, and her eyes turned watery. Her shoulders dropped, and she went from looking mad to seriously sad.

"Sorry, sweetie," she said. "I didn't mean to snatch. I just don't like this house." She stuffed the photo in her back pocket and pulled me in for a hug.

"But where is it? Have I ever been there?"

"It's called Belial House, and it's far away from here," she began. "It's a holiday home that belongs to your father, and no, you've never been there."

"Why not?"

She didn't answer me straight away, like adults did, just stared off in the middle distance, her eyes glazing as if lost in the memory.

"I've only been once, before you were born. Your father took me for a holiday, and I didn't like the house very much."

With wide-eyed innocence, I asked, "Why not?"

"Well, there was just something about it that I didn't like." She looked at me, her thick hair falling into her eyes.

"What didn't you like about it? Did it smell?" I considered it was like when I went to the dentist, and that horrible cleaning smell would cling to my throat and make me want to throw up.

"No, it wasn't the smell. It was a feeling. A creepy feeling, like the house had eyes and was watching me." Her voice got lower at the end of her sentence, like she was drifting away from me.

"Do you think it was haunted?"

"I don't know. Maybe."

"Well, that's silly." I folded my arms.

"Silly?"

"Yeah, there's no such thing as ghosts."

"You sound very sure of that," Mum said.

"At school, Milly Walters wrote in her journal that she'd seen a ghost, and Mrs Knight said that ghosts don't exist, so there must have been another explanation."

"And what do you think?"

"I don't think they exist. I think they're just in films and books, like unicorns and dragons." I'd been convinced Mrs Knight wouldn't lie to us, truly believing teachers weren't allowed to lie to the kids or else they'd lose their jobs.

"Then it doesn't matter what I think," Mum said, smoothing my hair from my face.

"Can we go to the house on holiday?" I wanted to look at the photo again, but she'd hidden it in her pocket.

Mum shivered before shaking her head. "No. I'll never set foot in that house again."

Now, scanning the room, I still can't quite believe I'm here—inside Belial House. I have no fucking idea what shit happened here, why the staff all think this place is cursed, and why my mum visited once and will never come back.

But I guess, seeing as how we've been dumped here for God knows how long, we're about to find out.

TWELVE

HAYAMI

A FAIRGROUND HAS COME TO ONE OF THE LARGE PARKS ON THE outskirts of Rothkor, and I've insisted on going as part of my campaign to ruin my father's plans for me. After the visit to the bar, I nearly abandoned the idea of fighting back. It was going to be too difficult, considering I had the Beast breathing down my neck.

I won't lie. I'd been intrigued by the bar I convinced Willa to let me go to, turned on in a way that I'd never imagined and only read about in the romance novels I devour. I'd felt drunk on lust watching the couple in the booth, surprised that it was Willa, not the Beast, who seemed more eager to steer me away. He'd stood behind me, watching, waiting, but not dragging me away by my hair or punching anyone in the face.

And there'd been a moment—when the woman invited me to join her—that I thought maybe the Beast was going to be okay with it. But something held me back. Nerves? Fear of the unknown? I don't know. Then Willa rocked up, and the moment was lost.

Since then, I've had to rethink my plans—until I saw the poster for the fair.

Bingo.

Strangely, my father has agreed to let me go, but only if I take two bodyguards with me. So, the Beast and Bastian have been given the delightful task of ensuring my safety for the evening.

What my father doesn't know is that I've arranged to meet up with someone—Cole Kilner, a new guy from university who arrived in Rothkor a month ago. He's nice. Cute. And, as far as I can tell, he either doesn't know who my father is or hasn't put two and two together and realised I'm Barrett Devall's daughter.

The fairground is noisy and littered with people of all ages. The smells of fried food and candy floss mingle with the garish clash of music genres and sound effects from the rides, as well as the riders' shouts and screams.

I imagine it's a bodyguard's nightmare. So much going on, so busy, too many things to pay attention to. The perfect place to get lost.

When we meet up with Cole, the Beast is furious.

"This wasn't part of the plan," he tells me, his scowl accentuating his scars.

I glare at him. "Sometimes life doesn't fit into a plan."

"We haven't done any background checks on this guy," he points out, not lowering his voice.

Cole just looks confused, his sandy hair flopping into his eyes.

Bastian comes to the rescue, his gruff voice highlighting how much he doesn't want to be here this evening. "He's fine. He goes to uni with her. We've done checks on all the students she has classes with. He checks out."

The Beast huffs as I smile at him. One–nil to me.

The pair stalk behind us, checking for signs of danger, hidden weapons, and whatever else they keep a look out for whilst Cole asks why I have two bodyguards tailing me. I try to convince him that they're overprotective family members, which doesn't wash. But I laugh it off and hope he doesn't ask any more questions.

By the time we've been on the Ferris wheel and the dodgems, I've relaxed a little. For a moment, it feels like this could be what life is supposed to be—slightly normal. Going on a date with a guy and enjoying myself. Cole is nice and good company. He's the kind of guy I can imagine sitting on the sofa with and watching a movie. Not the kind of guy who would pull my hair and tell me how naughty I've been, but beggars can't be choosers.

And the Beast and Bastian seem okay with how things are going. Well, Bastian does. The Beast is his usual sulky self.

But this all changes when we reach the line for the ghost train.

"No way." The Beast steps forwards, placing his arm in front of me.

"I beg your pardon?" I snap.

"There's no way you're going on that."

"Who made you fucking God?" I push his arm aside and move down the queue.

Cole looks from me to the Beast. "Hey, we can give this one a miss. It doesn't matter," he says.

"It *does* matter. I want to go on it." I stand my ground. The ghost train is the backbone of my plan.

"I can't see you in there. It's pitch-black. It's not safe. Anything could happen," the Beast explains.

"Do you think I'm going to get attacked on a fucking ride? Do you think someone is going to go to the trouble of following me on and then sticking a knife in me when it gets dark?"

The Beast doesn't answer.

"Or do you think Cole here is going to murder me?"

"Hey, I'm just here to have a good time." Cole holds both hands up and glances nervously at the Beast.

I look to Bastian, hoping he'll back me. Of course he'll back me. He wouldn't dare argue with me in case I complained to my father.

But Bastian says that maybe the Beast is right, and that's when my plan starts to unravel—the plan I've spent all weekend conjuring disappearing before my eyes, all because the fucking Hellhound says so.

The ghost train would have been the perfect opportunity for some action with Cole. I'd timed the ride. Seven minutes. There's so much you could do in seven minutes. And with no bodyguards watching over me, it would have been perfect.

Would have been. This was my only chance, and now it's gone.

And my head explodes.

"I'm sick of this," I spit, ducking out of the line. The last few months have finally caught up with me—the stress, the anxiety, the impending doom.

"Hayami!" Bastian calls, but I ignore him and keep on walking until I'm at the entrance of the fair.

I'm so sick of this life. So sick of the restrictions, of having everything decided for me. Of having some fucking prick in a suit tell me what I can and can't do. Is this how it's going to be for the rest of my life?

I already know the answer.

When I see the entrance to the woods ahead of me, I start running.

My calves burn and my ankles feel weak, but I keep going. Running through the trees, dodging the fallen branches, getting deeper and deeper until I have no idea where I am or where I'm going.

There's no fear of getting lost, because this is what I want. I want to disappear where no one will ever find me.

A new plan forms. Running. Run until I can't see what's behind me.

So, I do just that.

But he's behind me. Not Bastian. He's too old to run. But the Beast isn't. I can hear him. Every branch that breaks. Every scrunch of the leaves. Each sound only makes me run faster.

He *will not* catch me.

"Hayami!" he shouts, and I push on. My legs are flying now, running of their own free will to the point where I don't think I'd be able to stop even if I tried.

It's him against me, and fuck if I'm going to let him win. He won that day in the pool. He won't win this time.

Just as I think I might be able to outrun him, the trees thin out, and I come to a river. I only just manage to slow down so I don't run headfirst into the water.

Fuck.

I turn, and there he is. He doesn't even look out of breath.

"There's nowhere to run to, Hayami," he hollers.

I look all around. If I go left, he'll pounce—same if I go right.

Fuck.

"Give up?" He's stalking the ground, pacing like a lion before its prey, and somewhere deep inside, I feel the swell of something, a heat beginning to crawl up my insides.

"No!" I yell.

"There's no point running," he says calmly.

"Yes, there is," I pant, my lungs still in overdrive.

"Not from me, there isn't."

I glare at him, wanting to argue and ask him how the fuck

he would know, but then I look at his scars. Is he trying to run from the past that won't let him forget?

"You can run from me, Hayami, but I'll always catch you."

I eye the water.

"Don't," he warns, and it's enough.

Carefully, I step into the water, but I sense him move behind me. I try to run, but the surface is uneven and slippery, and I fall into the freezing depths.

"Shit!"

It takes him seconds to reach me as I scramble over the rocks, my hands numb, the cold attacking my body with sharp, razor-like teeth.

He grabs my arm.

"Get off me!" I scream.

"No," he says.

He's so cool, which annoys me more than him manhandling me.

"I said get the fuck off me!" I fall again, my hands sliding on the stones, the water tugging at my clothes.

"And I said no." He manages to get in front of me and scoops me out of the water like I'm made of fresh air. I've no option but to cling to him as he wades through the river and gets us back onto the embankment.

As soon as his feet hit the ground, I thump his chest.

"Put me down!" I shout, sobbing now, my voice having lost all its urgency.

He does as I ask, but he doesn't let me go. Instead, he holds me and dips his head.

"I'm not sure what you're running from, Hayami," he says, his voice low and gentle, no longer the angry growl I'm so used to, "but I don't blame you. I've been running for the past fourteen years, and I'm still running. We're all running from our past."

My body shakes, not just from the glacial water but from

his words, the look on his face, how it feels to be held by him, and from this first and only admission that his life has been anything but perfect. For the past five months, I've known nothing about this man. He's remained an enigma—until now.

My heart sinks because I want him to be right. I want to know that I can take the advice he's giving me and hold on to it, but I can't.

"I'm not running from my past," I tell him, my bottom lip trembling. "I'm running from my future."

He stares at me, lips parted, and I'm about to tell him what awaits me, what my father has in store, the kind of man he really is, but then—

"Hey!" Bastian's cry cuts through the trees as he emerges breathless and sweating. "I'm getting too old for this shit," he wheezes, placing his hand on the side of a tree.

The Beast lets me go. And I'm gutted. I feel like the lifeline has been pulled from my grasp—because he had me. He *almost* had me.

THIRTEEN
HAYAMI

IT'S WHEN THE DRUGS START TO WEAR OFF THAT THE REALITY of my current predicament kicks in.

Willa has made a pot of tea and found some biscuits, her effort at "settling us in." The Beast is off setting up the security system that's supposed to keep me safe from the nothingness that must be outside. Because who the fuck is going to find me when *I* don't even know where we are?

"So, how long are we expected to stay here for?" I ask Willa, pulling my knees up to my chest.

"I'm not sure. Until it's safe." She holds the black mug with two hands like it's a tiny fire keeping her warm.

"And how is my father intending to achieve this? By killing the entire Castro family and all their gang members?" I glare at Willa, who remains silent. "We both know what's going down here. A gang war."

Her grip tightens around her mug.

"Which is great if my father wins, but what if he doesn't?"

"Hey, it won't come to that."

"How can you be so sure?"

"When has your father ever lost at anything?" Willa scoffs. "Besides, it's not our place to be concerned about what's going on with him and the Castros. What we need to focus on is keeping you safe, which is exactly why you've been sent here."

It's my turn to scoff. "Of course he has. I'm his prized possession."

Willa's face screws up in confusion, as if the tea is too hot, just as the Beast returns. His black T-shirt pulls against his enormous chest, the dark combat trousers snug around his waist. And that face. One half angelically beautiful, the other monstrously scarred—he's a man of two halves.

He takes the tea that Willa hands him and scowls. I'm not sure why. Maybe this whole fucking set-up. I take a biscuit from the plate, avoiding Willa's quizzical gaze. She didn't know what I'd been talking about when I referred to my father looking after his investments.

What my father has been up to isn't common knowledge amongst the staff. I've contemplated telling her. She'd understand. She might even help me. But the Hellhound? I'd been close to telling him once, the day of the fair, when he found himself dragging me from the water for the second time, but then the moment was lost. I'm not even sure what he'd make of it all.

I have this belief that everyone who works for my father must have some level of respect for him; otherwise, why work for a guy like him? Then again, who *does* like their boss? Who works for someone just because they admire or respect them? Probably no one on this planet. Still, I can't imagine being a Hellhound without some degree of loyalty to my father—or at least the Devall name.

Or maybe it's not loyalty at all. Maybe it's just fear. Maybe everyone around him operates out of sheer terror at what will happen if they don't.

"Where the hell did you get tea and biscuits from?" I ask, eyeing the digestive, trying to distract myself from my thoughts.

"Markus mentioned something about a local store down in the town. He called ahead and got the owner to come up and stock the house with the essentials. Apparently, the store used to do it when your dad used this house for his holidays. It's just tea, coffee, eggs, milk, and bread by the looks of things."

"How long, then, before we need to start eating each other?" I quirk a brow.

Willa flips me an exasperated look.

"I'm kidding. We aren't going to be here that long, are we?"

She glances at the Beast and then quickly back to me— one of those looks she hopes I didn't notice.

"We don't know," she says. "But I'm sure it won't be long."

"And what about university? I've got lectures this week and assignments due."

I'd gone on to university after studying my A levels, even though there's no point in any of it, as there's no way my father will let me get a job in the real world. But he couldn't argue with staying on in education. Uni is the only time I get to feel like a semi-normal person, despite Bastian accompanying me to every lecture. He probably knows more about human biology than I do. I swear he pays far more attention.

"Your laptop bag is here. Maybe you could email your tutors and tell them you're ill, and they'll send you what you need. It'll be like distance learning, I suppose. I'm sure they won't object, not with how much money your father pays them."

This is one of the reasons why I love Willa. She's so practical and always thinking ahead. Distance learning is doable. The university organised it for a girl in my chemistry class who'd had a really bad car accident in the first term and broke both her legs. And yes, as one of the university's biggest donors, my father holds more sway than most.

But I don't like the ease of this answer.

I don't like that this is a solvable problem. I want a dilemma, something that can't be fixed at the click of an email or the flash of my father's cash. I need a reason why I can't be here in this fucking house. If I'm ever going to destroy my father's plans for me, it isn't going to happen squirrelled away on a mountain with my bodyguards.

"Fuck." I punch my fist into the sofa. "As if my life couldn't get any fucking worse, I'm now stuck here with you two." Willa doesn't react, and neither does the Beast. "Come on!" I all but yell. "You guys can't be happy about this."

Willa waits as if testing the water before saying, "Yeah, well, this is the last place I want to be right now." She pats my leg. "Marta's due date is next month."

My stomach squirms.

"Shit. I forgot about Marta. How the hell is she?" I ask, guilt swamping me that I'm not the only person here with problems, and some might argue that mine are worth shit compared to Willa. But I suppose we all think our own dilemmas are bigger than anyone else's.

"She's doing the best she can, but she hasn't been sleeping lately because she's so big."

"You sure it's not twins?" I joke.

"Yeah, it's just the one ginormous baby. But I hate being this far away from her when anything could happen." She stares at the cup in her hand.

"That sucks." I pick my tea up and take a sip, assessing Willa as she sets her drink down and starts to pull at her fingers. "Hopefully, we won't be here that long," I tell her, and she smiles, but it's not the usual Willa smile.

"What about you, big man?" I ask, turning to face the Beast. "You got some lovesick chick back home who'll be pining for you? Or maybe some hot dude who'll have to see to his own needs for the next few days?"

He glares at me, and I love it. It's like poking the bear with a stick through the bars of its cage. I've never asked him about his love life—that would just be weird. But when your bodyguards are with you so much of the time, it's hard not to get to know them.

Take Bastian, for instance. I know he's divorced, has no kids, and is dating a woman called Cherry, who has two kids from her previous marriage. I know he likes to fish. When I've asked him if he's had a nice weekend off, he'll tell me that he spent it at Lake Hanover, sitting on the embankment, catching absolutely nothing at all but having the best day ever.

And Willa, I knew about her and Marta wanting a baby and how they'd ruled out adoption. She hates horror films and wants to take up gardening to grow her own vegetables but has a strange fear of worms. You get to know these things through idle chitchat and general human curiosity.

But not the Beast. I know zero about him or his life, or his scars. Nothing that isn't written on his face.

With a stone-cold stare, he answers me. "No one."

And I believe him. Like the dog at the pound with no tail or a sparse coat, no one would want to own him.

"I forgot, you're married to the job."

"Speaking of which," Willa pipes up, "did you get the cameras working?"

"Yeah. They're all up and running," the Beast confirms.

Willa pivots slightly so she's facing me. "Okay, here's the problem." She pouts slightly like she's practicing how she's going to address her toddler when she has to break bad news. "We looked over the security layout on the flight out here, and I feel it only fair to let you know that there's a camera in your room."

"A *what?*" I hold the cup suspended in my hands.

"It's for your safety, I assure you. There could be any number of ways someone could try to get to you whilst you're asleep. It's been known for people to use drones, venomous insects, and all manner of things they could get into your room at night. So, Fenrir and I devised a plan. I'll stay up with you during the day to make sure you're safe, and he'll take the night shift, watching the camera from the security room."

I glare at the Beast. "I bet he put up a fight about that job, having to sit and watch me sleep all night. Where the hell am I meant to get changed? What if I need a little nighttime relief?" I don't break his gaze, thrusting the stick further into the cage. I'm practically poking at his fur, but he doesn't flinch. He doesn't even turn a shade of pink, which has me wondering if his scarred skin can change colour like the rest of his face.

"There's an en suite where you can get changed and… see to your needs," Willa explains.

"Yeah, and I wonder where *he'll* be seeing to *his* needs." I cock my head at him as Willa suppresses a laugh.

"That fucking mouth of yours will land you in trouble," the Hellhound says, and I'm not ashamed to admit that the hairs on the back of my arms stand up and a tiny flame ignites in my core, which I try to batten down.

"Is that so?"

Willa sighs. "Come along now, kids. We need to look out for one another, not fight amongst ourselves. We don't know how long we're going to be out here, and I, for one, do not want to have to referee you two. Do I make myself clear?"

I glare at the Beast, who stares back, and it's me who breaks. I glance at Willa and salute before the Hellhound just nods in her direction.

But the truth is, I don't want to behave, and he knows it. Over the past six months, there has been a strange energy between us. Something I can't fathom.

Eyeballing the Beast, I wonder what he's thinking.

I'm not sure what's going on between the two of us and what Willa will have to referee. I imagine the next few days are going to be so fucking boring that I'll have to find some way of amusing myself.

I've never been very good at toeing the line, and I'm not about to start now.

This could be fun.

FOURTEEN
FENRIR

PRESENT

THE HEAT FROM THE FIRE IS MAKING MY SKIN CRAWL. THE flickering flames lick at wounds that'll never heal, so I'm relieved when Willa suggests she show Hayami around the house. It means I can go and check to see if the cameras pick them up.

There's a small room under the stairs that houses a desk, a chair, and monitors. All allow the user to see what's going on around the house and grounds. When I set up the cameras, I'd done a full sweep of the house. It's grand but not ridiculously big, which is a relief. I was dreading having too many areas to cover with just me and Willa here.

I settle into the black leather chair, which'll be my vigil site every night. Willa and Hayami come into focus on the bottom screen from the camera in the foyer. There's no sound, just the image of them moving from the living room into the library, which sits on the left as you come in through the main entrance.

Hayami studies the shelves, her eyes wide, face full of

wonder, as Willa sweeps the room out of habit, looking for anything out of place.

"You picking us up?" Willa says into her cuff.

"Yes."

"How's the picture?" she asks.

"Clear enough," I reply as Hayami reaches for a book. She pulls it from the shelf, and I imagine her telling Willa she's read it or wants to read it or that they won't be bored here with all these books. But Willa isn't a bookworm. Not like Hayami.

A few months ago, Hayami bought me a book. She'd been in the bookshop for over two hours, which was unsettling. The space was so calm and quiet that I found myself relaxing, which isn't ideal when I'm supposed to be alert. She told me that books were her friends, which only confirmed her loneliness.

I understood what she was saying, but my face must have said otherwise, as she went on to ask me if I ever wanted to escape. I told her I did. I've spent my whole adult life trying to escape my past, but I can't seem to shake it.

I still haven't read the book she bought me. I don't know what I'm afraid of. Maybe that it won't work. That I won't find the escape that she surrenders to so easily within the pages of a book. Or maybe I'm scared that it *will* work. Maybe that's more frightening.

They leave the library and move across the foyer and into the sitting room, which is smaller than the formal living room. There are a few seconds where they aren't visible, tiny pockets of the house that aren't covered by any cameras. This is a worry. I don't like not having my eyes on her the whole time.

It's seconds before they reappear on the camera in the sitting room. They don't spend long in here, quickly moving on. There's another split second where they disappear, then reappear on the camera in the kitchen. Hayami looks in the fridge and takes out a bottle of water before heading into the dining room.

The pair then appear back in the foyer. They each grab the remaining bags I haven't got around to taking up. We packed in such a hurry, Devall giving us no time at all to prepare for a trip and no idea how long we were going to be away for. Nothing I wasn't used to. In the army, we could be deployed at a moment's notice.

Willa and I had been dropped off at our homes on the way to the airport and told we had twenty minutes to pack our personal belongings before the car would leave. Willa, I suspected, found this more stressful. Not only did she have to pack but also had to say farewell to her heavily pregnant wife, not knowing when she would be seeing her again.

And me? Well, let's just say there wasn't much to pack from my one-bedroom apartment. Ten years in the army means I haven't put down any roots, and it taught me to travel light. Possessions aren't important unless they can save your life. And I'm not sure what it meant when I found myself packing the book Hayami bought me.

Markus supplied all the security and surveillance equipment he thought we would need and talked me through the security system that's set up in the house. I recall the last conversation I had with him about not hesitating, being prepared, and wanting hourly updates.

Willa and Hayami appear on the monitor. They're in the main bedroom, which will be Hayami's. It's large with a king-sized bed in the centre of the room and a small sofa sitting in the far corner. French windows lead onto a balcony, which I don't like, for two reasons. The first is personal—my own dislike of balconies—and the second, and more relevant, is that they pose a security risk. They make an easy entry point for anyone wanting to gain access to the room. The balcony is situated at the back of the house over-looking the courtyard and garden, but we can't change rooms, as this is the only one with surveillance.

The camera is in the top right-hand corner, suspended from the ceiling, giving me the full view of her large bed, the French windows along the back wall, and the entrance to her en suite, which is over on the left. The only thing I can't see is a small section directly under the camera and the doorway leading into the room. But I'm relieved I have a visual of the windows.

"You still see us?" Willa asks into her cuff as Hayami drops the last of her bags on the floor and wanders over to the en suite.

"Yes," I answer.

"She seems to be taking this all in her stride," Willa says quietly as Hayami disappears into the en suite.

"She'll still be groggy after the sedative. I'm sure we'll get her proper reaction in the morning."

"By which point I'll be on duty, and you'll be catching up on your beauty sleep."

"I don't need much of that," I joke drily before adding, "Wake me if you need me. No matter what time it is or whatever the situation. You wake me."

"I'm not stupid." Willa lowers her arm as Hayami reappears. They say something to each other, and Willa points at the camera.

They both look up as if staring at me.

Willa waves, and Hayami sticks her middle finger up before they leave the room.

We meet back in the living room.

"Okay, guys, it's just after three in the morning, so I suggest Hayami and I go get some sleep if you're okay with staying on watch?" Willa asks me.

"Yes."

"You sure you can stay awake?"

"It won't be a problem," I reply. Willa doesn't need to know about my insomnia. That I haven't slept properly in the past fourteen years, and even when I do, my dreams are laden with flames and fire, the heat warping my skin, the screams piercing any chance of slumber.

"Okay, grab yourself a coffee, and I'll take over at about nine. That should give me a good five hours of sleep."

"Hey, you better get used to it," Hayami tells Willa. "Hell, you'll be lucky to get two hours when the baby arrives."

"Don't remind me." Willa laughs as she and Hayami leave the room.

I follow, but instead of making my way up the stairs, I shut myself away in my security room.

As soon as the door closes, the weight of the night hits me —the adrenaline that kicked in the minute we arrived in that fucking club is finally burning out. But the image is seared in my brain: Hayami, the strap of her dress off her shoulder, and that fucker's mouth clamped on her tit. I want to punch something just thinking about it. Try as I might, I can't get it out of my mind.

What the hell was she thinking? Why tell him to follow her? Why is she hellbent on letting any guy touch her? Because he's not the first. Over the past few weeks, she's all but thrown herself at any man with a pulse. If it hadn't been for me, she'd have been defiled by so many scumbags who aren't worthy of her time, let alone the privilege of touching her.

As much as I'm annoyed at our current predicament, it's a relief not to have to stop her from making a huge mistake with some filthy man who wants nothing more than to use her for his own gain.

But another thought plagues me. Hayami and I have never truly been alone. We've always been shopping or at a club. The only real moment we had was at the fair, when she ran into the woods. We were alone for what? Five minutes? In those five minutes, I felt like she was going to open up to me; I felt like *I* could have opened up to *her*. But then Bastian came bounding through the trees, and the moment was gone.

And now? There are only three of us in Belial House. What'll happen when Willa is asleep and Hayami and I are the only ones awake?

Settling into the leather chair, I stare at the monitor that shows the inside of Hayami's bedroom.

I guess I'm about to find out.

FIFTEEN

HAYAMI

PRESENT

THERE'S GRIT IN MY EYES, PROBABLY REMNANTS OF SMUDGED mascara after my failed attempt to get groped in a nightclub. If you'd told me seven hours ago that I'd be sitting in a creepy-ass house in the middle of nowhere with only Willa and the Beast for company, I'd have asked what planet you were on.

Once I'm in the room I've been assigned, I slump on the end of the bed before catching the red blinking light in the top corner of the ceiling.

He's there. Watching.

It shouldn't feel strange, as there's always someone watching me. Whether it's Willa hovering whilst I shop, Bastian sitting behind me at university, or even the Beast when I'm in a club, they always have their eyes on me. But at home, in my room, no one is ever watching. My bedroom has always been my haven, the one place where there are no eyes on me.

But not here. Not now.

He's watching.

I escape into the en suite.

Checking the walls, the cabinets, and under the toilet, I relax a little. No cameras. Willa had said there were none, but you never know.

I strip out of the clothes I presume Nita, our family's housekeeper who's always looked after me, packed. She's the only member of the staff who I'll allow in my room, and who I'll ask for more personal things. Like the time she had to cut chewing gum out of my hair when I was about seven, or when she helped me out of a dress I got stuck in only a few months ago, or when I started my periods and she was there with pads, two paracetamol, a hot chocolate, and a warm wheat bag. These are the things I should have gone to my mum for, but as I got older, it became clear that my mum had struggles of her own. Her grip on drink and prescription meds became tighter than it was on real life. She seemed distant, like she'd removed herself from reality, and it began to feel like she was out of my reach.

It saddens me to think of this.

And Nita is miles away. I wonder if she'll miss me like I miss her, or whether she simply sees me as a job, a part of her role, which is the way most of our staff see us.

Twisting the dial on the shower, I wait for the water to heat before stepping under the spray. I'm eager to rid myself of the grime of the night and the lull from the sedative.

It feels good—the pummel of the water on my skin, the heat burning off the touch of that guy in the club. *Sam? Tim?* I can't even remember his name—that's how memorable he was. But I'd been willing to give myself to him.

And he would have had me if the Hellhound hadn't broken down the door.

Water runs through my hair and onto my chest, gathering between my breasts.

A tingling buzzes between my legs, but not at the memory of Tim/Sam's tongue on my nipple, or the feeling of his hands squeezing my ass. No. The buzz pulses when I recall the Beast dragging the guy out of the cubicle by his collar and shoving the gun down his throat.

I gulp at how turned on I am, how turned on I *had* been by his brutality, by the way he handled that gun. Maybe I have a gun kink? Maybe I should do some research into gun kinks and whether they're an actual *thing*.

Or maybe, just maybe, it wasn't the gun at all but the man holding it?

No.

Absolutely not.

The Beast is just that: a menace, a creator of chaos. He was a Hellhound until my father had the great fucking idea of making him one of my bodyguards. It was no surprise that someone new was needed. Bastian's due to retire in the next year, and Willa had just announced Marta's pregnancy.

I can't help wondering if the Beast is loyal to my father. Is that where his dedication lies, in obeying my father's orders to keep me wrapped up in cotton wool, not to be touched or marred by human hands? Or is there another reason he keeps me guarded?

Whatever his motivations, he's sitting downstairs in the security room, waiting for me to come out of this en suite. I'd better get a move on. If he thinks I've been in here too long, he'll break the door down—which, I hate to admit, would only excite me.

After turning the shower off, I step onto the mat, grabbing a towel from the heater. Once I've secured the towel around my body, I'm about to exit the en suite when I remember his blinking eye in the corner of the room. There's a dark urge within me to strut through the door, let the towel drop, and walk naked through the bedroom, letting him see me, *all* of me. But even with the security of the lens, I chicken out and keep the towel wrapped around myself. If I'm honest, I'm not entirely sure what relationship the Beast and I have.

I've tried to treat him like all my security staff, just another punching bag, someone to absorb my daily rage. But somehow, he seems immune to my jabs. He doesn't respond like Willa or Bastian, batting my digs away as playful or simply ignoring them entirely. No—the Beast is different.

I don't know why or how. Maybe it's him, his scars, whatever it was that caused them, and whatever darkness burrowed deeper than the skin. Or maybe it's me. Maybe I'm seeing things that aren't there, feeling things I've simply imagined.

His actions are never clear. He's protective, but without treating me with kid gloves. He's possessive and violent, but never towards me. He can be brutal—unapologetically so. But I don't understand the reasons behind it. Is he simply a workaholic who takes his job too seriously? Willa told me that he was in the army, so is it that mindset—does he view me as a mission he refuses to fail? Or is he simply doing a job, just like Willa, just like Bastian and Markus, and just like Nita?

If that's the case, then why does it feel like he isn't working at all? Why does protecting me appear to come so naturally?

Does he annoy me? Yes. Is he a royal pain in my ass? Absolutely.

But do I hate him for it?

No.

I'm confounded by the man, by the Beast. And that's the problem. I don't know how I feel about him.

As I stare at the blinking red light in the corner of the room, I wonder if being alone in this house with him, I might be about to find out.

SIXTEEN
FENRIR

PRESENT

Eight minutes and seven seconds.

Eighteen minutes and twenty-three seconds.

Twenty minutes and thirty-one seconds.

How long does it take to get a fucking wash?

Hayami has been in the shower for way longer than is humanly necessary. I'm in and out in under five minutes—but that's mainly because I don't like having to look at my body for longer than I have to. It's been nearly half an hour. How long do I give her before I break the door down and face whatever she's done in that bathroom?

Because I'm in no doubt of what Hayami was doing that day in the pool, despite the lie she told her dad.

"I was just floating."

Lie.

The darkness that still surrounds her is a testament to that. And I've been under the impression that, like me, she's been running from something, a past she just can't shake.

That was until she confessed it wasn't her past she was running from but her future. I was sure she was about to elaborate when Bastian had come lumbering through the trees. I still have no idea what future she's referring to, but having been under the Devall roof for the past six months, I can guess it has something to do with her father.

She may not have attempted to take her life since the pool incident, but her behaviour has been erratic and downright scary at times. I've no idea what she's running from, but I'm determined to find out. I want to help her. I see so much of myself in her, it scares me.

It's also why I don't like her being out of my sight. It's hard enough to let the likes of Willa and Bastian watch over her when I'm not on shift. They don't know what they're looking for. They think the outside is the only threat, the only danger. They don't realise that Hayami needs saving from herself.

Admittedly, this makes it sound like I have some sort of hero complex, and that all people need saving from themselves. But in Hayami's case, it's true. And I don't judge those people who want to take their own lives because their existence is so painful that they would rather not exist at all—that, I understand. But Hayami is different. She's a victim of her father's choices, his actions, even of the name she carries. You don't need to be a trained psychiatrist to see it.

But does *she* see it?

Staring at the monitor, I mentally go over the check I did of the en suite after we first arrived at the house. There was nothing in that room she could have used to take her own life, but the thought of her filling the sink and dunking her head under is too much. I go to stand, readying myself to pull her from death's grip for the second time in six months, but then the camera blinks and she emerges through the door. A trail of steam follows her as she pulls the towel tight over her chest.

My heart rate drops, relief settling over my shoulders like my favourite T-shirt.

She sits on the edge of the bed and pulls one of her bags towards her.

The towel shifts, revealing more of her skin. It reminds me of the shift in our relationship. Before the ball, Hayami had been pushing me away, taunting me the same way she does Willa and Bastian. There was no way I was going to stand for her bullshit—only because I knew the mechanism myself: treat everyone like shit because that's how you feel.

I showed her, that first day in the changing rooms when she asked me if I wanted to come in with her, that she wouldn't belittle me. She wouldn't humiliate me to make up for how crappy her life is. And it threw her. After that little incident, she didn't know how to be with me.

But then came the night of the charity ball her father made her attend.

That night, things changed. She put her trust in me, and I delivered. She was different. Afraid. Disgusted, almost. I've never seen her like that before, and not with those kinds of men. I still don't know what the ball was all about and what made her feel so exposed, because she isn't like that at clubs or bars. There, she's the complete opposite—wanting anyone to touch her, giving herself away to any man who'll have her.

I don't understand what goes through her mind, and I am confused about my role in all of it.

And since the ball, well, things have been strange. I can't quite put my finger on it, but I know our relationship has deviated. I'm just not sure how.

Hayami pulls some clothes from her bag, stopping for a second before tilting her head up.

She stares at the camera like she's looking right at me, and it makes me wonder what she sees. A hideous beast? A monster?

Or a man who'll stop at nothing to protect her?

SEVENTEEN
FENRIR

PRESENT

Five days of the same walls.

Five days of the mountain view outside.

Five days of nothingness.

Only five days and I already feel like I'm losing my mind.

Other than what Hayami has had for breakfast, how much work she's done for her university course, what book she's currently reading, and how long she spends in the shower, there's been nothing to report.

She's been calm. There've been no attempts on her life, no hint of intruders or the house being watched, and there's been no strange activity. Nothing that explains why half the Devall staff hate this place and why Junko visited once and never wanted to return. I've even convinced myself that the hysteria surrounding this place must be due to its remoteness and the fact that you're cut off from the real world, so you start to think it doesn't exist anymore.

I've kept Markus informed, although there's been little to

share with him. I've asked for an update on the Castros, but Markus is remaining tight-lipped.

Willa has been on watch during the day, reporting to me on our handover that Hayami has completed her university work, listened to some lectures, and made pasta for lunch. She tends to sleep in the afternoon after watching something on Netflix and hasn't yet complained about her incarceration.

Willa has completed a full book of sudoku, and Hayami has persuaded her to read one of the books she found in the library. I take over around eight o'clock, with Hayami either watching TV or reading until she goes to bed around eleven. I've been keeping to the security room as much as possible, as I'm not sure how to be around her when Willa isn't here. I'm no saint, and having her so close with no one else to interrupt us is too much temptation.

There've been no tantrums. No explosions from Hayami. Willa even suggested that this break has done her some good, given her time away from her father. Willa said she seems relaxed here, which is more than can be said for us. Willa is either on her phone—keeping tabs on Marta—or shivering at the quiet of this place.

I'm not sure how I feel in this house. I try to sleep during the day, but it's difficult. My mind is plagued with too much for it to ever rest, so I've been working out in my room—doing squats, planks, sit-ups, push-ups, anything to keep my thoughts from straying to Hayami, of fires, of how fucking quiet it is up here. At night, I'm focused on the screens, watching a sleeping Hayami, wondering what dreams she's having and whether they will ever come true.

Tonight is no different. Hayami's reading in bed with the covers pulled up under her chin. The tiny lamp blares on the side. I note the jerk of her head, the dip of the book. It wouldn't be the first time she's fallen asleep whilst reading, and I've gone in and gently removed the book from her hands and tucked her in. But tonight, she gives in to sleep, puts the book on the bedside table, and pulls the covers back.

She's wearing T-shirt and shorts similar to the pair she wore on the first night. After swinging her legs out of bed, she makes her way to the en suite. Even in the dim light, I can make out the shape of her legs, the beauty of her frame, and it makes the walls of this room feel smaller than they are.

The en suite door closes behind her.

The time is eleven sixteen.

Over the last few nights, I've worked out that it takes her eight minutes in the en suite before she goes to bed. She must be brushing her teeth, flossing, using mouthwash, and maybe a last-minute application of face cream, but whatever she does in there takes her eight minutes.

If she goes a second over, I'll break the fucking door down.

The time is eleven nineteen.

I swivel the chair slightly, trying not to watch the clock but pay attention to the screen.

Eleven twenty-two.

A weather warning flashes up on my phone. Torrential rain for the next twelve hours. Nothing new. All it seems to do up here is rain.

Eleven twenty-three.

My hand brushes over my Glock resting on the desk. I've been itching to go to the firing range and wondering if there's anywhere out here I can set up a makeshift target. I hate the thought of getting rusty.

Eleven twenty-four.

Pushing the chair back, I ready myself to run, but as I palm my gun, the en suite door opens and Hayami emerges. I imagine the minty freshness of her breath and her glowing skin as she makes her way over to her bed.

But then she stops right at the foot of the bed and cocks her head at the camera as if she's thinking about what to do. She then turns to face the camera full-on and grins before pulling her T-shirt up and over her head.

My grip tightens on my gun. She's wearing a black bra, her perfect breasts held only by a scrap of lace material.

What the hell?

I'm mesmerised as she hooks her thumbs into the waistband of her shorts and shimmies them down her legs to reveal a black thong.

Fuck.

Kicking her shorts away, she looks directly at the camera, then blows it a kiss and appears to laugh before getting into bed and turning out the light.

Is this her idea of giving me something to watch? She'd joked about it on the first night—about me being bored. The only thing she's given me is a raging hard-on that I'll not bring myself to deal with here in this office when I have a job to do. No, there'll be time for that later, when I'm alone and can replay that little show in my head.

Right now, all I can wonder about is what game she's playing.

HAYAMI

What the fuck have I just done?

I sink into the mattress, feeling giddy and light-headed. I'll admit, when I stepped out of the en suite, I was hot. The central heating in this house isn't great—I've spent the last five days complaining about how cold I am at night, until the Beast found an oil-filled heater in the garage and set it up in my room. It's worked a treat, but now it's stifling.

I was about to take my T-shirt off when I remembered the cameras. Remembered *him*. And then something devilish washed over me.

It's been so quiet over the last five days. No news. No drama. In some ways it's been nice, but in others, it's made it all very dull. That's when it hit me: Would it really be so bad to strip in front of the camera? It's not like it's anything he hasn't seen—he saw me in a swimsuit that first day. Underwear isn't that different.

This would just be a joke, a bit of fun to lighten the monotony of what must be an incredibly boring job—watching me sleep.

And hadn't I said, on the first night, that I would give him something to watch?

So I did. I stripped right in front of the camera.

I won't lie. It felt good, knowing he was watching the scene unfold, hoping he wouldn't be able to take his eyes off me. The thought of him open-mouthed, hard, maybe even stroking himself, made me want to carry on and take off my bra and pants. But that would have been a step too far, and not something I would've been able to pass off as a joke.

And who's to say I do make him hard? For all I know, he could be gay or not interested in sex or women at all. And all I could have achieved with my little stunt was me getting excited.

It was just a little light amusement, I tell myself as I slide into bed. *A relief from the monotony that's become my new routine.*

Some people would love to be marooned on a mountainside. And I'll admit, there have been some positives to being stuck out here. I'm ahead with all my assignments and studying, and I've read at least three of the eight books Nita packed for me—God love her.

And then there's the absence of my father, which is the main reason I feel calm here.

So, yeah, maybe it was boredom that made me flash the Beast a peek. Or maybe it was the fact that we haven't had any real interaction for days—not with Willa under the same roof and the security cameras recording our every move.

I thought that once Willa went to bed and we were alone, something might happen between us. But he's stayed locked away in his little hidey-hole under the stairs, almost as if he's deliberately keeping out of my way.

I love nothing more than winding up my bodyguards, and he's no exception. I'm just not sure what would've been going through his head during my little tease.

EIGHTEEN

FENRIR

PRESENT

Hayami wakes at three twenty.

I sit up, having been slouched in the chair for the last few hours. Presuming she's just visiting the bathroom, I wait for her to switch the light on, but she doesn't.

She just sits upright, her head flopping to one side before she slowly slides a leg from under the covers. Her body twists awkwardly as she slithers from the bed.

Something's wrong.

Her arms hang loose by her sides, like they're attached by elastic bands. Her head droops forwards, her shoulders hunched at an unnatural angle.

Fuck. Is she sleepwalking?

As far as I know, Hayami has no history of sleepwalking. So what the hell is this?

She moves to the foot of the bed, her steps jerky, her head lolling slightly, dark hair veiling half of her face.

I lean in, wishing there was a fucking zoom on this camera.

Then, without warning, she runs her hands over her body, stopping at her breasts. She squeezes them, pushing them together, and exposes one of her nipples.

Fuck.

Is this another one of her stupid games? If it is, I'm not fucking laughing.

But no—there's something strange about her hands. Her fingers look arched, bony, almost clawlike.

Is she dreaming? Is this some sort of sleep-acting?

I don't feel right watching this, but I can't look away. Something about her movements isn't natural. There's no fluidity to her rhythm, no softness to her touch. It's stiff. Mechanical. Unsettling.

Her hands leave her breasts as she runs her nails up and down her arms as if she's cold. Her movements become faster and faster until she's breaking the skin.

Then her hands creep up to her lips. Her fingers scuttle like centipedes as they burrow between her lips and pull, forcing an inane grin.

I shudder. What the fuck is she doing? She's going to tear her fucking mouth open.

I need to get to her, but I can't stop watching. I can't tear myself away, but I must. This isn't right. *She* isn't right.

There's no sound coming through the cameras, but I hear her scream in my head as her mouth widens and her eyes spring open.

I run. Fucking fly up the stairs as her scream swells through the house.

I fling open the door and grab her. "Hayami, wake up."

Her eyes are glassy, not focusing properly. I pull her bra back over her breasts, covering her up before she starts to come to.

"What the hell?" Willa appears in the doorway wearing

grey pyjamas and an eye mask pushed up onto her head, her gun raised.

Hayami blinks, tears welling in the corners of her eyes, fear overwhelming her.

"It's okay," I tell her as Willa sweeps the room, her gun aloft.

"What's going on, Fenrir? Talk to me."

"I think she was dreaming."

"You sure?" Willa looks at Hayami, who's clad in only her underwear, me holding on to her, and I wonder if she thinks something else is going on here. She takes a step closer and notices the scratches down Hayami's arms. "Hayami, are you okay?"

But she doesn't answer, doesn't take her eyes from me as she grips my forearms.

"Do you want me to take over?" Willa asks Hayami, who appears to snap out of her trance, though her eyes remain locked on mine.

"No." Her voice is faint, like it doesn't quite belong to her, but I'm relieved she hasn't dismissed me.

"The cameras haven't picked up anything suspicious from the rest of the house, and there's clearly no one in here with her. I think it was just a nightmare," I explain.

Willa drops the gun and then looks again at the scratches on Hayami's arms. Glancing back at me, she seems to accept my version of events.

"You should go back to bed," I tell her. "I'll sort this."

"You sure?" Willa eyes the room like she might have missed something.

"Yeah, I got this."

She waits a beat, surveys the room one more time, then nods and heads for the door. "I'll do a sweep downstairs, just to be sure," she says before leaving.

Now alone, I look down at Hayami.

She's still gripping my forearms. A tremor runs through her body, down her arms, and into mine, like a conductor.

"It's okay. You're okay," I tell her, pulling the blanket from the foot of the bed and wrapping it around her shoulders.

"What happened?" she asks. The wobble in her voice is so unlike her that it almost doesn't sound like her at all.

"I think you were dreaming."

She looks at her hands, her bloodied nails.

"What did I do?" Her eyes are bulbous, the whites stark.

"You just got out of bed and started scratching your arms. Did you feel anything?"

"I just felt this dread, this horrible, awful dread, like something terrible was going to happen. And then you were in the room."

I glance at her bed.

She shakes her head. "I can't go back to sleep. Not after that."

"Why don't we get a drink?" I suggest.

"Yes. A drink."

I lead her from the room as she tightens the blanket around her shoulders. She's not the only one who needs a fucking drink.

HAYAMI

Rain batters the kitchen windows as if trying to get in. Its rhythm matches that of my heart still hammering in my chest.

Willa appears in grey loungewear, which just looks odd compared to her normal combats and T-shirts.

"Okay, everything's clear," she says to us both. "You sure you're okay?" she asks me.

"I'm fine," I lie.

Willa looks at Fenrir before saying, "I'll head back up if you're sure you're both all right?"

"We're good," the Beast replies.

Shivering despite the blanket, I sit at the large table as he pulls two glasses from one of the cabinets and finds a bottle of something.

"I can't imagine this was in the basic supplies that were delivered," I say, taking in the artificial glow of the under-cabinet lighting and the tea towel hanging innocently on the handle of the oven. This scene feels so different from the one in my room not five minutes ago.

"I brought it." He slides the glasses over the table and pours a generous amount into each.

I take the glass. "I didn't peg you for a whisky drinker." I've never had whisky before. My father drinks it, which has been enough to put me off it, but I'll gladly drink anything if it'll thaw the ice coating my bones.

"Sometimes, it's the only drink that'll do."

"And this is one of them?" I raise the glass to my lips.

"Sip it," he tells me.

It's hot, like drinking fire, waking up my dormant taste buds as the flavour explodes in my mouth.

"Jesus." I purse my lips. "People drink this out of choice?"

He almost laughs. Almost.

"Don't overthink it. Just let it do its job." He makes his way over to the sink, opens the cupboard, and fishes out a box. He rifles through it and finds a first aid kit.

Wordlessly, he lays the kit out on the table and finds antiseptic wipes. Then he stops and assesses me before speaking.

"Show me your arms."

I unwrap myself from the blanket whilst trying to keep my chest covered. Not because I feel like he's watching me, but I don't want him to feel uncomfortable.

He scans the scratches.

"Did I do this?" I ask, my voice breaking.

"Do you remember doing it?" He pulls a chair out and sits opposite me. As he takes one of my arms in his hand, he says, "This'll sting." Gently, he dabs at the wound with the anti-septic wipe.

I wince, and he pauses, the wipe held aloft. He looks at me, waiting. I nod, silently giving him permission to continue. He's so gentle, so careful, and it amazes me. Because he's so brutal, so fierce looking. I've never seen this side of him, this caring, careful Beast.

He continues to clean the wounds, and I begin to relax at the touch of his enormous hands.

When he's done, he pulls the blanket over my shoulders before moving around to the other side of the table and sitting down. He shifts in his seat, as if he's sat on something, then pulls a gun from the back of his waistband and places it on the table, facing the window. He reclines, resting his ankle on the other knee, cradling his drink near his crotch. He's in his standard black T-shirt and black combats—always the professional, always on the job—and I wonder where the real man is, Fenrir Therion, and whether I've met him.

Another gulp of whisky burns my eyes. The liquid trickles down my throat, thawing the frozen fear that's taken root.

"Can you tell me what happened?" he asks.

I take another sip, hoping it'll give me the courage to speak, evoke some words to describe the indescribable.

There was the stripping in front of the camera. How could I forget that little stunt? But then I got into bed and fell asleep to thoughts of him touching himself. Not a detail I can share right now.

After that, nothing.

No, that's a lie. There wasn't nothing. There was the

dread, this god-awful fear that wrapped me in cold arms and squeezed me.

And then screaming.

Someone screaming.

Pain.

Red-hot, searing pain.

New screams.

My screams.

Him.

He held me.

Covered me.

Told me it was okay when it was anything but.

No amount of whisky is going to spill these words.

"I don't know," I tell him. "I went to bed, fell asleep, and then you arrived. I was screaming, but I don't know why."

"Were you dreaming?" He tips his glass, the whisky circling the edges like it's trying to find a way out.

"If I was, I don't remember it. All I remember is a feeling." I tighten the blanket around me, feel the rawness of my arms under the material.

"What feeling?"

Bile rises in my throat as I stare at the bottle. I take another sip to try and push the nausea down. The alcohol works its way through my system as if trying to douse whatever is rising within me.

I gulp before looking at him. "Fear."

He stares at me. "What were you afraid of?"

"That's the strange thing," I say, the whisky fuelling me. "I've been scared before—as a kid. Afraid of heights. Afraid of the dark."

I stop there, even though the list continues. I'm scared of my father—scared of what he can make me do, what he's *going* to make me do, and what'll happen when he does.

"But this fear wasn't like being scared *of* something," I

explain. "It was different. This was soul-crushing. Black. Freezing. It was an all-consuming dread that had infected me—strangling me from the inside out. And there was nothing I could do about it other than let it take me."

I glance at his scars. "Have you ever felt fear like that?"

My pulse pounds in my ears, and for a second, I think I've overstepped the mark, but then he answers.

"Once."

"Of course you have." Again, my eyes land on his scars, but this time, I keep them there. I've no idea how he got them. Willa told me he was in a fire. I don't know how or why, but I can imagine his fear was ten times worse than what I've just described. He must have been caught, trapped, whilst the flames raged.

Sensing his need to change the topic, I move on. "Did you see anything on the camera?"

"No." His answer is too quick, too blunt, which makes me wonder what he *did* see.

"What do you think happened?" I ask, trying to change tack.

He blinks like he's considering the options. "It could have been a night terror."

"I've never had a night terror before."

"There's always a first time for everything." He traces the rim of his glass with his finger, and it sings lightly, making me quiver.

"Have you ever had one?"

"You have to be asleep to have a night terror." He takes a sip of whisky, and I note the ease with which he swallows it.

"You don't sleep?"

"Not for many years."

"Shit. No wonder you're such a grump."

There's that flicker on his face, the almost smile I've seen before.

"Do you think it'll happen again, the night terror?" I ask, the thread of dread still dangling like it's waiting to coil itself around me.

"I don't know. It's no surprise if you think about it."

"What do you mean?"

"You've had a stressful few days. Your life has been threatened," he reminds me.

"Please," I hiss.

I'm no stranger to death threats. You don't grow up being the daughter of a gangster without having some sort of threat hanging over you. I should be scared—most people would be frightened living this way—but I'm not. If anything, I feel coddled, stifled, and wrapped in so many layers I can't move. I'm in fear for my life, but not in the sense the Beast is referring to. I fear what is to become of it. That it's not my own life and never will be.

"But this is different. You've been moved out of your house. Cut off from your friends," he says.

"Do you see me with friends?" I ask, glancing around the kitchen at my invisible fan club. "Who wants to be friends with the daughter of Barrett Devall? I'm not allowed to go anywhere without my bodyguards. No one is allowed within an inch of me without having undergone a full background check. And no one wants to be accidentally killed just because they were hanging out with me on the wrong day. I've always been alone. That's never going to change. But don't feel sorry for me. I'd rather have it that way. I don't want to be responsible for someone else being hurt on my account."

He appears to consider this. "That makes sense."

"Do you know, when we arrived here, I was pleased."

He raises one eyebrow.

"I thought it might be my chance to run. I could get in the Jeep and drive off, never to be seen again."

Straightening, he puts his glass down.

I roll my eyes at him. "Don't panic. I'm not going anywhere. But do you know why I haven't tried to run from this sorry existence?"

He shakes his head.

"It's not that my father would find me. Though he would, let's face it. You can't outrun a man like him. It isn't even that I would spend the rest of my life looking over my shoulder, never being able to settle in one place, never being able to live the life I so desperately want. It isn't any of those things."

"What is it, then?" the Beast asks.

"He'd kill Willa. He'd kill Markus. He'd kill Bastian, and he'd kill you. All of you. Because you'd be the reason I got away. You'd be the people who failed him. You'd be the reason his precious daughter has vanished. It'd be your fault, and he'd make you all pay in the most heinous way possible. It wouldn't be quick. You wouldn't be spared. He'd take his anger out on every part of your body. He'd make an example of you. All of you. And that's the only reason why I won't run."

NINETEEN
HAYAMI

THE KITCHEN LOOKS DIFFERENT IN THE DAYLIGHT. GONE IS the glow from the under-cabinet lighting. The rain has fizzled to a misty drizzle—no rhythm upon the windows now, just an ominous presence. The whisky has been returned to the cupboard, where, hopefully, it won't be needed again.

After we'd finished our drinks last night, the Beast took me back to my room. He checked the cupboards, under the bed, the en suite—looking for what, I don't know, seeing as there's no one here but the three of us. Maybe he was just on autopilot, doing his job the only way he knows how.

I climbed back into bed, the sheets cold, the air stagnant, as if there was still a wisp of what happened a few hours ago.

But what did happen? A bad dream? A night terror? Whatever it was, I hope it was a singular event.

He stood by the bed, assessing me before he looked up at the camera. I wanted to ask him to stay. Fought the urge to beg him to sit with me, to hold my hand, to tell me he wouldn't leave—because I was terrified that I'd have to endure that night terror again.

"I'll be watching" was all he said before leaving the room.

That was the only thing that got me to sleep. Knowing that beyond the lens, he was sitting vigil in his little room under the stairs, watching.

I scour the pantry, trying to find something for lunch with the bizarre array of ingredients. I love cooking. I learned how to in high school food tech, but I was never allowed to test my skills at home due to Leo, our chef, hissing me out of the kitchen, telling me he would not hear of me preparing a meal for myself, even if it was only a slice of toast.

Having staff in your house means it never truly feels like home. It feels clustered and busy, like a place of work. Not that I've ever had a job in my life, despite asking my father if I could get something part-time in between my studies.

He'd laughed in my face before the scowl settled, and he said one word. The one word that was not to be challenged. The one word that was not to be misunderstood or debated.

"No."

I'm allowed to go to university because, and I quote him, *"You need something to occupy you."* Not that I need to enhance my learning or my chances at understanding the world I live in, or that I might want to follow a path where microphysics, biology, or engineering is needed. No. I just needed something to "occupy" me.

That's when I looked at my mum and wondered what was occupying her, other than the drinks she pours and the pills she swallows.

Our parents should inspire us. We're supposed to strive to be like them.

I don't want to be like my father.

And I sure as hell am not going to end up like my mother.

Or am I?

Selecting a tin of coconut milk, some lemon juice, and dried parsley, I try to recall how to make chicken Alfredo when I hear sniffling coming from the dining room.

Placing the ingredients on the counter, I tiptoe over to the doorway to see Willa, her mobile clasped to her ear as she stares out of the window.

"I'm sorry. I'm so sorry," she whimpers.

I've never seen Willa upset. Annoyed, yes, but not sad. Her distress disturbs me more than it should, and I have to hold back from scurrying over to hug her.

"I love you. Please believe me when I tell you that I love you."

I should leave, but it hurts to see Willa like this.

Her arm drops to her side, the phone clutched in her hand, and I have to speak.

"Is everything okay?" I edge into the room as Willa turns at the sound of my voice.

"Hey." She sniffs, wiping her cheek with the cuff of her hoodie. "It's fine. Everything's fine." She plasters on a Willa smile, but it's fake. I hate fake.

"Don't bullshit a bullshitter," I tell her, adopting one of my sterner tones. "You've seen me at my worst, kicking and screaming, biting and scratching, sobbing and snotty, so please don't give me the shit that everything is okay. We're stuck in the middle of nowhere with only each other. Right now, I'm all you've got, so please tell me what's going on."

She regards me before her head drops, and she bites her lip.

"That was Marta," she says, her voice small. "She's been to the midwife this morning, and they're concerned about the level of protein in her urine. It could be a sign of pre-eclampsia."

My stomach plummets. "Is the baby okay?"

"For now. But they've sent her to the hospital where they can monitor them both and take action if needed."

"Take action?"

"They'll induce labour or do an emergency C-section if they feel either Marta or the baby is at risk." Willa's voice trembles. "She's scared. I should be there with her, with both of them." Tears fall down her cheeks, and my heart cracks.

Then the anger arrives. "Shit. I'm sorry."

"Don't be. It's not your fault."

"Of course it is. It's because of me that you aren't with her now." Rage swims in my chest as I take in Willa's shaking hand, her swollen eyes, and her broken spirit, all because of me.

"You should leave." It comes out as if I hadn't meant it to.

"What?" Willa stares at me.

"We'll take the Jeep. I'll drive you to the airport so you can get the first plane out of here, and then I'll drive back before the B—*Fenrir* starts his shift."

"We can't do that. You know I can't leave." She shakes her head.

"Why not?"

"I have a job to do—"

"Fuck that. Fenrir is here. Do you think he's going to let anything happen to me? You know what he's like. A cold won't get within an inch of me if he's got anything to do with it."

"But he can't watch you all the time."

"I don't need watching all the time. We have a security system. We've been here for days, and fuck-all has happened. Besides, what's more important right now?"

Willa doesn't answer. She doesn't have to.

"I'll lose my job."

"So what? You'll lose your job. Jobs are two a penny." I want to add that her job isn't the only thing she'll lose, but

I'm not that cruel to point out the threat to her life when she's upset over her wife and unborn child. "You're an educated woman with a skill set to rival most employees. You'll easily get another job. And do you really want to be working for my father when your son or daughter arrives? You'd never get their birthday off or their first football game or their first dance show, because if my father wants you to work, you're working. Is that what you want for your family? For Marta?"

"I can't just quit. We have bills. Marta will be on maternity pay."

"Okay, then don't quit. But if you don't go be with your wife and child, you'll regret it for the rest of your life."

"Your father—" Willa begins to argue, but I cut her off.

"Doesn't even have to know. Look, if you leave now, you can go be with her, support her, and be there for whatever happens. You could be back here within the week, and no one has to know."

"But Fenrir will know."

"And he won't say shit."

"Of course he will. He'll report it straight away." Her voice quivers.

"Not if I have anything to do with it," I tell her. "I can be very persuasive."

"Hayami," Willa warns, but I bat her away.

"Come on. I'll help you pack, and we can work out the details after you've seen your wife."

I set off for the door, but she doesn't budge.

My shoulders settle. "Do you love her?" I know it's a cheap shot, a low blow when she's looking so terrified, but sometimes you just have to go for the balls. I've read enough romance novels to know that this is the moment where the word *love* needs to be used as ammunition.

She glares at me. "Of course I do."

"Then you'd do anything for her, right?"

"Anything," Willa confirms.

"Then what the fuck are you waiting for?"

————————

IT FELT STRANGE, DRIVING WILLA TO THE AIRPORT. I NEVER drive myself anywhere and had only managed to convince my father to let me get my licence because it'd give me something to do over the summer break.

For the forty-minute journey, Willa is a jumble of nerves, constantly telling me to keep to the speed limit, keep my baseball cap down, and watch the rear mirror for anyone tailing us. We'd deliberated over leaving the Beast a note, telling him where we were if he were to come out of his room, but then the idea of leaving a paper trail seemed like a bad idea. Willa had argued that he might call my father if he found us gone, but I knew he wouldn't. The Beast doesn't follow protocol. So we're chancing it, hoping I'll return before he realises we left.

"No one knows where I am," I tell her. "This is an impromptu journey, not planned, and no one knows where we're going, so stop stressing. If there'd been a sniper waiting to ambush me, then they'd have shot me the minute I stepped foot out the door, not when I'm driving on a busy road."

But the roads aren't busy, even when we reach the small airport. They're eerily quiet, the grey drizzle having kept everyone indoors.

"Go straight back to the house, no stops," Willa tells me as we unload her bags from the boot. "And be careful on that road back up the mountain. There were some pretty sharp bends."

"Stop worrying about me. You have enough to worry about, and I know how to drive. I'll take it steady. I promise."

She hugs me. Considering the number of times Willa has had to restrain me, I'm no stranger to her physical contact, but this feels oddly intimate. "Look after yourself, and don't drive Fenrir mad. You know what he's like when he loses his temper. Be nice to him."

"I will," I assure her as she picks up her bags. "Text me when you can, and I hope Marta and the baby are okay."

"Thank you." She turns to leave, then swivels, her expression serious. "It's selfless, what you're doing. Putting Marta's and my needs before your own."

"No, it isn't," I tell her. "It's just being human."

I watch her until she disappears inside the airport, and then my shoulders drop, and the tendrils of anxiety wrap themselves around my gut. What if my father finds out? What if he punishes her? But I know I'm right. Marta and the baby are more important right now; they're all that matters. Willa would never forgive herself if she's not there for them.

I send out a little prayer to whichever god is listening before I get back into the car and drive back to the house.

As I cruise down the deserted roads, I feel a strange sense of wonderment. I've never driven a car on my own, never been alone outside my house before. This is all so new, so refreshing that I can't help but smile.

How easy it'd be to just keep on driving.

The temptation to flee overwhelms me. But then reality sinks the dream. What would happen to Willa and Marta if I ran? Who would my father blame? Who would he punish?

Instead of running, I roll the windows down. Liberated by the fresh air and the drizzle that sneaks into the car, I enjoy that no one is telling me to roll the windows up, or to pull my cap further down over my face, or to do anything.

I've spent my whole life feeling trapped and alone, but this is the first time I've ever *been* alone yet free, and I love it.

Driving up to the house, I see it now in all its splendour.

The pitched roof, the arched windows, the pale stone, and the gnarled trees that look like an old person bent over with arthritis. Nothing is welcoming about this house. I could leave this place now, just turn the car around and put my foot on the gas, never to return.

But then I remember him.

After parking the car, I let myself into the house, keeping my steps light, like a teenager having snuck out for some illicit rendezvous—something I've never done, and would never have been able to do if not for today. I tick off another first on my bucket list. Today is shaping up to be a day of firsts.

The house is still and quiet, as if it knows what I've done and is keeping shtoom.

I figured that if the Beast had risen whilst we'd been out and discovered we weren't here, I'd know by the fury that would be permeating the walls—the devastation he'd have left in his wake if he'd found out we had gone. Especially after I'd confessed to having thought about running away.

Entering the sitting room, I sit on the window seat and wait for him to wake, for him to discover what I've done, and to face the repercussions.

TWENTY
FENRIR

PRESENT

Heat swells in the room. Smoke fills my lungs. She screams. And even though I know it isn't real—can't be because I've been here before, done this so many times—I can't wake myself from the dream. I can't pull myself from this hell that replays every time I close my eyes.

It's a rookie mistake that happens every now and then: I fall asleep. Proper sleep. Not just the thing I do when I close my eyes and try to rest, but the deep sleep that pulls me under and seems intent on tormenting me with the past, playing it over and over until I beg the flames to devour me.

But then I wake, bolting upright in the chair by the bed, hands gripping the armrests, my breath fast and tight.

Glancing around the room, I try to steady my breathing by focusing on the furniture. The double bed. The large set of oak drawers. My duffel bag I haven't unpacked. My boots sitting neatly by the door. After convincing myself the room isn't on fire and I'm not going to burn to death, I head to the en suite to shower.

Five minutes later, I return to the bedroom, changing into a fresh black T-shirt and combats before pulling on my work boots and lacing them tightly. Opening the door, I then step onto the landing and immediately know something isn't right.

The air is too quiet, too still. The walls are watching me as if they know something I don't.

Bouncing down the stairs, I flick my damp hair out of my eyes as I reach the foyer. Hayami's boots sit on the mat, the material dark from where they've got wet. She's been outside. *When? Where to?*

Then I notice Willa's boots are missing.

Fuck.

I head straight for the sitting room, where Hayami is perched on the window seat, book in her hand. As soon as she sees me, she puts her book down, which is not a good sign.

"What's going on?" I ask as I scan the room. "Where's Willa?"

Hayami swings her legs off the window seat and places her hands on her knees. She's the picture of peace, which I find all the more unnerving.

"I need you to promise that you'll stay calm." Her voice is low and level. My hackles rise.

"What?" A water droplet from my hair trickles down the back of my neck.

"Promise me." She glares at me, and I know by the severity of her words that she means them. I'm not going to get anywhere unless I play the good dog and obey.

"Okay." My teeth grind against the word, my mind racing with all the possible things she could be about to tell me, my imagination playing out the worst.

"There's a problem with Marta and the baby, so I sent Willa away."

"You did *what?*" I swear my teeth crack.

"I drove her to the airport and drove back here," Hayami says, but the words don't reach me, like a bullet that's missed the target board completely. I try to switch my brain into gear as she keeps talking. "She needs to be with her family right now, not stuck here babysitting me from a nonexistent threat."

Fuck.

Dragging my hand down my face, I open my mouth, ready to unleash every reason she shouldn't have done what she's just done, but Hayami puts her finger in the air, halting my deluge of profanities.

"You promised you'd stay calm."

"That was before I learned you sent the only other body-guard we have away. And not only that, but you also drove her to the airport, which means you drove back by yourself." I can't hide the snarl of my words, the anger blistering over my skin at how foolish, how reckless she's been.

"And I'm still alive. Would you look at that!" She flaps her arms out as if readying to twirl, and I want to scream at her.

"This isn't a fucking joke, Hayami."

"I'm not laughing."

I can feel the vein in the side of my neck pulsating.

What was she fucking thinking?

"Okay, you made it back alive and unharmed, but how exactly do you expect me to watch you every single hour of the day?" We were stretched at two of us, but now?

"I don't need watching. Today proved that. I'm perfectly safe."

"Today, maybe. But what happens if someone finds out where you are? What then?"

"Then you'll deal with them like you always do. Besides, you told me you don't sleep."

"I need to rest, Hayami. I can't be on alert all the time. I need to shower. I need time to reset."

"And you can. You're making a very big deal out of this." She scoffs at me as if I'm some minor irritant.

"Only last night you were telling me what your father would do to us all if you ran away. What do you think he's going to do when he finds out you sent Willa home?"

She bites her lip, the first sign of her being scared by what she's done.

"He won't know. She'll only be a few days, and then she'll be back here. No one will be any the wiser."

"Except me." I hold her gaze as if throwing down a gauntlet.

"Except you," she replies, throwing down her own. She's questioning my loyalty. Where does it lie? Here, with her, or out there, with her father?

"You want me to lie for you?" I ask.

She folds her arms. "Yes, I do."

"And why would I do that?"

"Because Marta needs her wife. Willa needs to be with her family. She won't miss the birth of her child because my father is such a tyrant that he sends a bodyguard into the middle of nowhere to protect his fucking investment when her wife is about to give birth. I won't be the reason Willa doesn't get the chance to see her child arrive in this world. I can't bear the thought of Marta having to go through whatever she's going through alone because, according to my father, my life is more important. That's why I'm asking you to lie for me. And if you have any ounce of humanity inside that fucking chest of yours, then you'll do as I ask."

Her words are heavy, hanging in the air as if she's testing me to see just how much of me is human and how much of me is the beast she thinks I am.

Fuck.

All the fight runs from my body, because who am I kidding? I will lie for her. I'll do as she asks. Not because I'm human. Not because it's the right thing to do. Not because I have any ounce of moral fibre in my being.

No.

I'll lie for her because I'd do anything for her.

Anything.

Dropping onto the edge of the sofa, I clench my fists, massaging my knuckles.

"You should have spoken to me first" is all I manage.

"And let you talk me out of it? No." She shakes her head. "It's done. I got back safe. End of story."

As much as it annoys me, she's right. There's no point going over the things she's already done. Right now, we need to think about moving forwards.

"So, how is this going to work?"

Hayami's shoulders drop, seemingly happy she's won the battle.

"You report to Markus like normal. You tell him everything is fine. I got Willa to leave her work phone here, so as far as they're concerned, she's still here in the house with us. We can send some messages from her phone and answer anything Markus sends her."

"And what about watching you?" I ask.

"I don't need watching."

"It's enough that you have me lying for you. I won't disregard my duties. Even more so now that I'm on my own."

"You're not on your own," she says, taking a step forwards. "I'm here, and I can help to keep myself safe. I'm not a complete idiot."

"Do you know how to look for traps? Do you know how to scan a room for tripwire? Do you know how to look for pressure pads that'll detonate a bomb? Do you know how to fire a gun?"

I'm hoping this'll hit home, but I know Hayami better than that. All she does is fold her arms and glare at me.

"No, but you can teach me. We've got nothing else better to do up here, and I'm a very good student."

Chewing the inside of my cheek, I consider this. It's not a bad idea. She's more than capable of holding her own. I know this due to the number of times I've had to restrain her, the times she's managed to run from me, and the times she's fought back.

It's not ideal, of course. I don't want her to have to defend herself at all. This is my job, what I'm here to do. But I can't be heroic about this now that I'm on my own.

"Okay. But I watch you still during the night. You're at your most vulnerable when you're asleep, as you can't alert me, and if someone is going to come for you, then the cover of darkness is the most likely time."

"When will you sleep?" She tilts her head to the side, and I swear she almost looks concerned.

"I'll grab a few hours here and there during the day, but only when you're in one room and you're going to stay there. I can fashion something that'll alert me if anyone opens a door or a window."

She rolls her eyes, all compassion gone. She doesn't take any of this seriously, but I have to. Not only because it's my job, but because I can't let anything happen to her. I can't go through that kind of pain again.

TWENTY-ONE
HAYAMI

PRESENT

"I'm going to head up and take a shower," I tell the Beast, sitting in the chair opposite me in the sitting room. He looks like a statue, his shoulders hunched, hands clasped under his chin.

It's been two hours since I told him I'd dropped off my only other bodyguard at the airport. Two hours of him probably catastrophising about what could happen to me.

Don't get me wrong, I value life. Just not my own. You have to have control of something for it to be yours, and my life has never belonged to me. It's bound in a direction I can't allow it to take, hence why I floated facedown in the pool.

But I know this: If I die on Willa's watch—or even the Beast's—it won't just be my life that ends. It'll be theirs. And I don't want anyone else's blood on my hands; my father has enough on his for us all.

I put my romance book down and push myself to the edge of the sofa. "You should check out the library."

"What?" I swear I hear his neck creak.

"I said you should check out the library," I repeat. "Did you read the book I bought you?"

"No" is all he says, but his mouth remains open as if he's going to add something. He must think better of it, as he closes his lips.

I'm not disappointed that he hasn't read the book. Maybe thrillers aren't his thing. Plus, he's never struck me as a bookworm. But I'd never pass up the opportunity to introduce someone to the world of books.

"Then you should check out the library," I say for the third time.

"Why do I need to check out the library?" The Beast furrows his brow, and I marvel at how the scars down the left side of his face don't move.

"Because for the last two hours, you have just sat in that chair and stared at me."

"It's my job, and you just sent your other bodyguard away."

"Yeah, well, it's boring, and also, I don't have any opportunity to pick my nose or scratch my bottom. When am I supposed to do these things if you're constantly watching me?"

There's a little quirk at the side of his mouth, the one I love to see because I know it takes a lot to make it appear.

"What's that got to do with me checking out the library?" he asks, the smile quickly fading.

"You should try reading a book." I wave mine at him for emphasis.

"I don't have time to read," he scoffs.

"There's nothing else to do up here," I tell him. "You're going to die of boredom if you don't find something to occupy you, and then who's going to protect me?"

He appears to consider this before speaking.

"The last book I read was in school, and I don't even remember it, so it must've been boring."

"More boring than sitting in this room staring at me, waiting for something that isn't going to happen?" I want to add. How does this guy unwind? No wonder he doesn't sleep.

"You've been reading the wrong books, then," I say as a devilish feeling comes over me.

I'm not sure what I expected now that the Beast and I are alone in the house. The dynamics have certainly changed between us over the last six months, but I still don't know how I feel about him. I can't deny there's something about him that fascinates me. There have been moments when he's made my skin heat and my core flip, but there have also been times when I've wanted to strangle him.

And what about the Beast?

Maybe he doesn't *feel* at all. He's gone all professional on me, reminding me that I'm a job, an assignment, and nothing more. But we're going to be stuck in this house together, and I can't stand the tension that's settled over the last two hours.

The naughty feeling begins to swell, so I flick open the pages of my book and select a paragraph.

I clear my throat and put on my best husky male voice as I read aloud. "'You want me, don't you, Kylie? Are you wet for me, baby? Do you want my big cock in your mouth—'"

I don't get any further, as he snatches the book out of my hand and scans the rest of the page, his face giving nothing away.

"No wonder you read so much," he says. "This is fucking filth."

"Yeah, well, this filth beats sitting around here doing nothing."

"You found this in the library?" He's still reading, his eyes roaming the words.

"No. Nita must have packed it for me."

The only time I've fallen in love is within the pages of a romance book. I'll never forget my very first book boyfriend. He did things for me and taught me things I would never have learned in real life. These books became my escape, became the only way I could live the life I wanted.

"It's porn," the Beast says with a tut.

"It's not." I snatch the book out of his hand. "And even if it was, we all have our needs. Don't tell me you don't have a stash of porn or a favourite website."

There's a ripple across his features, and I picture him, eyes closed, his hand working himself into a frenzy.

"I don't need porn," he says at last, his face darkening.

I've tried to embarrass him, tried to make him feel uncomfortable for my own amusement, and now it's going to royally backfire like all the times before when I've pulled this little stunt.

His gaze intensifies, and I swear I feel his eyes caressing my body before he says, "I have a very good imagination."

I gulp, heat flaring over my skin. What does he think about when he touches himself?

As if answering me, he says, "I thought you were going to take a shower."

Words escape me, so I just slip from the sofa and make my way up the stairs, knowing he'll disappear into the small security room to make sure no one attacks me when I'm in my room.

But is that all he'll be doing?

Entering my bedroom, I don't feel the release of his stare as I look at the corner of the room where the camera blinks. He'll be sitting there now, behind his desk, watching me.

A tingling awakens between my legs.

Maybe it's because of the book I've just been reading. Maybe it's because of the conversation we've just had. Or maybe it's because I'm thinking of *him*. I turn my back on the camera, bravery coursing through my veins as I pull my jumper over my head before easing my sweats over my hips and sliding them down my legs.

Is he watching? Is he gasping as I bend over to pull my feet through the legs of my pants? Is he stroking himself whilst looking at my backside?

And more importantly, do I want him to?

Kicking my discarded clothes away, I then turn to face the camera, letting him see me in my underwear. Letting him take in all of me. Letting him know that this is just for him.

FENRIR

There's no comical blowing of a kiss this time as Hayami turns to stare at the camera. She's enchanting. Her skin's the palest eggshell, her hair the darkest black. My cock twitches as she turns and disappears into the en suite.

She's just messing around. Just toying with me. This is nothing but a continuation of the conversation we were having downstairs about the type of books she reads. Nothing more than the flirtatious shit she pulls daily, right? I know the kind of clubs Hayami has been trying to get into these last few months. The kind where hands get busy under tables, where people go to have more than a drink and dance. They're the types of places where people go for one thing and one thing only.

And I still don't know what game she's playing or what goes through her head sometimes. But I sure as hell know that something is going on with her, something between us. Or am I imagining it? Is she just winding me up?

Maybe it's all wishful thinking on my part. Because there's no way Hayami could ever want me. Only weirdos are ever attracted to me, and people who see me as a morbid curiosity—the ones who want to tick "fucked a freak" off their bucket list.

I fight the urge to stroke my cock. I won't stoop to that level whilst I'm supposed to be working. This is a job. But after the revelation that Willa isn't here, I'm going to find it hard to remind myself of this.

After Hayami explained why she'd sent Willa away and my anger had settled, I realised what she was saying was right: Willa needs to be with her family, and Hayami has never taken her safety very seriously. I can't help admiring her for having the nerve to defy her father, and for standing up for what she believes in and what she thinks is right.

There are grown men who won't stand up to the likes of Barrett Devall.

The en suite door opens. I lean over the desk as Hayami emerges, towel-drying her hair, eyes on the floor. She doesn't look up, doesn't acknowledge the camera as she throws the towel over the back of the small sofa before she climbs into bed and flicks off the light.

Show's over.

I settle back in the chair and replay her stripping in my head over and over and over again.

TWENTY-TWO

FENRIR

It's twenty past two in the morning when Hayami stirs.

Sitting up, I focus on the screen as she slides one leg out of bed, followed by the other, and then pulls herself to stand.

My heart thumps erratically.

It's just like last night—her body not holding itself properly, like she's a puppet being manoeuvred, her head hanging to one side like she has a crick in her neck.

I brace my arms on the side of the chair, readying myself to run, but it's as if the image on the screen is holding me down.

Slowly, she makes her way to the foot of the bed and looks up at the camera. That same lopsided angle of her head makes it appear as if she isn't awake, yet her eyes glow wildly. Her arms rise, her fingers like tentacles as they reach for her face.

I don't breathe as her fingers crawl inside her mouth and pull her lips apart, spreading that inane grin I saw last night, her white teeth appearing razor-sharp. Telling myself it's just a trick of the light, my tired eyes fooling me into seeing things that aren't there, I lean in to get a closer look and then wish I hadn't.

Blood oozes from her open lips, pooling in the cavern of her mouth and dribbling down her chin.

The sight of the blood untethers me.

Taking the stairs two at a time, I sprint to her room, my pulse racing. My heart's ready to explode through my chest. I fling open the door and—

She's in bed, fast asleep, the rhythmic rise and fall of the covers stilling the painful throb behind my ribcage.

What the fuck?

Not convinced I'm seeing things correctly, I enter the room, stopping in the spot where, seconds ago, she'd been standing, staring at the camera like a woman possessed and pulling the sides of her mouth into that hideous grin, blood flowing down her chin.

Yet the scene before me depicts none of this. The carpet is clean, with no patches of fresh blood, and Hayami is sound asleep, as if nothing has happened.

Taking a step towards her bed, I bend down and examine her face, looking for traces of blood. There's nothing.

Her eyes spring open.

"Shit!" she gasps, sitting bolt upright.

I realise how weird this must have looked—Hayami opening her eyes to see me leering over her like some creep.

"Sorry," I say quickly, backing away. Straightening, I clear my throat. "I thought I saw something on the camera, so I came to check it out, but it's nothing," I lie. But *am* I lying? There's nothing here, nothing to see. But I saw *something*, right? Is the lack of sleep already starting to play tricks on me? Or is it this house, the tales that have been told about sinister goings-on?

Fuck knows.

Hayami gathers her legs up to her chest and glances around the room. "What did you see?"

"I'm not sure." My second lie. "Just a flicker of something. It could've been dust floating over the lens. But I wanted to check. Sorry to have disturbed you."

"It's okay. I'd rather you check these things." She scans the room again and then looks up at the camera.

"You can go back to sleep."

"No." She shakes her head. "I was having an awful dream."

"What about?" My question is too quick, and I'm not sure whether she picks up on it. If she does, she doesn't show it.

"I don't know. I just know it was awful." She lowers her legs, revealing her underwear, but she doesn't seem to notice. "Pass me my robe, will you?" She nods to the hook on the back of the door.

I fetch her robe and hand it to her as she swings her legs out of the bed. I note the fluidity with which her body moves compared to the stiff way she'd moved not five minutes ago on the camera. Did that really happen? What had I seen? Fuck, was I hallucinating? That's never happened before, but what else would explain what I thought I just saw?

Swallowing, I avert my gaze as Hayami stands and threads her arms through her robe. When I look back, she's tightening the belt and pushing her feet into her slippers.

"Fancy a drink?" she asks.

"It's almost three in the morning," I tell her.

"Didn't stop us last night," she replies, and I have to tell myself not to stare as the image of her from the video monitor creeps back into my brain.

It wasn't her.

It looked like her.

I watched her climb out of bed.

It can't have been her.

"Are you okay?" She folds her arms. "You look... concerned."

"I'm fine. Let's get that drink."

We make our way down the stairs. I'm glad she's up. I'm not sure I'm ready to go sit back in that room and watch the monitor that's just tricked me, or to trust my eyes, which could be making me see things that haven't happened.

The kitchen feels normal as I pad to the cupboard and pull out the bottle of whisky. Hayami takes up the chair she sat in last night as I pour two glasses and push one over to her.

She sips it carefully, her face squeezing slightly as I imagine the burn hitting the back of her throat.

"You're getting a taste for it," I tell her, downing my own and then pouring another.

"It's definitely an acquired taste, but I can see why so many people drink it. It's like you can feel it moving into your system and burning away whatever was there that was hard to swallow."

I glug my second glass, hoping to burn away the image of her standing in that room, pulling at the sides of her mouth as if she were trying to split her face in half. I should take it steady. Shouldn't really be drinking on the job, but that god-awful image is seared into my head, and I need it gone.

Last night felt different. She was sleepwalking, or what *appeared* to be sleepwalking. There were no sharp teeth, no blood in her mouth. And this evening, to have raced up the stairs and then found her sound asleep makes me question my sanity.

"What's it burning away for you?" I ask, hoping she isn't paying attention as I pour myself a third measure.

Hayami sneers. "Where to start." She tips the glass to the side as if trying to make the liquid dance. "The life I have, if you can call it a life. The life I'd like to have if my surname weren't Devall. What about you?" She angles the glass towards me as if it's a microphone.

I heave a sigh, unable to let the words fall from my mouth.

"Whisky doesn't seem to work for me."

"No?" Hayami regards me before she says, "Is it something to do with how you got your scars?"

I flinch.

"Sorry, I shouldn't be asking," she adds quickly, putting her glass down on the table.

"I'm surprised you haven't asked before. It's normally everyone's first question."

"Willa said it was a fire."

"It was."

"But there's more?"

"Isn't there always?" I gulp my drink, gearing myself up to speak of the night I try my hardest to forget, yet it clings to me night and day, robs me of sleep, of sanity. Of all sense of peace. If nothing else, it stops me thinking about what I've just seen, or what I thought I just saw, in Hayami's room.

"I was seventeen when it happened."

Hayami's eyes widen, and her shoulders brace. Everyone always assumes it happened whilst I was in the army, part of the job. But no. This was before then, when I was only a teenager.

"Seventeen?"

I nod slowly, that night coming back to me in all its horrific glory. The night the darkness touched me, and now crawls across my skin, never letting me forget, never giving me a moment of solace. The night that changed everything. Heat from the whisky permeates my insides, melting the bindings I keep these memories bound with.

"My mum worked as a cleaner at the hospital, and my dad was a delivery driver. Things were tight, but we got by. But one night, my dad came home late, pale, frantic. I was still up, but my mum and sister had gone to bed. He woke Mum up, told her to pack some things because we needed to leave, then told me to do the same. I kept asking him what was going on, but he wouldn't say, just told me to hurry up."

I tighten my grip on the glass, knuckles whitening as the blood leaves them.

"I was scared. I'd never seen Dad like that. Mum threw on some clothes and started shoving things into a suitcase as Dad stalked the house, pulling open drawers, stuffing money into a bag and a gun into his waistband."

I remember it all so clearly; how can I not when it's burned into my flesh? I take a drink as I gather my thoughts, the whisky loosening my tongue.

"I froze, didn't know what to do until we heard the smashing of glass coming from the front door. Dad shouted at me to go to my sister's room, to lock the door, to hide. His face was unrecognisable. I ran to Lilith's room. My sister woke up, and I told her we had to hide. She was sleepy and didn't know what was going on. I had no concept of time, no idea how long we hid in her cramped closet."

I take another swig of whisky as I hear the gunshots.

"The bangs of the gun… it was like I felt them, right here." I prod at my gut, the whisky sloshing against the emptiness that resides there. "We stayed in the closet, me telling Lilith that everything would be okay and that we just had to stay quiet until Dad came to get us."

I lower my gaze to the glass. The amber liquid looks so similar to the flames, as if I've captured that night in the tumbler.

"But he never did. I didn't know what was happening until I smelled something burning."

I blink, positive there must be smoke in the room, as my eyes start to sting. The periphery of my vision blurs, turning

Hayami's frozen figure into a hazy silhouette against the dimly lit kitchen.

"I ran from the closet, dragging Lilith with me. She was crying, and I could hear shouts from outside."

Their voices ring in my ears and echo off the wall cabinets. It wasn't until after that I found out it was the neighbours who'd gathered outside the building. They'd probably seen the smoke and called the fire brigade.

My throat begins to close as Hayami shifts in her seat.

"It was when I opened Lilith's bedroom door that I realised our apartment was on fire, and she and I were going to burn to death if I didn't get us out."

The weight of that responsibility still strangles my lungs, worse than the smoke did, and the words get caught up in the blaze.

Hayami remains silent, because what the fuck is there to say?

"I tried to get her out." I try to continue, but my chest squeezes as I feel the weight of Lilith's small body in my arms, her trembling, sobbing cries getting swallowed up by the greedy inferno.

"I had to break down her door and use it as a shield to get us through the apartment. But we were trapped." I let go of my glass, my palms drenched in sweat, the memory of the heat unbearable.

Hayami looks cold and pale, her lips almost blue.

"Then I remembered the Juliet balcony in the living room, the one my mum always fretted about when Lilith was a toddler." My mouth curls at the memory as it attempts to douse the flames, but they're too strong, too fierce for me to fight.

"I felt like I was on autopilot, like I wasn't consciously acting, just doing whatever needed to be done as I smashed the glass and told Lilith she needed to be brave, that we were going to fly just like birds, and that when we landed, we'd be safe."

The kitchen contorts, Hayami lost amongst the neighbours who were standing below, waving their arms and telling me to jump. And it was easy. No hesitation. No thought about the consequences, because when the flames are eating at your flesh, lifting the skin from your bones, there's no alternative.

"I jumped with Lilith in my arms. We landed on two neighbours who were standing below and said they'd catch us. We fell to the ground, and, for a second, I felt relief that I'd got us out."

I pause, my mouth dry, a bitter, charred taste clinging to the roof of my mouth. I reclaim my glass and down the remaining liquid, numbing the pain from the burns and fuelling myself for the rest of this sorry tale.

"You saved her," Hayami says, her expression soft, as if she's trying to convince me I'm the hero I've portrayed myself to be.

"I thought so." My voice trembles, betraying my hard exterior.

She thinks this is the happy ending.

I swallow, my teeth grinding against the inevitable. "When the firefighters arrived along with the ambulances, Lilith was awake, crying, with a broken ankle and a few scratches, but that was all. I thought I'd saved her."

My head hangs low, the glass now so heavy in my hand, I want to drop it.

"It wasn't until I was in the hospital, when I was still being treated for my burns, that a policeman came to tell me that my parents were dead, that they'd been shot, their bodies burned in the blaze." For the first time since I began, I meet Hayami's eyes. Her teary gaze peers back at me, and I wish I hadn't looked at her. "All I could think about was how my dad was going to teach me to drive, how my mum was helping me get through my A levels, and how young Lilith was to have our parents taken from her."

I try to fight the heartache with my anger, but I'm bowled over by the grief. The loving family I thought would always be with me until I was old were gone. They were taken from me.

Suddenly, I want to be alone, but Hayami is waiting. She must know by now that this isn't a happy ending. I can tell by how wide her eyes are and the hollows in her cheeks that she's bracing herself for the worst. I bite the bullet and get it over with.

"It was later, much later, when I was high on pain meds and wrapped in gauze like a fucking mummy, that a doctor told me that Lilith had passed away the third night after the fire." My breath catches as I remember how I argued with her, saying it wasn't possible because Lilith had been alive when I got her out, alive when they took her to the hospital, alive when I'd been stretchered off to the severe burns unit.

She'd explained that it was common in fires for death to occur later on, as it was the smoke inhalation that killed and not necessarily the burns.

I look up, making sure Hayami sees my face, sees the man I am, before telling her, "I didn't save her, Hayami. She died anyway. I'm not the hero you think I am."

TWENTY-THREE

HAYAMI

PRESENT

Blinking away my tears, I stare at this man who I've spent six months with—knowing nothing of what he's been through, nothing of what he's endured, nothing of who he was before he leapt into my swimming pool. The man before me is no longer a beast in my eyes—he's Fenrir, a tortured soul who has been through more pain in this life than I could ever even begin to understand.

This is the most he's ever said to me—to *anyone*, I'm sure. I've never seen him talk to Willa or Bastian. And it's no wonder he keeps to himself. No wonder he shudders when people ask about his scars. Because what he's just told me has left me feeling so numb, I'm not even sure I'm really sitting here and not still asleep in my bed, caught in some horrible nightmare.

Who lives through something like that and comes out okay at the other end?

No one.

"I'm so sorry." My words feel flimsy, as if they have no

power to undo what he's just told me. He lost everything. Everyone. At the age of seventeen, everything he'd ever known was taken from him. How do you live with that?

Fenrir doesn't respond, simply hangs his head and clutches at the tumbler in his hand.

"How did you go on with your life?" I ask, my eyes swimming at all the possible answers to this.

His jaw flexes, the scarring around his chin moving like a mask.

"I spent much of the first year in the hospital, recovering from my injuries. The burns team helped my skin to heal. I had specialists, doctors, nurses, therapists, surgeons, you name it; they were all involved in helping me to recover. So, when I was finally discharged, the thought of ending it all felt wrong because so many people had helped get me to where I was. What kind of repayment would it have been for me to undo everything that'd been done to help me? For the first few weeks, I was lost, but then I had some counselling, and my therapist said that I needed to channel my anger, find a cause, fight for something good. He told me there'd been a reason I didn't die in that fire, and that I just had to find the reason. That's when I realised what I had to do."

He waits, his eyes narrowing. I'm not entirely sure what he's referring to, so I ask, "You joined the army?"

"Yes. Two years after that night, I joined the army for one reason and one reason only." He balls his fist, flexes his fingers, and the penny drops.

He wanted training. He wanted to know how to fight. He wanted to be strong, an immovable force, someone who nobody would ever threaten. He wanted to become invincible.

"Revenge," I say quietly.

"I served ten years before I left. I told them I had a job to do, something I'd been meaning to do for the last twelve years." He slides the empty glass onto the table, the whisky fuelling his words.

"You wanted to find the people who killed your family," I guess.

"Yes."

"And did you?"

I feel the walls shrink, as if the whole room is waiting with bated breath.

"Yes."

His face is so cold now, I can feel the chill coming from him.

I don't want to ask, afraid of the answer, even though I know what it's going to be.

"Are they…?" I begin, and he must see my struggle, as he finishes my question.

"Dead?" He tips his head to the side. "Yes, all of them are dead." His eyes burn, a fierceness to his voice that I've only ever heard when he's mad with me or cross about something. The words he says next are like a knife to my gut.

"Morris Hamlin was the man who shot my dad and my mum. He's dead. Tyrone Miller was the man who poured the petrol and dropped the match. He's dead."

The names are familiar. I've heard them whispered at home when no one thought I was listening, and Fenrir mentioned them when we first arrived at Belial House. They are—*were*—members of the Castro gang, until they were killed. I never paid much attention to the gossip. This is my father's world, not something I choose to get involved in, but I am now. I'm in the firing line because….

I stare at Fenrir. It can't be. It's not possible, but his face is telling me otherwise.

I swallow hard as my next question works its way out of my head and onto my lips. "Robert Castro?"

"Was the man who gave the order." His gaze is hard, brutal, and unforgiving. "And he's dead."

It's not just the whisky now burning my insides. He's just told me that he was responsible for killing three members of the Castro family, the likes of which has now started a gang war.

"You?"

"Yes, Hayami. Me. I'm the one who killed them all. I'm the reason the Castro family are now sending you death threats. I'm the reason you're in danger. I'm the reason we're here." He holds my gaze as this sinks in, the enormity of it, before adding, "I brought this on you."

I want to respond, but my brain is struggling with this new information.

"Does my father know? Did he sanction their deaths?"

He doesn't blink, doesn't break eye contact as he answers, "No. No one sent me."

"I don't understand." I want another drink, but the bottle is half-empty and too far out of my reach. "If my father knew nothing of this, then how did you pull it off?"

"When I left the army, it was with the sole purpose of finding the men who killed my family. It took longer than I expected. But after tracking down some of my dad's old friends, I discovered that he'd been working for the Castros, delivering things for them and using his legitimate business as cover. But something went wrong. He messed up a delivery that cost the Castros a lot of money and put them in dicey waters with some other gang. Robert Castro wasn't happy with my dad, which resulted in two men being sent to kill him: Morris Hamlin and Tyrone Miller."

He pauses and drains his glass before slamming it down on the table.

"What I don't understand is how you ended up working as a Hellhound."

"Hamlin was easy to find, even easier to kill. He liked women and he liked to party, so catching him one night whilst he took a piss around the back of a club was like child's play."

About a year ago, I remember hearing something about one of Castro's men being found behind a nightclub. They thought he'd been jumped and robbed, but he'd been beaten so badly that they had to use his tattoos to identify him. I shudder, pulling my robe tighter around my body.

My next question slips out even though I'm not sure I want to know the answer. "And the other two men?"

"Very heavily guarded and very difficult to get to. I needed a different approach, and that's why I became a Hellhound."

"You joined the Hellhounds because you'd get inside info on the Castros?" I guess.

"And resources. The Hellhounds are very well equipped with all the latest tech and weapons."

"Oh my God." My body sinks further into the chair from the weight of all this new information pushing down on me. "My father really doesn't know any of this?"

He shakes his head. "I thought he did, the day he told me to come to the house. I thought he'd found out I killed Hamlin and Miller. But later on, he said he'd wanted to talk to me about a job, a job that only my face would fit. Then he assigned me to your security team, and I never found out what the job was."

"So, after you were brought onto my team, you still went ahead and killed Robert Castro."

"Things got more difficult when I was reassigned as your bodyguard. I wasn't on the front line with the Hellhounds anymore, and much of my time was spent guarding you. But the days when you were at university, I watched Robert Castro. I'd told myself he didn't need to die. I tried to convince myself that the two men who'd physically killed my family had been dealt with, but I couldn't let it drop. Working on your security team gave me some advantages. I started to look at Robert's security team, how they operated, how they worked, and I soon rooted out the weak spots. The bodyguards who weren't as eagle-eyed as they should have been. I knew Robert's routine. He visited his club, the Kaleidoscope, every Thursday afternoon. So, I positioned myself in an empty office overlooking the club, set up my rifle, and waited to get a clear shot. I'd done this a few times, and each time I never had him in my line of sight. Until last week. When he walked into the Kaleidoscope, one of his security guards dropped his phone. He stopped and bent down to pick it up, leaving me a clear shot of the back of Robert Castro's head."

The image plays in my mind. I've seen how good Fenrir is with a gun, how skilled a marksman he is, so this shouldn't surprise me, but it does. And it isn't just the killing itself; it's the repercussions, the chain reaction that Robert's death has caused.

"People have died. You told me the Castros killed a load of people in one of my father's clubs." My voice falters between sorrow and anger. What has he done? What has he set in motion?

"I know. And for that, I'm truly sorry. I never thought it'd start a gang war. I was careful, made every effort to ensure that it didn't point to the Hellhounds or your father."

"Jesus." I push my hair from my face, unsure how to process this. It's terrible, what he did, what he's done.

Then I look at his scars, the reminders he carries with him daily of what was done to him at seventeen, what he went through, what he witnessed, and how he lost his entire family at the hands of three men. My chest burns, my teeth clench, and I wonder if I'd have done the same in his position.

"What I don't understand is how you could work for my father as a Hellhound, dishing out the same sort of things that Castro's men dished out to your family," I say.

He lowers his gaze. There's no pride in where his journey has landed him.

"I don't kill people. I don't kill children. I don't burn families in their beds. The guys who killed my family were barbaric. They were ruthless. They were murderers. Somewhere in my twisted logic, I thought that if I could go and do their job properly, the way they were supposed to do it, just acting out the orders they must have had, then maybe my mum and sister would still be alive. There was no need for them to die, yet they did because of two fuckwits who took it upon themselves to burn them to death."

"Then what did you do for my father?"

"I broke bones, made people bleed. I spoke with my fists and my scars. I put the fear of God in the people who owed your father. I sent messages that were heard loud and clear. But I never killed anyone unless they were about to kill me or another Hellhound."

I've always thought myself a good judge of character, but I've misread this man completely. No matter how hard I try, I can't find any words or anything to say that'll make this all seem okay. There's nothing that'll put a different slant on his story, because it's fucking shit. Shit, shit, shit. Shitty life doing shitty things to people, and my father is just as culpable.

I want to scream.

"This is the reason you're so protective of me," I say at last. "You think this is all your fault."

Fenrir nods, glancing at me. I see it now, his need to protect. The way he smothers me with such force that I can't breathe. The way he won't let anyone near me. It's all because of his actions, because he knows he brought this to my door. But I also see something else on his face—the side without scars, the side that's Fenrir Therion, the seventeen-year-old boy who tried to save his sister and failed.

I want to tell him that I'm not his sister. That I'm a twenty-year-old woman who can fight her own corner. But this isn't the right time.

"You're just trying to do your job, and sometimes, I make it very difficult for you. I apologise."

"There's no need. I see your cage, and I know who put you there. I admire you. Fighting for what you believe in."

I want to laugh, because he doesn't know the half of it. "I don't think throwing a tantrum can be labelled as something so bold. I try my best to kick up a shitstorm where I can, but I'm not as brave as you think I am."

Fenrir eyes me, and I know I've hit a nerve.

"Are any of us?" he asks.

Sitting up, I can't help but wonder how right he is.

Silence trickles over the tiled floor, reminding me of how late it is and how this night has turned into something entirely different.

"Not the bedtime story you were after," he says, as if reading my mind.

"Don't say that," I scold, although he's right. I'm not sure I'll sleep after this revelation. "I'm glad you felt you could tell me." And I mean it. He's opened up to me and admitted what he's done and why he did it.

Something dawns on me. "Why *have* you told me?"

He cocks his head, confused, his eyes a little glassy from the whisky.

"Aren't you worried I'll tell my father?"

There's no hesitation as he answers. "No. I know you won't tell your father."

He's right, but… "How can you be so sure?"

"Because we both have secrets, Hayami. You sent Willa away and have sworn me to secrecy."

Touché.

"Besides," he says, rising from his chair and pushing it under the table, "I trust you."

There's a stab in my chest. I want to be able to reciprocate, share with him what awaits me when we get off this mountain, but this was his show and tell, not mine. I'll be damned if I'm going to overshadow his pain with my own sob story.

"You should get some rest." He angles his head, a softness brushing his skin as the light changes on his face.

"Why? Big day tomorrow?" I joke.

"No, but I need you to have your wits about you if you're going to learn how to fire a gun."

I sit up. "Really? You're going to teach me how to shoot?"

"I said I would," he says, "but only if you get some sleep."

"I can't argue with that." I slide off the chair and hug myself. "Are you going to be okay in the office?"

He nods and heads towards the door. "I'll walk you up to your room."

"Are you going to check under my bed?" I ask as he follows me out into the foyer and up the stairs.

"It seems stupid, but it's the basics," he says.

We reach my room, and he enters first, completing all his sweeping checks before letting me follow.

"I'll see you in the morning," he says before closing the door behind me.

And I'm left in the soft glow of my room that looks the same as when I left it, but I feel different. Everything feels different. And it shouldn't. He's the same man who beat the shit out of a guy who was trying to cop off with me in the toilets seven days ago. He's the same man who dragged me from the river one month ago. He's the same man who pulled me from the pool six months ago.

But he doesn't feel the same.

I see him.

I see what he is, what he can do, and his motivations behind it all.

He's a victim. A survivor.

And he's also a killer.

TWENTY-FOUR
HAYAMI

THE GARAGE IS GREY AND COLD, NOT A PLACE I WOULD normally wish to hang around, but shortly after getting up this morning, Fenrir informed me that today was to be my first shooting lesson.

I've no doubt this won't be my calling in life. I've never had the desire to handle a gun, and if I'm honest, I despise them. But if it puts his mind at rest that my safety isn't just in his hands, then I'll happily oblige. After all, I'm the one who sent Willa away and left Fenrir as a solo operative.

Yet, he's the reason I'm here in the first place. I can't help this thought overriding everything—his culpability in all of this. But then all I have to do is look at his face to remember why he did what he did. Why he felt the need to avenge his family.

A text arrived from Willa in the early hours of the morning, informing me that she'd made it to Marta, who cried when she saw her. They're still monitoring Marta and the baby, and I reassured Willa that they're all in the right place if they need to take action. She sent me a heart emoji and said she'd keep me updated.

"Have you spoken to Markus?" I ask Fenrir as he stacks boxes of varying heights at one end of the garage, then places disposable cups he found in the kitchen on top of the boxes.

"Yes." The one-word beast is back; last night's runaway tongue has been locked up. I blame the whisky.

"What have you told him?"

"As little as possible."

"Are they any closer to settling this war?"

"Markus just said they were making progress, but fuck knows what that means."

Wiping his hands down the front of his pants, Fenrir makes his way over to me. He looks the figure of fucking finery today in his black combat trousers and skintight black T-shirt. It's impossible not to blush.

He pulls a gun from the back of his waistband and holds it out to me. There's a second when I imagine what these hands have done, how he's taken lives with the curl of his fists and the pull of a trigger. How dangerous he can be. *Is.* Yet, I don't feel scared. I've never been afraid of him.

He must see the surprise on my face, as he thrusts it forwards and says, "It's not going to bite you."

"Yeah, but I might shoot your foot by accident."

"Not with the safety on."

I smile and take the gun from him.

It feels strange, like I'm not meant to be holding something like this, something that can take a life so easily.

"It's lighter than I thought it'd be," I say, turning the weapon over.

"Weight, ease of use, compactness," he says. "Guns have come a long way. But I don't want you to think about the gun." He takes a step back.

I'm not thinking about the gun. I'm thinking about him,

the soldier, the Hellhound, the killer. He looks all those things today and more.

"There's a ton of things to learn about firing a gun, but I'm going to focus on the basics. The first is stance. I'm looking for power. Something that'll anchor you to the ground. The best for shooting is a fighter posture. Think boxing." He steps closer and points at my feet, telling me where to put them before reaching for my waist, but then he stops and looks at me.

"Can I...?" I presume he's asking if he can touch me, which feels strange, as he's put his hands upon me many times before. But that was always in the line of duty. This is different.

"Sure." I shrug, trying to give off an air of nonchalance when inside I feel nothing of the sort.

As he slips his hand around my waist and twists my pelvis into a forty-five-degree angle, I try not to think about his hands on my body, the command of his words, and our proximity. This is serious stuff, and I want to learn. This shit could save my life.

"You're right-handed, so your left leg needs to be forwards and your right leg slightly back. That way, you have balance both front and back. See?" He moves my legs, then pushes me forwards and then back, showing me how grounded I am now that I'm standing in the correct position. "Good," he says, and my insides unfurl, wanting him to add a *"girl"* on the end, before reminding myself this isn't one of my smutty books.

"Now we need to look at your grip," he says, and I gulp. "The way you hold a gun depends on what type you're firing. For now, I just want you to grip it as tightly as you can. Firearms are powerful. They kick. They jump. So you need to hold it like you're never going to let it go. Let me see."

I raise the weapon and grasp it like he just said. I feel stupid, but he nods, seemingly impressed so far.

"The next is sight. There's front and back. You can't focus on both sights and the target, so for now, I just want you to concentrate on the front sight. Here, let me show you." He takes my hand and pulls it level with my eyes as he slides his body snugly against mine.

He's so warm, the heat from his skin making my hands sweat, and I worry I'm going to lose my grip on the gun.

"Okay, look here." He taps the front sight, and I focus on it. "And last is the trigger."

"I know this," I jump in, having read about this technique in crime books. "You have to squeeze it."

"Yeah, or I prefer to imagine rolling it. If you roll the trigger, it usually means the force will be consistent, smooth, and unified. You don't want to be surprised by the shot." He tucks himself in behind me, his breath on the back of my neck, and I tell myself to keep looking at the front sight and not think about how close he is or how much I want him to touch me.

"I'm going to take the safety off, and then you're going to line up the gun with the first target." He nods to the upturned box and the plastic cup sitting on top of it.

Wrapping his arms around my body, he pulls at the top of the gun, and it clicks. My mind is panting, yet I will myself to focus on the target.

"Okay, now line up the front sight with the middle of the cup." His voice is like the whisky running down the back of my throat, sending heat travelling right to my core.

Placing his hands over mine, he grips the gun with me, and I want to melt. His body feels hard behind me, like it's holding me in place, and I try not to think about what it'd be like to feel his arousal against me.

Trying to fish my mind out of the gutter, I concentrate on the target and the gun.

"Okay." He loosens his grip on my hands but doesn't pull them away completely. "Now roll the trigger and don't close your eyes."

Taking a deep breath, I pull the trigger.

It's like taking a punch. The kick of the gun has me reeling back on my heels, straight into the front of Fenrir. I'd kidded myself that maybe he was standing behind me just as an excuse to get close to me, but now I realise he'd been supporting me, as even with his instruction on my stance, there was no way I wouldn't have fallen backwards from the force.

"Okay, I was not prepared for that," I tell him as he lowers his arms, and I lower the gun.

"You'll get used to it." Fenrir steps to the side. "You did good."

"I didn't hit the cup." I nod at the box that took the hit.

"I didn't expect you to. But you will. With practice."

And this is what we do for the rest of the morning, until eventually, I hit the goddamn cup. It feels like I've won the lottery.

"Yes!" I shout, punching the air and jumping on the spot.

"Great job." Fenrir smiles, which only adds to my joy.

"It only took me eight hundred tries." I laugh as he smirks.

"Don't be too hard on yourself. You've done great. You've never even held a gun before today."

I can't help my smile spreading, and I'm about to hand him back the gun, but then I pause.

"Your turn," I say, holding the gun out to him with the barrel pointing at the floor.

He dips his head. "I don't need to practice."

"No, but I want to see how it's supposed to be done."

"I'm not a great role model," he says in a low voice that makes my insides tremble.

"Do as I say and not as I do?" I arch one eyebrow.

"Something like that."

I push the gun at him. "Please, for me. Just one shot."

Slowly, he takes the gun from my hand and stares at me before turning his attention to the remaining cup on the highest box.

He doesn't falter, doesn't hesitate. He just raises his arm, the gun an extension as he fires at the target, and the cup flies off the box.

Tipping my head to the side, I say, "Well, your stance was a little off, and I don't think you rolled the trigger, but it wasn't bad."

He smiles and turns the safety back on before sliding the gun into the back of his waistband. "You have to learn the rules before you can break them." His eyes remain on me. "Like I said, not a good role model."

We make our way back into the house as I remind myself that he's my bodyguard, here to do a job, and I can't let any attraction I may feel get in the way of that. One thing's certain: I felt things I usually only experience when reading my smutty romance books when Fenrir stood behind me, holding my arms, his breath licking my skin. I felt things that I never have with any other man before today.

After everything he's told me, after everything he's done, after knowing what kind of man he is, I still feel this bewildering attraction to him. But what *is* he?

A scarred beast or a broken human?

Or maybe he's both?

TWENTY-FIVE
FENRIR

MY EYES ARE WEARY AS I WATCH HAYAMI SETTLE IN THE LARGE chair, a book in her hand like a shield. The heaviness in them isn't purely from lack of sleep. I'm not sure how many glasses of whisky I drank last night, but however many it was, it was *too* many—my mouth had no restraint, unburdening my soul to the woman I've sworn to protect.

The whisky wasn't just to blame. I'd have done anything, *said* anything to rid myself of the image of her standing under the camera, fingers shoved into the sides of her mouth, pulling at her cheeks as if she were trying to stretch her face beyond all recognition. Then to have charged up the stairs to find her sleeping in her bed with no signs of the hideous show was enough for any man to question his sanity and push him to drink.

It's no wonder I ended up unloading my past on her and confessing my sins. When I returned to the surveillance room, I wondered if I'd done the wrong thing, shared too much, but I felt lighter somehow. I've spent too many years keeping everything to myself—never opening up to anyone. It's only fair for her to know what kind of man she's locked herself away with now that Willa is gone. She needed to know who I am and what I'm capable of.

I didn't expect her to run from me. I've known her long enough to see that she doesn't frighten easily, but she needed to know I'm no hero. I'm not her saviour, and I never will be. Only she can take up that role.

This morning, when she arrived in the kitchen, she looked at me differently. She sees the real me, and I don't know whether that's good or bad. I guess only time will tell.

After sending Markus an update from Willa's work phone, we grabbed some lunch and headed here to the library, Hayami insisting I get some shuteye.

"I'm fine," I tell her as she curls her legs under her body, adjusting herself in the oversized chair.

"You haven't slept at all. Just get an hour or so. I'll be fine in here. How can anyone not be safe surrounded by books?" She eyes the shelves as if they're a fortress.

"Fine, but I'm not leaving this room," I say, last night's vision still playing in my mind. Lowering myself into the chair opposite her, I cross my arms and close my eyes.

"You look about as comfortable as a gay man on a date with a woman." Hayami's voice lands in my lap as I open my eyes.

"I've told you, I don't need sleep, just rest."

She tuts, picks up her book, and brings it up to cover her face.

I close my eyes, rest my head back, and relive the moment in the garage when she'd had the gun in her hand and my arms around her. I thought I'd felt something—a heat, a reaction, a fluttering of her body—but I'm sure it's just wishful thinking on my part. Instead, I try to shake it off and recall all the things I was taught in the army when I first held a gun.

Miraculously, I doze lightly. I drift in and out of a restless sort of sleep, the kind where you feel like hours have gone by when in fact it's been mere minutes, before my eyes open. My brain refuses to shut down, and my legs feel like they're going to seize up.

I stretch, levering myself out of the chair and perusing the bookcases. Hayami's too engrossed in her book to even notice.

Various titles adorn the shelves. Nothing grabs me. Nothing screams out to be read. I'm about to give up on her suggestion that I find something to read when a spine catches my eye.

It's dark blue, with a soft texture, but the thing that stands out is there's no title.

I pull the book from the shelf and turn it over to reveal a blank front cover. One word's embossed upon it in silver font.

Journal.

Flipping through the pages, I note the journal has been written in. The first half is filled by simple penmanship that looks almost childlike in its heavy print. The words feel almost like Braille with the pressure that must have been applied whilst they'd been written by a heavy hand and a basic ballpoint pen.

Returning to the front, I open it to the first page and read:

Journal of Junko Devall, Winter 2003 — Belial House

Day One

Fuck.

It's her mother's journal.

My first instinct is to close the book. I shouldn't be

reading this. It's not my place. I should give this to Hayami. I'm about to hand it over, admit what I've just found, but I stop.

What if there's stuff in here about her father? What if there are details in here about their marriage, what he's done to her, what he's made her do, made her feel? What if there's sexual stuff? I can't imagine Hayami would want to read about that. I'm not even sure I do.

I go to put it back on the shelf, until I remember what Hayami said about her mother coming to this house with her father and then never returning. What happened here that made Junko Devall never want to set foot in this house again? Does it have something to do with what I've been seeing? Will it explain what's been happening to Hayami at night? I wonder if the answers are in these pages.

I should tell her what I've found, and I will. She deserves to know this exists, but I want to read it first. That way, I can prepare her if she needs it or burn it if there's something in here she never needs to know.

And so, for the first time in years, I read.

> *I hate this house. From the minute we arrived, I've had this feeling of dread, like something is going to happen. When I stepped out of the car, it was as if the house had been waiting for me, staring through its eyelike windows, clapping its hands in anticipation of my arrival. It felt cold, foreboding. I'd told Barrett when he'd slung his arm around me and asked me what I thought.*
>
> *"It's just the weather," he'd said, letting go of my shoulder and directing his staff to take our*

luggage into the house. "It doesn't look as dark when the sun is out."

I'd looked up to the sky, the thick grey clouds matted together as if they were shielding the blue from this house, and the thought came over me that this place has never seen the sun.

Inside was no better. Dark wood clads every wall, heavy drapes hang listlessly, and rich upholstery breathes. There's no light, no movement, and I shuddered as I was led through the many rooms, contemplating how I'd ended up here, the lady of the manor, the new Mrs Barrett Devall.

Barrett and I have been married for five months. He'd seen me in a nightclub whilst on a business trip with several high-powered men in Japan. I'd been working as a waitress, serving him drinks, my attention given only to his private party.

He's much older than I am, but still handsome. His skin's a little weather-beaten, as if he's been sailing on too many yachts. But he's charming and dashing, the kind of man who has women falling at his feet.

And I was no one.

He'd asked if I spoke English when I'd brought him his third drink of the evening.

I nodded. The manager of the club had told me to act demure. These men didn't like women who spoke, thought, or had an opinion. Barrett Devall wouldn't want to know that I probably spoke better

English than he did, something which usually occurs when someone has had to learn the language.

Every night of his three-week trip, he'd visited the club with his associates and dazzled me with his smile, his looks, and his velvety voice.

Rina, one of the waitresses and my closest friend, had said to me one night that he wanted me. All the staff had noticed how much attention he'd been paying me, and my boss had been happy for me to entertain a man like Barrett Devall, as, according to my boss, he was very wealthy and powerful and an asset to the club.

I smiled, told Rina that he probably only wanted one thing. She'd raised her eyebrows and told me that he had just lost his second wife and was, apparently, looking for a new one. I'd laughed and told her not to pay attention to the gossip that floated around the club. But I couldn't help the sense of excitement, the feeling of something brewing that there might be a life outside those walls.

On the final night, he'd told me, "How would you like to leave this place?" His words were like the opening of a new page of a book, the excitement, the anticipation of what was to come. "How would you like to live in a mansion, want for nothing, have everything?"

What would anyone say to that?

My friends at the club were so jealous. It was everyone's dream to meet a rich man who would sweep them off their feet with diamonds, jewellery, clothes, and the promise of a better life. And they were happy for me, over the moon, along with my family, who cheered and clapped at how I'd done so well for myself.

And I'd bathed in the attention, basked in the joy that this new life would bring. Because that's exactly what he did—sweep me off my feet.

It wasn't until he brought me to the city of Rothkor and his mansion that my feet started to be pulled down to the ground.

I'm wife number three.

This is how the staff refer to me.

Number Three.

From what I've gathered from the murmurings of the staff and overheard rumours, wife number one was a white woman of outstanding beauty, with flame-red hair, emerald eyes, and a smile so dazzling it could blind you. Barrett met her when he was in his thirties and, I believe, must have been the closest to love a man like Barrett Devall could have felt. Their marriage lasted five years. Some say she was feisty, a real fire-breathing dragon who gave Barrett a run for his money. Some say she was the love of his life. But for whatever reason, the marriage ended. Some say it was because she was infertile. Some say she didn't want children at all, and some tales tell of a woman who'd had enough of being Mrs Devall.

The knowledge of wife number one, I can cope with. She felt real, like they had met naturally and fallen in love. It was when I learned of wife number two that my bubble began to burst. I thought our story was unique, that he had seen me, fallen in love with me, and brought me here to live with him in his castle, but I soon learned that this is exactly how he met wife number two.

She was also a Japanese woman, just like me, although he met her in Rothkor when she'd come over here to work. Had he loved her? I think he must have. But it was sadly not to be, as number two died. I'm not sure how. The whisperings through the household tell of a fatal miscarriage, a birth gone wrong, or something along those lines. No one seems willing to talk about it. Apparently, Barrett's never really got over her death, because she was pregnant and carrying his child.

And I can't help thinking that he's simply replaced her with me. A carbon copy of the woman who almost gave him a child.

So, now I am number three.

"Third time lucky," one of the staff said when I arrived at his mansion, one small suitcase containing my scant belongings.

Since arriving in Rothkor and learning about his past wives, I realise now why I'm here. There's no love on his part. Lust, maybe. I am aware of the beauty I carry, and maybe that's what caught Barrett's eye that night in the club. But all he really wanted was a replacement for the woman who almost gave him what he truly desired. He married me for one thing.

An heir.

And that's why we're here at Belial House.

After five months of trying, I've failed to fall pregnant. Barrett said we should get away from the estate and get some peace. I liked the sound of that, something a little more normal, fewer staff floating about the place. I thought getting away from the mansion might bring back the Barrett Devall I met in Japan. That, away from his business dealings, he would be the man who captured my heart.

I had visions of a private beach with a luxurious holiday house or a fancy lodge at the edge of a lake, the kind of houses you see and only dream of. But when he'd told me where we were going, I'd shuddered at the name.

Belial House.

It hadn't sounded luxurious. It sounded depressing.

And I wasn't wrong.

There's something about this house. Something that makes me want to pack up and leave. Something that makes me want to cry, scream, and run—everything all at once.

I'm not the only one who feels it.

The staff feel it too.

I see it in the way they move around, their arms clasped around their bodies as if trying to keep warm, or when they're looking over their shoulder as if something is following them.

Because it's exactly what I feel within these walls.

Evil, as if the devil himself has built this place.

"Wow, this has got to be a first." Hayami's voice snaps me from the page, and I almost drop the book. I must look confused. "You're reading a book." She nods to the journal.

"Yes." There's a distinct tremor to my voice that, thankfully, she doesn't seem to pick up on.

"Any good?"

There's a second where I consider telling her, but I've made my mind up. I'll read it first. So I do what any discerning bodyguard would do—I protect her.

"It's nothing." I tuck the book into my back pocket.

She hesitates, as if she's going to push the matter, but then her shoulders drop. "I'm going to take a shower," she says, rising from the chair. "You coming to watch?" She smirks before I have a chance to reply. "Come on, big guy, you can at least stand guard by the door."

We make our way upstairs, and I look at the walls, studying them, wondering what evil Junko Devall felt whilst she stayed in this house—and whether I've already seen it.

TWENTY-SIX

HAYAMI

LUNCH HASN'T DILUTED MY ATTRACTION FOR FENRIR, AND reading about my latest book boyfriend burying his head under the skirt of the female main character has only added to the wretched state I now find myself in. A cold shower is the only solution.

As I step under the spray, the cool water pummelling my skin, I try to imagine my current book boyfriend, his mop of dark hair, his chiselled jaw, his perfect physique. But even when I close my eyes and concentrate, the only thing I can think about is Fenrir's hand on mine, the heat of him, the musky smell as he leaned into me and the firmness of his body pressed against my back.

Shaking my head, I try to rid myself of the image. I can't be attracted to my bodyguard, not to Fenrir, not to a man as savage as he is monstrous. His scars should repulse me as much as his actions. But they don't.

My hand wanders over my breasts, rubbing soap into my

hard nipples and then winding its way down between my legs.

He's all I can think about.

It's the isolation, I tell myself. *It's because he's the only red-blooded male within spitting distance.*

Whatever the reason, I give up trying to dispel the image of him.

I've no shame, no restraint as I picture Fenrir pushing me to the floor, spreading my legs, and telling me to be a good girl as his tongue works up the inside of my thigh.

Steam fills the small room as my pleasure builds with each movement of my hand, each image of him licking me, of how I wish my fingers were his tongue.

Pressing my palm against the wall of the cubicle, I steady myself as my climax snowballs, the heat building, the steam swirling. I bite my lip, the taste of blood mixing with desire. My thirst at wanting my lips on him, my mouth around him, my tongue flirting up his length sweeps over me.

Just as my orgasm starts to roll through me, ripping at my insides, the lights go out.

Shit.

It takes a second for my body to recalibrate.

Getting my breath back, I blink as if the lights have something to do with my eyes malfunctioning and not the bulb having blown.

Great. This is all I need.

Pulling the glass shower screen to the side, I wobble, the room shifting in this new dimension. I kneel, not wanting to slip on the wet surface and have to call for Fenrir to rescue me as I writhe about like a landbound fish.

I can just make out the outline of the small window, but the night sky is unnaturally dark tonight, the glass absorbing any light into the blackness that's now taken over the room.

It's a sticky dark. A rolling density. A black you could easily drown in.

Placing my hand on the floor, I feel for the mat, which sits outside the cubicle. It's not ideal, but it's better than trying to navigate my way around this nothingness naked. My hand meets the material, and I pull it to me, patting away the water that clings to my skin as if my body is the only sanctuary.

A tad drier, I ease myself to stand and throw the mat back onto the floor. I step out of the cubicle, my foot landing on the now-damp mat.

To my right, I can see the faint orange outline of the doorway. *Thank God I left the light on in my room.* I take baby steps, hands out in front of me, feeling for anything that shouldn't be there.

But there *is* something there.

It's not solid, nothing tangible, but it's there. It's a cold trickling at the base of my ankle, like a draft from an open door. The en suite is small, the shower having filled the room with hot steam, so this cold is unwelcome, like it shouldn't be here at all.

Moving quicker, I lunge forwards, finding the towel draped over the wall-mounted heater. Wrapping the cotton around me, I turn and press my hands against the door, running them over the panels, searching for the lock.

But I can't find it.

I imagine where it should be—right by the handle, the little brass mechanism that slides in and out. My fingers trail the wood like a spider's legs as the cold sensation climbs up the back of my calf, reaching under the towel.

What the fuck?

I try to calm myself, even as a palpable panic swells in my stomach.

This is my mind playing tricks on me, my imagination running wild due to the lack of sensory grounding.

The cold slithers further up my leg.

I'm just disorientated. Everything is fine. I just need to calm down and find the lock.

But it isn't where it's supposed to be.

Pressing harder against the panels, I search, trying to read the grains running through the wood.

Where the fuck is the lock? Why isn't it here?

The draft is now on the inside of my leg, rising with every second I'm stuck in this darkness.

Then I feel it. In my hair. Against my neck. On the side of my face.

Logic goes out the window, and I scream.

TWENTY-SEVEN

FENRIR

PRESENT

Hayami had been joking when she said I could watch her shower, but there was a split second when I'd hoped she wasn't. That I might get to glimpse her as she washed that perfect body—preparing it, ready for me to ruin.

She was likely teasing about me standing outside the door, something I considered until I realised how weird it was. Instead, I retreated to the security room, clock-watching her usual twenty-minute shower window, give or take.

Junko's journal sits in my back pocket, and for some reason, it feels more dangerous than the gun I carry.

What had Junko felt in this house? What was Junko like when she first married Devall? Whatever she was, it couldn't have been the same woman who walks Devall Mansion now, her face gaunt, her eyes haunted.

I pull the book from my pocket and place it on the desk before glancing at the screen.

Hayami's room is empty, the bedsheets roughly made, the

door to the en suite firmly closed. Flicking open the pages of the journal, I skim-read the next entry.

> *Day Three*
> *I hate it here. I want to leave. Even in the confines of the sitting room, the only room I seem to be able to tolerate in this house, I still have the urge to run out the door, into the forest, and never look back.*
>
> *Barrett and I sleep in the master bedroom, the room I feel most uncomfortable in. I'm not sure why this is, but as soon as I enter it, it's as if the whole room is closing in on me. I can't breathe, can't think. It's as if the walls are suffocating me.*
>
> *This evening, I asked Barrett if we could sleep in a different room, but he explained that the security cameras were only set up for this one, and it wouldn't be safe to sleep in a different one, as we'd only brought a scant amount of security staff with us. His response was direct and to the point, as if I were one of the staff. He never asked me why I wanted to move rooms.*
>
> *We'd just had sex. There's no lovemaking involved. This is purely practical. He wants an heir. Male. Someone to carry on the Devall name.*
>
> *Shortly after I married Barrett, I plucked up the courage to ask one of the staff what had happened between him and wife number one, the fiery redhead known as Eileen. It was tricky to work out which staff to ask. Most of them are incredibly*

loyal to Barrett, I think out of fear more than respect. But there is a maid, Sybil.

She's small, her back bent, with some sort of skin condition on her hands, which means she has to wear gloves, so most of the other staff keep their distance. But she's hardworking and has been with the household for years. She makes sure there are fresh flowers in my room, that my towels are soft, and that my bed is always turned down. She even got me a buckwheat pillow when it was clear to her that I was having trouble sleeping.

The next time we were alone, I asked her what had happened between Barrett and Eileen.

She didn't answer me. So, I told her that I wanted to be a good wife to Mr Devall and that I was a little afraid that I would make the same mistakes Eileen had.

Sybil sighed and said that as long as I followed the rules and was faithful, then I would not disappoint him.

I felt myself blush, then went on to ask about what had happened to her.

Sybil had been organising my dresser, moving things that didn't appear to need moving, when she told me their marriage was never destined to last. That all the staff knew it the minute he brought her here.

She explained that Eileen was a rare bird, beautiful and exotic, and Mr Devall was the collector. He wanted to own her, possess her, and show her off to the world. But she didn't want to be collected. She wanted to be free. One day, she was here. The next, she was gone.

I asked if she'd just left, and Sybil simply told me that was what she told herself. The thought turned me cold.

I'd then asked about his second wife.

Sybil recalled that no one knew exactly what had happened, but that she had been with child. Barrett had been pleased and was eager to give her the best care and all the attention she needed to ensure that the baby would be healthy. He took her away to one of his holiday homes, thinking the mountain air would do her good. Then Sybil had paled, her voice faltering, and my stomach sank. I had to press her, which I didn't like doing, but I could tell there was something she was holding back.

It was with a quiet voice that she told me that no one knew the details. Mr Devall had only taken a skeleton staff with him, as he wanted Noa to have the rest she deserved. But something happened with the baby, and because the place was so remote, they couldn't get her to a hospital in time.

I didn't ask any more questions about her because I knew the ending. Noa died. The baby died.

But there was one thing I did want to know.

I asked her which holiday house.

I'll never forget the way she raised her head and stared at me, clutching her cloth as she said, "Belial House."

So, you can imagine my horror when, after five months of marriage, Barrett announced we were to take a holiday to Belial House. Why would he bring me here? Why would he want to return to the very house where he lost his second wife and unborn child? It's ghoulish. I just hope my reproductive system is in full working order and I can give him what he wants and quickly. Because I don't want to be in this house any longer than I have to.

A woman and a child died here. I don't know how or why, but I feel as if the house is trying to tell me exactly what happened.

Junko's words have me in a chokehold, but something tugs at me. The stillness of the screen. The emptiness of Hayami's room.

I stare at the screen in silence, waiting for the door to the en suite to open.

Twenty minutes.

She's been in there for twenty minutes, and there's still no sign of her.

Last night's vision of her plays out: the gaping mouth, the way she'd thrust her fingers into the side of her cheeks and stretched them, the blood oozing from behind her teeth.

Twenty-one minutes.

Maybe I should take a stroll up there.

I open the small drawer in the desk and place the journal inside. I don't want Hayami to find it, not until I've read it and know what kind of content is in there.

Padding out of the security room, I make my way to the stairs.

A dull thudding noise resonates through the house.

My eyes scan the stairs, my ears straining, trying to work out where the noise is coming from.

As I climb, it gets louder.

Thud, thud, thud, thud.

It sounds like….

Fuck.

I run, leaping up the stairs, and fling open the bedroom door just as her scream rings out from the other side of the en suite.

My pulse pounds in my ears.

The door is locked.

"Stand away from the door!" I shout, bracing my full weight against it. "Stand away from the door!" I repeat before slamming my body against it.

It doesn't budge.

"Please, get me out of here!" Hayami's high-pitched screech travels from the other side of the door, panicked and raw, as if her voice is scraping the back of her throat.

This time, I back up so I can run at the door, throwing myself at it, but it won't open.

Fuck!

"Hayami, I need you to listen to me. I need you to stand in the shower cubicle. Can you hear me?"

"Yes," she whimpers.

"I'm going to shoot the lock. You can't be near the door, do you understand?"

"Yes."

"Move, now. Shout 'yes' when you've moved."

I wait. Seconds. Too long. Much too long.

"Yes," Hayami hollers.

Thank fuck for that.

Unholstering my gun, I aim it at the lock and fire. The explosion reverberates against the metal, making my ears ring.

Using my foot, I push the door open and step inside. The blackness has mixed with the steam, making it appear as if the darkness is swirling.

"Hayami!" I call out, and she comes bounding out of the black, a towel clutched to her body. Her hair's in wet tendrils around her shoulders, and her eyes are wider than I've ever seen them.

"Thank God," she says as she throws her arms around me, but I don't have time for embraces. I pull her from me.

"What happened? Are you hurt?" I scan her face, her body, her arms.

"I'm okay." She gulps. "The light blew when I was in the shower. I managed to find the door, but then I couldn't find the lock. I started to panic. It was so dark, and then I felt something on my leg."

"Someone was in there with you?" I arch my head into the doorway, ready to push her to the side and tackle whoever the fuck is in there. She must sense my thoughts, as she grips harder onto my forearms.

"No." She shakes her head, her reply sounding as if I'm being silly. "There was only me. I'm sure it was just a draft from somewhere, but when you can't see and you start to panic, your mind plays tricks on you. You start to convince yourself that something weird is going on."

"Fuck." Finally, convinced she's unharmed, I pull her back into me. Not even thinking, I wrap my arms around her and let out my pent-up breath.

"Sorry if I scared you," she says into the crook of my arm. "I scared myself."

"It's okay. I'm just glad you're all right." I push her back slightly, examining her face again to make sure I haven't missed something, before realising I'm holding on to her.

"Do me a favour," I say, quickly letting go of her and stepping back. "Never lock that door again, do you understand?"

"I won't. Although, I don't think there's much of the lock left."

We both glance at the door. It's on the bathroom floor, the handle completely blown off.

"I can rehang the door," I say.

Seconds pass, and I wonder if holding her or letting her go is what's created the silence.

She steps back and clears her throat. "I should get dressed," she says, pulling at the towel.

I nod and turn to leave.

"Hey, Fenrir," Hayami says.

I turn, more at the surprise that this is the first time she's called me Fenrir and not one of her pet names for me, such as Beast or Hellhound.

"Sorry for scaring you."

"You didn't scare me," I tell her before leaving the room.

It's not a lie. *She* didn't scare me. Her rational brain has already filed it away as hysteria, the normal reaction when one of your senses is deprived. But after what I've already seen and what I've just read in Junko's journal, I'm not so sure it can be explained away so easily.

Hayami didn't scare me.

But something did. Something in this house.

I just have no idea what.

TWENTY-EIGHT

FENRIR

PRESENT

Day nine at Belial House, and the last two nights have been quiet. Hayami appears to have slept well, but in the early hours of this morning, I could have sworn that there was someone in her room. I don't know why. There was nothing on the screen, nothing picked up by the camera, and she appeared to be sleeping soundly. It was more a feeling, a sense of dread climbing up my spine that she wasn't alone.

I raced up the stairs and pushed open her door to find the room empty and Hayami sleeping peacefully.

Tiredness can do strange things to the brain. Couple that with being alone in a house with only one other person and an old journal for company, and you've got a recipe for madness. With that in mind, I take the bull by the horns and make an executive decision—not only for Hayami's sake but my own.

"I think we should take the Jeep into town to pick up a few supplies," I say.

Hayami's eyes dart up from the book she's reading. Her

spoon is suspended over the bowl of dry cereal she's taken to eating because she isn't keen on the long-life milk.

"You mean, like, leave the house?"

"Is that a problem?" I hover by the kitchen door.

"No, not at all. I just thought you wouldn't want to leave because it's too risky. I'm all up for getting the hell out of here for a bit." She's already pushing her chair back and slipping the scrap piece of paper she's been using as a bookmark in between the pages.

"We could do with topping up a few supplies, and I think we both need a change of scenery." I try not to give too much away. Hayami isn't aware of the journal I've been reading or the things I've been seeing.

I'm a few days into Junko's journal, and I've built up a good picture of how she ended up being married to Devall and what she's learned of his previous marriages. But she's obsessed with the house and how it makes her feel, convinced that something is within the walls. I can't help but wonder if this was the beginning of her depression, the decline of her mental health, and whether being swept away from her job, her friends, and her family was the start of it all.

Or maybe there's something to what she writes about this house. That she really felt something when she was here.

I read a few pages in the early hours of the morning, Junko describing her sleep as fitful, as if something was knocking at her brain and asking to come inside. There was also an entry about seeing a face in the mirror that was not her own. She continues to talk about the house as if it's a person—a being occupying her thoughts, and a sense of evil she feels that's breeding under the foundations.

There've been no further disturbances since the night the light blew in the en suite. Although, having investigated the light after I rehung the door, it was clear the bulb hadn't blown, and the light had just gone out.

Hayami has recovered, brushing it off as one of those things when your mind plays tricks on you. She spent ten minutes explaining to me what happens to your brain when one of your senses is taken away from you and what panic can do to your body. For once, I'm happy she can explain the event away with her logical thinking. I, on the other hand, am not as easily convinced and need a break from these walls.

"We'll bring Willa's work phone with us and leave yours and mine here so that if Markus does a spot check on our locations, it'll look like we've sent Willa out for supplies and you and I have remained here. It'll also help to keep up appearances that Willa is here, and we're all functioning as normal."

"Sounds like a plan," Hayami says as she dumps her cereal bowl in the sink. "I'm a little giddy."

"We need to keep our wits about us," I remind her. "And you need to wear a baseball cap, keep a low profile."

"Sure. Body armour as well, or do you think that's too much?" She smirks. It isn't a bad idea, but before I can say anything, she's disappeared out of the room.

She returns ten minutes later wearing a large black coat, thick leggings, and winter boots along with her New York Yankees baseball cap.

"Is there a drill, a protocol you need to run through with me before we leave?" she asks, half joking, I think.

"Just the norm. You do what I say when I say it and don't question me."

"Yes, sir." Hayami mock salutes me, which is better than before this week, when she would openly argue with me, ignore me, or flip me off.

I wonder why she's suddenly showing a little more

respect. Is it because I shared my past with her, and she now knows the calibre of person I am? Or has she changed her tune because there are only the two of us here? She has no audience, no Willa to entertain, no shackles of the Devall house. But she's only swapped one cage for another—this house being her new prison. I'm not sure the reason, but whatever it is, this new Hayami is easier to work with. Although I miss the feisty Hayami I've become so used to.

I take a second before deciding upon my next move.

"I want you to take this."

Hayami spins around and stares at the gun in my hand. She looks up to me.

"Seriously? You're giving me a gun?"

"Just for the outing."

"Why?"

"Because I'm on my own here—no backup, no Willa. If something happens to me, which it won't, but if it does, I want you to be able to protect yourself."

We've continued with our target practice. Hayami is now able to load the gun as well as operate the safety. And her shots on target are improving.

"Wow, even after I shot the ceiling of the garage yesterday, you still trust me with this thing. I'm both honoured and really freaked out that our safety has come down to me."

"I wouldn't be giving you a gun if I didn't think you could handle it."

Hayami nods, and I hope that if something does go down, she'll do what I've taught her to do.

She takes the gun from me. Before putting it into her coat pocket, she checks the safety is on.

"Good girl," I tell her, nodding to the gun before leaving the foyer and heading for the front door.

TWENTY-NINE
HAYAMI

PRESENT

Good girl.

Good fucking girl.

I want to be cross with him for referring to me as a girl. But if two words can make me feral, it's those:

Good. Girl.

Trying to ignore the heat between my legs and the fact that I have a gun in my pocket, I set off to catch up with Fenrir as he hotfoots it out of the house.

After checking the car for bombs and trackers, we finally set off.

It's a clear, crisp day, the sky a hazy blue. It's so cold it scrapes against my cheeks, and I can't deny how good it feels to be out of the house, away from those walls that can sometimes seem like a cocoon.

Fenrir messes with the heating as I scan the road ahead, recognising it from the day I drove Willa to the airport.

It feels strange, leaving the house behind, like we're

escaping, doing something we shouldn't be, breaking the rules. I fucking *love* it.

"What are we shopping for?" I ask as Fenrir handles the car with such dexterity that I can feel my mind slipping, wondering what it'd be like to be handled by him.

"Essentials. Powdered milk. Bread to freeze. Any other food you want and maybe some firewood."

"I thought we had plenty in the store."

"We have, but the temperature is set to drop over the next few weeks, and I don't want to get caught out."

"Always with the planning."

"It's part of the role. To think ahead."

And he is thinking ahead. *The next few weeks.* Could we really be stuck out here for that long? We're nine days into this, and it still feels like a small holiday. But when will it stop feeling like that? What then?

We reach the main road that runs through the small town of Hellion Vale. It's a sleepy town, with a handful of shops all set around a square that's been made into a car park, which we pull up in. The shops look quaint, like this place has been frozen in time for the past fifty years. I wouldn't be surprised if the shop owners are wearing aprons and sporting handlebar moustaches.

As we exit the Jeep, Fenrir checks the surroundings like a watchful owl, his head swivelling in all directions. It must be exhausting to be on this level of alert all the time, especially coupled with the fact that he isn't getting much sleep.

Heading for the general store, Fenrir guides me, using his hand to steer the base of my back. I'm a little lost again, as this is something one of my book boyfriends would do and I'd completely lose my shit over.

We appear to be the only people in the store. I grab a trolley, and we start to load it with the essentials: candles, firelighters, powdered milk, eggs, bread.

Fenrir doesn't seem to notice—or if he does, he turns a blind eye—when I chuck in a couple of magazines and a few bars of chocolate.

By the time we reach the checkout, the trolley is piled high.

The man behind the counter looks relieved for something to do, but also a little intimidated by Fenrir as he clocks his size and his scars. But then his attention goes to me, and he scans our things a little slower.

I feel Fenrir tense behind me, his focus gone from loading the conveyor belt to whatever reason this guy is staring at me.

"Hey, are you guys up at Belial House?"

I read his nametag: Kevin, General Manager. I worry for Kevin with his receding hairline, kind face, and tortoiseshell glasses. He's probably just making conversation or trying to be nice or enjoying a break from the monotony of having spoken to no one all morning, but Fenrir has already slipped his hand inside his coat.

When neither of us answers, Kevin barrels on, and I only hope he isn't digging his own grave.

"I only ask because I'm the guy who brought all the supplies up a couple of weeks ago when Mr Devall called and said he wanted the house stocked up. You can imagine my surprise." His thick eyebrows rise above the rim of his glasses. "I haven't been called to stock Belial House in, God, it must be over twenty years. I wasn't the general manager then. My dad was still in charge, but he retired some time ago when things started to get a bit much for him. So, it's just me now and my husband, Al, but he's at the wholesaler's right now."

I don't know what to say. I'm hoping Fenrir takes the lead. This guy sounds genuine. Willa said the house had been stocked, but she never referred to Kevin.

I'm about to say something when Kevin speaks.

"I'm sorry for asking, and forgive me if I'm wrong, but you must be Junko's daughter."

My mother's name has my ears pricking up. How does he know her?

He continues to scan items. Fenrir keeps his hand in his jacket. But I can't stay quiet any longer.

"How do you know that?"

"You're the spitting image of her. You have her cheekbones. Is she not with you?" He glances outside as if expecting to see my mum loitering outside the shop, but the street remains empty.

"You know my mother?"

"Of course. I delivered their food the only time they came up to stay at the house."

"When was this?" I'm slowly packing things in the trolley, focused entirely on what this man is saying.

"Like I said, 'bout twenty years ago or so. I was the delivery boy back then, working for my dad in between studying. She and Mr Devall had just got married. They came up here for a few weeks, and I'd bring their supplies up as needed. Junko was so lovely. She always welcomed me in, and she'd make me this Japanese tea, which was the best tea I'd ever had. And we'd chat about things. I always got the impression she didn't like the house, though. Think she felt a bit lonely up there."

"She did?"

"Yeah, why else would she invite the delivery boy in for tea and cake?" He stops for a second. "She's okay, isn't she?"

I want to say, *Define okay.* She's breathing, yes. She's walking and talking, yes. But my mother is far from okay, and the scary thing is, I can't remember a time when she *was* okay. But here is Kevin, telling me there was another version of my mother, a chatty version who invited him in for cake and tea.

"She's fine," I lie.

"Tell her I said hi." Kevin looks at the till. "That'll be one hundred and eighteen pounds, please. Cash or card?"

Before I can whip out my card, Fenrir leans over with a wad of cash and hands it to Kevin, who counts it and then stuffs it into the drawer.

After handing the change to Fenrir, Kevin nods and bids us a good day.

"It was nice meeting you, and be sure to keep an eye on the weather," he says as Fenrir pushes the trolley out the main door.

"Can you believe that?" I say as we head to the Jeep.

"What?" Fenrir is scanning the car park, his shoulders tense, his eyes like lasers.

"That he knew my mother. She used to chat to him. Have you known my mother to chat to anyone?"

Fenrir doesn't answer, just starts to load the car up.

"I found a photo of the house once and asked her about it: where it was, why I'd never been," I tell him as I pass him bags from the trolley. "She said she just didn't like the house. But what I don't understand is, if it was their holiday home, then why did they never come back here?"

Fenrir shrugs and then says, "You heard what Kevin said. She didn't like the house."

"Yeah, but my father must've liked it, and he's never been one to take someone else's feelings on board, so why have I never been here until now? Why have my mother and father never come back to this house?"

Fenrir continues to load the car, but I swear he bristles as if a cold gust of wind has just rushed over the back of his neck.

We pack up the car in silence as I mull this over.

Why has my mother not returned to Belial House? Did something happen there that she can't face?

There's only one way to find out.

THIRTY

FENRIR

WE DRIVE BACK TO THE HOUSE IN SILENCE. HAYAMI'S PROBABLY lost in thought about what Kevin told her. She has that quizzical look on her face when she's trying to work something out.

This outing was supposed to help clear my head, put a bit of perspective on things. Instead, it's only fuelled my anxiety.

I don't like the fact that he knows we're here. Although Devall ordered supplies, he wouldn't have told Kevin who was staying at the house. When other people know your location, it can lead to trouble. Anyone could approach Kevin and force answers from him; in fact, you wouldn't even need to get the thumb screws out. He's a chatterbox and would unwittingly divulge anything to anyone.

It amazes me how some people are so unaware of basic safety, about not sharing personal information or asking too many questions. Then I remember that this is how most people live their lives, and I'm the exception because of the people I work for, the job I do, and what became of my family.

What he told us of Junko's stay at Belial House is new information to Hayami. I, of course, know about her one-time visit, but so far, I haven't come across anyone by the name of Kevin.

There's a temptation, as we make our way along the winding road that surrounds the large forest to the right, to drive in the completely opposite direction, to take this car full of supplies and head out somewhere no one would ever find us. Would she come willingly? She admitted to me that she'd thought about running away when she dropped Willa off at the airport, but the thought of Devall hunting down Willa and me and killing us in revenge stopped her.

What's to stop us now? What's to stop me from turning this car around and getting us both the hell out of here? Because even when this ends, when it's time to return her to reality, what awaits her?

"You're wondering about it, aren't you?" Hayami says, splintering my thoughts.

"What?" I keep my eyes on the road.

"About not going back to the house and driving off somewhere else instead."

I straighten in my seat, wondering how she knew.

"It's okay. I was thinking about it too. How easy it'd be just to drive to someplace else and forget about everything and everyone."

There's a strange feeling in my gut, and before I can think it through, I say, "Then why don't we?"

We're approaching the turn-off that heads up the mountain and to Belial House. It's ten feet away. Hayami eyes the road ahead. I ready myself to hit the gas, to keep on going. To never look back. Because I'd do it, without any hesitation. All she has to do is say the words, and we're out of here.

Instead, she looks down at her hands. "Because he'd find us," she says sadly. "We'd run and run and run. Never stop running. Never stop looking over our shoulders. We'd never be free. None of us."

"You'd rather live in your cage?"

"I'd still be caged. It'd just feel bigger. But there'd always be an end to it, a line I can't cross. He's made sure of that."

We drive in silence the rest of the way.

Once we're at the house, we unload the car and bring everything into the kitchen to unpack.

"I hate tinned food," Hayami says as she places various cans in the tall cupboard. "It all tastes metallic."

"Beggers can't be choosers," I tell her, retrieving my phone from the countertop where I left it and opening the weather app.

Between the lack of sleep, Hayami's strange nighttime incidents, and the en suite rescue, I've taken my eye off the ball concerning the weather, and Kevin's parting comment is niggling at me.

The app takes a while to load, and as I'm waiting, I notice Hayami placing the gun I gave her on the table.

"Won't be needing it in here, I hope," she says, eyeing the gun.

"No," I reply, but I'm focused on the weather report because, when it loads, the first thing I see is the red weather warning marked for the day after tomorrow.

I click on the alert.

A Red Weather Warning is in place for the local area for snow, ice, high winds, and freezing fog. Red Weather Warning means there is a threat to life, and you must not travel unless it is to reach safety or you are in immediate danger.

Fuck.

This is the last thing we need.

Hayami opens the fridge and places the chilled items inside.

There's a pang of something in my gut. I've already kept her mother's journal from her, so keeping this information from her as well feels like a step too far, even though the last thing I want to do is cause her to worry.

"There's a weather warning out for snow."

Hayami glances at me. "It feels cold enough. When for?"

"Two days from now."

"Did you bring a sledge?" She smiles. She doesn't see it. Doesn't realise we could be stuck up here for days, totally cut off from the world. Safe, at least, but stranded.

"I'll finish up in here," I say, moving over to the fridge. She eyes me suspiciously. "Haven't you got some work to finish?"

"Yeah." She sighs heavily. Her studies are the only thing keeping her focus right now, the only link she has to her life before this shit went down. I don't want her falling behind. "I'll set up in the library."

She leaves the kitchen, and I finish unpacking, relieved that I'll get a chance to pick up Junko's journal, as I'm eager to know if Kevin had been telling the truth or whether something else entirely is going on here.

THIRTY-ONE

HAYAMI

Relieved that Fenrir has given me an excuse to leave the kitchen, I make my way to the library. The large window frames the view outside, the towering trees that surround the house, and the tops of the mountain range opposite. I can already imagine what this view will look like when covered in snow.

Fenrir thinks I haven't realised the significance of snowfall—what it could mean to us up here.

No escape.

Right now, that's exactly what I want. I don't want there to be a reason to leave. I don't want things to return to the way they were. That would mean returning to a life I have no control over, a life I have no say in, and a future I want nothing to do with.

There'd been a moment, in the car driving back from the store, when I considered telling Fenrir exactly what my father has planned for me. The reason why he found me floating facedown in the pool, and why I've been acting so recklessly over the last six months. But I didn't. Because I know that if I'd told him, he would've taken the other road. Of that, I'm sure. And I can only imagine what that road would have led to.

Being hunted.

Being found.

Pulling my phone from my back pocket, I see a text from Willa.

> Hey, hope you're both okay and you guys haven't killed each other yet! All is well with Marta and the baby. I'm going to catch the next flight out and be back with you guys soon.

I type out a quick reply, telling her not to even think about leaving Marta, and that we're both fine.

My mind floats back to the conversation with Kevin. I register the time and wonder what state my mother will be in. Will she be drunk? High? Delirious? Neurotic? Any mixture of these is possible. But I have to speak to her.

The phone rings six times before she picks up.

"Hayami." She's breathless, as if she's been running.

"Hey, Mum."

"It's so good to hear your voice," she says as I try to work out whether her words are slow and slurred or fast and frantic. To my surprise, they sound relatively clear for my mum. "How are you?"

"I'm okay."

"And Willa and Fenrir? Are they both okay? Is everyone okay?" I hear it now, the panic, the desperation. She may not be drunk or drugged up, but there's a restlessness about her, as if she's been silent for so long and suddenly found her voice.

"Yeah, we're all good. Are you okay?" I ask. "How's Hanover House?"

There's a pause, and I wonder which of my two questions she's having to think about before she answers. "I'm fine. I've left Hanover House, though, and am back at the mansion. I couldn't bear to be away, not knowing what's happening."

"Oh, okay. Well, I was calling because…" I swap my phone to the other hand as I think carefully about what I'm about to say. "Willa popped out to the store today, just to stock up on supplies because it's supposed to snow in the next few days. She said that she got chatting to the guy who owned the store —Kevin, I think she said his name was—and he mentioned you. Told her he knew you and was asking about you."

I wait. She's still there. I can hear her breathing.

"Oh yes, Kevin. Gosh, it's been such a long time. Kevin was always so lovely. How is he?" I try to pick up on any intonations, but her reply is mechanical, careful even.

"Willa said he was okay, real nice, and seemed eager to chat. I just wanted to let you know. It sounds like he was a friend of yours." I try not to let this sound like a question.

"He was. He delivered to the house, and I was quite lonely up there. You're not lonely, are you?"

"No, Mum, I'm fine. I have Fenrir and Willa, and my studies are keeping me busy. To be honest, it's been nice to get away from things."

Another pause.

"I understand, but I need you to be careful." Her words are slow—not chemically induced slow, but as if she's treading cautiously.

"Because of the Castros?" I plant the seed, wondering if anything will grow from it.

"Not just that. I just want you to be… well, I just want you to be safe."

"I don't think it gets much safer than being in the middle of nowhere with two bodyguards for company."

I feel bad, lying to my mum about Willa being here, but she's holding back on me. She knows something and isn't telling me what it is.

"Of course, you're right. Your father has made sure you're safe up there."

I tut, then hope my mum didn't hear it. I'm under no illusion that she knows nothing of what my father has planned for me. Even if she did, she'd have about as much influence over his decision as I do.

"But there are some things your father has no control over…." Her voice trails off, and my heart sinks.

"What do you mean?"

That heavy pause again.

"I'm just talking about the things that no one has any control over, not even your father."

I roll my eyes and am glad she can't see me.

"Are you talking about the suspicions that this house is haunted? Because I can tell you that we haven't experienced anything up here." *Well, nothing that can't be explained with rational thinking*, I want to add, but I know that if I tell her about my nightmare and the light blowing in the en suite, she'll freak out.

"I wish you were here. I wish you weren't there in that house" is her only reply.

"I'm sure we'll be back soon," I tell her as Fenrir enters the room. I look up at him and nod, as if trying to tell him telepathically that I'm on the phone with my mum.

"I hope so. More than anything, I hope so. Stay safe, my baby girl. I love you. And Hayami…?" There's a beat down the line, and I want to give her the time she obviously needs to gear herself up for whatever she's about to say, but my impatience gets the better of me.

"Yes?"

"Don't let the house speak to you."

"What do you mean, Mum? Hello? Mum?" But all I hear is the drone of the dead line. I drop the phone by my side.

"Don't let the house speak to you." Jeez, she's really lost it.

Fenrir is next to me, his face grave. "What did she say?"

I shake my head. "Nothing much. She was being weird."

"Was she drunk?"

"No, that's what makes it even weirder. This was the most sober and clear-headed I've heard her in a long time."

"What did she say?" he repeats.

I glance at him, wondering what he'll make of it. "She told me not to let the house speak to me."

The muscles flex in his neck, his scars rippling as he remains silent. It's not the reaction I predicted. I thought he'd have sniggered at the ravings of a madwoman—a woman who spends most of her time high on prescription medication or doused in an alcoholic stupor. But no.

Instead, he remains motionless, like this all makes sense to him, as if he knows what my mother is referring to.

Why do I feel like he's in on the secret? Why do I feel like I'm the only one standing in the dark?

THIRTY-TWO

FENRIR

PRESENT

I HOPE HAYAMI DIDN'T PICK UP ON MY HESITATION WHEN SHE said that her mum had told her not to let the house speak to her. I didn't want to dismiss it as fanciful, or something that shouldn't be taken heed of, because I don't think that's the case at all. Junko might be under the influence of some pretty heavy medication these days, but she wasn't always this way. It appears as though her dive into madness began here, twenty-one years ago, at Belial House.

Junko knows more about this house than we do, and I'm determined to learn what that is.

So, whilst Hayami works at the desk in the library, I sink into the chair and return to the journal, and it isn't long before I come across Kevin.

> Day Seven
> Today, I met a lovely young man called Kevin. He
> works in the store in town that brings us our

supplies. It's a family business, owned by Nathaniel Hayes, a middle-aged man with salt-and-pepper hair and a birthmark on his right cheek. His son, Kevin, does the local deliveries for him. Kevin doesn't look like his father. His sandy hair and acne-marked skin must come from his mother's side, but I've yet to see Mrs Hayes. I'm guessing Kevin is around twenty years old. The slight awkwardness around adults and the hesitation I see is what I remember being like when I was that age, not so long ago.

I'm sick of being in this house by myself and crave some company, so, after delivering the shopping, I invited Kevin in for tea. He seemed reluctant, but then I told him my husband had left for the day on some urgent business, which seemed to put him at ease.

He stepped into the house, taking his baseball cap from his head and holding it in both hands as if he were entering some holy place. His eyes roamed the walls, and I thought he was taking in the Gothic architecture, the dense fabrics, and the dark colours. But when he shivered, I knew he wasn't admiring the décor but sensing something.

As we walked through the foyer, I admitted to hating the house.

He looked at me, not shocked at the statement, more surprised that I'd said it out loud.

I led him into the kitchen, where I put the kettle on to boil and assembled the tea things, and he asked me why I hated this place. I told him that

I wasn't sure why, but that from the minute I arrived, I could feel an oppression, a darkness that seemed to dwell here.

Kevin told me that I wasn't the first person to not like the house. I wasn't sure whether I was relieved to hear this or unnerved, and I was eager to find out if I was going mad or whether this house has some hidden past I was unaware of.

My skin prickled as Kevin described how one of the workmen died up here whilst the house was being built, which started off rumours about it being cursed. Maybe he saw my fear, because he then pointed out that this place is old, and that lonely houses at the top of mountains are always going to have some haunting backstory. If he'd said this to put me at ease, it didn't work.

I had to know more. This house, the feeling I have here, the way the floor creaks, the walls listen, and I feel like I'm being watched. There must be something to the rumours, so I asked if he liked the house and his body froze, his eyes widened, and his lips parted before he admitted that he didn't care for this house because of something that happened to his father here. I could barely hold my teacup, the matcha tea having gone cold, the smell of the ginger cake I'd served now repugnant.

It happened when Barrett was here on holiday with his second wife, Noa, and Kevin's father had fallen and broke his wrist, which meant Kevin had to do all the deliveries. He told me he was nervous and knew what a big account Belial House was, but that his father told him not to worry, as it would be Noa who answered the door.

He said she seemed kind, a little quiet, was heavily pregnant with porcelain skin, and had wide dark eyes. I could picture her standing with the door open, welcoming him inside. I was sure that Kevin recalled this too, as his face was soft, a gentle smile on his mouth until he dropped his cup on the table with a clatter that made me jump.

It was a few weeks later that Kevin returned to Belial House. He told me he hadn't been up to the house in a while, so he wasn't surprised when a large order came through.

He'd expected Noa to answer the door but recalled his shock that my husband answered. I felt all of Kevin's nerves as he described unpacking the order whilst Barrett observed. And just when he thought the job was done, Barrett had announced that the firelighters were missing.

Kevin's voice had trembled along with my own hand as he described showing the invoice to Barrett and explaining that there were no firelighters on the order. And I could easily imagine the burning in my husband's eyes, the way he would have stared at young Kevin with such anger at having the gall to question him.

So, Kevin had apologised and said he'd return with the firelighters immediately, which seemed to placate Barrett.

But when Kevin returned to the store and explained what had happened, his father wasn't happy about Kevin going back to deal with an irate Barrett, so he took the firelighters himself, leaving Kevin behind.

This was the part I felt that Kevin had been working up to, as I could see the tension in his face, the way he became lost in his memories... the horror he must have felt.

He said his father had returned home a pale and haunted man, a mere shadow of his former self.

My first thought was, what had my husband done to him? What had he said? But no. It was nothing to do with Barrett, who'd actually been grateful for the firelighters, offering Kevin's father a bottle of whisky for his trouble in returning. For once, Barrett was not to blame; instead, it was what Kevin's father saw on the roadside whilst leaving the house.

He'd swung his car around on the driveway when he'd seen someone emerge from the trees. He said that she just appeared, and he had no idea who she was as it was too dark, so he slammed on the brakes, the headlights illuminating her against the black of the night.

His dad had climbed out of the car, ready to apologise for not seeing the woman and to check she was okay, but then he stopped, not a foot from her. He'd said she had dark hair and was holding a mask over the lower half of her face. His first thought had been that it was Noa, but then he noticed that she had no swollen stomach. This woman was not with child, and Noa had been very much pregnant when he last saw her. He then wondered if she'd brought friends with her or family, or if someone had been sent to keep her company whilst she was staying here—which I knew wouldn't have been the case, as Barrett wouldn't allow anyone the luxury of companionship. His world is a very secretive one.

His father had asked the woman if she was okay. She hadn't replied, just stared at him until she asked him something, but he didn't understand, as she was speaking in what he thought was Japanese. He said it sounded like "Watashi kirei."

He told the woman he didn't understand her, and so she repeated it, to which he held his hands up and said he didn't speak Japanese and that he was sorry, but could he escort her back up to the house? But she didn't move. She'd just stood there staring through vacant eyes.

My blood ran like ice-cold water imagining how frightened he must have been. She asked him something else, something different this time that sounded like "Kore demo." Then she pulled the mask from her face and....

I'm not even sure I can write the words. I don't want to see the image again as Kevin described what his father recalled, but I must.

He said her mouth was large and wide, as if it'd been cut from ear to ear, the gaping wound red and raw, her teeth sharp and pointy, and her face that of a madwoman.

I'd begun to shake, the aroma of the tea suddenly sour, the air frighteningly still, and the house eerily quiet, as if the walls were also listening.

I only heard snippets of what Kevin said afterwards, about his father making it home and then never wanting to talk about it again and how he only made deliveries to the house in daylight and with Barney, their other member of staff.

My throat had gone tight, my breathing shallow as I'd tried to apologise, offer my condolences to his father for having witnessed such a thing, but inside, I'd been terrified. The cold blood had frozen in my veins, and I couldn't move.

Because this wasn't new to me. This is a story I've heard before, but not in this context. This is an old story. A legend. A myth. A story we told one another as children to frighten us during the hours of darkness. This is a story from my homeland.

This is the story of Kuchisake-Onna.

Hayami yawns loudly, and I almost drop the journal.

"I can't possibly type anymore about gene influence. If I do, I think my brain will explode," she says, shutting the lid of her laptop. "Oh, I forgot to tell you. Willa texted and said she's getting the next flight back here. I told her not to bother and that we're okay, but I'm wondering if *you* are okay. You look a little pale."

"I'm fine," I reply, though I'm anything but. How can I be after that entry in Junko's journal?

Kuchisake-Onna.

Who or what is Kuchisake-Onna? I can't risk asking Hayami, as I don't want to alarm her about something that could be nothing. But my gut is telling me this isn't nothing. Something is at work here in this house, and it has everything to do with what I've just read.

THIRTY-THREE

HAYAMI

PRESENT

"Have you slept yet?" I ask Fenrir. His features look drawn. Worry lines are etched across his brow that mingle with the scarring down the side of his face. I wonder if our confinement is getting to him.

"No," he answers quickly.

"Why don't you take a shower and then get an hour's rest? You can't keep functioning on so little sleep."

He's about to argue with me, so I add, "I'm fine here, but if it makes you feel better, I'll sit in your room whilst you shower and rest."

To my surprise, he nods, shoves the book he's been reading into his back pocket, and rises from the chair.

We make our way up the stairs and into his room, which is smaller than mine with less lavish furnishings. The bed is neatly made. A towel hangs on the radiator, and his large duffel bag is the only thing littering the floor. It smells of him, and it feels odd, being here, like I'm invading his personal space.

Grabbing a towel, he then roots around in his bag and pulls out a fresh set of clothes.

"I won't be long," he tells me. "Don't leave this room."

"I won't." I sit in the chair in the corner and watch as he disappears into his en suite.

I don't hear the door lock.

And then the thought of walking into the en suite to watch him in the shower takes over. The hot water running down his tight chest, the knowing look as I stepped under the water fully clothed. He'd take my head in his hands and kiss me so fucking hard that I'd grasp onto the side of the cubicle to hold myself up. He'd be hard for me. I'd press my hands against his chest and push him back. His eyes would narrow until I lowered to my knees and took him in my mouth.

Shit. I need to stop this.

Maybe we've both been in this house too long.

But as I pick up my book, I can't keep the fantasy from playing out. I can almost feel his length hit the back of my throat. It's just a hormonal reaction with him being the only male in the vicinity. But I'm starting to wonder how true that really is, and whether my attraction to Fenrir has been brewing since the day he pulled me out of that pool.

I've never been in love before, which is as much my father's fault as it is anyone's. You have to get to know someone to fall in love with them, and I've never been allowed to be close to or spend time with anyone for long enough for love to take root.

The only lust and longing I've ever felt has been in the books I read. I've never felt this attraction for a real person, one who's living, breathing, existing. How can I when I have a security team on my heels twenty-four-seven?

Fury burrows from within my chest and explodes across my skin.

As soon as I get out of this house, my plan will resume. I don't care how. I don't care at what cost. I won't comply with my father any longer.

But to achieve this, I'm going to have to tell either Willa or Fenrir what's going on; otherwise, I'll never manage it.

Willa isn't here.

That leaves Fenrir.

He's been so open with me about what happened to him when he was younger, about what he went through, and what he's done. But what will his reaction be when he learns what my father's plan is and what I've tried to do to thwart it?

As soon as I get out of this house.

Trying to rein in my imagination, I focus back on the words on the page. It's almost impossible. All I can focus on is the rushing water and the thought of Fenrir touching himself. Maybe he's even getting himself off in the shower. And fuck if the urge to touch myself right now isn't overwhelming.

FENRIR

When Hayami suggested I take a shower, I jumped at the chance. As the water heats, I pace the small en suite and google what I've just read in Junko's journal. My head is a mess, and I misspell the name, but Google knows what I'm typing, and the words pop up in the search list.

Kuchisake-Onna.

I scan the text, my heart speeding up.

Kuchisake-Onna is the Japanese urban legend and folklore of the slit-mouthed woman, who is believed to be the ghost of a woman who was mutilated, with a deep gash running from ear to ear, making her appear as if she is grinning. She appears at night, usually covering the lower half of her face with a mask. She will ask anyone who sees her if they think she is beautiful: "Watashi kirei?" If the person says yes, she will then remove her mask, revealing her hideous mouth, and ask, "Kore demo?" which means "Even with this?" If you answer no, she will kill you with whatever sharp instrument she is carrying, and if you say yes hesitantly, she will cut you in the same way she was cut. There is a theory that by answering "average" to the second question, you can buy yourself some time to escape her.

Legend has it that she was the concubine of a powerful samurai who caught her being unfaithful, so he punished her by slitting open her mouth from ear to ear. Another theory is that she was mutilated during a medical or dental procedure by a woman who was jealous of her beauty. Either way, you do not want to get caught alone with Kuchisake-Onna.

Lowering my phone, I note the tremble in my hand.

Fuck.

This can't be right. This is an urban legend. It isn't true. But even if it is, it's a *Japanese* legend. Why would Kuchisake-Onna be here on Hellion Ridge?

Maybe I'm looking at this all wrong. Maybe this isn't the famous legend. Maybe this Kuchisake-Onna has her origins here rather than in Japan.

Is it so unreasonable to think that the spirit that Junko felt in the walls is that of Kuchisake-Onna? Or is it all fabrication, something compiled by Junko's fragile mental health?

But what about Kevin's father? Is that story true? It's hard to say when the story is thirdhand. Did Junko really have that conversation with Kevin? He definitely knew her; otherwise, he wouldn't have said so when we met him in the store.

And then there are the things I've seen. That first night, when Hayami stood in front of the camera and pulled at the corners of her mouth. Then the following night, I watched her get out of bed and then stand under the camera, pulling at her face in the same grotesque way as her mouth filled with blood, yet when I ran into her room, she was fast asleep.

What the fuck is going on here? And why does Hayami not seem to feel it? Is it that her scientific brain won't let her believe in such things, or is it because she lives with such horrors every day that this is nothing compared to what she puts up with in her normal life? Or is it because nothing is happening at all other than what's going on in my sleep-deprived brain? Am I just like Junko and seeing things that aren't there?

Maybe I'm the one losing my mind.

HAYAMI

The water stops.

Five minutes pass before the door opens. Now he's in the room—T-shirt on, shorts hanging low, hair wet—and I can't breathe.

Towel-drying his hair, he stalks over to the bed. I've never seen him in anything other than workwear or a black suit. He looks natural, although his shoulders are square and the muscles on his upper arms seem tense, as if the shower has done nothing to abate his agitation.

Aware that I must be staring, I say, "You'll be glad to know I'm still alive."

He doesn't respond, just sits on the bed and places a pillow behind his neck.

I raise my book to cover my face.

"Hayami."

"Yes?" I lower my book. He's not looking at me but studying the walls. What the hell is he looking at? Surely he can't think the walls are bugged, or that there's a hidden trap moulded within the plaster, yet he's staring at them as if they're about to speak.

"If I do fall asleep and I…." He pauses. "If I shout out or say anything, wake me up."

I'm about to ask what he might shout, but then I remember the fire.

Of course he has bad dreams. I'm a little touched that he feels comfortable sleeping in front of me, and that he doesn't mind if I see this side of him. I think of all the sides of me he's seen. He's seen me at my lowest, my worst, the part of me that refuses to bow down to the life that's been shaped for me.

Or maybe he feels a little safer with me here?

"Of course." I nod, hoping to convey the concern and understanding that's rushing through me.

He takes a deep breath, then closes his eyes, his arms folded across his chest.

I try not to watch him, but I can't help it. There are two halves of this man—the brutally beastly side shaped by trauma, and the blessedly beautiful side, serene and still—and I wonder which one truly prevails.

I want to join him, to place my arms around him, stroke his face, bury myself next to him and sleep.

He's far from perfect, but that's what makes him all the more alluring. I could watch him all night. This goliath of a man, who's come into my life and taught me how to defend myself, how to keep myself safe instead of wrapping me in cotton wool. This man, who now trusts me enough to let me guard *him*, to let me keep *him* safe, because that's exactly what I want to do. I want to take all his hurt away and banish his demons, because he's just as vulnerable as I am.

My eyes grow heavy, but I fight them. I don't want to miss a single moment of him.

THIRTY-FOUR

FENRIR

SMOKE.

Behind my eyes, under my skin, in my blood.

The smell of it makes me want to wretch, but there's no time. I have to get her out. But I can't find her.

The rooms aren't familiar.

Doors aren't where they're supposed to be. Walls where they shouldn't be.

It's hot. So fucking hot.

Flames flare against my skin, making my flesh bubble.

I must find her.

Curtains cremated. Carpets incinerated.

She isn't here.

Yet, I know she is.

Heat hovers. Smoke swirls. Flames flicker.

Must save her.

My sister?

No, not my sister.

Hayami.

Smoke chokes me. Winds itself around my throat. Smothers my eyes.

Can't breathe.

So heavy, the weight on my chest.

I pull at my skin.

Try to breathe, but there's no air.

Can't breathe.

Can't.

Then the smoke drops, just like that.

And I see her.

Dark hair.

Darker eyes.

The darkest glare.

Hayami?

She holds a black scarf over her mouth.

I want to peel it away, but I'm frightened of what'll be underneath.

It won't be her luscious lips. It'll be sharp teeth, torn flesh, and oozing blood.

Her hand goes to the scarf.

Please don't take it off.

My chest is so heavy.

Please, God, no.

Can't breathe.

And my heart fucking stops.

My eyes snap open, banishing the gnarled nightmare as I'm thrust straight into another one, because the heaviness on my chest remains.

Hayami sits astride me, her hands pressing down on my ribs, her gaze boring into my face.

Under any other circumstances, I'd be flipping her over, pulling her under me, and showing her exactly what she does to me, but this is not *my* Hayami.

Her head is tilted to the side, that sickly grin across her face, her hair hanging like rags.

"Hayami?"

Her head twitches, and she grins that horrible, slimy smile, but it isn't her mouth. Her eyes shift, her hair grows longer, and her lips appear fuller.

"Who are you?" My voice is barely a whisper. I want to throw her off, but this is Hayami's body, and I won't hurt her.

She holds her finger up as if to shush me. Her hands move down towards the waistband of my shorts.

"Hayami, can you hear me?" I try to move, but she has me pinned to the bed.

Fuck. Panic floods me. None of my training has prepared me for this. *What the hell is going on?*

I try to move again, but it's hopeless.

She has to be dreaming or sleepwalking again. But it doesn't feel like it. I don't sense her in there. This is someone else, and I have a feeling I know who.

Kuchisake-Onna.

She stares at me. Then, as if a button has been released, the smile drops and her eyes widen, fear expanding them before she flops onto my chest like she's melted before me.

"Hayami?" I wiggle up the bed and pull Hayami up.

She opens her eyes. Blinks. She searches the room before her gaze lands on me, taking in that she is astride me.

"What the hell?" She lurches back, her face frantic.

"I don't know what happened. I woke up and you were sitting on me."

"Oh my God." She puts her hand over her mouth. "How? Why? I don't...."

"Did you fall asleep?" I ask.

"I don't.... I'm not sure. I don't remember. I was reading my book, and then...." She shakes her head. "Maybe?"

"I think you were sleepwalking," I lie.

"Oh my God, I'm so sorry."

"Don't be. It's fine."

She sits up on her heels. "It's not, though. What the hell is wrong with me? Why would I climb onto your lap?"

"There's no need to look for reasons. People do all sorts of strange things when they sleepwalk. It's fine, honestly."

"I'm so embarrassed." She places her head in her hands, and I pull them away.

"Listen to me," I say, holding her hands between us. "Don't ever be embarrassed in front of me. Ever."

"But—"

"No buts. There's no need to feel shame in front of me, Hayami. You've done nothing wrong."

"Except straddle you in your sleep. Oh my God, I didn't...." She gulps, assesses me. "I didn't *touch* you or anything, did I?"

"No. And stop this, now. It was nothing. Innocent sleepwalking, that's all."

"Jesus. What's wrong with me?" She glances over at the chair she was sitting in when we came into my room. Her book's abandoned on the floor. "I need to stop reading this shit. It's doing things to me, and not in a good way."

"Let's go downstairs and get a drink, shall we?"

My hand shakes. I hide it behind my back as she moves from the bed, and then I stand, frustrated that I'm lying to her, but she looks so embarrassed. She thinks she's losing her mind because of a bit of sleepwalking and a racy book. But what would she think if I told her what I saw and what I now think is happening in this house?

Kuchisake-Onna.

Maybe she'll think *I'm* losing my mind. As I sure as hell *feel* like I am.

We head downstairs and into the kitchen.

"What time is it?" Hayami asks as I pour two glasses of whisky.

"Just after twelve." I hand her one glass, which she takes, and I lead her into the large living room.

There's a chill in the air. Hayami pulls the long cardigan she's wearing around her shoulders and places her glass on the table before kneeling in front of the fire.

She works quickly, piling up the kindling and arranging larger logs on top. I'm grateful she appears to have picked up that I don't like to light the fire. I don't even like it burning, but the heating system isn't powerful enough to heat a room this size.

I make my way over to the window and reach for the curtain. "It's snowing," I say.

Hayami joins me. "I thought the forecast said tomorrow."

"When have you ever known the forecast to be right?"

She doesn't answer as we stare at the small flakes that flutter silently through the air as if they have no purpose.

"Do you think it'll settle?" she asks, tucking her hair behind her ear.

"It's dry enough." We've had no rain for the past two days, which has been a welcome break from the mist and drizzle. But now we're in for something completely different.

"Is there a chance we could get snowed in?" Hayami wraps her arms around her waist.

"Possibly." I don't mention the forecast, how bad they've predicted this snowstorm is going to be. You wouldn't think it, looking now at how light and lazy the snowflakes are falling—the calm before the storm.

"Wouldn't be such a bad thing," she says, and I note how small she appears standing next to me, arms cocooning herself as if this is her only line of defence.

"Wouldn't it?" I ask, closing the curtains.

"I could handle being stuck here for a bit," she says, wandering over to the fire and warming her hands. "Actually, I would love to be stuck here forever."

I don't pick up on what she's saying, not at first. "You'd be stuck up here with me."

She regards me. "You're not so bad."

A low chuckle rumbles in the back of my throat. "Even when I hauled you out of that cubicle at the club?" I pass her the glass of whisky, then move over to the sofa and sit down.

Hayami settles on the rug by the fire, sets her glass down, then pulls her cardigan over her knees. "You were just doing your job."

"Was I?"

She stares at me. Then her shoulders drop along with her eyes.

I feel bold. Not sure if it's the silence in the room, the dream I've just had, or six months of protecting this woman from herself. But I have to know.

"That day I dragged you from the pool."

She looks up, her eyes wide. And I feel bad for asking, but I need to know.

"You weren't just floating, were you?"

She swallows hard, her lips clamping shut, and I fear I'm riling her. I'm going to lose this connection we have right now, and I don't want to.

"It's a strange thing, surviving," I tell her. "When your whole family dies and you're the one who is left alive. You ask yourself so many questions that your head begins to spin. I spoke to my therapist about it, just after the fire, and he told me I was suffering from survivor's guilt, and that it was perfectly normal for me to feel the way I did, like I should have been the one to die. That I should have been the one buried, not my sister, not my father, not my mother. But I wasn't. I lived. And I've had to live with that knowledge. But the one thing it's taught me is that life is precious, even if we don't think it is. And when I look at you, I see an intelligent, beautiful woman who has so much potential. I know you're a Devall. I know the hold your father has on you, but he isn't going to be around forever. So why did you want to end it all?"

THIRTY-FIVE

HAYAMI

PRESENT

THE HEAT FROM THE FIRE BURNS MY BACK, BUT IT'S NOTHING compared to the shame I felt when I opened my eyes astride Fenrir, or the shame I feel now knowing I'm going to have to explain why I wanted to kill myself. Why my life isn't worth living, and why I've been behaving the way I have for the past six months.

It's time to tell him.

I pull at a loose thread on my cardigan, my head swirling as I try to coax out what needs to be said.

"The day you found me in the pool was the day after I'd had a meeting with my father." The words feel sticky, like they don't want to be said, but I know I have to do this. He needs to know. "I knew it was something important because he called me into his office."

Fenrir watches me carefully, his silence pulling more from me than any question ever could.

"He was behind his desk, his fingers steepled, his gaze making my skin itch. I felt like I was five years old and was being scolded for breaking a priceless vase or stealing cake from the kitchen." I wrap my arms around myself, the heat from the fire suddenly disappearing.

"He told me I'd be married by my twenty-first birthday. That he was arranging it."

Fenrir doesn't flinch. But I know he's listening—really listening.

"I asked him what he meant—if I'd heard him wrong. And then he told me there'll be an auction. That I'll be one of several women, and that he's set a price for me." I shake my head, bile rising along with the words. "He said my 'beauty and purity' would make me the most valuable."

The fire suddenly feels too far away, the cold creeping up my arms.

"I couldn't even respond at first. I just sat there, numb. And then I asked him, 'My purity?' Because—what the hell, right?" I glance down at my hands. "That's when he said he pays my bodyguards not just to protect me... but to keep me untouched."

I can barely say the words. My voice cracks around them.

"He said purity adds value. That it makes me more desirable for the men who'll be bidding. He called them buyers, not suitors. Not husbands. *Buyers.*"

I let out a slow breath. "There's a whole schedule already planned—events, meetings. All of it just for these men to assess me like I'm some asset. A fucking product."

I look back at Fenrir, my voice low, almost a whisper. "And that's why I was in the pool that day. Because for the first time in my life, I truly understood what it meant to be owned. And I didn't want to be."

I'm his daughter.

His flesh and blood.

And he's selling me to the highest bidder to keep his empire running.

"And do you know what stung the most?" I ask Fenrir, not waiting for him to answer because right now, he looks like speaking would hurt. "Just before I left his office, he told me not to fuck this up."

My eyes lift to meet Fenrir's once again. He hasn't moved. I don't think he's even breathing. There's a heat to his skin that I'm sure has nothing to do with the fire, as he looks to be seething, as if his anger is simmering on the surface.

"As you know, I don't like to bow out of a fight, and his parting words felt like a red rag to a bull. So, I thought about how I could fight him, how I could make sure I wasn't sold like a piece of meat to a guy I'd never met before and would have to live the rest of my life with. Even after my father's death, I'd still be shackled to this life, to a man I don't love, to a man I didn't choose. To a man who thought it was okay to buy his wife and her fortune. To a man just like my father."

Fenrir blinks. "So, you chose death."

I hold his gaze. "I chose death."

FENRIR

My jaw clenches so tightly I'm surprised my teeth haven't shattered. It's a good job we're hundreds of miles away from Barrett Devall. If not, I'd hunt him down and put a fucking bullet right between his eyes.

I can't promise I won't the next time I see him, because this is unbelievable. Although, it isn't. It's exactly the kind of thing a man like Barrett Devall would do—*is* doing. He's a powerful man, and powerful men don't get to where they are without doing some downright ugly things, some of which I've done for him myself.

But Hayami is his daughter, his flesh and blood, his

legacy. Why would he do this to her? Why would he auction off her body, her life, her soul?

I've seen evil. Smelled it. Felt the lick of it upon my skin. But that man.... *Fuck*. That man is on another fucking level.

"I thought death was the only way out. But then you saved me, and my father employed you as my bodyguard. Probably to keep me in line. I knew no one believed me when I said I was just floating in the water, and I know my father upped my security and alerted all the staff that I was to be put on suicide watch, so I had to come up with another plan. Some other way to get back at him."

Something clicks in my head.

"That's why you've been so calm about being here, because you've got away from him, away from whatever he's planning."

She nods. "The break has done me good. If I'm not there, I can't be paraded around dance floors for prospective buyers whilst thinking up ways to stop my father."

"Something other than killing yourself?"

"I did have a backup plan after I realised death wasn't the answer, but it was... stupid." She squints and wrinkles her nose, which, although it makes her look cute, infuriates me.

"You're a lot of things, Hayami, but stupid isn't one of them."

"Okay, reckless, then." She refolds her legs and runs her finger over the top of her glass. "I've been trying to get rid of my *purity*." She says the word as if it's a swear. Before the pieces can fully fall into place, she continues. "My father said I was worth more because I was still pure, and that he's made sure I've been unable to sully myself. So I thought the only way to fight back would be to *actually* sully myself."

Purity. The word burrows under my skin until it latches on, realisation dawning on me.

"You're a virgin?"

She bites her bottom lip, and her cheeks flush. I'm unsure if this has anything to do with the heat from the fire or the question I've just asked, but I take it as her answer.

"You wanted to lose your virginity to spite your father?" I say, her plan unravelling before me.

"More than that." Her eyes snap up to mine, that fire I've seen so many times back with a vengeance. "I wanted to get fucked. I wanted to be defiled. I wanted to ruin myself for whoever bought me. I wanted to know that I'd been touched by so many hands that I would lie there on my wedding night and laugh in the fucking face of whoever bought me, thinking I was this pure virgin when in fact I'd been fucked every which way because that was *my* choice. *My* decision. I wanted to have control over one fucking thing in my life. There was no way my father was controlling my sex life. No fucking way."

Then it hits me.

"That's why you wanted to go to the sex club. Why you kept coming on to those men."

"Yes." She lowers her head.

"Hey, don't look away from me."

She looks up. "You must think I'm desperate."

My heart pounds, my pulse thundering in my ears.

"I think you're very brave to stand up for yourself against a man like your father. You have more fight in you than some of the Hellhounds. I believe you're capable of so much more, and I'm furious that your father thinks he can take this all away from you."

She tuts, waving my words away. I imagine no one's ever told her this.

"And I'm sorry I foiled your plan. If I'd have known...." I can't finish that sentence.

"You'd have what?" Hayami presses. "You'd have helped me? You'd have let me fuck those guys?"

"Probably not," I admit, "because a toilet cubicle is no place to lose your virginity, and those guys were the scum of the earth. But maybe I wouldn't have gone so..."

She smiles as I struggle to find the right word. "OTT?" she offers. I roll my eyes but nod in agreement before she adds, "Maybe the gun in the guy's mouth was a bit much."

"Not by my count."

She tips her head to the side. "Why do you always lose it when I'm with a guy?"

"I don't," I snap.

"Yes, you do. There was that guy in Mojo's who tried to kiss me, and you marched over and kicked over his stool and told him that if he ever so much as breathed near me again, you'd ram your fist down his throat. You always lose your shit when any guy so much as even looks at me."

I swallow hard. "That ball you went to, the first night I escorted you, you told me not to let anyone touch you. I took it as a hard rule, meaning *anyone*."

Her face darkens. "That ball was the first function I attended where there'd be potential buyers. I absolutely did not want any of them even looking at me."

I nod. It makes sense.

"But all others were fair game?"

"Not with you around they weren't." She raises her eyebrows.

"I could say the same about you," I point out. "You always lose your shit when I'm trying to stop you from making a huge mistake."

"This hasn't been about a milestone, about remembering the most amazing first night of my life. That train has already left. Fuck, it never even pulled into the station. I'll never have the magical first time like everyone else does. My father made sure of that. This has always been an operation, a job that needs doing, and it doesn't matter with who, just so long as it's done."

"I understand your motivation, but do you really want to give your virginity to someone like those guys? They don't deserve it."

"Then who does?"

I grind my teeth. "Someone who respects you. Someone who views you as more than just a trophy fuck. Someone who'll treat you the way you deserve, who will give you what you need, not just take what they want."

The flames flicker behind her, taunting me, but I push them aside.

"And where the hell am I supposed to find someone like that? In one of my books? Because that's the kind of man you're talking about—a fictional man. And although I've learned a lot from reading romance, the one thing they've taught me is that men like that don't exist. Otherwise, why would books get written about them?"

I have no comeback to that, because she's wrong. They do exist.

Hayami's phone beeps from the side. She picks it up and reads the text before looking at me. "It's from Willa."

Great. She needs to get back here, as I'm struggling to man this show on my own, and a second opinion would be great right now as to what the fuck is going on here. But more importantly, I don't trust myself alone with Hayami anymore. She's too vulnerable. We both are. We're getting too close, and if the opportunity arises, I know I won't be able to stop myself.

I'm only human. And honestly, I want her too much.

I have no restraint where Hayami is concerned.

"What does it say?"

"Her plane's been grounded. They've suspended all flights

indefinitely due to the storm." Her eyes meet mine. "Looks like we're on our own."

THIRTY-SIX

HAYAMI

PRESENT

THE FIRE DWINDLES, ALONG WITH THE CONVERSATION, AS dawn on our tenth day here draws close, bringing with it the quiet certainty that we're truly alone up here—and likely to remain so.

I dreaded where the conversation was going, afraid of what I might do, considering I straddled him in my sleep. I'm not sure what came over me. Maybe it was my subconscious trying to complete the mission I'd set for myself all those weeks ago, or maybe I was acting out my most recent fantasies. Whatever it was, I need to tread carefully. Fenrir has shown no signs that he feels the same way about me. I don't want to make a fool of myself, especially since we could be spending a long time up here together alone now that Willa is definitely not coming back any time soon.

"I should go to bed," I say with a slow yawn. "I'm worried about you getting so little sleep."

"It's fine," Fenrir says, brushing off my worries. "I'm used to it."

"First thing in the morning, you're going to get some sleep. I insist," I reply, levering myself up from the rug.

He stands, picking up our glasses, which he drops off in the kitchen before following me upstairs.

Fenrir checks the windows of my room, under the bed, and the en suite. I wait dutifully outside until he gives me the all clear, then scoot into the room and gather my loungewear so I can take a shower.

"I won't lock it," I tell him, just before closing the door.

It's a relief to be alone, but also a torment. I don't want to be away from him, yet I need some air, some space, a second to collect my thoughts.

"Someone who will give you what you need, not just take what they want."

His words dance in my brain. I hadn't thought of it that way, but now that he's pointed it out, I see what he means. The guys I've tried to get with have always been interested in one thing: getting what they want. But I'm also guilty of this —purely using them to get one up on my father. They haven't been interested in me or my needs, but neither have I.

Do I want my first time to be built upon a mutual understanding in a toilet cubicle? No, of course I don't. If I had it my way, my first time would be momentous, with someone I care about. With someone who makes me feel like I'm the most special person on this planet. Someone who I can't stop thinking about, and who wants me as much as I want them.

I'm old enough, and enough of a realist, to know that I probably won't love the guy I lose my virginity to. That's old-fashioned, what you read about in fairy tales. It's not the real world. But I want it to be with someone I feel *something* for. Someone who makes my toes curl. Someone I respect. Someone who knows what they're doing. I don't want an inexperienced young guy, a selfish man. I don't want to be left wondering what all the fuss is about.

I want to be worshipped.

I want to be taken.

I want to be ruined.

Turning the shower on, I notice the hardness of my nipples, the goose bumps over my skin, and the fact that the door is unlocked.

And before I can stop it, the fantasy of Fenrir walking through the door and joining me in the shower is back, and there's no way I can stop it.

THIRTY-SEVEN

FENRIR

PRESENT

As Hayami showers, I pull out my phone to try and distract myself from the noise of the running water and that she's naked in there with the door unlocked. But as I scan the latest weather update, our conversation downstairs comes back to me. I'd had to push my anger down when Hayami revealed her father's intentions. And then again when she told me her plans to stop it by killing herself, then to try and sabotage her "purity" by throwing herself at the first guy she came across. *Jesus.* No wonder she's a volcano waiting to erupt.

I found it hard not to speak from my heart and tell her exactly what I thought: that if any man should so much as touch her, I'd rip his arms from his body and take pleasure in doing so. She doesn't see how precious she is or what she's handing to these men. But I blame Devall. This is his doing. He forced her hand with this ridiculous auction.

The door to the en suite clicks open and Hayami strolls into the room, her hair wrapped up in a white towel. She's dressed in shorts and a vest top, her skin slightly pink from the heat of the water.

"How's the snow looking?" she asks.

Sliding my phone into my pocket, I head over to the window and pull back the curtain. The white confetti has turned into fat flakes that swirl angrily in the air before landing on the now-white surfaces. The backdrop looks purple, the strange glow that always seems to illuminate the sky when the world has turned white.

"It's coming down heavy now." I close the curtain and turn to face her, and I freeze.

Hayami is by the bed, towel now in her hand, eyes on me. But behind her is a shadow on the wall cast from the lamp on her bedside table. But it isn't *her* shadow. It's taller. It's wider.

No. It's not possible. It's a trick of the light. It's my eyes playing games with me.

But as I try to rationalise what I'm seeing, I can't help but notice Hayami is stationary, yet the shadow moves towards her, its hands reaching out as if to grab her.

Hayami holds the towel to her hair, rubbing the long strands, completely oblivious—until I reach behind my back and pull my gun from my waistband.

HAYAMI

Fenrir stares over my shoulder, face aghast, his body rigid as if he's been frozen. I'm about to turn around to see what has captured his attention, but then he unfreezes, his arm contorting as he reaches into the back of his waistband.

He pulls his gun out and aims.

Cold fear drenches me.

What the fuck?

It takes a second for me to realise his gun isn't pointing at me. It's pointing behind me.

There's someone behind me.

"Fenrir." My voice sounds weak, and I don't mean for it to.

"Don't move." He's staring at the wall. His eyes don't leave the target, which is about a foot to my left.

Dread spools in my gut as I watch him aim the gun, arms straight and locked as he moves slowly, slowly, slowly, the target moving, getting closer to me with every second.

I haven't heard any sounds. I can't hear anyone else breathing or moving. There's no one in the room with us.

So, what the fuck is he pointing his gun at?

But then I recall Willa telling me about venomous insects and drones being used to kill people when we first arrived here, explaining why there's a camera in my room.

I swallow, and just before the gun reaches in line with my shoulder, I drop to the floor. Fenrir fires, the noise exploding off the walls and ringing in my ears.

Scrambling, I crawl to him, adrenaline coursing through my veins.

As I reach him, he puts out his hand and pulls me into his solid body, wrapping his arm around me. Confusion mixes with fear. Why aren't we running? Why is he not picking me up and getting me the hell out of here? Unless he shot them, whoever or whatever it was?

"What the fuck?" I ask as I turn to look where he still has the gun aimed.

But other than some cracked plaster and a bullet hole in the wall, there's nothing there. I drop my gaze to the carpet, expecting to see a venomous insect or some high-tech killing device, but again, there's nothing.

"What the hell?"

"I thought I saw something," he says at last, still holding me tightly.

"*Something?*"

"A shadow. I don't know." He shakes his head, his voice lacking any sort of certainty. He releases his grip on me, but I'm not ready to let go of him just yet.

"Jeez. You scared the shit out of me," I say, exhaling a large breath, but his reply niggles at me. *A shadow.* I recall the look on his face when he had the gun pointed at the wall. He looked at it for a long time. It wasn't a split-second glance; it wasn't a moment where something caught his eye. He *stared* at it. He must have known what it was. He was following it with his gun. It doesn't make any sense.

"Sorry." He doesn't look sorry.

"You really need to get some sleep. Sleep deprivation can do all sorts of things to the brain."

He looks like he's about to argue, but then seems to give in, his jaw tensing. He doesn't like not being in control.

"I'll get a few hours of sleep, and then we'll swap," I say, taking charge.

"No." He takes a step forwards.

"No arguing." I throw back the covers on the bed. "And I want you to stay in my room."

He glances at me.

"I don't want you falling asleep in that little room downstairs. At least if you fall asleep up here, I can wake you if something happens."

I'm starting to worry about him now. Is the isolation getting to him? Sometimes, I catch him staring at the walls or looking at something that doesn't appear to be there. Is this just his bodyguard mentality? He spends his entire time on high alert, never letting his guard down, never relaxing. But this feels different. This feels like a man who's had no sleep for so long that his brain is imagining things.

I'm suffering from delusions of my own, but of a very different nature. There'd been a second when Fenrir had his gun raised when his focus had been entirely on shooting whatever he thought he saw behind me, and I swear I would have dropped to my knees for him there and then.

Maybe we're both losing our minds.

THIRTY-EIGHT

FENRIR

She's looking at me like I'm a fucking nutjob.

Can I blame her?

But I know what I saw.

Her shadow?

No. Not Hayami's shadow.

Then whose?

Kuchisake-Onna?

It was making its way towards Hayami. If this is Kuchisake-Onna, then what is her purpose other than to put the fear of God into me?

I should tell Hayami what I believe is happening here, but I doubt she'll believe me, and she has enough going on without worrying about ghosts. I *will* tell her, but not until I have the full picture, and I won't have that until I've finished reading Junko's journal.

Hayami picks up her phone. "I'm setting an alarm for four hours. Then we'll swap." She places her phone on the bedside table before settling back onto the pillow.

I don't like the idea of being asleep at night. But she's right. There's no way I can stay awake for a whole eight hours. But can I trust her to keep watch?

Yes, of course I can. It's the other thing I can't trust.

Kuchisake-Onna.

The shadow had been about to devour Hayami. It had been about to slink into her body and take over the controls, just like I've seen on several occasions now, and I won't allow it. If I leave Hayami awake and vulnerable, it could do anything to her, make her do anything, and I can't take that risk.

I'm sure now that this is what stalks the walls of this house. Kuchisake-Onna. It's what Kevin's father saw the night he was leaving the house. Did Noa see it too? Did she experience Kuchisake-Onna, and that's what caused her to miscarry her child? Did she die of fright, of heartbreak that she'd lost her baby?

The only thing I do know is that nothing seems to happen during the day, only at night.

"I'll sleep when the sun rises," I tell Hayami. "That's non-negotiable." I settle on the small sofa in the corner of the room, sit back, and rest my ankle on my knee.

She throws me a stern look, one I've seen countless times before as she's geared herself up to argue with me, but then her shoulders drop along with her arms, and tiredness washes over her face.

"You drive a hard bargain," she says before turning off the small lamp and closing her eyes.

There's a gap in the curtains where I'd been checking on the snow. A purple glow slithers into the room, casting enough light for me to see Hayami's face. *Her* face. Not the contortion of that thing. Not the face of Kuchisake-Onna. Just Hayami's beautiful face.

I can still feel her arms around me after I shot the shadow, felt her heart beating against my chest as she clung to me as if her life depended on it. And I'd held her like she was mine. And the minute she let go, I felt bereft.

Hayami is right. Sleep deprivation is playing tricks with me, addling my brain into thinking things that aren't true, and I don't mean the ghost. I'm referring to the fact that I keep imagining that Hayami could be mine. That she might feel an ounce of what I feel for her, and that she might fall into my arms willingly.

What I wouldn't give to crawl under the covers and hold her, feel her skin against my own, let my hands claim what I believe to be mine, let my tongue take what it wants, and watch her unravel.

It will never be.

How could she ever feel that way about someone like me? Someone who wears my scars like armour and whose history is etched on my body like graffiti? She could never want me.

She *will* never want me.

I need to stop thinking like this, imagining things that'll never be, and concentrate on the very real problem of what is happening in this house. So, I pick up Junko's journal and pull up the torch on my phone, aiming it at the open pages.

Day Eight

Since hearing Kevin's story of what happened the night his dad dropped off the late delivery, I should feel more afraid of the house and what it hides.

I should be scared.

But instead, I'm curious.

How can a folklore, a legend from my home

country, be here with me on Hellion Ridge? For that is what I have always believed Kuchisake-Onna to be: a legend, a myth, a story. Not dissimilar to the bogeyman or Bloody Mary. They're just stories invented to scare people.

Is that what this is? A scary story? And how would that explain what Kevin's father saw? He wouldn't know anything about Kuchisake-Onna, so he couldn't have had any preconceived ideas that might influence his thinking. And if he didn't see Kuchisake-Onna, then who or what did he see? Because a grown man doesn't return home the way Kevin described when nothing has happened.

Is it this house? Is it playing tricks on me? Playing tricks on others?

Barrett appears immune to it all. He strides about the house looking perfectly content. The only thing that appears to rile him is if there's a problem with one of his businesses or something going on with his people. He doesn't tell me what he does, and if I'm honest, I don't want to know. He's a rich man, but he isn't a good one. I should never have married him, but I was blinded by his looks, his wealth, his charm, and the promise of a better life. Because who doesn't want a better life?

Day Eleven
It was the strangest thing, the strangest feel-

ing, as if someone had taken over my mind.

I went into the town to do some shopping and popped in on Kevin at the general store, who said I looked well, which I took as a compliment. I've been feeling a little out of sorts of late, but I've put this down to the house and being so cut off from the world up here.

The visit to town did me good. It stretched my legs and reminded me that there is life beyond this house and these walls.

Barrett was in the library for most of the day, making calls and sending emails. In the evening, I cooked us a meal, which he seemed to push around his plate as if trying to get away from it. Nevertheless, he drank the wine I bought and then told me it was time to make an heir.

We went up to the master bedroom, my food sitting heavily in my stomach. I performed my wifely duties. That's what it feels like. There's no passion, no romance, no attention to me other than to make sure his seed gets to where it needs to be.

As soon as it was over, he scurried off into the en suite and left me with my hips raised on a pillow, staring at the ceiling.

And that's when it happened.

There was something odd about the air above me; it pulsed before my eyes as if a great heat had penetrated the room, even though it felt cold.

I blinked several times, wondering if there was something wrong with my vision, that I was developing cataracts or experiencing an aura from a migraine, but no. The air continued to shimmer before me as if the colours in the room were mixing, like a painting that had been tipped up and wasn't quite dry yet.

And the ripples got closer and closer and closer.

I couldn't move for two reasons. First, I'm trying to get pregnant, as it's the only way Barrett will be happy, and second, I was mesmerised by the sight. The fear didn't arrive until it was too late, until the ripples were right in front of my eyes, and then they were behind them.

It was like being engulfed, swallowed whole, my body consumed by the shimmering light that had been hovering above me not seconds before.

Pain radiated through my body, searing hot torment across my face, and a spasm in my stomach, an emptiness that threatened to consume me. Desperation flooded me, mingling with darkness and sorrow.

Scratching at my skin, I tried to claw this feeling away, tried to pull it from my body, but it was stuck fast and wouldn't let me go. It held me in an iron grip until tears sprang from my eyes and stung the burning in my cheeks.

All I remember after that is Barrett standing over me, yelling at me to put the scissors down. He wrenched them from my hand. I had no idea what I was intending to do with them, but when he tore them from my fingers, it was like a slap to the face, like waking from a bad dream, and I was back in the room—me, Junko, not the darkness that had blinded me.

Barrett shouted, asked me what the fuck I was doing.

Pressing my hand to my face, I expected wet, oozing blood, but my fingers came away clear, only sweat coating my skin. I glanced down at my stomach, expecting to see a huge gash gushing with blood, but again, there was no wound. Quickly, I checked the scissors. There was no blood coating the blades.

I told him that I didn't know what I was doing, which was the truth, and he said I looked deranged. He started to say more but then stopped himself, as if he didn't want to say what or who I looked like. What had I reminded him of?

This is the only time I have seen him spooked. The only time since we arrived in this house that I've seen the businesslike façade slip.

What the hell happened to me? Was it Kuchisake-Onna? Had she visited me? And why had Barrett looked so afraid of me when it is I who am afraid of him?

LETTING THE JOURNAL FLOP IN MY HAND, I SEE NOW WHAT might be going on here.

Kuchisake-Onna is infiltrating their bodies. She did it to Junko. She's doing it to Hayami. And maybe she did it to Noa. Kevin's dad described seeing a woman by the side of the road, but she wasn't pregnant, so did he see Kuchisake-Onna herself? Is this why Junko relies on drugs and alcohol to get her through the days and has never returned to Belial House, because she'd been possessed by an evil spirit? Or is this all just a product of my sleep-deprived brain?

Maybe I'm the one who's being possessed, and none of this is real.

THIRTY-NINE
HAYAMI

PRESENT

I BOLT UPRIGHT, SLEEP SLIPPING FROM ME AS A SHARP SOUND fills the air, the vibrations of the noise having caused an avalanche through my body. We've been in this house for eleven days now, and I thought I'd got used to the creaks, the groans, and the other strange noises, but this was too loud for the house to be settling, too profound for the pipes to be complaining. It was deafening, like a fucking gun going off.

"What the fuck was that?"

Fenrir is on his feet, gun drawn, with the only light coming from a small gap in the curtains.

I've no idea how long I've been asleep.

Two seconds?

Two minutes?

Two hours?

I also have no idea what that fucking noise was.

"I don't know." His voice doesn't betray him. He's the pillar of composure, poised, gun aimed at the door. "Stay here," he says.

"Fuck no." I flip the covers back and fling my legs out of the bed. "I've seen those films where the murderer distracts the guy by luring him out of the room, leaving the defenceless woman on her own, ready to be slaughtered. No, thanks."

He fires me a warning look, then seems to be having some internal wrangling until he says, "Stay behind me. Stay quiet."

Carefully, I tiptoe across the room and position myself behind him. He signals for me to press myself against the wall. We edge along the plaster like searchlights until we reach the door.

Fenrir flattens himself and pulls his gun up so it's pointing at the ceiling.

"You wait until I tell you it's clear, do you understand?" he whispers.

I nod, not wanting to disobey his rule of keeping quiet.

He looks like he's counting in his head.

One. Two.

On three, he opens the door slowly, pointing the gun out before him.

Like I've seen the police do on so many TV shows and films, Fenrir checks the landing by aiming his gun at all areas before signalling for me to follow.

We make our way down the stairs, me staying behind him, Fenrir holding the gun out in front of us.

He checks the library first, but all we find are empty chairs, resting books, and a darkness that feels settled.

The sitting room and large living room are just as we left them, not a few hours ago.

It's when we reach the kitchen that I feel it—the charge in the atmosphere, as if someone has just been here and disturbed the air.

As Fenrir steps further into the room, the moonlight illuminates the table, glinting off the surface.

Flipping on the light, we stare.

All the drawers are open, pulled right out until they've reached the end of their runners, and all the utensils have been placed on the table in a neat line.

No, not *all* the utensils.

Knives. Cleavers. Scissors.

All the sharp things.

"What the fuck?" I hiss through my teeth.

Fenrir is still checking the room, pointing his gun at the walls, the window, the lights.

I take a step towards the table.

"Don't," he warns as if it could be a trap.

"What the hell is this?" I stare at the open drawers. "Have you been down here since I fell asleep?"

"No. I stayed in your room the whole time."

"I don't understand. How has this happened?" I certainly don't remember doing this. And Fenrir is running on fumes, not having slept properly for days.

Did he do this? Is this a product of a lack of sleep, his overtired brain operating on its own?

I can't say he's been acting rational these past few days. The other night, I woke to find him standing over me, convinced there was something in my room. Then, earlier today, he shot at a wall. These are not the actions of a level-headed man. But then I recall the night I woke, having had a bad dream, and not remembering getting out of bed. I wonder at what point I consciously decided to mount Fenrir when he was next to me on the bed.

Maybe neither of us is sane right now.

I run my hand through my hair as Fenrir steps towards the table and picks up one of the knives.

"There has to be a rational explanation," I begin, treading

carefully. "There are only two people in this house: you and me."

He glares, picking up on my accusation that this must have been him because I know it wasn't me. And if it'd been me who'd done this whilst I was asleep, then surely Fenrir would have seen me and stopped me, unless he also nodded off.

I'm going around in circles until he gathers all the utensils and shoves them back into the drawers.

"Come on, let's check the cameras," he says as he slams the drawers shut.

We cram into the small room under the stairs, and Fenrir works quickly, rewinding the camera footage from the kitchen. Surely it will show either him or me going into the kitchen and setting up this stunt. I'm not sure what I fear most: seeing myself or Fenrir on the camera.

He stops the recording at the right time and hits Play, and we see the kitchen, still, silent, smothered in darkness. Then there's a blip, a moment where all we see is a blank screen for one second before it flicks back to life. The drawers are open, and the knives and scissors are all lined up on the table.

"Fuck." I rub my eyes. I can't explain what I'm seeing.

Fenrir plays it back several times. I check the timestamp when the blip occurs, and there's no shift in time. The blip lasts two seconds before the kitchen returns, the drawers open and the knives having been placed on the table, not enough time for a person to have done this. Then what? It doesn't make any sense.

"There has to be a rational explanation," I repeat, more to myself than to Fenrir, who I know must be as stumped as I am.

Fenrir stares at the screen, playing it back again before moving on to the footage from my room. He rewinds the tape and plays it sped up. I watch myself sleep, turning over occasionally as Fenrir remains seated in the corner, engrossed in a book, looking up now and then to check on me.

And then I sit up as he springs from the small sofa and draws his gun. We must have heard the noise.

"Three o'clock," he says, pointing out the timestamp in the bottom corner of the screen.

Fenrir goes back to the tape of the kitchen and finds the moment when the screen goes black. He pauses it and checks the time.

Three o'clock.

It wasn't me or Fenrir.

So, who was it?

What was it?

"This can only mean one thing," I say, with less conviction than I'd hoped for. "Someone else has been here."

Fenrir doesn't answer. He checks all the other tapes to see if anything else has been picked up on any of the other cameras, but there's nothing. All the other areas of the house remain undisturbed.

"There's nothing on any of the other cameras," he says. "The snow is deep enough now to ensure that no one is getting up this mountain. And even if, somehow, they did manage to get up here and break in, why would they set this up? For what purpose?"

"To scare us?" I suggest.

He lifts an eyebrow because, yeah, it sounds stupid. Why would anyone want to do this? If it was someone working for the Castros, then why didn't they just come to my room and put a bullet in Fenrir's head and then one in mine? Why would they sneak into the kitchen to set up some freaky scene?

I wrap my arms around myself, wishing I'd grabbed my hoodie as goose bumps erupt over my skin.

"What the fuck is going on here?" I ask more sternly, hoping Fenrir will dignify me with an answer instead of his stony silence.

"I don't know," he says as he turns in the chair to look at me. "I don't fucking know."

There's a beat of silence before I say, "What *do* we know?"

As if answering me, Fenrir gets up and heads into the kitchen. I follow. He opens the cupboard and grabs the whisky and two glasses.

I shiver, the coldness hanging in the air like the aftermath of a horrible incident. "I'm not staying in here," I tell him.

"Neither am I," he says as he exits the room.

I follow him upstairs and back into my bedroom. He flips on the light and sets the bottle down on the tall drawers.

"Here." He hands me a glass.

"I'm going to be an alcoholic by the time we get out of this house," I quip.

"You and me both."

Sitting on the bed, I curl my feet under my legs and cradle the glass. Fenrir returns to the sofa, his glass held precariously by the tips of his fingers.

I take a sip and wince, still not used to the taste. I wonder how my mum tolerates this stuff. Then a thought occurs. "Hey, do you think it was this house that turned my mum to drink?" I ask.

He swallows hard before answering. "Who knows? I'd have thought being married to your father would be reason enough."

"You can say that again." I tut. "I often wonder why she stays with him, how she's lasted all these years, but then I suppose that I must be the reason."

"I'm sure it is."

"That and the fact that no one can ever leave my father. Not really. Only he decides that. But it doesn't stop me from wanting to get away from him. I'd give anything not to be a Devall."

"We have no control over the family we're born into, and I'm sure you aren't the only person who wishes they had a different family," Fenrir says.

He's right, again. I'm sure there isn't a day that goes by that Fenrir doesn't wish he'd been born into a family who weren't involved with a gang. He wouldn't have had to throw his sister over a balcony. He wouldn't have lost his mum and dad, and eventually his sister, who he tried so desperately to save.

He wouldn't have to carry this with him every day. He wouldn't have to be reminded of what he endured every time he looks in the mirror. He might have stood a chance of having a normal life, where he could walk down the street without being stared at, without having blood on his conscience, without having to deal out the retribution he felt he had to.

He could have been someone else entirely.

I glance at him, and it's in this moment that I wish I could give him that: a different life, one where he can be anyone he wants to be, where he doesn't have to carry the shit he's carried for so long.

"You should sleep," he says after downing his whisky.

"I'm not sure I can." I swill the liquid around the glass, then neck the lot, the burn working its way down my throat and into my stomach.

"Do you believe it's haunted?" I ask, immediately feeling foolish for even suggesting it.

"Haunted?"

"The house. Do you think it's haunted?" I repeat.

"You don't believe in ghosts," he reminds me.

"I don't." I place the glass on the bedside table. It doesn't escape me that he hasn't answered my question, but I won't push. "You'll stay?"

"If you want me to."

"Fuck, there's no way I'm going to be able to go back to sleep." I sigh, trying to shuffle under the covers.

"Here, let me help." He stands and makes his way over to the bed. I shuffle up when it becomes clear he's going to climb in next to me.

The frame creaks as he sits.

"Close your eyes," he tells me, and I do. Then I feel his fingers stroke the side of my face. "My mother used to stroke my face when I couldn't sleep. She also used to sing to me, but I won't make you endure my singing voice. But it never failed to get me to sleep."

I'm shocked at how soft his touch is, how gentle his fingers are for someone so large, so brutal. There's a tingling between my legs, and there's no fucking way I'm sleeping now as the touch of his hand smooths over my skin, igniting all sorts of fires within me.

It isn't the first time his hands have been upon me, but they've never been this careful, this light. It's like being stroked with a feather—the delicacy, the intimacy. It makes me want to grab him and kiss him.

Instead, I just lie here and let him stroke me, let him touch me, because this is what I've wanted all along. To be touched. To be caressed. To be wanted.

And I drift into a blissful sleep. The house, its ghosts, all of it forgotten.

FORTY

FENRIR

PRESENT

It doesn't take her long to fall asleep. I'm not surprised; I'd be out for the count in no time when my mother used to stroke my face this way when I was little. It used to frustrate me, as I'd fight to stay awake just to feel her fingertips glide over my skin. My body would relax, and I'd feel safe. But it was like hypnosis. No sooner did she begin, I'd be asleep, like she was casting a spell over me. I always wondered if this gift was acquired when you had kids or whether it was passed down through generations. I guess I'll never know.

The fluttering of Hayami's eyelids has stopped. Her breathing is soft and even, and her face looks peaceful. Even though she's asleep, I continue to stroke her face.

She hadn't put up a fight when I suggested this technique. She just let me. I wonder if Junko had a way of settling Hayami when she was younger. For some reason, I doubt it.

I'd only just put the journal down when I heard the noise downstairs. It was so loud that I felt the house shake. Hayami had woken instantly, and this time, I knew it wasn't just my sleep-deprived brain or the influence of what I'd just read that was messing with me.

She heard it too.

And while the scene in the kitchen was so fucking bizarre, all I could think about was Kuchisake-Onna—the mutilated woman—and Junko's journal entry.

One thing's for sure: I'm going to have to tell Hayami what's going on. Before tonight, she thought this was all in my head, a product of no sleep, but there was no way I could explain what happened in the kitchen. It was why I checked the cameras, to prove to her that I hadn't moved from her bedroom. Her logical thought process was that *I* had done it. That *I* had wandered from her room in a sleepless fog and set up the scene.

But right now, I continue to stroke her face because I don't know when or if I'll ever get the opportunity to touch her like this again. And I must stay awake. The night is too dangerous, too precarious for me to drift off. And what better way to keep my vigil than right here next to Hayami watching her sleep?

The hours of darkness creep by unnoticed as I'm lost in her. Time slips by until the moon finally disappears and the grey sky returns, a shift in the light through the small gap in the curtains.

Morning has arrived.

It's safe.

She is safe.

Only now do I allow my eyes to close, let sleep take me as I lie curled up next to Hayami.

FORTY-ONE
HAYAMI

THREE, FOUR, FIVE, MAYBE? I DON'T RECALL HOW MANY TIMES I wake, but when I do, all I can feel is the heat from Fenrir's body, the feel of his arm draped over my side, and the safety that encompasses me as I float in between sleep and wakefulness.

It's morning. A dull glow seeps through the gap in the curtains, but I'm so tired, so relaxed that I don't ever want to move from here. I don't ever want his arm to leave me, so I stay within his reach.

In and out of sleep.

I've never felt so safe.

In and out of sleep.

Until I wake to a different feeling, something hard against my lower back. I didn't register it at first. I've never lain in bed with a man before, so I have no idea what things feel like or what is normal, and it isn't until I wake fully that I realise what this must be pressing into the base of my back.

Oh my God.

He's hard.

Trying not to flatter myself, I recall reading somewhere that most men wake with a hard-on, so this has no direct bearing on me. But even so, I tell myself it's *because* of me. I've done this to him. Me. This is the way I make him feel.

How I wish this were true.

It starts to brew. The feeling between my legs, the hot wetness that pools when I imagine what I'd like to do to him, what I'd like him to do to me. I'm not even aware of it, but I must start to grind against him because he stirs, nuzzling his head into the back of my neck.

I push back.

God, I want him. I want him so badly I could cry.

His erection presses harder into my back, and I reciprocate, pushing out my bottom and wanting to touch myself, to ease the burn that's flared up.

He must wake, as he sits up, pulls back, and I feel the cold immediately rush over my skin.

The bed moves, and I hear him shuffling behind me and feel the shift in the weight of the mattress.

I wait a beat before opening my eyes, rolling over to see the en suite door ajar as I hear water running in the shower.

Quietly, I climb out of the bed and tiptoe over to the door. I shouldn't be doing this, but my feet command me, deaf to the protest of my conscience trying to convince me that this is wrong. The water is loud, the pressure high, steam already building as I slip my head around the door and stare.

He's in the shower, his beautifully naked body soaked from the spray. I can make out the scarring down his side, how it grips his skin and rolls down his tortured torso. It should repulse me, but it doesn't. His head is down, eyes closed, as his hand works himself.

Steam clings to the glass door, obscuring his size. By the length of his strokes, he must be well endowed.

I should go, stop watching him. This isn't right. It's an invasion of his privacy. He thinks I'm asleep. But I'm not. I'm here, watching him take care of his needs, watching him touch himself, and I can't stop, can't move. Because I want to touch him. I want to be brave enough to walk in there, open the door to the shower, and step in with him, lowering to my knees and taking him in my mouth and finishing what he's started. But I can't. I've never done anything like that before, and I'm afraid he'll push me away, tell me to stop. Then I'd know that this isn't what he wants. *I* am not who he wants.

So, I just watch him, like some Peeping Tom, all whilst my pulse races and my thighs clench as I imagine taking him in my mouth, what it'd feel like to swirl my tongue around him. My hand moves between my legs. I'm so wet. My fingers flirt over my clit, the swell of desire only intensifying as I touch myself whilst I watch Fenrir.

His hand speeds up, and I dip my fingers, wanting my touch to be his.

He places his hand on the wall of the cubicle as if steadying himself, and he lifts his head. Sensing he's about to come, I press my hand to my clit, wanting to feel what he feels, but then his head turns, his eyes snap open, and he looks directly at me.

Fuck.

I dart from the door and fling myself back onto the bed.

My heart is pounding, my pulse throbbing at my temples.

Did he see me? I don't know. Maybe. Possibly.

Shit.

The water stops running.

I lie quietly, closing my eyes and willing myself to calm the fuck down. I've done nothing wrong.

That's bullshit. I just watched him masturbate in the

shower. It's very wrong, but so fucking hot I can still feel the tingling between my legs.

I hear the door open and then gentle footsteps padding into the room before they leave.

Panic strikes me as I open my eyes.

He's gone. *Where the fuck has he gone?*

I'm about to get up when he comes back into the room. I squeeze my eyes closed, but then I hear him shuffling on the other side of the bed, so I open them again.

He comes into my line of sight, shins clad in black combat trousers, his feet bare. Then he bobs down and stares at me.

There's a second when I think he's going to say something along the lines of "I saw you" or "What the fuck did you think you were doing?" or "Do you get off on watching people in the shower?" But instead, he just stares at me until I have to speak, because if I don't, I'll crack.

"Morning." I smile.

"Yes, it is."

"I didn't mean it like that." I drop my smile.

"I know."

I can't read him. I don't know what he's thinking. Did he see me looking at him? Does he know I was touching myself?

Shit. This is awful.

Willing myself to carry on, I think of the most mundane thing to say.

"What's the weather looking like?" I ask.

"White."

Okay, so he's in one-word mode.

I'm about to say that I'm going to jump in the shower, but then I stop. I don't want to mention showers. Instead, I sit up and yawn loudly as Fenrir stalks to the other side of the room and tells me he's going to leave me to get dressed.

As soon as he's gone, I slump over and place my head in my hands.

I've no idea if he saw me. *Should I confess?*

No, absolutely not. The best thing to do is to carry on as normal.

But what is normal around here?

FORTY-TWO

FENRIR

PUTTING ON SOME DEODORANT AND THEN RUNNING A COMB through my hair, I wait ten minutes for Hayami to get dressed.

It wasn't the dream of her sitting on my face that woke me. No, it was the reality of her grinding her ass against my hard-on. Because that wasn't a dream. That was real. She was curled up next to me, rubbing herself against me, and there was no way on this earth I could lie there any longer without crawling on top of her and taking care of whatever dream she was having.

It must have woken her, my hotfooting it into the en suite and turning on the shower, but I was too wrapped up in taking care of my needs to think she would get out of bed and come watch the show.

But she did.

It should have made me stop, should have dried up all my carnal desires when she ducked from the open door. Instead, it only made me come harder. The only thing I'm unsure of is how she felt when she was watching me. I'd like to think that if she'd been repulsed, she would've stopped looking and moved away well before the end. Or was it like a car crash where you couldn't help but stare even though you didn't want to? Besides, I have no idea how long she'd been there, so I guess I'll never know.

Whatever she felt, the atmosphere is now thick and palpable, and I'm not sure how long we'll be able to keep up this façade that everything is normal.

Checking my watch, I head back into her room to find her dressed in leggings and a hoodie.

"Wasn't sure what's on the agenda for today, so I went with casual," she says, running her fingers through her hair. "I thought we were going out for lunch to some fancy restaurant, followed by a little shopping spree before catching a show, but then I remembered we're stuck on a mountain in a snowstorm and also hiding from gang lords, so I put back the Versace number Nita must have packed for me."

She's opting for humour—her defence mechanism when she doesn't know what else to do—and I'm relieved. Her only other line of defence is attack, which I've been on the receiving end of far too many times to count, so I'll settle for the comedy.

"We're digging a path to the wood store and then probably target practice, but only if that fits in with your agenda."

Hayami raises her eyebrows. "My agenda consists of drinking hot chocolate and reading for most of the day, so, yeah, I suppose I have a window. Have you seen how bad the snow is?"

I edge over to the balcony doors and pull back the curtains.

The glare hurts my eyes, the white so bright it's almost glowing.

Everything is covered in snow.

The trees. The ground. The bushes.

"It's like someone has dusted the whole place with icing sugar," Hayami says as she joins me. "It's so quiet. Why does snow make everything silent and peaceful?"

"I suppose it's the white," I say. Hayami looks confused, so I add, "Colour of innocence."

"Wow, that's a little philosophical for this early hour," she points out.

"It's eleven o'clock."

"Okay, maybe not that early, but I think you're right. White just makes everything look so clean and calm. I almost don't want to ruin it by going outside and making footprints."

"I don't think they'll remain for long at the rate the snow is still falling," I tell her.

"Then why are we going out and digging a path to the wood store if there's more snow forecast? Shouldn't we wait until the worst is over?"

"We need more wood. Better to go now than when it's doubled in depth. We'll salt the walkway to try and discourage it from settling. Although, I don't think it'll make much difference."

There's a beep from Willa's phone, which is on the bedside cabinet.

Striding across the room, I reach the bed and pick it up. There's a message.

"Markus wants an update."

Hayami joins me and takes the phone from my hand. She's better at pretending to be Willa than I am. Markus would know the second I replied that something was amiss, as I have no way of filtering my answers.

"What should I tell him?" she asks.

"Tell him that we're all okay and stuck in the house due to

a snowstorm. Tell him that this helps our situation, as no one could reach the house even if they wanted to."

Hayami types out a text and then passes it to me.

> Nothing to report other than two feet of snow surrounding the property. No need to worry. We have supplies. The only good thing about the snow is that no one is getting within spitting distance of us, as all the roads are impassable. Hayami is fine. She's been busy with her coursework. Over and out.

It's perfect—businesslike enough to be an official report of what's going on, but also with the little chatty side of Willa. You don't work within a team without getting to know one another, and Willa has been working for the Devalls for the last six years. Markus told me that Willa is the longest-standing female bodyguard Hayami's had who hasn't left after one of her tantrums.

Feeling like I'm detonating a bomb, I hit Send and we wait several seconds before the phone beeps, making me jump.

We read it together.

> Keep an eye on the weather and keep me informed.

"Markus is so miserable," Hayami says, pocketing Willa's phone.

"He has a stressful job," I tell her. "And he has to answer to your father."

"Don't we all?" She moves over to the door. "Come on, this snow isn't going to shovel itself."

HAYAMI WIPES HER FOREHEAD, PUSHING HER WOOLLY HAT UP and squinting at me.

"Fuck me, this is hard work." She pulls a strand of hair from her face and tucks it into her coat. "I can't see shit because of the snow, my back is killing me, and my hands are red raw even under my gloves."

We've been clearing the path for just over an hour. It's one of those jobs where you feel like you're getting nowhere, like trying to clear sand from the desert.

"Go inside. I'll finish up," I tell her as I heave another mound of snow to the side.

"I'm not quitting. I'm just saying that this is no fun."

"There aren't many things in life that are fun."

"No, I guess not." She leans on her shovel. "You ever had a snowball fight?"

I stop and look at her. Her eyes are narrow, and there's a hint of a smirk at the corners of her mouth. My heart rate spikes.

"Not since I was a kid."

She lays down her shovel and picks up some snow.

"Don't even think about it," I tell her, but she just grins. "This won't end well."

"I don't doubt that," she says, rolling the snow into a smooth ball.

"You throw that at me, and I'll come for you." There's a growl to my voice that isn't intentional, and I can imagine that neither is the flush that works its way up Hayami's cheeks. I wonder if she's thinking the same thing as me, about how much I'd love to chase her.

HAYAMI

I gulp.

This wouldn't be the first time Fenrir has chased me.

The last time I ran from him was at the fair, when he stopped me from going on the ghost train with a guy I'd met at university. I'd been trying to run away from my problems. When he'd caught me, I asked him how I could escape my life.

He never answered me, as we were disturbed by Bastian. But here, now, with a snowball cupped in my hand, I wonder if I can outrun him this time.

With a shriek, I launch the snowball right at his face. As soon as it leaves my hand, the adrenaline pumps down into my legs and sets me off running.

But the snow is so deep that I barely move. I try to wade through it, but it's up past my knees, and my boots aren't the best for quick movements.

When I reach the edge of the drive, that's when I feel the snowball hit the back of my head. Ice slithers down my neck.

"Shit, that's cold," I say as I turn. He's right behind me, balling the snow casually, just striding up with a devilish look in his eyes that makes my knees go weak.

I bend to pick up some snow, but he's too close. I try to run again, but just as I pick up my pace, another snowball hits the back of my coat, and I scream and laugh.

As I turn, I hold my hands up in mock defence, and just before he reaches me, I say, "I surrender. You got me."

But he's already got me, already has his arms around me. I hold on to his forearms, and his smile disappears.

Dropping my arms, I step back. What's happening here? Why do I feel this attraction to him? And does he feel it too, or am I just a job to him?

I've no way of knowing the answers.

He presses his lips together and says, "You shouldn't start things you can't finish, Hayami," and I'm not sure whether he's referring to the snowball fight or something else entirely.

FORTY-THREE

HAYAMI

PRESENT

FENRIR FINISHES CLEARING THE PATH TO THE WOOD STORE, and I head inside to make us some soup, because I need to get away from him, his words running on a loop.

Don't start things you can't finish.

I don't understand what he meant by that. Was he referring to the snowball fight, which was only a bit of fun to lighten the mood, or was he referring to this morning when I'd watched him in the shower?

I've no idea, but I'm hoping cooking will distract me.

The kitchen feels different this morning. No shadows are clinging to the corners of the room. There are no drawers like monsters with their jaws open wide, and no sharp objects like teeth waiting to bite. It seems strange that this happened only hours ago, and now there's no evidence of it, like it never really happened at all.

After tying my hair back, I roll up my sleeves and assess the ingredients I have to work with.

It isn't long before the kitchen smells of tomatoes, basil, and hot bread.

Right on cue, Fenrir arrives in the kitchen, shrugging off his coat and hanging it over the large radiator. His right cheek is flushed pink with the cold, yet the left side of his face remains pale, the scarred skin never changing colour.

"Just in time," I say as I place a steaming bowl of soup on the table.

A nod is all the thanks I get as he sits.

We eat in silence that's fractured by the scraping of spoons and the tearing of bread. He doesn't look at me, and I can't seem to look away from him. All the while, a tension brews that began the minute his head turned towards the open doorway to the en suite this morning.

I've tried to ignore it. Tried to pretend it didn't happen. I've tried to be funny, light-hearted, and comical to ease the tension that sits at the table with us, but it hasn't worked.

As soon as I've finished, I clean the kitchen and head upstairs. I don't tell him where I'm going. He'll work it out for himself, but I need to be alone, and this is the only place I can be alone in this house.

Closing the door to my en suite, I lean against it, taking in large gulps of air as I try to clear my thoughts. People can go crazy when cooped up for long periods, and maybe that's what's happening here. Fenrir and I have been alone for several days now. Throw in the bizarre occurrences, and no wonder we're starting to act strangely towards each other. Maybe that's all this is, just cabin fever setting in.

I turn on the shower and allow the water to heat before stripping off and stepping under the stream.

I close my eyes and let the hot spray warm my body. This is what I needed. The snow had chilled me, the ice down my back had been almost painful, and my hands had been so red when I'd come back inside. Cooking had thawed me out a little, the soup defrosting my insides, but the water now washes away the icy atmosphere that accompanied our meal, and it's bliss.

Dipping my head under the faucet, I let the water run over my skin, cleansing away the little niggles, the silly thoughts, and the strain at the table. I remain this way for several minutes, just letting the water do its job, until I hear a noise.

The door opens.

I freeze.

What the fuck?

I'm relieved when Fenrir steps into the room, but it's quickly replaced with confusion.

What is he doing here?

He says nothing. His face gives nothing away. He just leans against the far wall, arms folded, watching me.

Okay. Okay, I get this.

He *did* see me this morning watching him in the shower. No wonder the atmosphere has been frosty. But this? What is this?

Then it hits me.

This is payback.

I watched him, so now he's watching me. Fair is fair.

Don't start things you can't finish.

Is he punishing me? Is he trying to humiliate me? Is that what he thinks I was doing this morning, embarrassing him?

Shit. I've no idea what's going through his head. I haven't a clue what to do, so I do the only thing I can think of, which is to carry on taking my shower and try to show him I'm not fazed.

So, I wash my hair, taking my time to lather up the shampoo and rake through the conditioner, trying to ignore the mix of nerves and desire that mingle like the soap and water. Then I wash my body, rubbing the sponge up and down my legs, over my breasts, and down my arms, all whilst feeling him watching, which sends an erotic charge running through me.

But I have to ignore it. Two can play at this game, and I won't let him think he's rattled me, because that's all this is—purely a game. This can't be anything other than him trying to get under my skin, payback for my Peeping Tom act this morning.

When I'm done, I turn off the water, brace myself, and open the cubicle door.

There's a second where I'm standing naked, facing Fenrir, all of me on display, no shower screen to hide behind. Then he takes a step forwards, pulls the towel from the heater, and holds it out to me.

Slowly, I step into it and say, "I think that makes us even now."

It feels clever, the right thing to say, and I want to believe I have the upper hand, have survived his little payback.

But then he leans in and whispers in my ear, "Not quite," before wrapping the towel around me and leaving the room.

FENRIR

Exiting the en suite, I've no idea of the can of worms I've possibly just opened, but then I recall that I wasn't the one who started this.

And I've had enough. There's too much going on in this house for me to be playing mind games with Hayami. The stunt in the en suite wasn't planned. When I realised she'd gone for a shower, I had a feeling it was now or never.

We could be stuck up here for days, even weeks, and with the strange shit going on, I don't have the patience to try to resist her any longer. I know what her plan was: to lose her virginity and destroy her father's business deal. But now, we're hidden away here, with no chance of her executing this plan, and that only leaves one thing. One person who can help her out.

Me.

Does she want me to do the job of taking her virginity, ruining her father's plan of selling her as a "pure" woman? I have no fucking idea. But she said that she'd happily let anyone take it from her, determined to piss off her father and whoever her future husband might be.

Although this isn't the way I want her, I can't help but think this might be the only way I can have her, and the thought of someone else doing it makes me want to crush something. I've no doubt she was serious about her plan, considering the calibre of bloke she had clamped onto her tits when I busted the door down in the toilets the night we got the code red. It still makes my blood boil just thinking about it. If she'd been willing to let some scumbag like him take her virginity, then she'd stoop as low as letting someone like me, someone who looks the way I do. Hell, all she'd have to do is close her eyes.

I'd do anything for her. Anything.

The stunt in the shower was me setting this in motion, placing the piece on the board and letting her make the next move.

I'm just not sure whether it'll be checkmate or game over.

FORTY-FOUR

HAYAMI

STORMING OUT OF THE EN SUITE, I FOLLOW HIM INTO THE bedroom, where he turns and faces me. I can't read him. I have no clue about his thoughts, but I'll be damned if he's going to get the last word.

"What the fuck is that supposed to mean?" I say, folding my arms over the towel I've tucked around my body.

"You tell me," he replies. It should sound condescending, but he doesn't look smug, more inquisitive.

"Okay, I admit, I watched you in the shower this morning, okay? There, I've said it, owned up, confessed to being a pervert. But you were the one poking me in the back with your fucking hard-on."

I wait for him to grin, to acknowledge that he's made me confess, but he doesn't. Instead, he just stares at me until he speaks.

"And whose fault was my hard-on?" There's no joke intended.

"I don't know. Some dirty dream you were having? Some

woman you've left behind? Your last lay? How the hell would I know?"

"There's only one woman who gets me hard, Hayami."

I want to say, "Lucky her," but his gaze is so intense, I can almost feel it touching my skin.

One woman.

Was he thinking about this woman whilst I was grinding myself against him? God, I feel so embarrassed—until he takes a step forwards and something clicks.

One woman.

Me?

I'm about to ask, because I can't stand this pressure.

"You."

He says it, throws it out into the room like a fucking bomb, and I think my body is going to explode.

Fuck.

I'm lost now. I don't understand. I thought he just tolerated me. I thought he saw me as a job and nothing more. But no. What he's saying is that I make him hard, that he must think about me in the way I think about him. And right now, I don't know what the hell to do with this.

It's not hearts and roses; it's not a declaration of any kind of feelings other than carnal lust, a basic reaction that most hot-blooded people have when they find someone attractive. I need to remember this. He's also been cooped up in this house for days with no sleep and no sexual outlet. Of course I gave him a hard-on this morning. Then the poor guy tried to take care of it, and I thought I'd sit back and watch the show.

"I didn't know," I stammer. "I shouldn't have watched you. And I know that's why you came and watched me just then, to get even. So, we're even now."

"We aren't," he says, still no smirk at playing me like this.

"Why not?" I shift my weight from one foot to the other.

"Because you watched me masturbating. I watched you take a shower. That isn't the same."

My cheeks heat, and I hope to God he doesn't see the redness that must be spreading across my face.

"So, Hayami, how are we going to even out the balance?"

Oh my God.

My whole aim for the past six months has been to have sex, to be rid of my virgin status. I've been waiting for this moment for so long, but now that it's here, I've frozen.

Is that what Fenrir is doing? Offering to solve my little problem? If he is, then all my fucking Christmases have come at once, because I'd sell my soul for this man to kiss me, let alone fuck me. Maybe it's the reason I can't move, can't think, because I *actually* want this. The other guys were just a means to an end, a way of getting what I needed. But this? This is different. *He* is different, and now I feel like a little kid wanting to play with the older, cool kid.

"You want to get yourself off whilst I touch myself, is that it?" I swallow hard, wishing I felt as brave as my words, but this is unknown territory for me. All I have to go on is the smutty books I've been reading for the past few years.

Now he smirks, and I want to slap him. *This is the part he chooses to laugh at?*

"If only it were that simple," he says at last, and I can't stand it any longer.

"What, then? What do you want? Are you offering to help me out here, be the one who's going to take my virginity? Do you want to fuck me?"

He clicks his tongue to the roof of his mouth, and my heart sinks when he says, "No, Hayami, I don't want to fuck you."

I want the room to swallow me whole.

I'm such a fucking idiot. Way out of my depth. He must hate me. Really fucking hate me, and he's chosen now to reveal his true feelings: that he despises me and thinks I'm just some rich spoiled bitch who has tantrums because she can't get her own way.

But before I can charge at him, I note the darkness in his eyes, the way he's staring at me like he wants to devour me... the step he takes towards me, which makes the rest of the room disappear as he says, "I want you, Hayami. I want to taste every bit of you, touch every inch of you, worship every part of you until I don't know who I am anymore. I want to consume you until all you can feel is me, inside your head, between your legs, and on every word you utter. I want to devastate you, ruin you, blind you with such pleasure that all you see is me. But I know if we do this, I won't be happy with just one fuck. Once won't be enough. I'll want more. So much more, and I'm not sure if that's what you want. So, I'm asking you now, is this what you want?"

Heat pools between my legs, and my chest swells with the breath I've been holding.

I want to worship you.

I want to ruin you.

All this time. All this time, I didn't know.

Once won't be enough.

He's asking me. Giving me the choice. Is this what I want?

Without thinking, without hesitating, I drop the towel.

FENRIR

Fear. That's what I felt after I told her what I want. Gut-wrenching fear that she'd walk away. Laugh in my face. Spit at me. Tell me this isn't what she wants, because how could she? How could *anyone* want such a monstrous person?

But when she drops that fucking towel, my heart erupts, and I have to hold myself back.

This will be her first time.

I have to remember this. Six months of fantasies are clawing to get out, but I have to take it slow.

I *will* take it slow. Just this once.

***

HAYAMI

There's a second where he doesn't move, doesn't say anything, just stares at my naked body. Even after his declaration, I have a moment where I think this could be a trick, a stupid game, a way of humiliating me. Then he looks me in the eye and I see it—the hunger, the need—and I'm shaking.

"Are you ready?" he asks.

I nod, afraid of what words might spill from my mouth.

"Show me."

What? I don't know what he means, and he must see my panic, as he says, "Show me you're ready."

My pulse pounds in my ears as I register what he wants me to do. Taking a deep breath, I slip my hand down my stomach and then between my legs. Slowly, I push two fingers inside myself. I'm wet, warm, ready.

I bring them out and show them to him.

He eyes them carefully and then tuts.

"You're not ready, Hayami. This is your first time, and you saw the size of me this morning. I won't be responsible for ripping you to shreds. Come here." He beckons me with the crook of his finger, and without thinking, I move towards him as he sits on the edge of the bed.

His head is level with my stomach, so close I can feel his breath against my skin.

"Place your foot on the bed." He pats the side of the bed next to him.

I do as I'm told, lifting my leg and placing my foot on the bed. I should be feeling shy, embarrassed even, but desire engulfs these emotions to the point where he could ask me to get on my knees and beg, and I would.

With both hands, he grips my waist and pulls me towards him.

Slowly, so fucking slowly, he runs his thumb down my stomach and continues until it reaches my pussy. He stops for a brief second.

It's agony, and I have to stop my hips from involuntarily thrusting towards him. That is until he slides his thumb down and over my clit, and something explodes behind my eyes.

Oh my God.

No one has ever touched me here. No one. And it feels like magic. It feels like I'm under a spell. It feels like nothing else matters as long as he keeps touching me.

I bite my lip as he lightly circles my clit before dipping his thumb inside me. He was right. I wasn't nearly wet enough for him. But I am now as his thumb slides in and out of me, his finger now toying with my clit as my breath catches in my throat.

He's gentle, the pressure so light it only makes me want it more. My head spins, my fists clench, and I think I'm going to come, but then he pulls his hand away.

What the fuck?

I panic. Is this the part where he pulls back and tells me this was all a joke? When he laughs in my face and says this was all to humiliate me?

And just when I think this is all too good to be true, he pulls my hips towards his face and his tongue does one long lap of my pussy.

The leg I'm standing on buckles.

Holy fuck.

I've read about this in so many books, but nothing could have prepared me for what it feels like.

Fuck!

Sparks ignite in my pussy and travel through my body as I grip his hair and push his face into me.

It's animalistic. It's brutal. And I can't get enough.

His tongue laps at me, flicks my sensitive spot, and then dips inside me, and the whole room melts away. His hand squeezes my bottom as the other guides my hips forwards, and I think I'm going to pass out.

My leg wobbles.

"Fuck, I can't stand," I say through ragged breaths.

Fenrir pulls back and I'm bereft, devastated that he's stopped, taken away my pleasure when it was building so fucking high. He grabs my waist and twists me onto the bed, then takes hold of both my ankles. He stares at me for a second, appearing to take in my splayed legs, my heavy breathing, and flushed cheeks, before kneeling and placing my legs over his shoulders.

Picking up where he left off, his tongue flicks over my clit. My back arches as he slides two fingers inside me, and I grab his hair and hold his face still as the first orgasm anyone has ever given me shatters through my body.

"Holy shit." I clench my teeth as my breath rushes from my lungs, trying to steady the roll of euphoria washing over me. My stomach clamps, my legs tense as I ride through my orgasm. "Holy fucking shit," I say as the last tremors pulse through me.

Fenrir inches back, sitting up on his heels as he regards me. I thought he'd look smug and pleased with himself, but no. He looks focused, like the job isn't done yet.

Reaching for his belt, he asks, "Are you on birth control?"

Pushing myself up on my elbows, I answer, "Yes." His eyes narrow, so I explain. "My mum took me to the doctor not long after I started my periods because they were really painful. The doctor put me on birth control to help with the pain. Nothing to do with my sex life, as I was fourteen at the time. I've been on it ever since, and I obviously don't have any diseases."

"Me neither," Fenrir says and continues to unfasten his belt.

I sit up and push his hands away to try and take over, but he stops me.

"Not this time," he says, and must see my confusion. "Your first time should be about you and only you. I can wait."

Looking up at him, I frown. "But I want to."

He sighs, shakes his head slightly, then moves his hands away. I remove his belt and pull his zip down.

His black boxers are tight and do nothing to hide the bulge. He closes his eyes momentarily as if steeling himself before I hook my fingers over his waistband and pull them down.

Holy shit. He isn't going to fit in my mouth, but I will certainly try.

Wetting my lips, I slowly take the tip of him into my mouth and flick my tongue over his head whilst gripping the base. He lets out a low growl, which spurs me on. I'm already wet, but with each lick, each little suck of him, heat pools between my legs and only makes me want him more.

His breathing gets faster as I get a little braver, taking more of him into my mouth, his head hitting the back of my throat. I speed up, my hand and jaw working in tandem until he grips my hair and pulls my head back.

"I don't want to come in your mouth." He pushes me back onto the bed and climbs on top of me. His eyes are intense, fuelled with desire. There's a second when I feel I should be afraid.

"I'm ready," I say, gripping the sheets, as if having something to hold on to will help brace me.

"I'll take it slow because it will hurt, but only for a second. If you want me to stop, you need to tell me, and I'll stop."

I nod to show him I'm paying attention when all I'm really thinking about is how badly I want this. I've never felt like this before. All the times I've tried to get laid, it's always been about getting the job done, ticking the box. But this is different. *I want this.* I want *him*. If I don't get him, I'll fucking scream.

He positions himself as he takes hold of both my ankles in one hand, then rubs his cock up my centre.

My eyes flutter closed, but I don't want to miss anything. He continues to rub his cock over me, coating it in my pleasure before he gently places the tip at my entrance.

"Look at me, Hayami," he says. I meet his gaze. "It's going to sting, but I'll help." He drops my ankles, my legs flopping onto his shoulders as he pushes deeper inside me. And there it is, the fucking sting, but as the pain builds, he places his thumb on my clit, and I moan.

"Oh my God."

He pushes on, slowly dipping all of him inside me until I feel his thighs against the back of my legs. Then he pulls back, continuing to massage my clit, and I think I'm dying, think I'm in heaven and he's a fucking angel.

None of the books I've read have prepared me for this. None of them.

"Hayami," he snaps.

"Yes."

"Do you want me to stop?"

"Fuck no. You dare stop and I'll scratch your fucking eyes out." I grip his legs, pulling him into me.

He smiles, and I swear to God, I've definitely died.

And now he fucks me, slow to start, then faster, deeper, pushing into me and then pulling out, toying with me, playing with me until my body can't hold back any longer. As my back arches and my breathing ceases, I feel him swell within me, and that's enough to tip me over the edge. My orgasm crashes through me as Fenrir holds himself deep inside me, the feeling of him pulsing only prolonging the ecstasy that rolls through my body.

"Fuck, oh fuck!" I cry as Fenrir exerts one final thrust before dropping beside me, his face in the crook of my neck as he catches his breath.

Seconds pass. I feel weak yet powerful, as if I've just discovered a superpower I didn't know I had. I never thought it would feel like that, never expected it to be so intense, and I now know why he said he wouldn't be able to stop at only doing it once.

He pushes up on his arms and pulls out, then tells me to wait. He stands. I want to look at him, to marvel at his body, but I'm exhausted and still catching my breath. He must go into the en suite, as when he returns, it's with tissues, which he uses to clean me up.

I sit up, my legs shaking, my arms like cooked noodles. I feel different. It's cliché, I know, but I do. I feel like a whole new world has been opened up to me, one I've only read about in books, and this man has led me there by the hand. I want to kiss him for it.

But we haven't kissed. Is that strange? I'm not sure. It feels wrong not to have kissed him, too clinical, like this was just a transaction between two people. I want to kiss him. I want to smother him with all of me. I'm not sure whether the two orgasms have made me feel brave, but I grab his head in my hands and lean in. He freezes under my touch, my hand covering his scars, and for a fleeting second, I think I've done the wrong thing, touched him in a way he isn't comfortable with, but I'm lost in this heady moment, post-orgasmic pleasure leaving me feeling drunk and slightly giddy.

"Thank you," I whisper before I place my lips on his and kiss him like I'm starving, like he's the only food I need. He tastes of me, but I don't care. I want this. I want him. I want him to know how much this means to me. Wrapping my arms around him, I pull him closer, his clever tongue setting me on edge again.

His mouth moves down my neck, giving me the chance to inhale some much-needed air.

"I want to do it again." My voice is breathy, my words heavy with desire.

"We will, but you need time to recover," Fenrir says at last.

"I don't," I protest.

"Yes, you do, because I told you before that I was only going to be gentle this one time." He pulls away, a warning look flashing over his face.

"And then what?" What does he mean? I wasn't taking it all in before. I was so nervous, so wrapped up in this moment that I'd imagined for so long, that I wasn't thinking about what he was saying.

"Then, Hayami, I will fuck you how I know you want it."

"How do I want it?" I'm confused now. What the hell does he mean?

His eyes narrow, and his head dips. "All those times, Hayami, when I've had to restrain you, when I've held you down and you've bitten me, scratched me, fought me as if your life depended on it, tell me it didn't turn you on."

I gulp.

Because he's right. Nothing made me wetter than when I've fought with him, when he's chased me, when I've known he'll catch me, and when he does, I'll get to feel his hands on me, rough and unyielding.

"How?"

"I could see it in your eyes, felt it in your body. You wanted it that way, and I'll give you what you want, but it'll be different. There will be rules."

"What rules?" Just talking about this is getting me worked up again.

"You need to remember that it's all part of the game, the things I'll say to you, things I will make you do. And it might go too far. So, we need a safe word."

"Can't I just say stop?" I'm shaking now. Fear, adrenaline, anticipation, all of it one big fucking cocktail.

"'Stop' won't cut it," Fenrir says. "You'll be telling me to stop, begging me to stop, when really you don't want me to stop at all. That's all part of the game. We need a word that we both know means that it has to end. One word. It can't be mistaken for anything else, a clear word. You need to tell me what that word is."

Shit. This feels so heavy, yet I've never felt desire like it. One word. *Think.*

And then I have it.

"Kemono."

"Kemono," Fenrir repeats. "What does it mean?"

"It's Japanese for 'beast.'" He quirks his eyebrow. "That's what I called you in my head when we first met. I called you the Beast."

"I should feel hurt."

"Don't. It was a compliment. And now I know it's true. You are a beast. *My* beast."

FORTY-FIVE

FENRIR

PRESENT

"MY BEAST."

Those two little words unhinge me.

Hayami looks at me and then down at my torso.

"Can I touch them?"

She's referring to my scars. Apart from the ones on my face when she'd held my head earlier, she managed to avoid touching the ones that run down the side of my body whilst I fucked her. I'm not sure if she intentionally avoided them, but even so, the fact that she's asked for permission shows she knows how sensitive I am about them.

"Why would you want to?"

"Because I find them beautiful. I know that must sound strange because they were made by something terrible, something that hurt you and took your family from you, but they're part of you, which makes them yours. And I find everything about you fascinating."

The thought of anyone touching my scars sets me on edge. Anyone but her.

Holding her hand, I place it on my chest before letting go. She keeps it there, smoothing her fingers over the gnarled skin.

Her other hand joins in, tracing my burned flesh, exploring the knotted surface. I don't feel her fingers—the nerve damage means I have very little sensitivity left. But inside, I feel her touch; it goes deeper than the surface of my broken skin.

She kneels, reaching up to follow the scarring onto my face before cupping my head in her hands.

"Has anyone ever touched them?"

"No. Only you."

She nods, seeming pleased with this as she kisses me gently on the lips before moving her mouth over my scars. Her lips stroke them, caress them, her tongue carefully licking over the skin as if she's trying to heal my flesh with her mouth. I don't feel the tingle of her tongue. I feel something else. That she wants to touch the worst part of me, wants to taste it, wants to be near is so amazing that I can't look away.

"I'm scared," Hayami says, pulling back from me.

For a second, I think she's referring to the strange goings-on that have been happening, but she cocks her head to one side.

"I'm scared about what happens when we leave this house."

"What do you mean?"

"I mean that, as long as we're here, we can do this. I can touch you. I can kiss you. We can fuck. We can be this way. But when we leave…?"

I push her hair from her face. "When we leave here, you won't want me anymore."

"That's not true," she says.

As much as I want to believe her, she's only saying this

because I'm here now. I've just given her what she's wanted for so long. She thinks I'm the only man who can give her this. And as much as I'd like to think she's right, she'll change her mind the minute we leave this place.

"Let's not worry about anything else. Right now, it's just you and me and this house."

"I don't ever want to leave this house," she says as she rests her head on my chest. "As long as you're here, I don't ever want to leave."

As I sink into her embrace, reality checks in. Will she feel the same after she reads Junko's journal? Because I have to let her read it. I know this now. We can't remain in this house any longer without Hayami knowing the truth about what stalks these walls. But I'm torn between keeping her here and setting her free.

What if I can't do either?

FORTY-SIX
FENRIR

I TURN ON EVERY LIGHT, KEEPING EACH ROOM ABLAZE AS THE night sky frames the snow and turns the white world into a purple hue. It's surreal, the way the darkness pollutes the purity, turning the enchanted scenery into something much more sinister.

We've spent the evening doing target practice in the garage. I found it hard to focus on the lesson, to not be distracted by the sight of Hayami gripping my gun, her stance near perfect, her shots so much more accurate. And I know she's been looking at me differently. I can feel the way her gaze slides over my body, like she's eyeing up what she wants. I wanted to fuck her in the garage, to set up our first scenario, but it's too soon and it isn't safe, not with loaded firearms. I need her to take the guns seriously. She also needs time to heal, for her body to recover. I wasn't joking when I said I wouldn't be gentle.

I know what I've done is wrong.

I can't keep her.

She doesn't belong to me. She doesn't even belong to herself.

She belongs to Barrett Devall.

When the snow clears and we get the go-ahead to return to the mansion, my dream will shatter, and things will have to go back to the way they were. We've been secluded up here for so long that the real world is slipping from our grasp. I want to live in this fantasy for as long as I can, so I'm trying not to think about what happens when our time's up, when the snow melts—and this dream along with it.

In the evening, we curl up on the sofa in the large living room and binge-watch a series on Netflix, sharing a large bag of crisps, something I've never done with any woman. It surprises me how intimate it feels, how normal. I've never felt anything like normality, and I can't imagine Hayami has either.

Just before midnight, she decides she wants to go to bed.

I follow her up the stairs, her hand held loosely in mine as if she's afraid that if we aren't touching, I might disappear. This new contact is something I'm going to have to get used to. Before, I had boundaries I couldn't cross, no matter how much I wanted to.

But now?

Now I have her.

All of her, any time I want. The thought is dangerous, all-consuming, and so incredibly powerful that I almost don't know what to do with it.

She disappears into the en suite, leaving the door wide open as she gets ready for bed. I hear the tap running, the splashing of water as I climb onto her bed and settle myself on one side, resting my back against the headboard. Junko's journal has been stuffed into my back pocket for the entire evening, reminding me that there's still more to be learned before I can tell Hayami about what I've found.

Guilt nips at my skin at keeping this from her, but I need to be sure of the outcome. I need to be positive that what I'm about to learn can be tackled, dealt with, and addressed. I'm not looking for a happy ending—Junko's mental health is a testament to that—but I am looking for a solution.

Hayami appears in the doorway, drying her hands with a towel and only wearing a tiny T-shirt. My cock stirs, and I tell it to heel. Curbing my feral thoughts is nothing new. I'm a master at keeping these feelings under control, but it appears as though Hayami isn't. I see the look in her eyes, the way she licks her lips as she tosses the towel to the floor and saunters over to the bed.

Straddling me, she flicks her hair over her shoulders and bites her bottom lip before grinding her pussy against my cock.

"I'm not tired yet," she says, her hands finding their way under my T-shirt.

"And I said I wouldn't fuck you again today, Hayami," I remind her.

"And I respect that," she replies, her hips swaying to an invisible tune, my cock getting harder the more she touches me. "Technically, it's after midnight, and you didn't say anything about *me* fucking *you*. And I owe you."

"Owe me?"

"I watched you pleasuring yourself. Now you get to watch me," she says.

Like the fucking temptress she is, she pulls the T-shirt over her head, and my resolve lands with it on the floor.

FORTY-SEVEN

HAYAMI

IT'S OFFICIALLY THE TWELFTH DAY SINCE WE ARRIVED, AND I don't know who this person is, this version of me, sitting astride this hunk of a man, fingers tugging at his belt as if trying to pick a lock. I don't recognise myself as I pull at his waistband and slide his boxers down his hips, his cock springing free. For someone who's only done the deed once, I don't feel like this is something I should be doing—taking the lead, setting the tone—but I've been held back for so long, my romance books my only guide in this sexual world. Now I feel like a panther who's been set free. I've been caged for too long, pacing the bars, watching this strange world from afar, and now Fenrir's unlocked the door, swinging it wide open, and I want nothing more than to explore.

He said no more sex today, but it's past midnight, so it's a new day. Now it's my turn to show him what I know, what all those books have taught me. And if I get my kicks whilst I'm at it, then that's just a bonus.

"How wet are you?" Fenrir asks as I lower my mouth over his cock.

"Wet enough," I reply, then flick my tongue over the tip.

"I doubt that," he says, his eyes closing for the briefest of seconds as he runs his fingers through my hair. "You need to be really wet, Hayami, if it isn't going to hurt."

"I've only just got started. By the time I'm done, I'll be dripping for you." I smile as I see the confusion pass over his face. He thinks I know nothing, that my romance books are all heaving bosoms and face fanning.

Sitting up on my knees, I grab the base of his cock and position it below my pussy, as if I'm going to lower myself onto it. Instead, I slide myself down it, the wetness coating his cock. The tip rubbing against my clit sends a blaze of pleasure coursing through my core.

I repeat the motion, allowing his cock to linger at my entrance, pushing slightly inside before sliding back up and over my clit. Spitting on my free hand, I then swap and rub the wet hand up and down his shaft.

"Fuck," Fenrir hisses, his eyes glued to me, my body, taking in what I'm doing to him, what I'm doing to myself.

"Can you feel how wet I am now?" I ask.

"Fuck, yes." He leans his head back against the headboard. "But you need to be punished."

"Do I?" Keeping to my rhythm, I continue to slide my pussy up and down his cock, slipping him inside me briefly with each dip of my hips.

"I told you no more today, which you ignored, and now you're teasing me with your cunt," he moans.

"Are you going to punish me, then?" The urge to sit on his cock, to have him fully inside me, is getting to be too much. I'm not going to be able to hold out much longer. But I love the fact that he's getting as worked up as I am, and this is the only thing stopping me from fucking him like I want to.

As if in answer, he slaps lightly at one of my breasts, sending a jolt of desire surging through me. He glances at me, trying to read my face, trying to assess whether I'm okay with this.

"Is that all you've got?" I tease, placing one of my palms flat on his chest.

He doesn't answer, simply takes one of my nipples between his fingers and pinches it hard whilst slapping my other breast.

"Oh God." I don't recognise the moan that leaves me.

"This is only for starters, Hayami. I will punish you properly when I'm in control. Right now, I will let you have this, but only because you owe me," he says.

"And I always pay my debts."

He slaps at my breast again. Not hard enough to hurt, but enough to make it sting. I want more. I want to feel the buzz of pain, the rawness on my skin. I've been punishing myself for so long—it's nice to have someone else do it for a change.

I've picked up the pace, dipping his cock deeper each time, my clit throbbing. I'm going to come. I'm so close, so wet that he's slipping in my hand.

"Sit on my cock," Fenrir says. "I want to come inside you. I want you to feel what you do to me."

I almost come at his command, but I manage to slip him inside me just in time. He grabs hold of my hips and a fierce look crosses his face as he pounds into me from underneath, hitting that spot inside me like a detonator, making me come so fiercely that I have to put both hands against his chest to steady myself as the waves of pleasure ripple through me like thunder over the sky.

FORTY-EIGHT

FENRIR

IT DOESN'T TAKE HER LONG TO FALL ASLEEP, WHICH IS NO surprise considering what she did to me just forty minutes ago. It was wild. I've never had a woman take control like that. I didn't think I'd like it if I'm honest. But fuck me, it was so blindingly hot, I can still feel the aftershocks, still feel her thighs gripping me, the clench of her pussy around my cock as she came.

But now, she's sleeping next to me, her hair a dark sprawling mass like a halo, her breath so light compared to the heavy breathing she'd been doing earlier. And I take the opportunity to read some more of Junko's journal.

Day Twenty-four
The days are blurring together. Aside from the
store deliveries, nothing marks the passing of time
here—just the switch from day to night, and the
nights are always the worst. I fill the daylight hours

pressing wildflowers, making dorayaki, writing in this journal. But when darkness comes, I feel it—the house pressing in, a presence I can't name.

Two nights ago, I woke outside. No memory of leaving my bed. Just cold air, stones under my feet, and a knife in my hand. There was blood on the blade. I don't know whose. I don't know how I got there. I only remember the fear—fear that I'd hurt someone, fear that the house had taken hold of me. Barrett found me. Markus was there too, his hand on his holstered gun. They say I was sleepwalking. I let them believe it.

Barrett locked me in a guest room "for my own safety." But I saw the looks he and Markus were giving each other. They think I'm mad.

Maybe I am. Or maybe it's this house.

I lay awake all night afraid of what Barrett would do with his mad wife, if this was to be my new life—locked away here, or later in some hospital. In the morning, I feared the worst, that this room would be my prison, until I realised I'd missed my period.

Scrambling through my toiletries bag, I was relieved to find a test but terrified to use it.

The test confirmed it: I'm pregnant. I'm not sure how I feel, but it's not the way I expected to feel—excited, jubilant. Instead, I feel afraid. Afraid of what this means, of how this changes things. It isn't just about me anymore. But here and now, the child changes everything.

I can't be sent away.

As soon as Barrett came to the room, I wasted no time and told him, with as much delight as I could muster, that I was carrying his child. His reaction was cautious, but I could see a degree of pleasure on his face. He'd finally got what he wanted, and so he agreed we can leave this house today. For that alone, I'm truly grateful.

Because I'm convinced something in these walls is trying to consume me.

And if nothing else, this baby has saved me from an unknown fate. But what awaits us both, I have no idea. All I know is that we are going home today.

This will be my last entry. I'm leaving this journal here in the library. I don't want these memories coming with me, and if anyone finds it, they'll know what lives here.

Kuchisake-Onna.

FORTY-NINE

FENRIR

THERE'S A TREMOR IN MY HAND AS I LAY THE JOURNAL DOWN on the bed.

The baby must have been Hayami. The timing is correct.

Fuck.

I'm not sure what to do with this information. I need to tell Hayami, but no matter how I construct the words "Your mum believed the house was haunted and her body was being possessed by Kuchisake-Onna," I can't seem to get over how ridiculous it sounds.

It'd probably be better for Hayami to read the journal herself, but I don't know how she's going to take it. She's seemingly unaware of what's been happening to her, her scientific brain refusing to consider the occult or paranormal as an explanation for what's been going on in this house.

But what happens when she does? What happens then?

I need to get her out of here, but we're snowed in, and the weather is getting worse by the second.

I smooth my hand down the side of her face and she stirs,

leans into my touch, then seems to settle back into the rhythm of sleep.

What the fuck am I going to do?

The pressure in my bladder tells me I need to pee. I haven't moved from the bed in hours. As carefully as I can, I slip from the bed and pad to the en suite, leaving the door open as I relieve myself.

Tiredness washes over me. I really need to sleep. But when? When can I let my guard down? I could wait until dawn, catch a few hours before Hayami wakes like I did the other morning, but I'm nervous after what I've read. Then there's the whole reason why we're out here in the first place —the very real threat from the outside, the gang war that Hayami has been caught in, the gang war that I instigated. Although I doubt we're in danger from gangsters in the middle of a snowstorm, I still have to remember my sole purpose for being here.

After washing my hands, I check the weather app on my phone. The snowstorm is set for the next few days, but there's a let-up in the snowfall coming up, which appears to last a few hours before the snow starts again. But even after the snow stops, the temperatures won't get above freezing, which means the snow will freeze into hard blocks of ice, so it'll be treacherous and difficult to dig out.

My phone pings in my hand, and I pause before returning to the bedroom as Willa's name pops up with a message.

> Proud mother of this little fella. He was born by C-section at 12:06 and weighs a healthy 7lb 3oz. Marta is a little sore but doing well. Love to you all, and we can't wait for you to meet him. Name TBC, as the name we chose doesn't seem to suit him now he's here. I'll keep you all posted.

It's a generic message probably sent to all her contacts.

Along with the message, there's a photo of a scrunched-up baby that could be either gender, with a red face and closed eyes, swaddled in a thick cream blanket and wearing a hat that looks like a tea cosy.

I'm not a baby person. They all look the same to me. I like kids once they get a bit older and can answer back. I'm tempted to reply, offering my name as a suggestion, but I'm sure Willa is tired and fending off a thousand other replies from her friends and family. Besides, I have more important things on my mind right now.

Slipping my phone into my back pocket, I head for the doorway, reminding myself to tell Hayami as soon as she wakes, as she'll want to know that Willa's baby is here safe and sound. But as I reach the doorway, I freeze.

The bed is empty, a dent in the mattress the only reminder of where I left Hayami. But this isn't what makes my blood stall.

Hayami is still in the room.

She hasn't left it.

She's floating on her back, two meters above the mattress.

I've never been paralysed with fear, not even when my family was burning to death. Terror usually spurs me into action, sends a jolt of adrenaline through me, the fight-or-flight mode activated. But here, now, watching her float above the bed renders me so utterly afraid that I can't move, can't breathe. All can do is stare at her body like it's a hideous magic trick.

Should I speak? Try to wake her?

But what if it isn't her? Then what?

A tingling sensation works its way up my arm and into my chest.

I need to do something.

I take a step into the room, and as I do, Hayami starts to turn. Her T-shirt hangs from her legs, her arms by her sides, her eyes remaining closed as she rotates from her back onto her front.

Quicker now, I move to the bed, looking underneath her, above her, trying to find the strings, the wires, the invisible ledge that'll reveal the trickery that's at work here. But there's nothing but air, nothing but space, nothing but the unbelievable notion that Hayami is suspended by… nothing.

There's the urge to touch her, to pull her down, but I don't want to wake her, frighten her, rouse the sleeping beast if she isn't Hayami, if something else is occupying her body right now.

Do I want to be faced with Kuchisake-Onna?

But I can't stand here and do nothing.

Just as I'm about to climb onto the bed, Hayami's eyes open, and she screams.

FIFTY

HAYAMI

THE SCREAM IS SO LOUD IT COULD LACERATE MY EARDRUMS, making me feel like they're bleeding. It takes a second before I realise that the scream is my own, just before I drop and land on the bed.

"It's okay. You're okay. I got you." Strong arms encase me, warm and familiar, Fenrir's voice bringing me out of the fog of the dream.

"What happened?" I ask breathlessly, my chest heaving as if a thousand volts have just been fired through my body.

He holds me like I've just broken, and he's trying to keep the pieces of me together.

"You were asleep and…." He regards me with such a pained look that my fear comes thundering back into my ribcage. I've never seen him look afraid. Never.

"I was dreaming. This horrible dream," I begin, because the look on his face is telling me that he has no idea what just happened either. "It was dark. Terrifyingly dark. The kind of blackness that clings to your skin and doesn't let go. I was scared, so fucking scared, but I'm not sure why. I'd done something, betrayed someone, and I was about to pay the price."

Fenrir stares at me.

"Then pain," I say, remembering the next part of the dream. "Bloodcurdling, searing pain. My face felt like it was on fire, the burn reaching my ears. My mouth felt raw and wet. And just as it felt like I couldn't take it anymore, that was when I screamed."

He waits as if this isn't enough, and it takes me a second to find the words, because dreams I can understand. Nightmares, night terrors—call them what you will—have been around since the beginning of time. They're nothing new. But what I saw when my eyes opened scared me the most.

Glancing at him, I swallow. "When I opened my eyes, I wasn't on the bed. I was above it, looking down at it. And then I fell and—" The terror reaches inside me, grips my vocal cords, and cuts off my words as Fenrir pulls me into his chest.

"It's okay," he tells me, but I push back.

"No, it's not okay. The sleepwalking is one thing. *That* I get. People sleepwalk. The dream is another. People dream. But they don't wake up floating above their bed. They *do not.* So either I'm going mad or something else is going on here." My eyes search his as if there might be a recording of what he saw behind those black pupils. "What happened when I screamed? Why were you out of bed?" Tears join the fear, swirling with a manic anger that threatens to consume me.

He blinks, takes a second, and then appears to compose himself.

"I got up to use the bathroom, and when I came back...." He closes his eyes, and I wonder if he's recalling what he saw or blocking it out.

"What? What did you see?"

FENRIR

She looks so scared, so afraid, but I don't know what's worse: knowing that what she saw really happened or that she was hallucinating. I falter. I don't know what to tell her. I don't want to frighten her any more than she is already, but the truth is, I'm scared too. I'm scared about what's going on here, about what she's becoming. About what or who is taking over her body and doing these things to her.

There's nothing else to do.

I pull Junko's journal from my back pocket and hand it to her.

FIFTY-ONE
HAYAMI

PRESENT

I SHOULD BE DELIGHTED WHEN FENRIR HANDS ME A BOOK.

I remember him finding it in the library only a few days ago, and I watched him read it after I told him to try reading something to pass the time, having no idea what it was.

"What is it?" I ask as I take the book from him.

His face looks haunted as he takes a breath and tells me that it's my mother's journal from the only time she stayed in this house, before I was born.

My mother's journal.

My eyes swim, and my hands shake. Normally, I love nothing more than to read. I can spend hours lost in the pages of a romance. But the reason why I love to read is that I know it's not real; it's all just a figment of some author's wild imagination. And no matter how much shit the author throws at the main characters, there'll be a happily ever after at the end of it all.

This, however, isn't going to be a light read. This hasn't been recommended by bookish fans. Because this isn't fiction. These are the words of my mother when she stayed in this house. Everything I'm about to read is real, and I can tell by Fenrir's face that it's not a happily ever after.

I give him no reaction as I take the book, open it to the first page, and begin to read.

PINS AND NEEDLES CREEP UP MY LEGS AS I SHIFT THEM OUT from underneath me. My body has seized up from sitting in the same position for God knows how many hours.

Fenrir has brought me cups of tea, toast and jam, and crackers with peanut butter, all of it untouched. I haven't been able to tear myself away from the words on the page, the words of my mother.

It's fascinating to hear inside my mother's head because, for most of the years of my life, she has been an enigma—disguised behind a fog of pills, blurred beneath the rippling glug of alcohol, the true person never quite finding her way to the surface. But here, within these pages, is a time before all that, when my mother was Junko—when she had a personality and hobbies. She liked to make tea the traditional way, enjoyed clothes, sewing, and took walks in the woods. This was my mother. *Is* my mother.

But everything is overshadowed by what else these pages contain.

By the time I reach the end, I'm numb.

I set the journal down on the bed.

Fenrir stares at me.

My legs are numb, my hands tingling from the lack of blood flow. I should move, get the circulation going again, but it feels as if my heart has stopped altogether—stalled by what I've just read, by what my mother believed lived within the walls of this house, by what she believed was trying to take control of her.

Kuchisake-Onna.

"Have you read it all?" I ask, biting the side of my cheek.

"Yes." His voice is so small, I barely hear it.

"And you're only showing me it now?" Rage brews in my stomach.

"It was never my intention to not tell you what it was," he begins. "I just wanted to read it first to make sure there was nothing in there that would cause you harm or distress."

The rage bubbles.

"Are you for real?" I spit. "So, what do you think I've just read, some light-hearted family saga? An emotional epic about a newlywed embracing the start of her married life?"

"Look, I know that contradicts what I've just said, but in light of what's happening here—"

"And what *is* happening here? What do you think *this* is?" I wave my hand over the bed, the place where, hours ago, I face-planted onto the mattress, having been asleep two feet above it.

"I don't know exactly, but I believe that Junko knew."

"You believe this?" I pick up the journal by the corner.

"I'm not sure. All I know is that things are happening in this house that also happened over twenty years ago, and not just to your mother but to others. Maybe it's time to look beyond the realms of the normal, beyond the realms of the living, because I can't explain what the hell is going on here."

Unable to process this, I drop the journal onto the bed. My logical brain is fighting it. I don't believe in spirits. I don't believe in ghosts. I don't believe in the supernatural. But I also can't explain what is happening in this house. I thought Fenrir was sleep-deprived. I thought I'd started sleepwalking—a perfectly natural reaction to upheaval, a perfectly reasonable trauma response. But my mother?

"You've had this journal for days," I accuse him. "You say you care about me, yet you kept this from me."

"It's *because* I care about you that I kept it from you. And not in the sense that I want to wrap you up in cotton wool, and that I don't think you have a right to know. I am, after all, your bodyguard. My job is to keep you alive. And knowing what a tough job that's been in the last six months, I thought it'd be best to vet the material before I gave it to you, but again, only to decide how best to tell you or present it to you. There could have been anything in there about your mother and father."

"And there is," I point out.

"But nothing about them and their relationship that you don't already know."

"No, just the fact that she was scared of him after he locked her up in a room and was probably going to section her." I almost laugh.

"And that's why I've sat here with you, remained by your side as you read every page, brought you drinks and food, reminded you that I'm here, that I will always be here for you no matter what."

"Because it's your job to keep me safe," I echo his words.

"Because keeping you safe goes beyond the bullets and death threats. Your well-being and mental health matter to me, even if they don't to you," he says. "Look here."

He leans over to the bedside table and picks up my current read. He flips to the front, finds what he's looking for, then spreads the pages and turns the book to face me.

"Think of me reading the journal before you as a list of trigger warnings." He taps at the page that lists the trigger warnings for my current read, which includes a whole host of stuff, some things I've never heard of. "I had no intention of keeping anything from you, of not letting you read the journal. I just needed to know what was in there before I gave it to you so I could prepare the trigger warnings."

I take a second, letting this sink in. He's being protective, that's all. And yes, I'm annoyed that he read it before me, but I can't argue with his intentions. If I'd have found it accidentally, then maybe I would have more to be cross about, but he just handed it to me. Besides, there's a part of me that knows it's stupid to fight with him. We're stranded in this house together. We only have each other. Not to mention the things we've shared, the emotions that now bind us, and there's a whole load of shit going down—most of which is inexplicable—so fighting with the only person who's here to help me is probably a bad move.

"Okay." I snatch my current read from his hand, worried my bookmark might fall out.

"Thank you."

The words sound strange coming from him. I don't think I've ever heard Fenrir say thank you for anything before— but that having been said, I've never had to forgive him.

"We need to move on to the more pressing matter of what the fuck we think this all means."

He draws his hand down his face. "I don't know. I don't know what or who to believe. The only thing I do know is what I've seen, what I've felt. Whether it's supernatural or not, something's going on here."

Even though my head is rattling—loose parts jangling because I don't know how to put them back together again— what he's saying does make sense.

"Okay. So this prompts the more important question: What the fuck are we going to do about it?"

He sits back on the sofa and lets out a long breath. He'll have been thinking about this, surely. This is his job: to fight the bad guys, to keep me safe. But this is something else. The usual bad guys are blood and bone; this is mist and mirage, an invisible threat we know little about—and one I'm still sceptical of because my brain refuses to believe such things.

But the sensation of opening my eyes to find myself staring at the mattress—the feeling of weightlessness, and then being dropped from a height—still lingers. I can't explain it, except to say I must have still been dreaming, even though I felt awake. And the other night, when Fenrir and I were upstairs and heard the noise in the kitchen, only to come down to find the drawers open and all the sharps laid out on the table—I have no logical explanation for that either, except perhaps some sick joke on Fenrir's part, altering the security camera footage. But what would he gain from that? And why would he do it? To make me think I'm going insane? Or because he is?

"Any suggestions?" I ask as Fenrir chews on his lip.

He sits up, as if he's going to say something profound. Instead, he just lets out an audible sigh before saying, "I'm not sure."

I stare at him. He's always known what to do, always has a plan, even when it involves sedating me, restraining me, or chasing me. So why doesn't he have one now?

"Okay, the way I see it, if this shit's real"—I slap my hand on the cover of my mother's journal—"then we have no other choice but to leave."

His eyes snap to mine. "We can't. Not in this weather."

"I get that we can't drive off the mountain, but why can't we leave on foot?" I shrug.

"Because there's a blizzard outside, which means visibility will be next to nothing. We don't have the right clothing for a snowstorm, and I'm not even sure how long it'd take us to reach the bottom of the mountain, by which point we'll have probably died of hypothermia. So as much as I agree with you that we need to get out of this house, to do so in this weather would be signing our death warrants. We need to remain here where we have shelter, heat, and food."

This is more like the Fenrir I know, the one who's looked at all solutions.

"Okay, so it's agreed: We stay put until the weather subsides. So, how do we deal with whatever shit we're dealing with?" I ask, pushing my hair behind my ears.

"I think we both need to agree on what exactly is going on here," Fenrir says, eyeing me carefully.

Inhaling deeply, I consider this. What do I think is going on here?

"Do you believe what my mother wrote in her journal?" I ask. We need to get to the bare bones of this, the million-dollar question.

"Yes," he replies.

"Why?" I shoot back.

"I don't know. It feels genuine." He scratches his chin.

"She could have made it all up. The ravings of a madwoman who'd been secluded in a house for too long with a tyrant of a husband," I suggest.

"She could, and if I'd have read the journal, having not been in this house, having not witnessed the things I've seen over these past few days, then I'd argue that yes, she was deluded, confused, seeing things." He leans closer to me. "But I have seen things too, felt things, watched you do things I can't explain. So now I have my own experiences to add to hers. And the more I think about it, the more it all makes sense that what she wrote was true. The question you should be asking yourself is: Do you believe in ghosts?"

He holds my gaze because he already knows my thoughts on this topic.

There are no such things as ghosts.

But before I get a chance to answer him, a phone rings.

FIFTY-TWO
HAYAMI

PRESENT

WE STARE AT EACH OTHER BEFORE OUR HEADS SWIVEL TO where the sound of the ringtone is coming from.

It's Willa's work phone.

"Shit," I say as Fenrir strides over to the mobile sitting on the bedside table. Panic swells in my chest.

This isn't a social call, one of her friends checking in. This is her work phone, so there can only be a handful of people calling her and expecting her to answer.

Fenrir picks it up, and we stare at the name on the screen. Markus.

"What do we do?" I ask, my voice quivering.

He takes a deep breath. "We answer it."

He presses Answer and places the phone to his ear. My stomach coils in on itself as I lean in to hear what's being said.

"Hello." He doesn't flinch, and I'm amazed by how calm and cool he appears.

"Fenrir?" Markus asks, then doesn't give him time to answer before he says, "Where's Willa?"

"She's in the shower," he replies, glancing at the open door where the shower stands empty.

"Okay," Markus says. I can taste the tension in the air, feel it humming down the phone line, and I pray that Markus remains oblivious, because right now, we are fucked. "Well, as soon as she gets out, tell her to call me."

"Of course." He angles his thumb over the End Call button, but Markus's voice carries through the air.

"Everything okay up there?"

"Yeah," Fenrir says, and I mime my hand churning, trying to silently tell Fenrir to give Markus something, anything to break the strangeness that's coating this call. Fenrir rolls his eyes at me, then says, "Besides the weather."

"The forecast looks pretty bad. You guys holding up all right?"

"Yeah. Other than being bored."

"And Hayami?" Markus enquires.

"She's fine."

"Good. Mr Devall is getting a little restless about the weather."

"If anything, it's doing us a favour," Fenrir explains. "The roads are impassable. There's no way anyone is getting anywhere near this house without a snowplough."

"As soon as the snow stops, Mr Devall will send a plough out to clear the road up to the house. He's already been on the phone with the company to remind them that it needs to be done as a matter of urgency." A bit of static crackles down the line, and I see Fenrir contemplating this. "Get Willa to call me as soon as she's out of the shower."

"Will do." This time, Fenrir doesn't hesitate. He ends the call and throws the phone onto the bed as if it's about to explode.

I run my hands through my hair as he stares at the device.

"Why do you think he wants to talk to her? Do you think it's something to do with Marta?" My brain is racing with possible reasons why Markus would want to talk to Willa.

"It might be about her maternity leave. Speaking of which, Marta's had the baby."

"What? When?" I throw my hands in the air.

"She messaged in the early hours," he says.

"And you're only telling me now? It's nearly dawn."

"I was going to tell you when you woke up, but then things got a little sidetracked. If you check your phone, I'm sure she messaged you."

Stepping away from him, I grab my phone that slipped under the covers and see the unopened message on my screen.

Opening it, I'm faced with a photo of a tiny baby and a message from Willa. Relief washes over me. Willa was there with Marta when she gave birth to their child. Willa got to see her son come into this world. Despite the bullshit we're currently dealing with, I remind myself that this is the one good thing to have come out of all this.

I did the right thing in sending her away. I repeat this mantra, trying to convince myself that it's true.

I reply quickly, sending my congratulations and best wishes, forgetting for a few seconds the shitstorm that Fenrir and I are heading for, and I don't just mean the weather.

After hitting Send, I throw my phone back onto the bed.

"What are we going to do?" I ask as I watch Fenrir chew on his bottom lip. "Markus is expecting Willa to call him. What happens when she doesn't call back?"

"I don't know." He begins to pace a small square of the room.

"We could call her, ask her to call Markus back," I suggest.

"But it'd be from her personal phone, not the work number."

"We could ask her to say that she's lost it," I offer.

"In the space of twenty minutes? Besides, there are trackers on all our phones. Markus knows this, and so does Willa. It wouldn't make any sense for us to tell him that she lost her work phone. No, there's no way around the phone situation." His face is stoic, though I feel like the stress is radiating from my skin, fooling no one that I'm really starting to panic now.

"Shit. Shit! What the fuck do we do?"

He stops pacing as if he's come to a decision.

"We don't do anything… yet. We wait for him to call us back," he says calmly.

"That doesn't solve our problem." I'm spiralling, overrun with thoughts of Willa being hunted down by my father's men, discovered in the maternity ward, and then Fenrir being held accountable for a decision *I* made.

"No, but it buys us some time."

I slump onto the bed, averting my eyes from Fenrir and the mess I've thrown him into.

"We could tell Markus that, before the storm, Marta went into labour, so I sent her to the hospital. I'm sure he would understand."

Fenrir glares at me, and I know, even as I said the words, that Markus *would* understand, because Markus is a man, a human being with emotions and feelings and empathy.

But my father is not. My father would only see the disobedience, the insubordination, the defiance, and the deception.

"What the fuck have I done?" I place my head in my hands.

Thick arms envelop me.

"Hey, stop this. You did the right thing. Willa was there

when Marta gave birth. She was there with her wife and got to watch her baby being born."

"Yeah, and I've put a goddamn price on her head and yours. When my father finds out what I did, it won't just be me who pays."

His grip tightens. "I won't let anything happen to you, Hayami."

I pull back, staring into his eyes.

"I mean it. I'll protect you until my very last breath."

Silence drenches the room until the wind whips at the windows and rushes down the chimney, reminding us of the storm that's raging outside.

FIFTY-THREE
FENRIR

PRESENT

THERE'S A SECOND WHEN ALL I SEE IS HER. HER LONG, DARK hair, her pale, shimmering skin, and those large, brilliant eyes that are afraid, full of fear and sorrow and anger. She's twenty years old and has never known anything else. She doesn't deserve this life. She deserves so much better.

Snapping into action, I pick up Willa's phone. Hayami's eyes track me.

"What are you doing?" she asks as I slide out the SIM card.

"Taking the SIM card out," I tell her. "We'll do the same with all our phones. With a bit of luck, Markus might think the lines have gone down with the storm."

"Does that even happen these days, what with Wi-Fi and stuff?" Hayami picks up her phone and takes her SIM card out, and I do the same with mine.

"I have no idea, but it's worth a shot and will buy us some time."

"To do what?" Hayami swallows.

I stop messing with my phone and look at her steadily. "Leave."

"You said we can't, not in this weather."

"Not on foot, but you heard what Markus said," I explain, knowing this isn't what she's going to want to hear. "They'll clear the road as soon as the snow stops, which, according to the weather report, will be in the next couple of hours. I'm not sure how long it'll take them, but I guess they'll try and get as much of it done before nightfall as possible. That gives us a fair few hours for me to get some rest, pack up, get the snow off the Jeep, and drive down to the main road before the sun goes down." I stop, waiting for Hayami to catch up.

"And then what?"

I give it a second before I answer. "We run."

She swallows again, this time harder, as if she has something lodged in her throat. I take her hand in mine.

"I wish there was another way. I wish we didn't have to, but I don't see what choice we have."

Hayami winces like she's in pain, and I wonder if she's not only thinking about us but the danger this poses to Willa and her new family. But I can't think about Willa now. Hayami is my priority. Has always been my priority.

It feels like an eternity before she nods and squeezes my hand.

"I'm sorry," she says at last, her eyes pooling into watery swirls.

"You have nothing to be sorry for," I tell her, squeezing her hand back.

"This is all my fault. If I hadn't sent Willa away, if I'd just kept quiet and done as I was told, then we wouldn't be here."

"You seem to forget the reason why we're here in the first place," I say, reminding her of my culpability in all of this. "And if you hadn't sent Willa away, she would have missed the birth of her child, and we'd still be sitting here under the authority of your father, and you'd still be on the path to having your life auctioned off. This way, at least we might have a chance. And that has to be worth something."

She nods, and something cracks in my chest. She doesn't want to run. I don't want her to *have* to run. Running isn't living. It's surviving, and that's all she's ever done. Survived. Until it was too hard to even do that.

I pull her into me, and she rests her head against my chest. Smoothing down her hair, I ask, "Are you with me?"

There's a beat, a second where I doubt her answer, worry that it won't be the one I want to hear, and then she speaks. "I'm with you."

Unsure whether I'm relieved or just shit scared, I hold her head.

"Good, because we have to be out of this house by nightfall."

She tenses, and I feel bad because I've reminded her that her father isn't the only thing we're now running from. It seems that everyone is out to get us. But I know who I'm more afraid of.

We decide to try and rest whilst the snow still rages. I want to get moving, clear the car and the drive and get packed up, but I haven't slept in so long. But as we lie on the bed, wrapped in each other's arms, I hope Hayami isn't thinking the same thoughts as me, which is that this whole thing is fucking hopeless.

We have no money on us. I'll have to stop at a cashpoint to withdraw as much as I can, which Devall will know about. Hayami said she'll take all the money she has out of her account, which I pointed out will probably be frozen by her father the minute he suspects that something isn't right.

The Jeep has a tracking device, which I'll disable. But even so, it won't take Devall long to alert his people to be on the lookout for it, so we'll have to change vehicles, which will probably mean stealing one. That'll mean we won't just have him on our case but the police as well.

And there's our appearance. Hayami will be able to change how she looks. But me? How the fuck am I going to hide all my scars?

All this comes before we even try to find somewhere to hide. And even if we do manage to slip through the net, how long will it be before it closes in again? How will it feel to spend every day looking over our shoulders—for the man who, if I'm lucky, will put a bullet in my brain, and who will, in the blink of an eye, snatch his daughter away?

Hayami was right that day when she said there's no running from a man like Barrett Devall.

I hold her tighter. It's cruel—I've only just got her, after all the waiting, watching, and longing—only for it to be cut short. I have no illusion that this plan will work.

We're fucked.

HAYAMI

We're on the bed, holding on to each other as if we're on the *Titanic* and the water is rushing into the cabin. And it's awful to think that I'd prefer that. Death would be the better option right now.

I've never been afraid of dying.

I've always been afraid of my father.

He'll find us. Fenrir knows it too. I can see it in his eyes, hear it in his voice, feel it through the tightness of his embrace.

And he'll kill Fenrir. It'll be slow, painful, the worst way to die, and it'll be my fault.

I'd welcome my death. But my father will not grant me

this. The deal will be tarnished, the goods spoiled, my purity now sullied. There's no way my father will believe that nothing happened between Fenrir and me. So, not only will I have cost him money, but I'll have embarrassed him, brought shame down on our family and him specifically. I won't be let off lightly.

If he had other children, I'm certain he'd kill me, dispose of me like he's done so many others who've disobeyed him.

So, as I lie here in Fenrir's strong arms, I wonder what my father will do to me and whether I'd rather face the ghost of this house than endure his wrath.

I haven't forgotten that feeling of being weightless, of floating above the mattress. And having read my mother's journal and the things she experienced, I wonder if what happened to her is happening to me. She described the feeling of having someone else in her head. I can't say that I've felt this, but there've been the dreams, the horrible, vivid dreams of such terror, such dread, that I wonder now if this is similar to what my mother felt.

Kuchisake-Onna.

And let us not forget the whole reason I'm here in the first place. The threat that was made by the Castros. I was sent here because this was supposed to be the safest place for me—somewhere the bad guys wouldn't be able to find me. But my father knows where I am. Kuchisake-Onna knows where I am. And I'm sure if the Castros looked hard enough, they'd find me too.

It seems I'm destined for death.

Maybe I've always been doomed to die; after all, aren't we all heading in that same direction? Just some of us quicker than others.

After the first attempt in the pool, I hated Fenrir for saving me. Even now, I wish he hadn't, and then I wouldn't be in this predicament, having brought him and Willa along with me. But there's part of me that wonders if this was fate's way of giving me one thing—one little box ticked before I reached for the hand of death.

Before I met Fenrir, I'd not felt attraction. I'd not felt the need for another person the way I need him, and I'd have died a virgin—my book boyfriends remaining the only experiences I had with men. But now? Now I know what it feels like to be held, to be kissed, to be touched. And in its cruel way, I wonder if this is worse, knowing what those things feel like and that I will never feel them again.

Is this love? Is what I feel for Fenrir the real deal? I wouldn't know. But I would certainly like the opportunity to find out.

Someone once said it's better to have loved and lost than to never have loved at all.

Right now, I'm not sure if that's true.

FIFTY-FOUR

HAYAMI

PRESENT

WITHIN TWENTY MINUTES OF US GIVING UP ON RESTING, Fenrir has thrown his duffel bag into the foyer and tells me he's going to start clearing the drive because it'll be the longest and hardest job.

"What can I do?" I ask, needing to keep myself busy so I don't stop and think about what's waiting for us when we leave this house—what we'll be running from, and what, if anything, we'll be running towards.

"Once you've packed, you can start clearing the snow from the Jeep." Fenrir nods towards the garage. "There's a scraper and snow shovel in there. And don't be tempted to pour warm water on the car. It'll freeze instantly and make the job harder."

I nod, biting my lip and thrusting my hands inside the sleeves of my top. I've dressed with care, layering as much as I can—not just for warmth but so there's less to pack. My coat isn't designed for snow. I've never paid attention to tog ratings and water-resistant properties before, always buying whatever was in fashion, confident a bodyguard would hold the umbrella or the car would be waiting at the door. But I do own a North Face, bought at university because everyone else wore one, and God bless Nita for packing it.

Fenrir wears his black base layer with a black zip-up jacket, cargo trousers tucked into his boots. He'll work up quite a sweat when he starts clearing the drive.

When it's clear neither of us has anything else to say, he edges to the door. Three locks click, and the cold hits me, sharp enough to make my eyes water.

It's biting fresh, with a zing that makes me feel as if my face is stretched tight against it. The snow has stopped, but the wind still whips through the trees, knocking off the freshly laden snow like tiny avalanches. It's beautiful, this white world of wonder that looks so fragile, so innocent, yet is just another danger.

As I watch the tiny fragments of snow being blown off the scrawny branches, I can't help but think of the larger drifts waiting to slide down the mountainside, consuming whatever's in their path. The whole mountain is a death trap —a beautiful, dazzling death trap.

HOURS SLIP BY IN BLISTERING COLD, DAMP FEET, AND FROZEN hands. It takes me over an hour to clear the Jeep properly, and then I start helping to clear the rest of the drive, by which point, Fenrir's been shovelling relentlessly. He's made progress, and by dusk, we've reached the road that leads onto the mountain road.

In all the time we've been clearing the drive, we haven't spoken.

It feels like there's nothing to say.

The sky is greying, the light from the snow appearing to

lose its vitality, a stark reminder that we need to leave before nightfall.

I stop for a breather, leaning against the shovel that feels fused to my hand, my palms raw, blisters threatening to bloom. As I wipe my forehead, I catch the blink of orange lights and the low rumble of an engine.

Fenrir has already seen it and is walking over to the road as the small plough makes its way slowly up the hill.

Time seems to move in a strange way up here, and the plough is no exception. It's methodical and gentle, yet ruthlessly pushes the snow to the edges of the road.

As it reaches the boundary of our land, the plough stops, the engine cutting out, the lights still flashing on the top of the vehicle. Fenrir edges closer, regarding the driver before turning to me and silently telling me to stay where I am.

The driver tugs down his beanie before swinging his door open and dropping from the cab.

"Hey there," he calls, his black boots landing on the crisp snow that's piled up, his jacket and trousers oversized in fluorescent orange waterproof material luminous against the white backdrop.

"Hey," Fenrir replies as he stands taller and spreads his chest as if he's a peacock preparing to wage war.

If the man is disturbed by Fenrir's appearance, he doesn't show it. He merely nods at the driveway and says, "You've been busy." His navy woollen hat is pulled low to his brow, and the collar of his jacket is worn high as if he's Elvis. What remains of his face is dark, his skin a road map of lines, as if every job he's done has been weathered into it.

"Thought we best make a start at clearing it whilst the snow's on hold." Fenrir eyes the man, then looks towards the road. "What's it looking like?"

The guy glances behind him as if to remind himself before he turns back to Fenrir. "It's not great. The plough has cleared the bulk, but it's frozen underneath, and what isn't frozen now will be by nightfall. I was instructed to clear the road. God knows why. You'd be a fool to try and drive down it." He scratches his chin and then nods at the Jeep. "You going somewhere?"

I can feel the tension coming from Fenrir. He's not sure of the situation, and neither am I. What must this look like? Who in their right mind would plan on leaving the mountain in these conditions if there wasn't some kind of emergency?

Fenrir takes his time before he answers. "We might have to."

The man whistles through his teeth, shakes his head, and then raises his eyebrows. "Well, I hope you have four-wheel drive and the best tyres money can buy. If it weren't for me needing this goddamn job to keep a roof over my family's head, I'd have refused this suicide mission." His eyes rise to the upper height of the mountain that looms behind us before resting back on Fenrir.

"You've managed to clear the road," Fenrir points out.

"Yeah, but I gotta get back down, and I reckon we only have twenty minutes before we're going to be in total darkness." This time, his eyes rise to the sky before landing back on Fenrir. "Now, if you don't mind, I have a family to try and get home to." He claps his hands together and then grabs for the cab door. "Mind if I use the drive to turn around?"

Fenrir nods as the guy climbs back into the driver's seat. He starts the engine and then leans out the open window. "If you're good to go, you can follow me back down; might be the sensible thing to do. I'll be gritting as I go, so you'll have a better track to drive on."

Fenrir glances at me and then looks back at the guy. "Sure thing. We're nearly ready."

The man leans back into the cab and appears as if he's about to turn the vehicle around when he pops his head back out the window. "I ain't waiting, though. We don't have much light left, and I'm not hanging around on this godforsaken mountain any longer than I have to. If you ain't behind me, I ain't stopping, do you hear?"

"Yeah." Fenrir grips the shovel, then turns and makes his way over to me. "You ready to go?" he asks as I turn and walk with him, picking up speed to match his brisk pace.

"Yeah. I was going to get changed because I'm soaking, and I need the toilet. Other than that, I'm ready."

He doesn't break his stride as he approaches the Jeep and flips the lid to the boot. "Scrap the change of clothes," he says as he slides the shovel in and closes it. "The guy is right. We're losing light, and it won't be long before the grit he spreads will be useless. This might be our only chance to get off this mountain safely."

"Okay. I'll just go to the toilet." I head back into the house, fear and dread twisting in my gut.

Needing the toilet wasn't a lie. I should go now, because who knows how long it'll take us to get off this mountain, and I'll get the chance to stop and use a restroom. I've also forgotten something: my mother's journal. It remains in my bedroom, discarded on the bedside cabinet after I'd finished reading it. I hadn't packed it, thinking it belonged to this house and needed to stay here. But something is telling me to get it. I'm not sure if it's because it was my mother's or whether I don't want other people finding it and reading it. Maybe it's just because this might be the only thing of hers I have left.

We're running from my father, and that means running from my mother. What if I never see her again? My chest tightens at the thought.

Glancing at the house as I run back inside, I note the arched windows, the grand entranceway, and then, as I bound up the stairs, the swirling banister. I try not the think that these might be the last things I see if we don't make it off this mountain.

Darting into the bedroom, I grab the journal from the side and then duck into the en suite. I try not to think about anything as I relieve myself quickly, imagining Fenrir sitting in the Jeep, revving the engine, warming the car for whatever lies ahead.

When I'm done, I reach for the toilet roll, and that's when the lights go out.

Shit. Not again.

This is not what I need right now.

Grabbing for the toilet paper, I tear off a piece and wipe myself quickly, hoping my eyes will adjust to the gloom, the sun not yet having fully descended.

Once I'm done, I go to stand and wobble, my balance thrown. I place my arms out, but the fading light throws shadows across the room as if trying to disorientate me. I pull my leggings up and try to ground myself by placing my feet in a solid stance as if I'm on a boat. I've been here before, and I'm not about to panic like I did the first time.

Besides, this time, although it's fading, there's light coming from the window, and the door is wide open, so I make for the grey hole that I know is the exit.

Taking a deep breath, I pace forwards and clear the doorway, the bedroom looming before me. This room is darker, and I can just make out the shape of the bed, the long curtains, and the dim light from the balcony doors.

Aware that Fenrir is waiting, I take a step, and the cold hits me.

It's like a slap to my face, my cheeks raw.

What the hell?

Focusing on the doorway to the landing, I try to move, but the room slides, like the whole house has been tilted on its side.

I brace myself, hands out in front of me.

Slowing my breathing, I try to process this rationally. Is this a fucking earthquake? That can be the only reason why the room suddenly feels like it's slipping beneath me.

My heart races in my chest and pounds in my ears, my blood rushing around my body like it's being chased by a mountain lion. And just when I think life is playing cruel fucking games with me, I hear a noise like the swishing of a skirt, the rustling of movement.

But I'm the only person in this house.

The knives on the table flash before my eyes, the kitchen drawers opened by nothing. Fenrir poised, gun aimed at the emptiness behind me before he fired into the wall. The bed lying two feet below as I floated above, nothing holding me there.

Stop it.

Must move. Must get out of here.

Steadying my footing, I take a step, but the room laughs at me as it tilts me further towards the bed.

Holding both my hands out, I try to grab onto something. As I do, an eerie feeling creeps up the back of my neck, cold and uninvited.

It's just your imagination. Ignore it. Find something to hold on to.

The bed. My fingers trail over the smooth wood of the headboard, reading it like it's Braille, telling me a haunting story where a girl gets trapped in a house of tricks and shadows.

Stop it.

It's just an old house. The lights have tripped before. This isn't the first time I've been stuck in the dark.

But I'm panicking. It's no wonder after recent events. My heart rate is already elevated.

I'm stressed and hyper-aware of what's going on. But as I

tell myself this, the cold creeps over my neck, and I swear my hair moves.

I slap the back of my head, pulling my hand down my hair and over my neck. I continue to shuffle forwards, using the bed as a guideline.

Not far until I reach the doorway, which is six, maybe seven paces away.

Just get to the end of the bed, then run.

Five paces, four.

I'm almost there.

As I edge forwards, my gaze fixes on the open doorway to the landing. The banister is just visible, running from the stairs along the hall. I brace to run, drawing in a deep breath—

"Where are you going?"

The voice slices through the air, freezing my heart, my body, my soul.

FENRIR

Starting the engine of the Jeep, I watch the plough turn into the drive, then swing back out slowly onto the road, the driver not giving me a backwards glance.

I've kept myself busy all day because if I'd stopped, I wouldn't have been able to fight the anxiety burrowing under my skin about whether we're doing the right thing. The mountain is dangerous, the road precarious. Thoughts of getting trapped under an avalanche or the Jeep sliding off the road and down the side of the mountain have been plaguing me since we decided we'd leave the house. But the alternative isn't much better.

By now, Devall will know something is amiss, having

been unable to get in contact with us. Yes, I could explain the issue with the phones as the connection being disrupted by the weather, but how the fuck would I have explained why Willa isn't here? Why she couldn't come to the phone?

I keep trying to justify the decision to run since Hayami mentioned the idea herself, but I always come back to the fact that she hasn't run. Because she knows how it'd end. We both know what will be at the end of this.

The whole time we've been digging, I've been avoiding looking at her. For the past six months, Hayami's carried the darkness around with her—the one I presume arrived the minute I pulled her from that pool. But today, it's grown darker, as if the shadow's swarming her, watching, waiting, growing stronger by the second, knowing death is near.

I haven't looked in a mirror in years. If I were to do so, my own shadow would be the same—pulsing around me like it's clapping its hands. It knows we're doomed.

So, I'm sitting in the Jeep, revving the engine, heater on full, prepping myself for the most dangerous drive of my life. We've chased off death before, so I'm hoping we can do it again. We have to try.

The plough moves slowly, reaching the corner of the road where it will disappear, its lights blaring against the dark backdrop.

The dark.

Fuck.

I dip my head, analysing the sky that's changed from a lucid grey to a penetrating gunmetal in the last few minutes. I give it ten more minutes before it'll be pitch-black.

Come on, Hayami.

I look back at the house.

I wait.

Nothing.

No Hayami.

Impatience drums at my insides along with something else—a nagging familiar feeling that has nothing to do with the icy road, the treacherous drive, or the death run we're about to embark upon, and everything to do with the shit that's been going down in that house.

The door is wide open, Hayami having not bothered to close it after she ran inside. I can only just make out the dying headlights of the snow plough.

The sky is closing in on us. There's no more time.

As I fling open the door to the Jeep and swing my legs out, the house goes black. All the lights have gone out.

Fuck.

I jump out of the Jeep and run towards the front door, trying not to pay attention to how dark the inside of the house looks.

"Hayami!" I call as I race into the grey foyer. No reply.

Fuck!

Stupid, Fucking stupid. Why did I let her go inside by herself?

Stepping further into the house, I can't ignore the drop in temperature, the sinister feeling that envelops me as soon as my feet hit the floor.

"Hayami!" I call out again. My senses are playing tricks on me, as I swear I see something move by the stairs, a flicker of something dashing by me.

It's just nerves, just the tension of this situation playing mind games with me.

Stay alert.

Stay focused.

Get Hayami.

Get the fuck out of here.

Making my way to the rear of the house, I wish I had my phone turned on so I could use the torch, as a thick blanket of darkness covers the interior with such menace that I can't help but wonder if it's natural or is being pumped out like a smoke machine.

"Hayami?" The change in my voice isn't lost on me, the way her name sounds like a question. I reach the downstairs toilet, which I presume is the one she chose to use, with it being the closest, but all I find is the door wide open, the bathroom empty, no running water from the cistern, and no residue in the basin from her having just washed her hands.

Shit.

What the fuck has happened to her? Where could she have gone?

Stop it.

She'll be upstairs.

She'll have gone to use the bathroom there for reasons best known to herself.

Despite the darkness, I pick up my pace and jog through the house and up the stairs.

As I stalk the long hallway, I shove open doors to spare rooms, the large bathroom, and my room until I reach the master bedroom. The door is already open. The icy chill of a breeze brushes over my face as if trying to warn me of what's to come.

"Hayami!" I call, shoving the door open. The room is drenched in darkness that climbs the walls, hovers in plain sight, and clings to my skin.

But the darkness isn't all I see.

I'd been convinced the draft was supernatural—an icy introduction to the malevolent spirit that roams this house— but I was wrong. The breeze is real, pouring in from the open balcony doors.

Hayami stands with one leg over the railing, her hands gripping either side of the ornate stone façade, her hair whipping in the wind, the darkness buzzing around her as if ready to swallow her whole.

And I freeze.

I don't want to scare her into falling, and I'm not entirely sure who this is.

"Hayami?" I say her name gently and put out my arm as if to pull her back, using the force of my hand alone.

"Stay back," she tells me. Her voice. Hayami. She isn't being possessed. I can tell by the way her head moves, the way her eyes pin me down. This is Hayami. *My* Hayami. She isn't crying, but I can tell she has been. Her eyes are glassy, and her cheeks are stained.

Holding both hands up to show her I'm no threat, I take a slow step towards her. "What are you doing out there?" I ask, hoping to distract her from the step I've just taken.

"I said stay back!" she insists.

I stop, keep my hands up where she can see them.

"Okay. But just tell me what you're doing." My gut churns.

"You know what I'm doing, and don't you dare try to talk me out of it." She's spluttering, anger mixed with fresh tears.

I thought we were over this—the desire to take her own life. I thought I'd given her something to live for. But I think we both know that's a lie.

"Okay," I say with as much conviction as I can muster whilst she dangles on the edge of a thirty-foot drop. But I've got her attention, and now she stares at me, probably trying to work out my game plan, just as I'm also trying to figure it out.

"You're not going to try and stop me?" Her eyes narrow, her grip on the balcony flimsy at best.

"No, but I'm going to ask you to tell me why. I need to know why this is the only option." I lower my arms, hoping it will make her think I'm staying put.

Her head tips to the side, her gaze fixed on me before she inhales.

"I saw her. She was here," she tells me in a shaky voice.

"Who?" I ask, even though I have a good idea who she's talking about.

Kuchisake-Onna.

"The lights went out, and then I felt something, a freezing-cold air on the back of my neck, and then I heard a voice —*her* voice."

Hayami's eyes dart around as if checking to see that we're still alone, even though I don't think we've ever been alone here.

"I thought I saw something, a dark shadow. It was hard to tell, as there was just blackness, but I swear I saw the flash of eyes."

Her words come quicker now, as if she needs to set them free.

"I tried to run, but there was this burning in my chest, as if I was being flooded by something invading my body. My limbs weren't mine. I had no control over what my body was doing. And then my thoughts were not my own."

Her eyes settle on a spot on the balcony, her hair billowing behind her as the wind whips at it and the darkness caresses her skin.

"Memories came to me—not my own, someone else's. It felt like a movie playing in my head." She glares at me, but it's as if she isn't seeing me, her eyes glassy, her face drawn as she tells me exactly what she saw in a haunting voice that barely resembles her own.

"I was in the master bedroom," she says, voice flat, almost mechanical—not her words but the words of whatever had consumed her. "It was evening. I remember shaking, hiding behind the en suite door because I knew he'd found out." Hayami's hands tremble. "Barrett… he was hammering against the door and shouting. 'Whore.' 'Bitch.' 'Cunt.' He kept hitting the door until it splintered, and that was when I saw the tip of the axe. I was afraid, not for myself but for the baby." Her hands drop protectively to her stomach. "I deserved this. I'd been unfaithful in order to get pregnant, to give Barrett the only thing he ever wanted from me. But my baby was innocent." She snarls like a dog guarding its pup, then raises her hand. "I smashed a mirror, grabbed a shard of glass, but—" She swallows hard, eyes flicking past me. "It was too late. He was in the room, laughing like a fucking maniac, spitting insults at me, swinging the axe like a pendulum."

All too clearly, I could picture Barrett Devall, lord of the manor, betrayed, mocked, and in a fucking frenzy.

"He told me about Kuchisake-Onna—the legend from my country about a concubine who was unfaithful to one of the samurai. And as punishment, he slashed her mouth from ear to ear whilst she was still alive." Hayami's arms drop, eyes glazing over as she stares at nothing, but I see the horror, the bloodless pallor of her skin. Her hands move back to her stomach as if shielding an invisible child. Then she looks at me.

"He said I was a cheating whore. That he'd make me look like her. Then he grabbed the shard of glass from my hand."

She touches her face like she can still feel the cut. "It was like a hot poker slicing through meat, tearing the flesh from my cheeks." She hesitates, a gargled sound coming from her before she continues. "I stopped screaming when the blood gathered under my tongue, stopped breathing when it ran down the back of my throat and choked me until I couldn't breathe."

She blinks slowly, one hand cupping her jaw as if she's trying to hold it on, the other rubbing over her stomach as if trying to soothe the baby she felt was there.

Her voice fades, like she's lost all power, all purpose, because she knows this is the end. "The last words I heard him say were that no one ever defied him and got away with it, not even me, his wife."

Hayami stares at me, eyes awash with memories that are not her own.

"Noa Devall," I confirm, placing this detail amongst the others, letting it settle into the picture as if placing the last piece of the jigsaw. "Your dad's second wife."

She nods. "I was told she died in childbirth. Always believed that was the case. But now I know. I saw it." Her eyes widen, fixing on me as if daring me to challenge her, even though she knows I'm not the one who needs convincing about the spirit of someone plaguing this house. Hayami has always been the sceptic, the one who reaches for an explanation, science, and facts. I thought, along with Junko, that it was Kuchisake-Onna. But no. It was never the legend that roamed this house. It's the ghost of Noa Devall haunting this place due to her barbaric murder that happened in this very room.

"I felt it." Hayami gulps the freezing air. "I felt it all, the glass on my mouth, ripping my skin as the shard cut through it. I tasted the blood, felt it pooling in the back of my throat, couldn't breathe, couldn't scream, and all the while, I was looking into his eyes—the eyes of my father." A sadness swamps her as she carries not only her own hurt but that of everyone who Devall's destroyed.

"After Noa left my body, I wondered why she'd done it, why she was here and trying to communicate with me. Then I realised she was warning me, showing me the kind of man my father is, what he's capable of and what he'll do when he's betrayed—just as she tried to do with my mother, although Mum never figured out who she was or what she was trying to tell her before leaving this house."

Hayami looks out over the mountainside, and something in me crumbles, because she's right. This is what will happen to her. I don't care what happens to me; I've been on the brink of death, felt the lick of the flames, felt the heat of hell. But Hayami... I can't let Devall find her. I can't let him do this to her. I won't. But how do I protect her from a man with eyes everywhere? A man who will tear the world apart to get what he wants?

She's right. Her sensible scientific brain has worked it out, has come up with the only solution to the problem. The only answer that'll ensure that he doesn't get what he wants, doesn't find her, and doesn't win this war.

It's why the dark shadow stalks her aura. It knows her time is almost up. Death's so close now. There's no escaping it.

My heart sinks as I look into her eyes. "You're right," I tell her.

Her eyes widen. It's not the response she expected.

"This is the only way to stop him." I take a step towards her, and she clings to the balcony.

"What are you doing?" she asks, watching me warily.

"I'm doing what we both need to do—the only thing we can do—because you're right: Your father will find us and kill us. I don't care what he does to me; I'll probably take great pleasure in the pain he dishes out, because I deserve it. I've failed you, just like I failed my sister."

Hayami opens her mouth, but I cut her off. "We don't have time for you to argue with me. This might be the last chance I get to speak to you, so you're going to listen to me, Hayami."

She purses her lips.

"My sister was innocent. You're innocent. Victims of this fucked-up world of gangs and guns. I've killed, done heinous things that can't be forgiven. But you? You've done nothing— just like her—and yet you'll die at the hands of a man who never deserved you, never deserved a wife or child. And you're right: Taking your life is the only way you'll defeat him, the only way to fuck him over for the final time. But it kills me, Hayami, to know that it has come to this, that this is the only way to be free of him. I swore to protect you with everything I have, with every fibre of my being. I'll keep that promise. I won't let you die alone. Without you, there's nothing left for me. Without you, I don't exist."

HAYAMI

My knees are weak, my legs shaking against the railing, my hands numb from gripping the cold stone for so long.

He's close now, close enough to take my hand. And I give it to him freely, because I know he understands, sees things the way I do, because there's no other way. There's only death, and I'll be damned if my father gets to dish mine out.

If I am to die, it will be my way, my choice, my demise.

Heart-wrenching loss splinters my chest as Fenrir wraps his arm around my waist and places his head against my forehead.

"All I ask is one thing," he says. I pull back and stare at him. "I've already thrown myself from one balcony when I jumped out of my burning home cradling my sister. I can't do it again. I can't leave this world that way, Hayami. There are other ways. Quick. Painless. We will die together. And we'll remain in this house together forever." He swallows hard as agony rips through my body.

I'm about to argue. He doesn't need to die too. He doesn't need to do this with me. But then I think about what my father will do to him. Fenrir isn't stupid.

It's the only way.

And I want to tell him that I wish things could have been

different. I wish I'd met him in some other place, some other time, some other body, but there's no point in making wishes that are never going to come true. Instead, I haul my leg over the balustrade, Fenrir tightening his grip as I regain my balance. Taking my hand, he leads me back into the bedroom, where we stop and hold each other.

"Thank you," I whisper.

He places his thumb under my chin, tipping my head back. "What for?"

"For everything," I begin. "For showing me what pleasure is, for making me feel things I only thought possible in books, for listening to me, for saving me." I stroke the side of his face, my fingers tracing his scars.

"It's been my duty, my honour, and my pleasure, Hayami Devall."

He lowers his head and kisses me. Softly, gently. But I need more. This is going to be the last time I feel his mouth on mine, the last time I taste him, so I need to make it last. I pull him closer, press my body against his, and thrust my tongue into his mouth.

Why does this feel so right—like I belong here, like this is the place I'm meant to be?

We kiss for longer than we should, but it doesn't matter. Nothing matters anymore other than the feel of his arms around me and his mouth upon mine. The wind blows through the open doors, the chill sprinkling the room in an eerie cold, yet all I feel is the warmth of Fenrir's body, the heat from his mouth, and the pressure of his hold.

As he holds me, he says, "Hayami, before we do this, I need you to know that everything I've given you, everything I've shown you, has been real. You might think that I took you because I thought I was helping you, but it wasn't just that. It was because I wanted you. I've wanted you from the moment I pulled you from that swimming pool. I'm not sure if you feel the same, but I'll tell myself that you do. I want to be the only thing you think about, the only thing you breathe for, the only thing you live for, and the only thing you're willing to die for, because you, Hayami, are already all of those things for me. I'm yours, Hayami. Always will be. Always have been. Now and even in death. You are my all."

I bite my lip, tears pooling in the corners of my eyes. I can't let him die not knowing. I can't die without telling him.

"I've never been in love. I don't know what it feels like. But if wanting to die in your arms is love, then please, hold me."

My heart aches as his grip tightens around my waist. He tips my head back, wipes my tears with his thumb, and then places his hand around his back and produces the gun that's been tucked into his waistband.

I pull back because I know what this means.

It's time.

His eyes well with tears.

"I want to kiss you again," I blurt. "I want to taste you as I die. I want my last breath to be yours."

He stares at me before he speaks. "I'm not sure if I can pull the trigger, Hayami. I can kill myself, that isn't a problem, but I can't shoot you. I won't be able to." He passes me the gun.

"I can't." My voice wobbles as I shake my head, realising what he's asking me to do.

"I only have one gun, Hayami. One of us has to go first."

I thought he'd shoot me, then himself. It never occurred to me how impossible that would be for him. Because if it were the other way around, I wouldn't survive it either—not the sight of him falling, not the sound of his last exhale. I can't take a breath in this world without him.

"I can't do it," I tell him. "I can't watch you die. I can't be in this world without you—not even for a heartbeat."

And still—beneath the panic, beneath the grief—there's the truth I can't ignore: I don't want to die. I don't want to put that gun to my head. I want to live. I want to grow. I want to experience the world the way that I choose. And I choose him, because I don't know how to live without him.

He nods as if understanding.

"Then we do it together." He lets go of me, and I'm bereft at the loss of his touch. He disappears from the room. My heart thumps furiously inside my chest, reminding me it's here, and it wants to beat, but only for him.

When he returns, he's holding another gun.

He presses it into my hand. It feels cold, brutal, yet necessary.

Tears stream down my face as he strokes the side of my cheek and raises his gun to his head.

"You're the most beautiful person I've ever met. I'm ready to die for you, Hayami. Ready to give my life for you, because you're the only thing worth living for." The barrel pushes up against his temple, his finger tracing the trigger.

Something swirls in my stomach. It isn't fear. I've been ready to end my life for so long, I'm not afraid of it. And I've felt fear, smelled it, tasted it when I saw what happened to Noa Devall at the hands of my father. I welcome death if that pain is the alternative.

What I feel is loss.

The loss of a life I could have had—the sadness at not being able to spend more time with the one man who's shown me what living is, who's taught me more than any of my college lectures, has shown me who I can be, who I want to be.

I just never got the chance to live that life.

"I love you," I tell Fenrir, and he nods, a tear rolling down his cheek. I catch it with my thumb as I raise the gun to the side of my head and press it against my temple.

"Kiss me," I tell him.

He lowers his head as my finger finds the trigger. His lips meet mine and I savour him, devour him.

The last thing I'll feel, the last thing I'll experience, the only place I want to be as my finger tightens on the trigger is with him. I need to fire my gun first. I can't be a second behind. My last feeling can't be of his dead body in my arms.

I look into his eyes. His beautiful eyes.

The only man I've ever loved.

The only man I will ever love.

My first and my last.

FIFTY-FIVE

FENRIR

THE NOISE IS SO LOUD IT SHAKES THE HOUSE. THERE'S A second where I think Hayami has pulled the trigger, got there before me, but her body goes tense, not limp. Her fingers grip my forearm as I pull away from our kiss, and she lowers her gun.

Her eyes search my face, probably thinking the same as me, that I pulled my trigger and that was what the noise was. We remain where we're standing, holding onto each other for dear life.

"Fenrir?" she says, her voice a light rasp as if she doesn't trust it to be hers.

"I'm here. We're both here," I tell her, lowering my gun.

"That noise," she says, glancing around the room. "What the hell was that?"

"I don't know." It could have been anything, but it was so loud, it shook the foundation. "It came from downstairs." I stare at the door, then slip the gun into my waistband and take her hand. "Come on." I pull her from the room and jog down the landing, Hayami behind me, her gun still in her hand.

We reach the stairs, run down the first set, then turn and begin our descent on the second set. Then we both freeze, Hayami one step behind me.

Fuck.

She sees it.

I can tell she does because her arm tenses, her hand grips mine, and her body goes rigid, mirroring my own.

She sees *her.*

And I don't know why I'm shocked by this, by *her.*

There's been so much weird shit going on that this shouldn't be a surprise. But she's never appeared before us. Not even Junko saw her. The only person who did was Kevin's father. But she's here, clear as day, her body floating ten inches above the ground, her hair coiled around her shoulders, the gash across her face like someone has thrown a can of red paint at her beautiful portrait.

There's no expression. How can there be when half her face is missing? But her eyes are wide, ghastly, as if she's the one who's afraid of us.

"Fenrir," Hayami whispers, her voice barely audible above the beating of my heart.

"I see her. Do you see her?"

"Yes."

I'm not imagining things.

We can't just stand here. I hold up my hand, palm flat out in front of me, ready to say something.

"We come in peace. We mean you no harm. What the fuck do you want?"

I have no idea what to say to the ghost of this house, to the woman who was brutally disfigured and murdered by her husband, the spirit who seems intent on telling us something, on trying to speak to us from beyond the grave.

But before I open my mouth, she turns around with a graceful fluidity to face the door. I don't have time to wonder what she's doing before the door opens.

FIFTY-SIX
FENRIR

It hits me—it isn't fear I've been feeling in this house. Well, that's not strictly true. I've felt fear before: core-crunching, adrenaline-pumping, sweat-inducing fear. But not my own. This house contains fear—it's drenched in it—but it's never been one that felt harmful. I've never felt in danger.

Until now.

We stare at the figure in the doorway, his large frame obscured by the darkness of the night sky behind him.

Hayami's hand tenses in mine, and I squeeze it, letting her know I'm here and I won't let him near her, because Barrett Devall is standing in the entrance like the goddamn devil himself.

Markus arrives on his left, gun trained, trying to push in front of his boss until his eyes land on the apparition. Then he backs off. Junko enters on the right, her eyes wide in terror as she sees the floating spectre. But Devall is frozen, feet in cement as he stares at the ghost of his dead wife.

The silence is thick and dangerous, Noa with her back to us.

"Noa?" Devall asks, barely a whisper, as if he can't quite believe his own eyes.

Then it happens in what feels like slow motion. Noa turns, like a tornado shifting direction, and she flies over to us, her face a contorted rage. I don't have time to act, no time to think, as Noa flings herself at Hayami.

Hayami stumbles back at the impact as Noa disappears.

She gasps, eyes wide, and she drops my hand.

"Hayami?" I call, but she doesn't respond, because it's not Hayami now standing next to me.

Her head twitches, her shoulders rolling as she stands up, takes one step forwards, and glares at Barrett Devall before raising the gun in her hand and pulling the trigger.

FIFTY-SEVEN

HAYAMI

WHEN WILLA, FENRIR, AND I FIRST ARRIVED IN THIS HOUSE, I woke up here in this very room. The large living area felt spacious and grand, yet now it feels full and claustrophobic as my mum flanks me, tucking a blanket around my shoulders. Markus paces before the unlit fire. It isn't until Fenrir arrives, bobs down in front of me, and places a glass in my hand that I feel the world sink back into me.

"Drink this," he tells me, holding the glass with me as I move my shaky hands to my mouth.

The whisky burns, but it's nothing like the feeling of… of what? Having a ghost inside me? Having a spirit take over my body and then shoot her husband, *my father*, with the gun in my hand?

"It's done. You are free." Noa's parting words as she left my body, and I'd realised what she'd done, ring in my ears.

Fuck. It's going to take more than a shot of whisky.

"Hayami, my darling, it's okay. We're here for you." My

mum's voice isn't one I recognise. It's clear, concise, reassuring. I like it. It feels more like the voice from her journal.

"I don't mean to push things, but someone needs to start talking about what the fuck just happened out there." Markus stops pacing and runs his hand through his thick, greying hair. I've never seen him look ruffled, but I guess he has just seen a ghost use my body to shoot his boss.

Fenrir stands. "Why don't you start by telling us what you're all doing here."

Markus eyes us warily before speaking. "We thought something was wrong after I called you wanting to speak to Willa and she wasn't available. Then, when I called back twenty minutes later and none of your phones were switched on, we knew something was going on. So, on a hunch, I called Rothkor General Hospital, and they confirmed that a Marta Gatsby was staying on the maternity ward." He raises an eyebrow, glancing from Fenrir to me. "I figured out what happened," he says, a little softer. "You let Willa go to her wife when she went into labour."

There's no need for me to explain the details, so Markus continues.

"I had no choice but to report this to Mr Devall, and, as you can imagine, he went berserk and said he was coming out here. I explained about the weather, and he said that the road up the mountain would be cleared in the next few hours. I tried my best to advise him that flying out here wasn't the best idea, but as you know, there's no arguing with him."

Markus takes a breath, and my mum uses the opportunity to speak.

"I've been worried sick every day since you've been gone. I'm the only person who knows what this house holds." She runs her eyes over the walls as if they're listening. "I needed to see you so badly. So, when I heard your father was flying out here, I insisted on coming. Barrett didn't have time to argue with me. There was no way I wasn't going to come and help you. They were worried about the Castros. I was worried about something entirely different."

I squeeze my mum's hand, and she squeezes it back as Markus picks the thread up.

"We flew in on the jet, picked up a car, and headed up here. By the time we hit the foot of the mountain, it was late and already getting dark. The road had been cleared, so we started the climb, but it was still slick—ice all over.

"About halfway up, we ran into the guy with the plough heading down. He stopped, said he'd seen you at the house and that you were supposed to follow him down—but you never showed. By then, Mr Devall was spitting feathers, so we eased past the plough, carried on up, parked, got out, and made our way to the front door."

Markus stalls, and I wonder if he's replaying the events, trying to imagine what he could have done differently, how culpable he is in my father's death, seeing he is—*was*—his bodyguard.

"I tried to tell him to get behind me, to let me scope out the situation before he went in, but he was having none of it. We got inside the house, and the rest you know." Markus drops his hand by his side and looks at Fenrir.

Fenrir gulps and glances at me, then back at Markus.

"Tell me what you saw when you walked through the door," he says.

Markus scratches his head. "I know what I *thought* I saw. *Who* I thought I saw. But it doesn't make any sense."

"You saw the ghost of Noa Devall, who was murdered in this very house by her husband," Fenrir tells the room.

"Wait, no." Markus shakes his head. "Noa died here, yes, but she died in the middle of the night. There were rumours amongst the staff that it was pretty horrific." He halts.

We all wait for him to continue. He presses his lips together, concentration on his brow as if he's trying to retrieve his memories.

"There were no staff in the house that night. Mr Devall had given us all the night off, as he said Noa wasn't feeling well, and he wanted the house to be quiet for her. A handful of us were called in the next day, and all we were told was that she'd gone into labour in the middle of the night, but there were complications. The baby was breech, and the ambulance couldn't get up the mountain in time. Devall told us she'd been delirious with the pain and that things hadn't ended well." Markus assesses us, maybe hoping this will be enough of an explanation as to what happened that night.

"Did you see her body?" my mum asks, eyes narrowed at Markus.

"Of course not. No one did." His face pales, his eyes darting between the three of us.

There's more. He's holding back. Fenrir glares at him, holding his stare until Markus's shoulders drop.

"The rumour was that Noa panicked. She thought her baby was going to die, so she'd tried to cut it out herself with a shard of broken mirror, and that was why there was so much blood in the bedroom and why no one was allowed to see her body; he had it privately cremated." Markus looks at the floor as I digest this horrific fabrication of events.

"Bullshit. All of it," Fenrir interjects. "Devall murdered Noa when he found out she had slept with someone else to get pregnant. He cut her face open, and she choked on her own blood. She died in this house, and her body was probably burned by Devall himself somewhere in the woods. Noa tried to warn us that Devall was here, and that was when she took over Hayami's body."

Everyone looks at me, and I know I have to speak. It's my turn to explain.

"He's right. She came into my body. She shot him."

The room spins. I close my eyes, remembering the moment she flew at me, her face feral, her eyes blazing. I was so scared, but not of her. I was scared of what I might feel, and what she would show me.

Even though she was transparent, the figure of lucidness, she hit my body like a ton of bricks. And then it was like someone taking over the controls. I wasn't myself anymore. My thoughts were not my own. They were hers. I felt it all.

The rage, the hatred, the burning desire to avenge my death and the death of my unborn child, to kill the man who had ruined my life and was about to do the same to his daughter. I knew I would never get this chance again. So, I took it.

Noa took it. She fired the gun.

Markus clicks his tongue and shakes his head.

"She isn't lying," Junko says. "I felt her presence the last time I was in this house. I thought it was something else, a legend from my homeland, but when I walked through that door and Barrett said her name, it all fell into place. It was Noa. She came into my body and tried to warn me of the man I'd married, of what he was capable of." She glances at Markus, who still looks sceptical. "Don't you remember the night you found me in the woods with a knife in my hand?"

"You were sleepwalking," he begins to argue with her.

I interrupt, saying, "I don't care whether you believe us, Markus. I get that this all sounds so fantastical that it can't possibly be true, but it is. It *is* what happened."

Markus crosses his arms. "I don't know what the hell I saw. I don't even want to try and understand what happened here, because I don't think my head will ever accept it. But I've worked with Mr Devall long enough to know that some things are not always easily explained. But my question is, what do we do with the dead body in the entranceway? And what the fuck are we going to tell everyone else?"

Fenrir straightens like a soldier standing to attention. "We tell them the cell service went down. You came here as backup when I reported that there had been an intruder on the grounds. We don't name the man; we don't affiliate him with any gang. We say he was a crazed stalker of Hayami's and that he threatened her life. That's why we brought her out here. He arrived at the house at the same time as Devall, and in the scuffle, he was shot."

"That could work," my mum says, nodding at Fenrir and then glancing at Markus, who doesn't look convinced.

"It'll work," Fenrir confirms with a snap. "People will believe what we tell them to believe."

"But what about the repercussions? What happens to the business?" Markus asks.

And for some reason, they both look to my mum.

She sits up and arches her back as if this is the first time anyone has noticed her since she married my father.

"Normally, it would go to his heir."

She glances at me, and I close my eyes. That's the last thing I want. I'm not a gang lord, a criminal, or a tyrant. I have no qualifications for the role, and my mother knows this.

"I think I speak for my daughter when I say she wants nothing to do with her father's empire. So, it'll be up to me to decide what happens from here on in."

Markus stares at my mum, a hard stare that I'm sure she must feel under her skin.

"I'm not sure how that'll work," Markus begins, but my mum is ready, as if she's been thinking about this for longer than the twenty minutes since I killed my father.

"That's my concern and not for you to worry about." She looks sharply at Markus, then softens a little. "Barrett's death will send shock waves through the city. People will be stunned. And what better time for us to declare peace and an end to the bloodshed and the corruption?"

"What about the Castros?" Markus asks.

"The Castros will be happy that Barrett is dead. They'll take it as a win, even if it wasn't at their hands. Hopefully, once they realise we're no longer a threat to them, they'll leave us alone. But right now, they aren't my main concern. My daughter is the priority."

The room is silent, everyone probably wondering where we go from here, because as long as we've all been alive, we've only known one thing—my father's reign.

What this new future will look like is anyone's guess, but it'll be a hell of a lot different from what my own looked like earlier tonight when I had held a gun to my head.

"If you'll excuse me, I'm going to change my clothes," I announce, shrugging the blanket off and pulling out of my mum's embrace.

I stand, and she looks at me with such concern, her eyes the clearest I've ever seen them. "Do you want me to come with you?" she asks, but Fenrir steps in.

"I'll go with her." It isn't a question, and my mum sees his hand move to my lower back, sees me lean into him, and she smiles. She knows. She sees it. She understands that this man is my world, and I am his.

Markus nods at Fenrir as if giving his blessing as we exit the room.

FENRIR

We make our way to the Jeep, our eyes avoiding the covered body of Barrett Devall in the entranceway, Hayami gripping my hand like it's the only thing tethering her to this new reality. We don't talk as I pull her bag from the car and bring it back inside the house. The silence accompanies us up the stairs and waits patiently as we enter the master bedroom, where we'd been prepared to take our lives in each other's arms.

I've been on the brink of death; I know the feeling of having cheated it. But Hayami? I'm not sure how close she's come, how tight death's grip was on her before I pulled her back from the depths of the water. And this time?

As I place her bag on the floor, Hayami flops onto the bed. I kneel before her. "Talk to me," I say.

She shakes her head.

"Don't give me the silent treatment. You have to talk, have to let it out; otherwise, it'll destroy you. You just killed your father," I begin, but her eyes dart to mine.

"It's not that. I have no memory of that. All I saw was Noa coming towards me, and then it was *her* feelings, *her* thoughts. I didn't consciously raise my hand. I didn't actively pull the trigger. It was *her*. She was inside me. I felt her pain, her sorrow, her hurt, but then it changed.

"I'm not sure what she did, or how she managed to interfere with what I saw, because the only thing I saw was you. You filled my head, and that's all I can remember until I heard her voice in my mind telling me it was done, that I was free now. Then the room came back into focus, and I saw my father on the floor."

She gulps. I let her gather her thoughts, rubbing gentle circles on her thighs.

"I have no memory of shooting him, no recollection of pulling that trigger. I didn't see him get hit, didn't see him fall. But when I did come back and I saw him lying on the ground, the blood spreading over his chest, all I felt was relief." A tear rolls down her cheek. "I'm glad. Happy.

Fucking ecstatic that he's dead, because everything will be different now. Noa's given me a chance, given me a life that wasn't mine, and not just me but my mum and you and Willa. She's saved us all."

Placing my finger under her chin, I gaze at her, relieved she has no memory of what happened, that Noa had the foresight to protect Hayami from something that could have scarred her for life.

"I'm glad you see it that way, the way it is—an evil man eradicated from this world. But he *was* your father."

"He was my father by blood and DNA. Those things don't make a dad."

I let out a sigh, hopeful that my rational Hayami is still operating the controls. But we aren't out of the woods yet, because there's another topic to tackle.

"Hayami," I start, treading carefully. But she knows what I'm about to say, must feel it in the air, because there's no escaping what we were about to do in this room.

"I can't help thinking about what would have happened if Noa hadn't made that noise downstairs. That must have been her, right? She had to have been stopping us. She knew what was coming, somehow knew he was on his way. Even if she didn't, she made that noise to stop us. But what if she'd been too late? What if I'd pulled the trigger? What if you'd pulled it before I did? What if—"

I press my finger over her lips.

"What if I hadn't got out of that burning building? What if my sister hadn't died, and I'd never come to work for your father? What if your mother hadn't got pregnant with you when she did? What if we'd have set off down the mountain and been hit by an avalanche? What if? What if? What if?" I repeat. "I could go on forever, giving you all the what-ifs, but all it'd do is drive you to madness, and I think you've already been there."

She laughs. It's small, hardly a laugh at all, but it's something.

"So, promise me this." I take her head in my hands. "Stop thinking about the what-ifs and think about the what now. Where do we go from here?"

Her eyes soften as I stroke the side of her cheek with my thumb.

"I don't care where we go, just as long as it's together."

She wraps her arms around my neck and pulls me to her lips. I kiss her passionately, desperately, as if her breath is the only thing keeping me alive. Because there's one thing I've noticed: The dark shadow surrounding her doesn't appear as dark anymore. In fact, it's almost gone. And when I went to the Jeep to pick up her bag, I checked my own reflection in the mirror, and my shadow has also faded.

I've always thought it cloaks the people who've come close to death, but I wonder now if it remains, hovering and waiting, until it can fully take you as it knows that death's near, that you cheated it once but won't do so again.

For now, it's gone for good. It'll return, of that I'm sure, but not now. Not for a long time.

Deep down, I know she might change her mind when we leave this place, when she starts to live the life she should've always been able to live. But I take my own advice and stop worrying about the what-ifs.

All I need to know is that she's here now with me, and that's where she wants to be.

EPILOGUE
HAYAMI

FIVE MONTHS LATER, BELIAL HOUSE

Warm sunlight beats through the window of the library, heating my face and sending a cascade of calm around me. I finish the chapter of the romance book, stuff it down the side of the chair, and close my eyes to soak up the warmth.

I can't believe how much my life has changed in the past few months. After my father was declared dead, there was this strange stillness, like no one knew how to feel or behave without him pulling the strings. Even the Castros were oddly quiet. No rebellious outbursts or push to take over the city. Were they in shock? Maybe. Mourning? Definitely not. It felt more like a truce, like a new chapter had begun.

My mum has been, well, my mum. The one I got snippets of when I was younger. The mother she's always been under the fog of drink and pills, which she no longer takes. She's been here, with me, in the present, helping me get to the end of my degree and looking at options for jobs when I finish.

I want to go into drug research, maybe looking at cures

for diseases. Maybe. But underneath all the science, what I really want is to help people like me. People who've been coerced for so long that they've forgotten who they are.

That's why I've been volunteering with a local charity. They support people who are still trapped in that life—or just finding their way out—because I know what it's like. I've been there and survived.

We've not done all this alone. Soon after my father's death, my mum called her brother and sister, my Aunt Emi and Uncle Michi, both of whom I'd never met. They flew over for the funeral and stayed for weeks to help my mum sort out the businesses. After three weeks, Aunt Emi returned to Japan, but Uncle Michi stayed. He has a good head for business and said he had some lost years to make up for where his sister and niece were concerned.

Together, my mum and Uncle Michi have restructured the Devall empire, ensuring that all the businesses are running legitimately. They also set up a personal security firm called PIP, which stands for Personal Inclusive Protection. It's headed up by none other than Markus and Willa, who returned to us after taking a month's maternity leave with Marta and Oscar, their very healthy five-month-old son who grows cuter by the second.

The Hellhounds were redistributed amongst the businesses and put to work in other areas, such as security guards in some of the office buildings, but most of them have been employed within PIP. They now work as security for victims of crime, vulnerable people who don't feel safe going out alone. Because I won't lie, the city is still a hotbed of crime.

The Castros may have accepted their new roles, but rival gangs have been moving in to try and take advantage of the changes. They've used the breather to stretch their legs and take over the territory that my father held. But I can live with that, as we're not the cause, and the Hellhounds have been helping people feel safe.

And then there's him.

As thoughts of Fenrir wash over me, I sink further into the chair. The smell of him. The feel of him. The taste of him. *My* Hellhound. *My* beast.

He's remained by my side through everything—counselling sessions, revising for exams, even celebrating my twenty-first birthday with my family. He'd been shocked when I suggested coming back to Belial House for spring break.

My mum wanted to sell it, but I said no.

Whilst my thoughts on the supernatural have changed drastically, I still approach life rationally, and I can't quite believe that memories can seep into the walls of a building. That said, this house holds some horrendous memories. Noa. My mother. And who knows what stories it holds from before my father bought it? I've got my own terrible memories here—though the worst aren't even mine. They're the ones from when Noa Devall took over my body and showed me what my father did to her.

But I can't ignore the amazing things that happened here.

This house is where Fenrir and I were first alone. Where he showed me what my life could feel like. Where he taught me to be the person I *want* to be, not the one I was raised to be. Where I learned what people will do—what they're willing to sacrifice—when they love someone.

I fell in love whilst in this house. That's why I couldn't let my mum sell it. That's why I brought us here for spring break, and why I'm sitting in this chair now, soaking up the early sun.

Of course, I had reservations about coming here. We both did. But as soon as we stepped through the door, we felt the house breathing, like it had a new lease of life. Because she's gone. Noa Devall doesn't roam these halls anymore. She left the night she killed my father because her job was done.

"It's done. You are free."

And I hope she's somewhere bright and full of warmth, where she can smile like she used to before she married my father. That's my wish for her.

My head lolls to the side, sinking into the cushion. I didn't hear him come in, didn't hear his footsteps because he was a soldier, a Hellhound, and would never announce his presence so clumsily, but I'll let him think I can't smell him, that I don't know he's watching me the way that I watch him when he's sleeping, the way that I look at him and wonder what I would do without him—and hope I never have to find out.

Behind the darkness of my closed eyes, I feel his stare roaming my skin, his gaze upon my body. A buzz of energy rushes through my core. How does he do this? How can he make me feel these things without me even seeing him? Without him touching me, without him saying a word?

Then I feel him, standing over me, his breath coming closer to my face.

"I've been looking for you," he whispers.

My heart skips. I know by the tone of his voice, by the way he's breathing, deep and lustful, that this is only the start.

"You found me," I reply, trying not to grin, the anticipation of the game already buzzing under my skin.

"And you've been reading again." I hear a rustle next to me, feel his hand brush my side as he plucks the book from the chair. I hear the flick of pages. "Tell me what you've been reading about," he says, feeling him tuck the book back where he found it.

"It's a romance," I say. I'll draw this out as long as I can, because this is the part I love—the game we play so well.

"What kind of romance?" His fingers skim my leg gently, so gently it almost isn't a touch. I shiver, pleasure already simmering under my skin.

"A filthy, smutty romance," I tell him, and though I wish I could see the look in his eye, the intent on his face, I keep my lids closed. It heightens my other senses and builds the anticipation.

"What makes it a smutty romance?" Something brushes my face. His nose? Is he smelling me? I feel his lips ghost over mine, so faintly, so subtly, for the mere briefest of seconds, but it's enough to send my head spinning.

"There's lots of touching, kissing, licking." I clench my hands between my thighs, aware that I'm squirming in the chair.

"And do you like that?" he asks, knocking my hands away.

"I do," I tell him. "But I prefer it in real life."

Silence spins. He's waiting, drawing it out because I know what comes next. Adrenaline is already pumping, desire swarming like a frenzy of bees, and I can't wait. I'm giddy, light-headed, and buzzing as I wait for his words, his command.

"Are you ready?"

On your mark.

I crack open my eyes. He's moved back, standing by the chair, his arms folded, baseball cap pulled low over his brow, the bulge in his combat trousers visible through the dark material. He's perfect, every fucking inch of him, and I almost don't move. I'm almost grounded by how beautifully beastly he is, by the thought of what he's about to do to me.

But I know it'll be so much better after the chase.

"I'll give you a thirty-second head start."

Get set.

His face is impassive, which makes it all the more exciting. He gives nothing away. No hint of what's to come. No clue as to what he has planned.

And then, like the shot of a starting pistol, he says the word: "Run."

With a squeal, I leap from the chair and dart from the library. I have thirty seconds before he'll chase me. Thirty seconds until he'll come after me. Thirty seconds until he'll find me, and then….

Fuck.

FENRIR

Thirty, twenty-nine, twenty-eight….

She'll head for the stairs. She always does.

When I found her in the chair reading one of her books, I couldn't resist. I know the type of things she reads, know what it does to her, and I'm more than happy to give her the real thing.

I'm just glad she seems okay here, back at Belial House. When she suggested coming here during her break, I was reluctant, for many reasons. What if it brought it all back— what happened, and what *almost* happened? What if Noa was still here?

But she isn't. The house feels cleansed, like the walls have been scrubbed, the blood gone, the memories just that.

At the time, I couldn't take in the house's majesty. But now, leaving the library and moving towards the open staircase—Hayami's heady scent in the air—I can fully appreciate the architectural beauty.

And the only thing it stirs in me about what we almost did… is the fact that we didn't. Which means now we get to do the things we want. Live the lives we were always supposed to live.

Together.

Hayami's been concentrating on her studies, getting ready to make a career choice when she graduates this summer. Whatever she decides, she'll put her all into it, because that's who she is, who she always was.

And me? I'm with Junko's new security company, training new recruits. And the rest of the time, I spend protecting Hayami. It isn't my job—it's my life. I'll always protect her, no matter what. Because without her, being alive doesn't mean a damn thing.

And this game, well, it's what we do. It's who we are. Because what is love without a dose fear?

Stopping at the foot of the stairs, I flex my hand and contemplate my next move. I'd hoped to catch her on the stairs, but I seem to have given her more time than I anticipated.

I start with the ground floor.

She's not in the main living room.

Not in the kitchen.

But she's been here. I can smell her.

Checking the walk-in pantry, I wonder if she's gone outside. But just as I stalk towards the back door, I see a flurry of movement out of the corner of my eye.

She darts from under the table and springs out of the room.

Without hesitating, I run after her, pulse pounding in my eardrums.

She's in the foyer. She swings herself around the banister to the stairs and sets off up them.

This is perfect.

I'll have her just where I want her.

I follow, flinging myself up the stairs, taking them two at a time. Hayami is fit, but her strides are no match for mine.

I reach for her leg, careful not to pull her back so she falls, but strong enough to stop her in her tracks.

She stumbles forwards, putting her hands out on the step above to stop herself.

Standing on the step below her, I run my hands up her legs. "That wasn't very difficult, Hayami," I tell her. "It almost makes me think you wanted to be caught."

"I don't." Her breath is all raspy, just the way I like it. "I'm just toying with you."

"Is that so?" My hands smooth up the insides of her legs, her leggings hugging their shape. "You know the rules," I say, gliding my hand over the curve of her ass. "You aren't the one who gets to toy with me."

"I like breaking the rules," she replies, and my hand twitches.

"You know what happens when you break the rules, Hayami."

This time, she nods, and I hope to God she can't get her words out because she's so desperate to feel me.

There's only one response to this.

I slap her on her ass, the crack reverberating off the high ceiling.

Then, silence.

She does nothing.

Says nothing.

There's a split second, like there always is, when I flounder, wonder if I've been too hard, but all the times we've played this game, she's never once uttered the safe word. I wonder if today will be the day and I've gone too far.

Then she speaks.

"Do it again."

I exhale, smile inwardly, and pull her leggings down to reveal her thong and her ripe, round cheeks.

I smack her again, harder this time, the sound louder on her naked skin. Her flesh turns pink. A gasp flies from her mouth.

"Maybe this'll be a reminder of how you should behave. How you should give yourself to me without all this running."

"Or maybe it'll just make me run faster." She springs from the step, catching me off-guard as she hauls herself forwards, dragging her leggings back up as she sprints up the remaining stairs.

And all I do is watch as she runs into the bedroom that used to be mine when we stayed here for the first time, a few months ago.

Slowly, I climb the stairs.

I can already smell her in the room—jasmine and honey-suckle, sweet and inviting. It's cold and feels unused. The bed's neatly made in grey linen, the en suite bathroom door closed, the wooden floor polished to a glossy sheen.

I wade deeper into the room, glancing at the curtains, looking for her silhouette, listening for her heavy breathing. As I reach the window, I catch a glimpse of her darting from under the bed and racing for the open door.

Like a hound with the scent in my nose, I set off, chasing her out of the room. She doesn't make it to the stairs. I catch her on the landing, pulling at her top as she struggles to get herself free.

"I'd love nothing more than to let you run a bit longer, but I need you to have enough energy for what I'm about to do to you," I tell her, pushing her arms behind her back and securing her legs with my own. She lets out a little grunt, her hair plastered to her face.

Stepping in front of her, I throw her over my shoulder, then turn and make my way to the master bedroom.

She thumps her fists against my back, crying, "Put me down!" as I reach the bed.

"Gladly." I throw her onto the bed.

She scrambles up the mattress, gripping onto the headboard, and I almost laugh as I pull her back down by her leg and flip her over.

"The more you fight, the more fun I get to have with you," I say, catching one of her arms in midair as she grapples with me. Holding her by one wrist, I pin her to the bed, then grab her other wrist and hold her down. That's when she looks at me and grins.

"I'll just have to keep fighting you, then," she says as she tries to wriggle from my grasp.

"You can try." I tighten my grip.

When I feel her relax, I move her wrists together, holding them in one hand as I take off my belt with the other in one swift move. The snap of the leather makes her eyes widen. I know she loves this; she told me so weeks after we left this place, and we started to play this game.

"Not the belt," she says.

I wink at her.

"You know what happens when you struggle." I wrap my belt around her wrists, securing them above her head. When I know she can't free herself, I let go of her wrists, sit back, and admire her bound underneath me.

"Fuck me, if there's a nicer sight than this, I've yet to see it," I tell her, biting my bottom lip. I consider what I'm going to do with her, all the ways I could take her—different ways to show her what she's worth, what she is to me. That she's everything and always will be.

"What are you going to do to me?" Even though she could bring her bound hands down, she keeps them above her head. When all's said and done, she's a good girl when it comes to the game.

"If I tell you, I'll have to fuck you." I bend down and lick the inside of her neck.

She shudders. "Tell me, please." Her voice is all sexy, her breathing already pitching at the thought of what I'm going to do to her.

I should hold out, but she asked so nicely, so I tell her, "I'm going to undress you, remove everything whilst following each touch with my tongue. I'm going to lick every inch of your skin. Then, when you're naked, I'm going to bend you over my knee and smack that smart ass of yours—one hit for every minute I spent trying to find you. Then I'm going to lay you down, spread your legs, and admire the view. And I'll wait until I can see just how wet you are before I lick your pussy until you're so far gone you'll be begging me to fuck you." I drag my finger over her nipple.

"But I won't—not yet anyway. I'll flip you over and push my fingers inside you as you curse me, call me all the horrible names you can think of because all you want to do is come. It'll only make me fuck you harder with my fingers. I'll thrust them deep inside you until you're screaming for me to let you come. But I won't. Not then either." I lower my head and nip her lips between mine as she bucks beneath me, trying to rub herself on the bulge between my legs.

"Lie still; otherwise, I won't tell you what I'm going to do to you," I say, lowering my voice so she knows how serious I am.

She stills, and I know it's killing her.

"Good girl," I praise her. "Now, where was I? Oh yes, just as you're about to break, I'll take my cock out and stroke it, long and slowly, showing you what you want, what you need. Then I'll fuck your mouth, just to stop you cursing me. And

I'll fuck it hard, Hayami. I won't hold back. I'll fuck your mouth until you're choking on me."

Her lips part, as if she can already taste me, and my cock twitches.

"By then I think the burning between your legs will be unbearable. If it isn't, then I'll make sure it is by licking your pussy out again until you're crying, screaming for me to put you out of your misery. I'll wait to see the tears streaming down your face, and then I will finally fuck you so deep, you won't even know where you are."

Hayami moans as I lower my mouth to her ear and whisper softly, "Then, and only then, I'll let you come on my cock. I'll feel you squeezing my length with your pussy until I come inside you, my name on your lips as you cry out for more."

She's panting now, her chest rising and falling rapidly, her cheeks flushed. I can almost feel the heat from her body.

"What are you waiting for?" she says.

"This day, Hayami," I reply. "I've been waiting for this day my whole fucking life, so forgive me if I want to take my time."

And I do just that. I take my sweet, sweet time with her. I make it last.

Make it last forever.

ACKNOWLEDGMENTS

Firstly, I'd like to start by thanking you, the reader, for taking a chance to get lost in my world. I just hope it was worth it.

It's fair to say that this book wouldn't even exist if it weren't for my wonderful editor, Kristin Scearce, who I know loves nothing more than the macabre, particularly Stephen King. And that's where this book began, when I was wondering how nice it would be for Kristin to work on a romantic horror inspired by the work of Stephen King. Hey, presto: *Beautifully Beastly*. So, thank you, Kristin, for sharing these little nuggets of your life with me, chatting with me via email about our favourite books, and for being obsessed with reading all things dark and delightful.

Beautifully Beastly certainly lived up to its name, as it was an absolute BEAST to write. I knew that Hayami and Fenrir's story began in that club, but getting from there to where the story needed to be whilst filling in the backstory wasn't an easy task. Then throw in Junko's backstory, and I found myself in a bit of a pickle. Luckily for me, editor and author Becky Johnson undertook the first round of edits, and boy, what a great job she did! Like an elite puzzler, she took it apart and put it back together in a way I never could have, so thank you, Becky, from the bottom of my heart.

And don't even get me started on the amazing cover. I had every faith in Claire at BookSmith Designs, but she really captured the essence of the book with this one, and I am forever grateful for her creativity and vision.

This book would not be what it is without my wonderful

beta readers, Andrea Altvater, whose comments warmed my heart. And Mandy Pederick, who is ever the detective—my aim in life now is to write a plot twist you won't see coming! Thank you both so much for casting your eagle eyes over this one and picking up the loose threads.

I will never write a book and not acknowledge my wonderful author friend Kerry Williams, who has been with me on this author journey from the start. I'm so glad she's with me, every step of the way.

I am indebted to all the book bloggers and influencers who have read and reviewed *Beautifully Beastly* and shouted about it on their socials. Without your support, my book would be lost, so thank you for helping it to get found.

And lastly, eternal thanks to my family, my husband, my children, and my dog. Because you all lose a little bit of me every time I sit down to write, or when you're talking to me and I'm busy plotting in my head or imagining a new scene. Thank you for allowing me to follow my dreams, even when they're a tad dark!

ABOUT THE AUTHOR

Maria Dean is an author from Yorkshire in England, where she lives with her husband, two boys, and her faithful Boston terrier. Her short stories have appeared in various publications and range from fantasy, sci-fi, and the supernatural, but for the long-haul, her heart remains rooted in romance.

WWW.AUTHORMARIADEAN.COM

instagram.com/author.maria.dean
tiktok.com/@authormariadean
bookbub.com/authors/maria-dean

ABOUT THE PUBLISHER

Hot Tree Publishing loves love. Publishing adult romantic fiction, HTPubs are all about diverse reads featuring heroes and heroines to swoon over. Since opening in 2015, HTPubs have published more than 350 titles across the wide and diverse range of romantic genres. If you're chasing a happily ever after in your favourite subgenre, HTPubs have you covered.

Interested in discovering more amazing reads brought to you by Hot Tree Publishing? Head over to the website for information:

WWW.HOTTREEPUBLISHING.COM

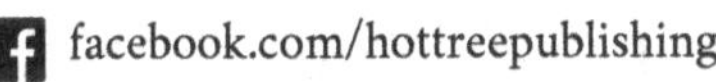 facebook.com/hottreepublishing

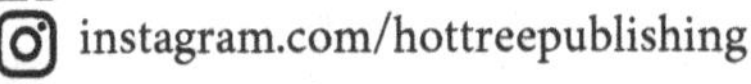 instagram.com/hottreepublishing

 tiktok.com/@hottreepublishing